A KINGDOM UNDER SIEGE

WARDENS OF ISSALIA, BOOK FOUR

JEFFREY L. KOHANEK

FALLBRANDT PRESS

COPYRIGHT

ISBN: 978-949382-14-3
PUBLISHED BY:
JEFFREY L. KOHANK & FALLBRANDT PRESS
www.JeffreyLKohanek.com

BOOKS BY JEFFREY L. KOHANEK

Runes of Issalia

The Buried Symbol: Runes of Issalia 1

The Emblem Throne: Runes of Issalia 2

An Empire in Runes: Runes of Issalia 3

* * *

Runes of Issalia Boxed Set

* * *

Heroes of Issalia: Runes Series+Rogue Legacy

* * *

Rogue Legacy: Runes of Issalia Prequel

Wardens of Issalia

A Warden's Purpose: Wardens of Issalia 1

The Arcane Ward: Wardens of Issalia 2

An Imperial Gambit: Wardens of Issalia 3

A Kingdom Under Siege: Wardens of Issalia 4

* * *

Wardens of Issalia Boxed Set

* * *

ICON: A Wardens of Issalia Companion Tale

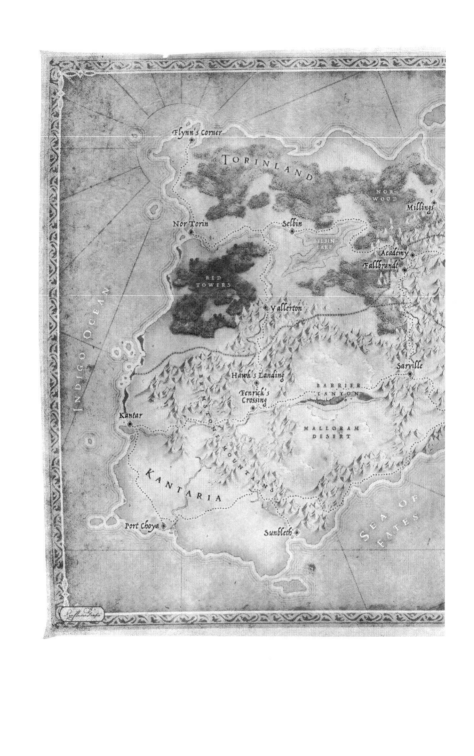

From the records of the Issalian Empire, 2nd Dynasty

For two centuries, The Hand kept the evil of Chaos buried – hidden and unable to tempt mankind with its power. Then comes a boy, a nobody, masked by a veil of lies, tricking others into believing he was something he was not. He somehow discovered the secret we had locked away where nobody should have found it. This boy, this deceiver, used the power of Chaos to beguile others and to build himself into a king.

While King Brock sat on his throne, basking in riches and glory, the members of The Hand, including myself, labored in a secret prison, living as if we were animals. Many of us died in those prison tunnels, but enough survived, clinging to the faith that Issal had not abandoned us. Our chance finally presented itself after thirteen nightmarish years of incarceration. We escaped and headed east to begin anew with gold and power and our faith restored.

I made a promise that day – a promise to right the wrongs I had suffered, to end King Brock's reign, and to see Chaos banished for good. Now, six years after achieving freedom, I sit at the helm of a new Empire, guiding the most powerful nation in Issalia while the tortured ghost of my enemy moans in his fiery after-life. With King Brock dead, Issalia belongs to the Empire. Soon will come the time when the kingdoms lay down their swords and accept their destiny.

When that time arrives, I will see the end of Chaos. Forever.

The Avatar of Issal,
  Archon Meryl Varius.

PROLOGUE

Brock Talenz climbed out of the carriage and squinted into the wind-driven snow. The bite of it was refreshing – a reminder that he was very much alive. Cinching his grey wool cloak into his fist to block the wind, Brock turned toward his longtime friend, Cassius DeSanus, who was seated in the carriage.

The king of Torinland was a shell of what he had once been. Before his tenure as king, Cassius had carved a legendary career as a captain in the Holy Army. Now nearing sixty, Cassius' hair had gone gray and the lines on his face had deepened. But, the years were not the cause of the man's condition.

A foiled assassination attempt had robbed Cassius of his strength, leaving him barely able to stand. The citadel minister had acted with urgency, using her skill with Order to save the man's life within seconds of his attack, but blackbane was extremely lethal. A drop of the poison could kill in less than a minute. Although the poison had run through his veins only a short time, his nervous system suffered permanent damage and left him unable to walk without a cane, his hand now rarely able to hold steady. Still, Brock respected the man for his mind and integrity. Not even poison could sap those resources.

"Issal willing," Brock said, "I'll see you in the spring."

Cassius, nodded. "Until then, my friend, be well."

When the carriage door closed, the driver snapped the reins, and the horses lurched into motion bringing King Cassius back to the Nor Torin citadel.

Brock turned toward his son, Broland. "Let us board so we can escape this wind."

Twenty Torinland soldiers marched behind Brock and his son as they headed toward the nearest pier. Flakes continued to drift down from the grey clouds overhead, leaving a blanket of white over the city of Nor Torin. Despite the winter storm, the docks were busy, filled with dockworkers loading ships.

Four ships hugged this particular pier, two on either side, each vessel rocking as the water roiled. When he reached the Razor, Brock led Broland up the plank and onto the ship's deck. Half of the guards followed while the remainder continued to the next vessel.

A pair of sailors unhooked the mooring lines, ran up the plank, and pulled it on board while others scurried about the ship under the direction of Captain Tenzi Thanes. When Tenzi spotted Brock and his son, she turned toward one of her trusted crewmembers, gave the man instructions, and descended to the main deck, walking purposefully toward Brock and Broland.

"Welcome aboard Razor, your Majesty," Tenzi said as she bowed.

"Thank you, Captain." Brock said firmly before stepping close and lowering his voice. "I'm sorry we could not depart sooner, Tenzi. I know you are eager to free Parker and Dalwin, but...I must consider the bigger picture. There are far more than two lives at stake."

The frustration on Tenzi's face was apparent. "I just hope they are still..."

Brock put his hand on her shoulder. "As do I. Both men are my friends, but my crown does not allow me to place a higher value on their lives than on those of thousands of subjects."

She turned away. "I know. I just feel so...helpless."

"We will recapture Wayport. And when we do, Chadwick and Illiri will pay for their betrayal."

"Oh, they will pay. If I have my way," she drew a knife and ran her finger along the blade. "It will be a very drawn out payment, one that might take days or weeks to complete."

"Tenzi...I cannot condone torture." Brock's tone was harder than steel.

"Fine," Tenzi sighed. She sheathed her dagger as a gust of wind struck, forcing her to grip the brim of her black hat. "I have a ship to sail. Why don't you two rest in my cabin? It is warm in there now that I finally got the hole repaired. At least *that* came out of sitting here for eight days."

"Very well," Brock said.

Tenzi turned and climbed the stairs to the quarterdeck while Brock and Broland ducked into her cabin.

Dim light seeped through the window along the outer wall, joined by the pale blue glow of a lamp on a wall sconce – both light sources fighting to keep the shadows at bay. While Broland crossed the room and sat on the bed, Brock grabbed a chair beside the small round table and withdrew a map from his coat. Unfolding the map, he spread it across the tabletop and considered his plan.

"How long will it take to sail to Wayport?" Broland asked.

Brock looked up at him, blinking in thought. "Remember, we have stops to make at Port Choya and Sunbleth. Even then, it depends on the weather. All things considered, I expect to land in Wayport ten days from now."

Seemingly satisfied, Broland fell silent. Shifting his focus back to the map, Brock withdrew a pen from the inside pocket of his leather coat. Not just any pen, this one was a gift from Pherran Nindlerod – a memento from the day Brock first met the kind old engineering master. Unlike others, this pen contained an internal inkwell. As Brock stared at it, a smile crossed his face – a rarity over the previous five weeks.

The assassination attempt against him and his family left Brock brooding. A desire for vengeance gnawed at him, something he repeatedly pushed aside. Varius and the Empire had made the war personal with that attack, which made it difficult for him to remain pragmatic when planning his response.

He closed his eyes and sought his center, sinking into the peace he found within his own source of Order. *I must remember the goodness in this world and not allow this war to harden me.* Brock thought. *Well, not too hard, at least.*

The ship rocked, the motion causing Brock to open his eyes and slip from his meditation.

"We hit the breakers," he said to Broland. "This might be an unpleasant journey with the storm over us."

Razor was now beyond the relatively smooth harbor waters, and the waves had grown tenfold. Everything tilted as the ship rocked. Clanking and banging of hanging cookware came from the galley next door.

"I don't feel well." Broland's face had gone pale, his hand pressed against his stomach.

"Seasickness." Brock nodded, knowingly. "This is only your second voyage, and the last was quite tame. I suggest you go back outside and watch the shoreline until your stomach settles. It helps."

Without another word, Broland stumbled toward the door, opened it to the howling wind, and slammed it shut. Alone, Brock studied the map and considered his plan. An armada of eight ships had just departed Nor Torin, each vessel loaded with ten Torinland warriors and ten civilians in addition to the crew. Those civilians were special – his secret weapon.

With the help of Cassius, Brock had collected almost every arcanist in Torinland, from Millings to Flynn's Corner, from Selbin to Nor Torin. Among those civilians were people he had freed from imprisonment a lifetime ago. They had fought a war for him once. He swore he wouldn't ask them to do it again.

While it is a wound against my integrity, these people may be the difference between freedom and death. Regardless of their participation, their lives are as much at risk as mine should we lose.

With stops planned for Port Choya and Sunbleth, Brock hoped to double the size of his force, including troops and magic users, by the time they reached Wayport. He would need them once he retook the city, a thought that brought up another problem.

Recapturing Wayport would be easier if collateral damage were not a risk. *I must find a way to remove Chadwick and those most loyal to him with as little violence as possible.* The soldiers and citizens of Wayport were his subjects. He needed to protect them, not kill them. More selfishly, he would need them for the struggle to follow. With that goal, he set his mind to the task. *Chaos is assuredly the answer, but how to best leverage it? How large of a force will be required?* He closed his eyes and imagined Wayport, considering his options.

The ship continued to rock from side to side, the motion beginning to affect Brock as nausea set in. He opened his eyes, folded the map, and slipped it into his pocket as he made for the door.

Stepping outside, he found the sails filled with the gusting wind and the snow changed to a steady drizzle. Two ships ran even with the Razor while the other five in the armada trailed behind. To the port side, Brock then noticed another fleet nestled in a protected bay.

Brock turned and climbed the quarterdeck as sailors scurried about the distant narrow-bodied longships. "Ri Star? What are they doing down here?"

The Ri Starian crafts raised anchor, the oars at their sides moving the longships toward deeper water as the Razor and the trailing armada sailed past. Tenzi called for another sailor to take the helm while she dug out a tube with glass on each end. She aimed the tube toward the ships, looking through it as the Ri Starian vessels unfurled their sails.

With shock, she gasped. "Flash cannons! They plan to attack!"

Considering what he knew of Ri Star, Brock recalled his previous interactions with Queen Olvaria. In his two decades as King of Kantaria, he had only met Olvaria three times. Despite her polite exterior, Brock had always sensed a hard edge to the woman. She often argued that her queendom was small and lacked resources. If not for their diamond mines, Ri Star had little bargaining power when it came to trade.

With Ri Star consisting of nothing but Ilsands nestled in dangerous waters, they had naturally developed Issalia's premier navy. Manned by tough, experienced sailors and a crew of oarsmen below deck, Ri Starian longships were the fastest in the world. Having those vessels armed with flash cannons was a frightening prospect.

A flash of green fire and a puff of smoke billowed from the lead Ri Starian ship. A boom followed, and a projectile hit the trailing vessel of the Torin armada, sending a blast of splinters into the air.

"This is bad." Brock's tone was grim. "Queen Olvaria has thrown her lot in with the Empire."

Another longship fired, also striking the trailing Torin ship, this time near the waterline. The wounded vessel rocked, tilted to one side, and turned toward shore, but it was too late. The ship was sinking while sailors and passengers scrambled for the lifeboat.

"We have to stop them!" Brock put his hand on Tenzi's shoulder. "Slow down so the rest of the armada can pass us."

She turned back toward the enemy fleet. "Once we are in range, they are going to fire at us."

"I know, but I don't have a choice. Just trust me."

"Fine." With her face in a scowl, Tenzi bellowed out orders, sending sailors up the masts to lower the upper sails.

Brock leaped down to the main deck where he spotted Stein. The man stood at the rail watching the trailing ships, his attention shifting toward Brock as he drew close.

"Stein! I need you to run below deck and instruct the other arcanists to begin applying Reduce Gravity augmentations to the deck. I want a large rune drawn near the bow, one in the middle, and one near the quarterdeck. Have them stack augmentations."

"Stack them? You know what will happen." Stein's expression revealed his doubt.

"Just do it."

As Stein ran to the stairs and disappeared below deck, Brock darted back to Tenzi's cabin. He burst in and searched the room, his gaze falling on the small, round table bolted to the floor. With his boot heel against it, he gave it a shove but it didn't move. He then picked up the chair and swung hard. The chair smashed into the table, scattering broken wood pieces onto the bed and across the floor. Brock gripped the tilted tabletop and lifted, tearing it off the base with a loud crack. He then set the tabletop on the floor and began to carve a symbol into the wood with the tip of his dagger. Once finished, he picked up the tabletop and ran back outside.

The drizzling rain continued, driven by the wind and leaving the deck slick. Razor had fallen behind most of the fleet, and the last remaining vessel was nearly upon them. Stein and the nine other arcanists were on deck with a group at the bow, a group in the center, and a group right beside Brock, near the stern. A man in the nearest group hurriedly traced a symbol with a chunk of coal. The diameter of the rune was half the width of the ship.

"Be sure to get the symbol exact!" Brock warned. "A misdrawn rune will kill us all!"

Still clutching the three-foot diameter table, Brock scrambled up the stairs to find the Ri Starian fleet less than a quarter-mile behind them.

"Tenzi!" he hollered. "Raise the sails the moment you see this rune activate!"

Without waiting, he closed his eyes and embraced the anxiety of the moment. The raw and angry energy of Chaos surrounded him, and he drew it in as easily as drawing a breath. Within seconds, a raging torrent of raw power surged throughout his body, threatening to tear him apart. Brock opened his eyes and gazed upon the rune he had etched into the table. It flared to life with a fiery glow, and Tenzi commanded her crew to raise the sails.

Brock ran across the quarterdeck and, with a grunt, threw the tabletop toward the Ri Starian fleet. It spun like a disc, the charged rune etched in the wood pulsing and fading as the tabletop struck the water.

A *boom* and a blast of green flame burst from a cannon on the bow of the nearest enemy vessel, launching a metal ball toward Razor. The projectile hit just below the quarterdeck with a massive *crack* that sent Brock, Broland, and Tenzi stumbling. It smashed through the rear of the captain's cabin and emerged out the other side, destroying the quarterdeck stairs in a burst of splintered wood.

"No! Not again!" Tenzi roared in frustration.

The floating tabletop then turned pure white and the churning ocean around it began to freeze. A thunderous *crack* came from the ice and it expanded in a roar of *pops* and *snaps*. The air over the center turned the drizzle to snow that thickened into a swirling localized blizzard.

Razor rocked and began to rise out of the water, sending those on board stumbling as the craft lifted upward. Brock leaned against the rearmost rail and watched the expanding ring of ice race toward them, far faster than the ship sailed. He glanced backward to see the Reduce Gravity runes on the deck, again pulsing with the next augmentation about to take hold.

"Come on. Just a little more lift," he urged, nervous that the ice would reach them too soon.

The ship lurched and rose up higher, tilting as the hull came out of the water and the wind pushed against the sails. Broland fell into Brock, both of them rolling across the quarterdeck until they wedged against the port side rail. Tenzi held tight to the wheel. The sailors and arcanists toppled to the deck, many sliding across it before slamming into the rail. A sailor on the main mast slipped, spun, and dangled by a rope briefly before falling into the ocean.

Brock pulled himself up and peeked over the rail. The ice ring had expanded beyond their position, the ocean now a white, choppy, uneven surface of frozen waves. The trailing fleet crashed into the ice in a massive collision, damaging hulls and launching crew members overboard. The sailors who landed on the ice did not move.

As the Razor floated away, tilted at a hard angle a hundred feet above the ocean, the ice continued to expand. In the distance. Brock spotted a lifeboat from the sinking Torin vessel, fighting the churning waves as it headed toward land. Between him and the ship, the sea had become an Island of ice, two miles in diameter. Ten Ri Starian longships were locked in the ice and would remain there until the augmentation expired. Even then, Brock suspected that most of those vessels were too damaged to make it to shore. *Those ships will no longer be a problem.*

"That was too close," Broland said.

"I can't steer!" Tenzi spun the wheel with no response. "The rudder is useless! We are drifting toward the cliffs!" She cupped her hands to her mouth and bellowed, "Lower the sails!"

Tenzi leapt off the quarterdeck and ran toward the main mast, which was unmanned. The sailors in the other two masts worked frantically to lower the sails while Tenzi scaled the main mast. Brock climbed his way up the angled deck to the starboard rail and looked down. They had passed most of the fleet with only the lead ship still ahead of them.

"Broland, follow me." Brock leapt over the broken stairs and landed on the main deck, almost falling on the slippery, tilted surface.

With Broland following, Brock bolted to the closet beside the galley and opened the door to reveal three ballistae, three-foot long bolts, and long coils of rope. As the sails came down, the deck began to level, making it easier to stand.

Joely appeared beside the door. "What can I do?"

"Both of you, help me with this," Brock said as he lifted one of the heavy ballistae.

Once the weapon was out the door, Brock returned to the closet, grabbed two coils of heavy rope, and threw one over each shoulder before scooping up a ballista bolt with a grappling hook on the end.

"Broland, Joely, Stein," Brock said as he moved past them. "Carry the ballista to the bow."

As the trio scrambled to pick up the ballista, Brock looked up to find only the lowest sails still unfurled. The ship had slowed and leveled but was still headed toward the cliffs.

With Broland, Joely, and Stein in tow, Brock led them to the prow. The Razor was now even with the leading ship – the craft a few hundred feet to the starboard side and a hundred feet below them. Kneeling, Brock tied the two coils of rope together and then tied one end to a massive cleat normally used when docking. As he secured the other end to the eyelet on the ballista bolt, he issued instructions.

"Rest the ballista on the rail and hold tight." He turned to Joely. "You know this weapon. We only get one shot. Make it count."

Joely nodded, eyeing his target while Brock cranked the launch mechanism back, inserted the bolt into the ballista, and held on tight.

Joely tilted the ballista upward and moved it slightly to the right. He pulled the release trigger, and the bolt launched, the recoil sending Brock, Broland, and Stein stumbling to the deck. The coil of rope rapidly unwound as it slid over the rail, chasing the projectile.

Brock scrambled to his feet and watched the bolt fly toward the other ship. It hit a sail, tearing it. Reaching the end of the rope, the grappling hook recoiled and leaped backward, spinning around the main mast before latching on. The rope drew tight and the Razor lurched, causing everyone on board to stagger.

Razor's prow dipped and tilted toward the ship towing them. Their direction altered slightly, but the cliffside was approaching fast. The cliff drew close…too close to avoid. A deep grinding sound came from the hull. Razor lurched and shook as it scraped across the cliff face. Moments later, the sound ceased and the ship slipped free.

A glance over the rail provided a wave of relief. They had cleared the obstruction and were now heading toward open waters. Brock wiped his brow and turned to find Tenzi glaring at him, her fists on her hips.

"What's wrong?" he asked.

"I have a hole in my ship, thanks to you." She gestured back at her cabin and the broken stairs.

Looking through the opening, Brock was able to see the cliffs behind them, slipping into the distance. "Yes. I'm sorry about that."

Tenzi crossed her arms and stared north, toward the trapped longships, now appearing as dark specs in a field of white. After a moment, she sighed. "I know you did your best. I just wish they would stop firing flash cannons at *my* ship."

Brock moved closer and put his hand on her shoulder. "I'm sorry, Tenzi. However, look around you. We are a hundred feet above the water. You may have a hole in your cabin, but I am willing to bet that Razor is also the first flying ship. Ever. It should make a great story next time you're having drinks with other sailors."

1

A TASK

D rip.
       Drip.
Drip.

The sound echoed outside Parker Thanes' cell and repeated in his head. He had become convinced the leaking pipe was intentional –a torture of insidious design.

Through the small window in his door, he had spent many hours watching the pool of water collect on the floor and run toward the nearby floor drain. The image arose in his mind as he lay on the pallet in his dark cell. He imagined bursting through the door and licking the pool of water until it was dry – anything to quench his thirst. *Have they turned me into some sort of animal, like a stray mutt digging through the trash for food?* The thought sent his stomach growling.

Parker was not alone in his misery. Dalwin Pretencia occupied the neighboring cell, Hex in the cell beyond. Days had passed to become weeks and now Parker had lost count. Tenzi had escaped. Of that, he was sure. The day after his capture, Duke Chadwick had visited Parker's cell. The questions asked and the fear in the man's eyes informed Parker of the truth – Tenzi's ability to elude the duke had created frustration. Chadwick was afraid of what might come of her escape.

Good, Parker thought. *You have good reason to fear her, Chadwick.*

Since that day, Parker had seen nobody other than the three rotating jailors. He missed Tenzi and hoped she might find a way to rescue him. Yet, he worried about what she might try. After all their years together, she still tended toward brazen, dangerous actions rather than safe ones. He had to admit her attraction to danger was among the reasons he loved her.

From the dim light coming through the small barred window in his cell door, Parker knew morning had come. If not for the meager light, there was little to differentiate the days from the nights. With the morning came breakfast – gruel and a cup of water. Lunch and dinner were repeats of the same – a disgusting meal that did little more than keep him alive.

Sometimes, surviving was the most one could hope to achieve.

The door at the end of the corridor opened, creaking noisily, followed by the tapping of boot heels on the stone floor. His brow furrowed when he recognized the sound of multiple footsteps. With an effort, he rolled off his pallet and rose to his feet, a groan slipping out.

He pressed his face against the small window in the cell door and blinked at the light coming through the high, grate-covered window. Six guards stood in the room, arranging themselves along the wall opposite from his cell. Chadwick entered the narrow room with two more guards at his side.

The man wore a double-breasted green coat with gold buttons, cinched tight at the waist with a gold gilded leather belt. Parker had always considered Chadwick a bit of a fop. Recent events had proven him a traitorous fop.

"Good morning, gentlemen," Chadwick said with a smile.

Parker wished he could squeeze the weasel's throat and wipe the smile from the man's face with his fist.

"Have you finally come to your senses, Chadwick?" Pretencia said from his cell. "Are you here to free us? You know we have done no wrong."

"What you have or have not done is immaterial, Dalwin," Chadwick replied. "Your identity remains the reason behind your incarceration. Perhaps you will find some relief in the knowledge that you will not rot in this cell."

Parker blinked at the statement and wondered if he dare hope for his freedom.

Chadwick drew a letter from his coat, unfolded it, and began to read aloud.

Duke Chadwick,

I am pleased that you have formally committed to our cause. The events that will soon unfold require your full support. As a means to demonstrate your dedicated loyalty, I give you a task.

My son informs me you have King Dalwin and Parker Thanes in your custody. Somehow, Dalwin found a way to escape the Sol Polis dungeon. Do not allow him to repeat such a feat. Having a rogue king on the loose could cause difficulties the Empire wishes to avoid. As a result, you are to execute these prisoners in a very public manner. Use it as a demonstration to galvanize the undivided loyalty of your citizens. Make them aware that the Empire will exact a steep price from any traitorous action, but fealty will bring rewards to all.

Expect to hear from me soon, for this is but the beginning of our war against Chaos. More will be required of you and your people to ensure a better future for Issalia.

The Avatar of Issal,
Archon Varius

Chadwick folded the note and slipped it into his pocket. "When we captured you, I was unsure of how to proceed. In fact, I spent an undue amount of time considering that very question. Archon Varius has solved the problem for me. The only decisions I had to consider were the manner and timing of your demise.

"It has been many years since a public execution has been held in Wayport. So I considered the means carefully. Though other methods might be faster, a good old hanging is apt to linger in the minds of witnesses. The choking, the kicking, the process of watching someone's life drain away…it sends quite an effective message, don't you think?"

"I think you're a traitorous weasel," Pretencia growled.

Chadwick shook his head. "Oh, come now, Dalwin. Certainly, we can be civil. As you can see, I am merely following orders, and your death is a matter of practicality."

"Let me out of this cage, Chadwick," Parker said with a snarl. "If you don't, I'll be sure you find the practical end of a sharp blade."

"Tsk, tsk, Master Thanes. That is no way to speak to a duke...one who will soon govern all of Kantaria." A smile clung to Chadwick's face as he stared into space. After a moment, he put his finger to his lips. "Where was I? Oh, yes. The date of your hanging. A new gallows platform is already under construction, and notices are being posted throughout the city.

"We will make the event a spectacle, held right here in the citadel plaza. Enjoy the next eight days as you consider what might be in store for you in the next life, should Issal wish it so. On the ninth day, you will die."

The man and his guards left the room, with his words hanging in the air. Even after they were gone, Parker stared through the bars, and his thoughts turned toward Tenzi. Of course, he missed her. However, he also feared for the impulsive woman. *If she hears of the execution, she is bound to try something rash.* Chadwick might be a weasel, but Parker knew the man had a cunning streak.

A public execution was also likely to be a trap.

2

THE ABYSS

Rena Dimas huddled on her pallet inside the cavern, rocking with her arms about her knees and her eyes closed as she sought her center. Where the Order rune should be, she only found shadow, as if an abyss waited to swallow her should she dare to venture too close. Rather than finding her center, she had failed. Again.

Meditation was growing more difficult with each passing day. Whatever had taken residence inside of Rena had invaded even that place of solace.

She did her best to forget the dome of rock above her and the mountain beyond, pressing downward with an immense weight that was sure to crush her and everyone else with the slightest shift. Repeatedly, she found herself wishing she were far from Vallerton and the horror haunting the town. People surrounded her, but she felt alone.

Alone. I am tired of feeling alone.

Thoughts of Torney arose and left her desperately missing him. She prayed he was well and hoped she would see him soon.

Yet, the darkness and fears inside her remained, slipping tentacles of terror through her defenses and penetrating deep into her soul. That terror lingered from her nightmares, which had grown worse.

A hand touched her and she jumped with a start, opening her eyes to a girl staring at her. The girl was young, certainly no older than ten summers, and had brown hair and large, brown eyes. Somehow, the girl and the other children in the tunnels behaved as if nothing were amiss, as if living below millions of tons of rock were normal.

"Didn't you hear me?" Tian asked. "It's time for dinner."

Rena collected herself, attempting to appear calm despite her racing pulse. "Sorry, Tian. I was focused on my meditation." *You failed, Rena. What if you fail when they need you?*

Tian stood and tucked her long, brown hair behind her ear. "When we get out of here, I would like to go to Fallbrandt one day. Perhaps I can learn magic, too."

Rena forced a smile. It felt like a lie. "I hope so, too, Tian."

The girl said, "Come along before it gets cold."

Gathering her will and doing her best to smile, Rena stood and followed Tian across the cavern. She passed dozens of makeshift pallets to her left and right, each covered by blankets and furs. The surviving citizens of Vallerton slept here, as did Rena and the other wardens who had come to help the townsfolk. Over a week had passed since she had first entered the mining tunnels – ten days that felt like years. Rena wondered if she would ever see the sun again. Without natural light, it had become impossible to know if it were day or night outside. *Does it matter? Does anything matter?*

Following Tian, she approached an open spot at the end of a bench. The women and children seated at the tables were sharing stories as if they were at home having a simple family dinner. *How many of these families remain intact? How many have died?* Somehow, Rena's thoughts grew darker. *How many will soon join the dead?*

A woman named Marta placed a steaming bowl of goat stew before Rena, the scent stirring hunger that been buried beneath her anxiety. She picked up her spoon and gripped it like a weapon. *I don't even know how to wield a knife,* she thought. *Without magic, I am helpless.*

Noise from the tunnels caused everyone to fall quiet, even the children. All eyes stared toward the dark opening…waiting. Movement shifted within the darkness and Grady emerged, the big blacksmith removing his snow-covered fur hat to reveal the wisps of his remaining gray hair. Kwai-Lan, Bilchard, Nalah, Kirk, and the surviving men from the village trailed behind Grady.

Kwai-Lan pulled down his hood and removed his cloak. "It must be tonight, Grady. We are limited on food and cannot wait in here forever."

Grady turned toward him with a scowl. "I prefer to discuss this in private."

Despite standing a head taller and outweighing Kwai-Lan by a fair margin, Grady looked away from Kwai-Lan's grimace.

"Fine." Kwai-Lan waved toward Rena. "Wardens with me." He then turned back toward the tunnel.

Kirk shrugged and followed the man into the shadows, with Bilchard and Nalah trailing. Realizing she had best join them, Rena stood and left her warm stew behind. Grady waved the men of Vallerton along as he followed Rena to the neighboring cavern. When they arrived, the other wardens were already seated and Kwai-Lan was tapping the table with his fingers, appearing impatient.

"We cannot wait any longer, Grady. You know it as well as I do." Kwai-Lan's tone was resolute. "The trap is set. We must now add the bait and attack when the monsters appear."

Grady ran a hand over his balding head, his eyes searching those of his Vallerton neighbors – men who had come to rely on his leadership. "What say you, men? Are you ready for this fight?"

The men eyed each other in silence until Tindle cleared his throat.

"Will it work? Can we kill them?" Tindle looked down, his long blond hair falling over his face as he spoke toward the ground. "I...I don't want to die."

Grady put his thick hand on Tindle's shoulder, his tone somber. "I cannot promise anything. We have done our best to prepare..." He turned and met Rena's gaze. "And we have magic on our side. Perhaps it gives us a chance."

Rena turned away, her breath coming in rapid gasps. She tried to calm herself, but she could not stop imagining the entire village dead, torn apart by the monsters waiting outside...everyone betrayed by the monster lurking inside her.

The night was still, no movement but a thin swirl of fog with each exhalation. Bilchard stood beside Rena, holding his wool cloak tight against the chill. Beneath the cloak, the tall wildcat wore his full armor.

To Rena's other side, Nalah leaned on a massive bow, thick and matching her in height. Arrows the size of ballista bolts stood beside the bow, the arrow points soaking in a bucket of naphtha. Rena pinched her nose to the smell of the accelerant.

The trio stood atop the second-story inn roof. Waiting.

It was dark, but the snow-covered ground made it easy to see the outline of the buildings across the street. To the south, a fire simmered in the middle of the road, the coals still hot. A metal stake stuck up from the frozen ground a few strides from the fire. There, a tethered goat stared nervously toward the darkness, bleating in fear. *Even the goat realizes this is madness*, Rena thought.

Just past the fire was a barricade, standing two stories tall and connecting the houses on each side of the road. Similarly, the gap between every building on both sides of the street had been walled off, leaving the road from the north as the only way in.

The destroyed smithy, or what remained of it, stood just behind the barricade. Beyond the smithy was the keep. That was where they were to go if anything went wrong. Rena prayed it wouldn't come to that. She shivered when she recalled the mad constable who still lived there. *Am I going mad as well? Will I become like Hardy?* Somehow, the thought seemed worse than the idea of monsters eating her. Monsters. She could think of no better term than what they were to face. *We have all gone mad for intentionally seeking out these beasts rather than fleeing.*

A call in the distance drew her attention. Moments later, two forms materialized from the night, tromping through snow as they ran into town. The men stationed on the rooftops across the road leaned forward as they watched Kwai-Lan and Kirk hurry toward the inn. Kwai-Lan stopped before the door and turned toward the waiting men, cupping his hands around his mouth.

"Ready yourself," he bellowed. "The lure is in place!"

Kwai-Lan disappeared into the building. Moments later, Kirk emerged from the trap door they had cut in the roof, and Kwai-Lan followed soon after.

Although Kwai-Lan was short of stature, the man was a weapon master and had more fighting experience than everyone else combined.

His knowledge and skills were why he had been chosen to lead the expedition.

The weapon master addressed the three wardens before him. "The stew is in place, simmering on coals. If things go as planned, the scent will draw them soon. When they reach town, they will go after the goat. When they do, we strike." Kwai-Lan turned toward the tallest person in the group. "Are you prepared for this, Bilchard?"

Bilchard, whose face was now covered by the patchy blond scruff of two-week growth, nodded. "I've been training hard, sir. I'm ready."

Kwai-Lan's voice lowered. "Combat training and fighting rabid monsters differ greatly. Both a puddle and a storm are wet, but there is little to fear from a puddle."

"I'll...do my best."

Kwai-Lan patted Bilchard's shoulder. "That's all we can ask."

Kirk squatted near the roof edge and looked down. "Thank Issal there is no wind tonight. It's cold, but not as bad as it would be with a breeze."

"The lack of wind will make it easier to aim as well," Nalah noted as she eyed her bow.

Rena found her gaze drawn toward the dark end of the road, where she imagined monsters charging in from the darkness. She had heard stories about them – massive, psychotic rabbits with glowing red eyes. Images of the beasts tearing people apart arose in her mind, leaving phantom torn limbs on the street below.

A hand on her shoulder made her jump with a start, drawing her back to reality. "Are you well, Rena?" Kwai-Lan asked.

She shook her head. "It's...nothing."

"You are the only arcanist we have. The only healer as well. I need you to focus and prepare yourself."

"I know."

"What I ask of you...it's dangerous."

"Yes. It is a path only for the desperate. I believe this situation qualifies."

He nodded. "Stay away from the eaves. Distance is what will keep you alive. Besides, if you push too far, you are likely to faint, which would be bad if you were standing near the edge."

Rena took a deep breath, hoping she might inhale some courage. The cold air instead chilled her lungs and fed the fear inside her. Finally, she nodded and he stepped away.

Her gaze shifted to the weapons piled atop the roof: spears made from long saplings sharpened to a point, rocks the size of her head, and arrows three times the diameter and length of a normal arrow. Naphtha from the mining tunnels had been painted on the spears. Heat runes marked each of the rocks, two dozen in total. Rena couldn't imagine holding enough Chaos to charge them all, yet she was the only arcanist they had. *These people have no chance without my help. Even then, what hope do we have?*

A gasp from Nalah sent a chill down Rena's spine. She looked down the road as black shapes entered town, moving in fits and spurts. Their eyes glowed red, but otherwise the monsters appeared like nothing more than vastly overgrown rabbits – rabbits the size of bears. More rabbits emerged from the shadows, all advancing with caution. The bleating goat began to frantically tug at the rope around its neck.

"May Issal strike me blind," Kirk swore. "There must be a dozen of those things."

"Rena, it's time." Kwai-Lan said, his tone grim, his attention focused on the approaching monsters below.

With the terror Rena felt inside, reaching for Chaos was as simple as drawing a breath. A torrent of raging energy filled her. She held it for a moment and wondered how long she could do so until it tore her apart. Her gaze fell on the symbol drawn on the back of her hand – a rune she had never tested before, a rune that carried a heavy price.

She released the energy into the Stamina rune and it began to glow. Exhaustion replaced the Chaos as it flowed out from her, leaving her weak and her breathing ragged. The glow pulsed and faded from the rune. An icy shock of cold ran through her, causing her back to arch and her eyes to bulge. It then dissipated as quickly as it had risen, a warmth rushing through her as if she had just slipped into a warm bath.

Rena instantly felt…refreshed. In fact, she felt wonderful. Turning toward Bilchard, she again reached for Chaos and, amazingly, it did not slip away.

"By Issal's breath," Kirk swore again. "Look at them all."

With the Chaos expended and the rune on Bilchard's cheek glowing, Rena turned toward the road. The breath caught in her throat.

A tide of blackness rushed into Vallerton, amid which were hundreds of glowing red eyes. The monstrous rabbits rushed in, filling the street in a moment. Crazed and frenetic, they weaved about, smashed into walls, and broke windows as the swarm headed toward the frightened goat.

"Bilchard, the tree!" Kwai-Lan ordered.

"Right!"

Bilchard jumped to the next building and continued north, hopping from building to building in Chaos-powered leaps.

Kwai-Lan gripped Rena's shoulder and spun her toward him. "Charge us. Now!"

She nodded, grasping her fear and drawing Chaos in before charging the Power rune on the man's head. Without pause, she drew in Chaos and charged Kirk before moving on to Nalah.

The fore of the monsters reached the goat as its bleats became high-pitched with fear. The beasts at the front attacked the goat as one, tearing it apart in seconds. By then, the entire herd had entered town, rapidly filling the space between town's edge and the barricade.

To the north, Bilchard carried the massive pine they had cut down the previous day. Moving with haste, he laid it across the road and then disappeared.

"Kirk, Nalah. Loose!" Kwai-Lan shouted.

The combat master then hefted a ten-foot long spear and launched it toward the mass of monsters. With strength augmented by a Power rune, the spear became a missile, skewering the monster through the back and pinning it to the ground. The beast fought to break free but the effort was futile. Kirk joined Kwai-Lan, throwing spear after spear toward the mass of monsters below. Nalah joined them, using her oversized bow to launch thick, naphtha-coated arrows into the horde.

Bilchard landed on the roof just two strides from Rena, startling her. He was panting, his breath coming out in thick puffs of steam. Their eyes met and he nodded.

"I'm ready."

The tall wildcat then picked up one of the rocks and spun it so the Heat rune faced her. Two seconds later, the symbol was glowing red with Chaos. Bilchard cocked his arm back, turned north, and took aim. With a grunt, he heaved the rock and it burst into white flame, lighting the night as it sailed toward the far end of town. It landed just before the downed pine and crashed into it. The dead tree lit immediately, the intense heat of the rock turning the tree into an inferno that blocked the road and sealed the trap.

Bending to grab another boulder, Bilchard held it toward Rena as she charged it. He then threw the boulder toward the milling mass of monstrous rabbits. The rock burst into flames and smashed into a rabbit, crushing the beast before it bounced into the next monster and set it aflame. Terrifying, high-pitched squeals arose from the rabbits as they frantically tried to escape the flames.

As Kwai-Lan and Kirk continued to launch spears, Nalah fired arrows into the mob below. When fire reached the naphtha-covered weapons they would instantly ignite, burning hot and fast. The panicking rabbits began to climb atop one another, jumping up to reach the second-story roofs. Men stationed on rooftops urgently used long poles to shove the rabbits away. One of the beasts reached the top of the roof across the street and Grady attacked it, smashing the rabbit in the eye with an axe.

All the while, Rena continued to charge Heat runes drawn on rocks that Bilchard then threw at the monsters. The barricade at the south end caught fire, as did one of the buildings across the street. Black smoke filled the air, causing Rena to cough and cover her face, but she continued to charge runes as the others desperately fought to keep the monsters corralled. The squeals grew in volume, and the monsters began to furiously slam into surrounding buildings. Massive thumps came from the inn below Rena's feet and she staggered. The melee grew more intense, the smoke thickening, the squeals pealing loudly, the building shaking violently.

A massive crack came from the building across the street, and it collapsed. The men stationed on the roof screamed as they tumbled into the mass of burning monsters. Everywhere Rena looked, buildings and monsters were on fire while black smoke rose into the orange-lit sky. Structures were collapsing, roofs caving in, lives ending.

Weakness wracked Rena's body – an exhaustion causing her to fall on her hands and knees, her vision turning to spots. She wobbled in a haze of smoke and weariness, struggling against the invading darkness.

"Everyone off the roof!" Kwai-Lan shouted in alarm. "Now!"

The others turned and leaped away to land somewhere behind the building. Rena tried to crawl but fell on her side, her face striking the rooftop. Kwai-Lan appeared, standing over her.

"I'm here, Rena," he said, reaching toward her.

A loud crack came from below, the shock of it causing Kwai-Lan to stumble. The building beneath them shook again and collapsed.

Rena felt herself fall into the abyss, the darkness consuming her. Death beckoned as her nightmares welcomed her, enveloping her in a chilling embrace bereft of hope or light or love.

3

DESPAIR

Death was cold – cold and lonely – much like the box Rena's father had locked her in when she was nine years old. Trapped in that dark box, she had feared she would never see the sun again. This box was worse, nebulous and undefined, leaving her unable to grasp its nature. She pounded on invisible walls and screamed in silence. It wasn't that she believed she might escape. There was no escape from death. Rather, she wished to discover if the afterlife had anything more to offer. Other than despair, she found nothing.

She grew aware of a light and realized it had been there for some time, hanging dimly at the edge of her vision. Slowly, the light shifted until it was directly before her, bright and intense and…warm.

The heat of the light soothed the side of her face. It felt like…life. *Is this Issal? Has god come for me? Will he judge me for what I've done – for what I am?* Rena knew condemnation would follow such a judgement. She was evil. Her father had been sure to hammer *that* truth into her brain.

Something wet dropped into her eye and caused her to blink. She opened her eyes to the morning sun shining on the right side of her face. A drop of cold water ran down one cheek as another drip landed on the bridge of her nose. *Snowmelt*, she thought.

When she tried to move, she found it very difficult. Something, no, someone lay on top of her, limp and heavy, weighing her down. She tried to shift toward the sun, but something sticking up beside her prevented it. Feeling it with her hand, she found it to be wood, damp and sticky. Sliding away from it, she was able to pull herself from beneath the other person and roll onto her stomach, jerking her hand away when a splinter impaled her palm. She pulled it free and tossed the shard of wood aside. Broken and charred boards surrounded her, jutting up in every direction.

When she spun around, she found Kwai-Lan staring at her, his gaze lifeless. A broken board, the end covered in blood, stuck up from the man's back. Rena realized that he had fallen with her when the roof collapsed and ended up on top of her. Somehow, she had survived, despite the fall, the fire, and the cold weather.

Rising to her feet, Rena studied what remained of Vallerton.

Most of the buildings had collapsed and burned. The barricade was nothing but a pile of charred wood, similar to the front wall of the inn. The charred remains of the monstrous rabbits littered the street, many pinned to the ground, others lying atop one another in piles, charred and pink with burns and occasional patches of black fur. Nothing stirred. There was no sound, not even the wind. Rena found herself wondering if anyone had survived. She didn't even know how long she had slept. A jolt of terror shook her core when she realized that the survivors might have already left town, thinking her dead.

Alone. I can't be alone.

With a sense of urgency, she climbed from the wreckage, over what was left of the blackened front porch, and onto the gravel road. The snow was gone from the area, melted away by the fire. She picked her way through the slain animals, unnaturally oversized but now appearing as innocent as any other rabbit. Seeing them in the daylight, she found their numbers beyond what she had anticipated, exceeding a hundred in total.

Dead men lay among the monsters – or parts of men in some cases. Bloody, broken, burned, every one she passed was undoubtedly dead. The bright sun above seemed out of place amid such horror.

A pile of ash is all that remained of the massive tree they had set ablaze. The heat of the Chaos-charged rock, coupled with the naphtha applied to the trunk, had fed the inferno and left less behind than one might expect. The rock, so blackened it seemed to absorb the surrounding light, lay among those ashes like a marker for the pyre that had consumed the tree.

Once she was thirty feet beyond the remains of the tree, she found the road covered in snow – snow filled with massive rabbit tracks.

She followed the road to the intersection and turned east, stepping in the tracks created by frequent trips between town and the mines while the men were constructing the trap. Despite the surrounding snow, the sun was warming her and causing the surrounding pines to drop white clumps from their boughs as she passed by. The forest was quiet without even a bird chirping as Rena followed the trail down into the mining pit and crossed to the familiar tunnels.

The darkness of the tunnel welcomed her, and the fear of being left alone bubbled up, rising to a crescendo as she reached the door. She took a deep breath, said a prayer to Issal, and knocked.

Silence.

With her heart racing, she knocked again. The echo made the tunnels sound hollow, lacking the life she prayed would be waiting.

Tears began tracking down her face and she slumped to her knees, her head hanging as she stared toward the tunnel floor. Hope had fled her, despair returning in full force.

A sound caused her to open her eyes. She looked up and found Tindle holding a glowlamp in one hand, an axe in the other. He blinked in shock.

"You...you're alive?"

Rena looked down at herself. Her coat was covered in Kwai-Lan's blood, her hands blackened with soot. *I wonder how bad my face appears*, she thought.

Swallowing in an attempt to wet her dry throat, she gazed up at him and wiped her eyes dry. "I guess I am." She croaked. "Did anyone else survive?"

He dropped his axe and scrambled forward, putting his hand beneath her arm and helping her to her feet. "You should come in and sit down."

4

DIRE NEWS

Ikonis Eldarro picked at his food, the crab on his plate eyeing him. Somehow, Iko fought the urge to use the side dish of boiled seaweed to cover the crab's face. His mother loved seafood. He did not. However, Sol Polis was a seaside city and seafood was common. Worse, beef, lamb, and farm-raised crops had become rare and expensive, with much of the supply reserved for the Imperial Army. He suspected the situation would only grow worse as they prepared for war.

He glanced toward his mother, Archon Meryl Varius, to see if she was watching. Her dark hair was now streaked with gray and the lines on her face more apparent, but little else about her had changed since their day of freedom six years past. Even while they were in prison, Iko knew his mother as a leader – someone others respected. Nothing surprised him about her rising to become the most powerful ruler in Issalia.

General Kardan sat beside Iko's mother. The man's hair had lightened over the years, from brown to gray, and it was trimmed short enough to stand on end. Despite his advancing age, Kardan had retained the build of a warrior – muscular with broad shoulders and a barrel chest. His dark blue uniform made him appear more formal, and his appearance remained fearsome. The three of them were alone in Kardan's office, discussing a report that had arrived that morning.

"It was a chance worth taking, Leo," Varius said. "The attempt cost us nothing."

"Not exactly true." Kardan wiped his face with a napkin and sat back in his chair. "We had a full squad hidden in the Kantar Citadel. Other than the two men who arrived this morning, those soldiers are dead and the opportunity to use them, lost."

Iko's mother sat back with her fingers tented and pressed against her lips. A moment of silence passed before she spoke. "When Filbert reached out to us, I found the chance to gain Kantar without a siege too compelling to ignore. At the same time, I know Ashland well. She is smart and has the will of a survivor. That she foiled Filbert's scheme is not surprising. Yet, two dozen guards is a pittance to pay for taking the city. We had to take the chance, even if Filbert did not succeed."

Kardan nodded slowly. "I forgot that Ashland was your assistant."

Iko's mother turned toward the window and she stared toward the bay with a distant look in her eyes. "I had much hope for the girl back then. In her, I had foreseen a powerful ecclesiast. Ironically, the only person who was stronger in channeling Order was Brock. I had hoped to bring both into the fold as members of The Hand. That was before I knew of their true nature. Discovering they were both Unchosen, tainted by Chaos, cut me to the quick. That particular betrayal still stings today, decades later."

Kardan put his hand on hers, drawing her attention. "At least we no longer need worry about Brock. Of the two, he was always the more dangerous."

"True," she agreed.

Proceeded by a brief knock, Sculdin stepped into the room with a scowl on his face that made Iko alarmed.

"Captain Sculdin," Varius said with a growl. "I assume you have good reason for barging in on our meal."

Sculdin dipped his head. "I apologize, Archon. However, I have dire news to share."

With a furrowed brow and her lips pressed together, the Archon gave Sculdin a nod.

The tall captain ran a hand through his hair, a gesture reeking of exhaustion. Iko noted the bags under Sculdin's eyes and a button uncharacteristically missing on his uniform coat. *He is pushing himself too hard*, Iko thought.

"The messenger I sent to Corvichi just returned. When she arrived there, she found the castle destroyed with only a portion of the wall still standing. The rest was nothing but charred rubble."

Iko stared at Sculdin, stunned. He turned and found shock on his mother's face, her jaw dropped open. Kardan recovered before she did.

"What of the troops stationed there?"

"Only seven survived. She found them camped just outside the wall, preparing to leave for Yarth. With what remains…there is little need to hold it."

"Seven? The castle housed two hundred soldiers and almost as many workers." Kardan clenched his eyes closed, his tone shifting from denial to acceptance. "Did they say what happened?"

Sculdin opened the letter in his hand, his eyes scanning it for a moment. "Apparently, someone infiltrated the grounds. Jarlish alerted the guards, who stormed the foundry. Moments later, the castle exploded. In the light of the fire, the guards stationed on the wall detected enemies just outside the compound. They gave chase, but the invaders were able to escape."

Iko's mother leaned forward, her face like stone. "What of the weapons? The flash powder?"

"We've been continually receiving shipments with most going to Hipoint or to the garrison outside of Yarth. However, half of our supply was still untapped according to my last report. We can assume that supply has now expired in the fire."

The room fell quiet save for the gentle beat of Iko's mother tapping the arm of her chair. He knew the sound well, a habit that arose when she was deep in thought.

Finally, she spoke and broke the spell. "We will receive no more weapons," she stated it as fact. "And we are unlikely to recruit more fighters. There is nothing to be gained by waiting, so I suggest we accelerate our plans."

Kardan shook his head. "Spring is not yet upon us. A march up the Greenway through snow will cost us lives."

"True," she responded. "However, our unseen enemy continues to move game pieces while we bide our time. If we wait another month, what else might occur that damages our plans?"

The general stared at Iko's mother with eyes narrowed in thought. The silence in the room was thick, matching the tension. Kardan then took a breath and turned toward Sculdin.

"Send a missive to Olvaria. I need more Ri Starian ships as soon as possible. Continue everything else as planned. We won't move quite yet, but we must be ready to advance as soon as I give the word."

5

HOLIDAY

Brandt Talenz held the wooden staff before him and stared into Quinn's eyes, normally a deep blue. Now, he found them a steely gray. *She is serious*, he thought.

Quick as a flash, she lunged with a sword. He spun his staff and blocked her strike, dancing aside to avoid her other sword. She twirled around with a low swing, a sword coming toward his ankles while her tail of blond hair sliced through the air. When Brandt leaped over her strike, he found Quinn's other sword trailing the first but in a higher arc. An urgent twist allowed him to block the strike, sending a loud *clack* throughout the stable yard behind Pintalli's Inn. He landed off balance and stumbled. Quinn drove forward, pressing until he tripped over the hitching post and fell on his back. The breath shot from his lungs in a grunt. He rolled onto his side and gasped for air that refused to obey.

Quinn lowered her wooden practice swords and stood over him with a furrowed brow. "Are you all right?"

Finally, sweet air refilled his lungs, coming in deep breaths. The shock of pain in his back eased and he sat up, nodding. "I'll be fine."

The clapping of hands caused Brandt to turn toward their audience – Mason and Hinn, the two stable hands. Mason, a thick-bodied teen with brown eyes and dark curls, stood and walked toward them with Hinn a step behind.

"Where did you learn to spar, Quinn?" Mason asked.

Hinn, a thin boy who stood a half-head taller than Mason, ran his hand through his long, dark hair and smiled. "I wish I could learn to use a sword."

Quinn shot a questioning look at Brandt as he rose to his feet and dusted himself off. The two stable hands seemed innocent enough, as did their line of conversation. However, Brandt and Quinn had secrets to protect.

Brandt shrugged but remained silent. She frowned at him before turning toward the boys.

"I spent some time at the military academy in Fallbrandt," Quinn said. "Among other things, I trained with swords while I was there."

Mason's large eyes grew even wider. "TACT? You were accepted to TACT?"

Quinn shrugged and tossed her wooden swords aside. "Yes."

Hinn grinned. "How did you get in? Did you have to know your way around a sword first?"

"No," she shook her head. "I had never used a weapon before my trial, so I opted for a fist fight." She flashed a wry grin. "I was over-matched, and it was a bloody affair, but my determination convinced the recruiter to extend me an invitation."

Brandt found himself grinning as he imagined what it must have been like for the recruiter who had faced her. Quinn's bold nature and tenacity made her unexpectedly dangerous. The man had likely antici-pated an easy bout and then discovered a fierce warrior beneath her pretty exterior.

Brandt, his sister's voice rang in his head.

Hi, Cassie, he replied over their telepathic link.

Delvin just stopped by, pressing me for information. Her frustration carried through the connection. *It's been over a week and they are eager for an update.*

A sigh slipped from his lips, and Quinn looked at him with one brow cocked.

Tell them to gather at sunset. We will give an update then.

Thank you, Cassie sent. I'll talk to you soon.

Brandt realized that Quinn and the two boys were staring at him, her with her brow still raised in question, them with confused expressions.

"I received a note from my sister," Brandt said, constructing his message carefully. "We are to meet her and the others for dinner. They are interested to hear about our journey to Yarth."

Quinn nodded. The two boys glanced toward each other and shrugged.

Brandt gestured to Quinn. "If you are finished beating me with those sticks," a grin crossed his face, "I thought you might like to go for a walk."

She put a finger to her lips and looked toward the sky, as if contemplating his request. After a moment, she smiled. "I suppose I could join you."

He chuckled. "I feel so honored, oh great warrior."

The comment earned him an elbow in the gut.

"If you boys could watch our practice weapons, I would appreciate it," Quinn said.

Mason eyed the swords and bit his lip. "Do you think we could give it a try?"

Quinn shrugged. "Suit yourself. However, don't beat each other too hard or you'll find yourself at the local temple, seeking a healer."

Brandt snorted. "Not that you would know anything about that."

She grinned in response. "Yes…well. Sorry about your ribs."

"I'm sure you are. While it was painful, the required donation of silver piece still hurts. It's no wonder the temple here looks like a palace." He turned toward the stable hands. "Take care, boys. Store the weapons when you're finished."

"See you tomorrow, boys." Quinn said.

Brandt took Quinn's hand and led her from the stable yard, taking an alley leading to a wider street. They paused as a farmer's wagon rolled past, the workhorse pulling it at a slow, methodical pace. The wagon was empty save for a few potatoes that wobbled around the wagon bed. Following in the wagon's wake as it forced foot traffic aside, Brandt and Quinn headed west, passing shops that had become familiar sights.

The past week had been cathartic for them both. While Brandt enjoyed action and sometimes even sought danger, he couldn't deny that his time of living as a spy in Sol Polis had worn on him. Living under the enemy's roof, hidden behind a false identity required constant vigilance accompanied by an overdose of anxiety. When he looked at Quinn, she noticed and shared a smile. Since their arrival at Yarth, her smiles were far more frequent, as was the amount of time they were able to spend together. It was clear to him how much she enjoyed their respite. He felt the same way.

The smell of freshly baked bread stirred the hunger in his stomach. He pulled Quinn toward the open bakery door.

"Time for a snack," he said, smiling.

She smiled in return. "You read my mind."

Once inside, the smell grew thick and left Brandt feeling as if he could eat the air itself. An overweight, middle-aged woman stood behind the counter, kneading a hefty chunk of dough. Her brown hair was tied in a bun, her cheek, smock, and hands covered with flour. She looked up, smiled, and dusted her hands off on her skirts.

"Well, if it isn't my two favorite new customers."

"Good afternoon, Pyrene," Brandt said. "We tried to pass by, but our stomachs forced us in, demanding a taste of whatever was teasing our noses."

A hurt look crossed her face. "You would pass by without saying hello?"

Quinn chuckled. "Saying hello isn't the issue. Our funds continue to dwindle and a fair share ends up here."

Pyrene shrugged. "I would apologize, but your weakness is how I pay my bills."

"We completely understand. What do you have for us today?"

She grabbed two small towels, turned toward the warming racks above the oven, and spun back with a baked roll in each.

"They are filled with custard – a new recipe I think you'll enjoy." She held them out. "Careful. They're hot inside, so you had better exercise patience."

Brandt accepted one while Quinn did the same. He gave Quinn a sidelong glance. "Hmm. Quinn may be in trouble. She has many wonderful qualities, but patience is not among them."

The comment earned him an elbow, but the chuckle from Pyrene made the price worth it. *It's funny what I'm willing to pay for a laugh,* Brandt thought in a moment of self-awareness.

"What do we owe you?" Quinn asked.

"Nothing. They are my gift to you."

"What?" Brandt frowned. "Why?"

"Three times in the past week, I have had new customers come in and make sizable purchases. All three mentioned hearing of my bakery from a young couple dressed in black." Pyrene gave them a smile of adoration. "You are my only customers who fit the description. I thank you for the added business."

"No need to thank us, Pyrene," Quinn said. "We were only telling them the truth. Your bread and pastries are amazing."

"True," Brandt added. "We talk about them because we can't help ourselves."

The woman laughed. "All the same, take the pastries. They are a gift."

Brandt stepped toward the door. "Thank you. Have a good evening."

"Bye, Pyrene," Quinn added, following Brandt outside.

The couple ate as they meandered the streets of Yarth, chatting and laughing and enjoying being together. At some point, Brandt led Quinn down an unfamiliar street that opened to a square. Beyond the square was the north gate, bracketed by two towers.

"It was your idea to come here." Quinn narrowed her eyes at him. "I assume there is a reason behind it."

He grinned. "I tell you you're beautiful, and you know I love your spirit. However, you continually impress me with your cleverness. It's rare for anything to slip past you, and I find that as attractive as anything else."

Quinn's hand went to her hip, her head tilting. "I feel like you are flattering me for a reason. What did you do?"

He laughed and held his hands up in surrender. "I've done nothing. At least, not this time."

"What is it, then?"

Watching the gate, he sighed, his voice lowering in volume. "Despite my desire to continue our little holiday here, we are wardens, and we have responsibilities. When we meet tonight, our friends in Fallbrandt will expect more from our stay here than stories of pastries, afternoon strolls, and wine." His grin reappeared. "Unless they are interested in our recent evening adventures *after* the wine."

Quinn's eyes grew wide and she punched him in the shoulder. "You had better not."

"Ouch." He rubbed his arm, but the grin remained. "I was only joking."

"All right. What do you suggest?"

"We have seen a fair number of Imperial troops in town."

"Yes."

"Have you noticed that they always head north when they leave?"

She shrugged. "I guess."

"What do you say about a little scouting?"

Quinn looked toward the open gate as a wagon rolled in, pausing while the guards on duty inspected it. "All right. I am interested, but won't it look strange if we head out and return an hour later?"

"I have a better idea. It's a bit more dangerous, which means it's also more fun."

She smiled. "That's the Brandt I love."

His smile fell away and his stomach quivered nervously. "Love?"

Quinn blinked and stammered. "Well...I...it's a saying, you know?"

He stepped closer, touching her cheek with his fingers. His hand shifted, and he cupped her chin as he leaned in for a kiss. The surrounding world and all the problems that came with it ceased for a moment – a moment he poured his heart into before his lips pulled away.

"I'm not afraid to say it, Quinn. I've always been bold, but I was never the person I could be until I met you." He stared into her eyes, deep blue like the ocean, full of life and energy and spirit. "I love you."

The words hung in the air, lingering, waiting for a response. He didn't breathe, couldn't breathe, not until he knew if he had opened a door or poisoned a well.

Finally, she smiled. Her whisper was for him alone. "I love you as well, Brandt Talenz."

Breath returned to his lungs, his heart leaping in his chest. "Those are the sweetest words I have ever heard. However, please be careful using my name. I *am* famous after all."

She snorted. "No. Your parents are famous. You are just vain enough to think you deserve the same adoration."

He laughed. "Perhaps I am. The difference between me and who I was when we first met is that I am now satisfied with the adoration of just one person."

Quinn held her hand to her chest and spoke in a sarcastic tone. "Me? Could you be referring to *me*?" Her hands went to her cheeks and her mocking intensified. "Oh, my. What did I ever do to deserve such a prince?"

Laughing, his hand covered her mouth as he held her close. "Quiet. You can stop, now."

Her muffled voice came through his palm. "Fine. I'll stop. But you had better move your hand before I bite it."

With a yelp, he yanked his hand away. "You wouldn't."

She arched an eyebrow.

"Never mind." He held out his elbow and she took it. "Come on. The sun is nearing the horizon, and we have scouting to do."

Strolling at an easy pace, he led her toward the gate. Another wagon was approaching, this one fully loaded with a tarp covering whatever was in the back. Brandt noted that the driver was armed with a knife and had a crossbow on the seat beside him.

As the guards drew near the wagon, Brandt called out. "Alarm! He has a knife!"

The guards jerked to a halt and drew their weapons as they surrounded the wagon. Brandt pulled Quinn aside, out of the guards' view and backed against the tower. The door beside him opened and four Imperial soldiers poured out, their backs to him as they ran toward the wagon.

"Now!" Brandt whispered as he darted into the open door with Quinn on his heels.

Like the tower outside, the room was rectangular. Two tables surrounded by chairs occupied the middle of the room. Chain mail, tabards, and helmets hung on one wall. A set of stairs leading upward stood at the far end of the room.

Brandt grabbed a chain mail cuirass and handed it to Quinn. "Put this on."

She lifted it, frowning. "It's lighter than it looks."

He nodded and pulled it over his head, slipping his arms through. "I noticed. I wonder what they use to make it."

The chain mail came down to their thighs, as did the white tabards they donned over it. They each then added a black leather belt with an Order rune on the buckle, matching the blue rune marking the tabards.

Brandt then gave Quinn a helmet before sliding one over his head. When he turned toward her, he smiled.

"You look like one of them."

"So do you, but isn't that the point?"

"Yes." He waved her to follow as he headed up the stairs.

"Where are we heading?" she asked, her voice coming from behind him.

"The top, of course."

They climbed two stories, opened a door, and stepped onto the wall. With Quinn following, Brandt walked a couple hundred feet from the guard tower and stopped.

The sun hovered over the western horizon, reflecting off the blue water of the Sea of Fates. The land to the north was wooded with a seaside road heading toward the northwest. Inland about a mile was an area recently cleared of trees. The peaked roofs of buildings could be seen past the wooden palisades surrounding the area. Swirling pillars of smoke arose from inside the walls while guards patrolled the outside. At each corner of the palisades was a square turret standing higher than even the trees. Something was positioned on each turret. From the distance, Brandt couldn't be sure, but he guessed that something might be a flash cannon.

"What do you think it is?" Quinn asked. "It's almost the size of the city itself."

He nodded in agreement. "Yes. That level of effort means it's important."

Quinn sighed as she gripped his hand. "I believe our holiday has come to an end."

6

THE FORGE

With leather mitts protecting his hands and goggles to shield his eyes, Everson Gulagas gripped the crucible handle and lifted it from the hot coals. The liquid metal in the crucible wobbled as he turned and carefully poured shimmery bronze into eight castings. With the crucible empty, he set it aside, pulled the mitts from his hands, and removed the goggles from his sweat-covered face.

The air cooled as Everson walked away from the forge, a welcome relief after working in the heat for the past hour. He stopped beside a pair of workbenches, each occupied by a person focused on assembling bronze components into a ball-shaped object. Bronze panels, thin flint strips, and vials of dark powder sat on the work surfaces.

Master Benny Hedgewick sat at one table, completely fixated on his work. Over the past few weeks, Everson had grown more comfortable being around the man. Spending many hours a day with Benny had slowly whittled away the legendary inventor status Everson had held toward him. He now acknowledged Benny Hedgewick for who he was – an intelligent man with a good heart. The fact that Benny had invented things such as the Hedgewick Flyer and the original flash bomb still lingered in the back of Everson's head, but it no longer made their conversations awkward.

Ivy Fluerian sat at the other table, focused on the meticulous assembly before her. She absently tucked her long, dark hair behind an ear and bit her lip, her gaze intense as she poured dark, sparkling powder into the device. After setting the vial of flash powder aside, she secured the last hexagonal piece, one of the eight that included an inlaid piece of flint. The piece snapped into place, completing the bomb. She set the eight-inch diameter ball into the padded basket beside her and sat back with a sigh.

Everson smiled when she turned toward him. "This is nerve-wracking work, isn't it?"

Ivy nodded and wiped her forehead with her forearm. "The idea that one wrong move could blow us all up continues to cross my mind, again and again. I feel like I've aged three years since we began this process."

"Yet, it's only been one week." He grinned.

Her brow furrowed. "Is that all?"

Benny finished the bomb he had been building and set it into a basket before turning toward Everson. "This process brings back memories of when Karl and I built the first flash bombs, almost two decades ago. We were nervous wrecks the entire time and that lasted only a few days." He ran a hand through his thick, dark hair. As often happened, the man's rectangular spectacles were askew and made his head appear lop-sided. "Based on the flash powder remaining, we could be at this for another week or more. I'm not sure if my heart can handle the anxiety."

"You don't have to help, Master Hedgewick," Everson said. "We can finish this work."

"Pfft. Nonsense." He stood and stretched. "If it comes to war, which appears to be the case, then this is the least I can do. It is about time we leaders join this fight. If the Empire wins, we all lose."

The door to the forge opened, and Everson turned to see Cassilyn Talenz entering. She stopped, her gaze sweeping the massive room until it landed on him. Walking with purposeful strides, she crossed the room. The girl's brown curls covered the shoulders of her gray dress, her green eyes locked on him.

"Hi, Everson," Cassie said. "I suspected I would find you here."

"You determined that all on your own?" he said with a grin. "Perhaps you should become an espion."

Cassie stopped and frowned at him. "How droll. You sound like my brother with your sarcasm. I expected better from you, Everson."

He glanced toward Ivy, his smile faltering. "Well, I..."

Cassie touched his arm. "Easy, Ev. I'm just joking."

An exhale of relief came from Everson's lips. He had been making an effort to be a bolder version of himself – to be more like his sister, Quinn. Years of shyness, and unusual politeness for someone his age, had derived from his disability. With the thought crossing his mind, Everson looked down at his metal-encased legs. Mechanical constructs made it possible for him to stand – devices powered by Chaos Conduction, his greatest discovery. Inside those contraptions were his scrawny, useless legs. Despite Everson's brilliance and his impressive inventions, his disability had been a shadow over him most of his life. Harnessing Chaos energy, along with a fair bit of ingenuity, had changed that.

"Ev?" Cassie asked.

He looked up, blinking when he met her eyes. "Yes."

Cassie smiled, mirth reflecting in her green eyes. "I thought I lost you, there."

Ivy laughed. "It's not you, Cassie. He does the same thing with me. Issal only knows where his mind might take him next."

Everson did his best to wear a hurt expression. "You do know I'm standing here, right?"

Ivy stood and put her arm around Everson's waist. "Don't worry, Ev. We still adore you, despite your wandering attention."

With her body pressed up against him, he found himself unable to resist a smile. His gaze locked with hers and he saw adoration in her large, brown eyes. He then recalled the childhood crush toward Rena, a misplaced affection that had kept him from noticing Ivy for far too long. Now, he couldn't imagine being with anyone else. *How could I have been so blind?*

"Master Hedgewick, I'm glad you're here as well," Cassie said, drawing Everson back to the conversation. "I came to find Everson because my brother and Quinn have finally agreed to provide a full report."

Benny stood, his glib expression growing serious. "It's about time. Delvin has been chomping at the bit about their mission."

"I know," Cassie replied. "He cornered me earlier and convinced me to press Brandt. When I contacted my brother, he said they would give their report after sunset."

Benny's gaze swept the room and he frowned. "I forget there are no windows in here." He looked at Cassie. "How much time does that leave us?"

"I'd say two hours at most."

His brow furrowed. "I had better go, then. I need to send word to the others so we are all present."

The man headed toward the door and Cassie turned toward Everson. "They need me present in order to communicate with Brandt, but I wonder if they will continue to allow you to sit in with us."

Everson nodded. "I have been wondering the same thing, but I don't dare broach the subject. I'd hate to be the one who spoils it."

Cassie moved closer and whispered, "If it comes to that, I'll relay messages to you. Quinn is your sister, and I'm sure you are as concerned about her as I am about Brandt."

"Thank you, Cassie. I appreciate it."

She gave him a warm smile. "I'll see you in the briefing room after dinner."

As she walked away, Everson wondered what Quinn and Brandt had been up to since their last report. *I'll find out soon.*

A glowlamp on the table and one beside the door lit the briefing room, each with a blue nimbus casting shadows in a different direction from the other. Everson sat in one chair and Cassie sat beside him. The other chairs encircling the table were occupied by ICON's leaders. The room was quiet, the mood one of impatience as they all waited for Brandt to begin relaying his report through Cassie.

Elias Firellus sat across from Everson, his dark, almost demonic stare targeted at Cassie, who sat beside Everson. The man still made Everson nervous, as if he were something other than human. The master arcanist had a serious, brooding nature that left Everson wondering if he were ever happy.

Beside Firellus sat old Pherran Nindlerod. The small engineering master was the opposite of Firellus in many ways. Quirky, comedic, and loveable, Nindlerod had a knack of making those around him feel at ease.

The stern and impressive Captain Goren, leader of the Torreco Academy of Combat Tactics, sat beside Nindlerod. Since the military academy stood two miles from the Arcane Ward, Goren only joined important meetings. With war approaching, Everson assumed the man's attendance would become a more common occurrence.

Salina Alridge, master of the arcane arts, sat beside Goren while tapping her long, elegant fingers on the table. With dark hair, mocha-colored skin, and curves that drew men's attention, she carried a serious intensity that challenged anyone who might step out of line.

Abraham Ackerson sat beside her, rubbing his graying beard, his squinty eyes appearing to contemplate something serious. As head-master of the Fallbrandt Academy of Magic and Engineering, the man had played a key role in Everson's life since he arrived at the school. As a leader within ICON, his presence became a constant Everson found comforting.

The man beside Ackerson was rarely serious. Instead, Delvin patted his own chest to a beat, as if listening to music nobody else could hear. With dark hair slicked back and a trimmed goatee, Delvin behaved as if he didn't have a care in the world. However, Everson knew the man was not what he seemed. Of anyone at the table, Everson suspected that Delvin held the most secrets. As a master espion, the same man who had trained Quinn and Brandt, Delvin heard whispers others wouldn't hear, went places others did not go, and pulled strings others didn't know existed. Everson trusted the others around the table, but he couldn't find it in his heart to trust Delvin Garber.

"Is he ready yet?" Benny said from his seat beside Cassie.

She opened her eyes and turned toward him. "Just a moment, Master Hedgewick. They are moving to a private location."

"Do you know where they are now?" Delvin asked.

"Brandt says they are in Yarth."

Delvin's eyes narrowed. "Yarth. Interesting."

The comment stirred three conversations at once, involving everyone present other than Delvin, Cassie, and Everson. When Cassie held her hand up, the room fell silent.

"They are ready." She closed her eyes and then began reciting Brandt's report. "Once assigned the task of destroying the Imperial weapon facility, Brandt and Quinn concocted a scheme that might make it possible for Quinn to return to Sol Polis as the Archon's bodyguard. Leveraging her assignment to locate any spies within the palace, Quinn crafted a missive before she and Brandt slipped away. The note was addressed to Varius and implicated Brandt as the spy before outlining Quinn's plan to follow him in hope of discovering who was behind the assassination attempt on the Archon. To further sell the story, they planted the stolen map in Brandt's room before they left Sol Polis."

Delvin nodded. "Good thinking. The position Quinn had as the Archon's bodyguard holds value and leaving the door open to return might become important."

With her eyes still closed, Cassie resumed her tale. "Brandt and Quinn then journeyed to Vinata for a brief stay before departing for Corvichi. They arrived to find the castle heavily guarded. Using guile and stealth, they snuck in and found that it, indeed, was where the Empire was making its new weapons.

"Karl Jarlish was there, as were workers who built the weapons. In addition, Brandt and Quinn found the stores of flash powder, including eight barrels filled with the stuff. While preparing to destroy the weapons, they were discovered and surrounded by armed guards." Cassie gasped. "The situation forced Brandt to test the Speed rune on himself. That desperate act not only enabled them to escape, but they were also able to sabotage the castle in the process. The stored flash powder ignited in a massive explosion, destroying everything, and everyone, within.

"The Speed augmentation made Brandt's movements quicker than thought, his perception of time altered such that a second felt like minutes to him, but it also expired far faster than other augmentations. Worse, when the effects wore off, Brandt found himself weak and exhausted.

"While Brandt and Quinn escaped the blast, Imperial soldiers at the castle gate attacked, using a new weapon called a...musket. Quinn was shot in the arm as she and Brandt fled. Thankfully, they found a boat and took it downriver, eluding the pursuit."

The tale had been harrowing, but discovering Quinn had been wounded stirred dread inside Everson. *Is she all right?* He missed his sister and couldn't imagine losing her.

"When Brandt woke the next day, Quinn's condition was dire, her body hot with a fever, and she had lost a lot of blood. He cut a chunk of metal from her arm and...and he healed her using Order."

Thank Issal, Everson thought.

"The river took them to Yarth, where they now reside, recovering from their mission."

As Cassie finished, Everson's gaze swept the table, studying the faces of ICON's leaders. Some rubbed their chins in thought; others narrowed their eyes while staring at Cassie. Delvin leaned in and folded his hands on the table.

"Cassie, ask Brandt what they have discovered since their arrival in Yarth."

Closing her eyes, Cassie, again, began to relay Brandt's message. "Something big is happening in the area. They have seen squads of armed warriors heading toward a newly constructed compound about a mile outside the city."

Delvin peered across the table. "What do you think, Goren?"

The military captain crossed his thick arms and grimaced. "It could be a garrison for the army, giving them a place to gather and train as they prepare to launch their campaign."

Delvin nodded. "My thought as well."

"Hold on," Benny said, turning toward Cassie. "I would know more about these muskets. Please ask your brother to share more information. Can he describe them and how are they used?"

With a nod, Cassie closed her eyes. A moment later, she said, "Similar in size to a crossbow, they also use a release trigger. However, rather than firing a bolt, they have metal tubes and a striker that ignites flash powder inside the tube. A chunk of metal then flies from the tube – just like the one Brandt cut from Quinn's arm."

Benny whistled and sat back.

Everson leaned forward and shared his theory. "Muskets are like miniature flash cannons. They are using controlled explosions to launch metal balls in both cases." As he said it, he knew it to be true. "However, muskets are small and light enough to be carried. The energy generated by igniting flash powder could make the range of these muskets four times that of a bow. I just wonder if their aim is reliable." Something else then occurred to him. "Regardless, healing someone with a chunk of metal in them would be impossible, and removing something like that is far more difficult than pulling an arrow free."

"I agree, Everson," Benny said. "Flash bombs, flash cannons, and now these muskets – these creations could greatly alter battle strategy." An uncharacteristic sadness reflected in the engineering master's eyes. "What good is a sword against such weapons?"

7

HARRIERS

The sky above was gray, the air chilly enough for Quinn to require her wool cloak. When the line ahead of her moved, she shuffled forward a step. Brandt stood beside her, neither having said a word since they had joined the line. At the time, there had been fifty men and women ahead of them. Thirty minutes later, that number had been whittled down to four men while a line of more than twenty extended behind her. Standing in the heart of the square outside the Yarth citadel, the sight of citizens going about their daily lives stirred Quinn's childhood memories of Cinti Mor.

Wagons were lined against the citadel wall as farmers sold fresh fruit and vegetables to the citizens of Yarth. Tinkers stood beside blankets filled with trinkets as they called for passersby to come and inspect their wares. Men and women carrying buckets approached the circular fountain in the heart of the square, filling the buckets before retreating. Amidst all this activity, Quinn found her attention repeatedly drawn to the children.

Divided into two groups and of ages from five or six summers to their early teens, the children's shouts and laughter had Quinn missing her brother. One of the groups was playing Captain May I, the captain standing alone beside the fountain, his back to the other children as they took turns advancing. Quinn, Everson, and the other children in Cinti

Mor had often played the very same game. Watching these young citizens of an enemy nation play the familiar game had Quinn realizing that the citizens of the Empire were not evil. *The fault lies with their leaders.* If, somehow, the mindset of the Empire leaders could be altered and their tireless fight against Chaos set aside, war would not be necessary.

Brandt leaned close, his voice drawing Quinn from her reverie. "If you had told me six months ago I would be joining the Imperial Army, I would have laughed in disbelief."

Quinn snorted. "Same here. However, life is unpredictable."

His arm wrapped around her back and he pulled her close, whispering, "Regardless of what happens, I'll always cherish our time in Yarth."

She smiled. "As will I. Too bad it had to end, but at least we had those seven glorious days to ourselves."

The line advanced again, the two men ahead of them approaching a table where a man sat, wearing a dark blue outfit that reminded Quinn of Sculdin's uniform. Armed guards dressed in the familiar chain mail and white tabards of the Imperial Army surrounded the man, surveying their surroundings with wary eyes. After a brief discussion, the seated officer handed a sheet of paper to each of the two men at the head of the line. When the two men stepped aside, Brandt and Quinn approached the table.

The seated officer finished recording something in a ledger before looking up at Quinn and Brandt. His head was shorn and he had a well-trimmed brown beard. Quinn noted the stripes on his shoulder, one less stripe than what she remembered from Sculdin's uniform.

"You are here to join the Imperial Army?"

"Yes, Captain," Brandt said.

The man shook his head. "I am not Rorrick. He is at base camp. My name is Lieutenant Killian, Rorrick's second in command." His gaze shifted to Quinn. "You wish to join the army as well?"

"Yes, sir."

"What's your name, girl?"

"Jacquinn Mor."

"A Hurn name."

"Yes. I grew up in Port Hurns."

His gaze lowered to the sword on her hip, the one remaining after she had been forced to sell the other so she and Brandt could survive. "Do you know how to use that?"

Quinn followed the man's gaze, her hand going to the hilt. "Yes. I have some skill with a blade."

The man's brow furrowed. "You appear too young to have been in the army."

Quinn had her lie ready and recited it without hesitation. "My uncle spent time in the Holy Army. He gave me this blade and taught me how to use it."

"And what brings you here?"

"Until recently, I was working as the bodyguard for a merchant in Sol Polis." She frowned. "It turns out that a sword can't protect you from poison. When a deal went bad, the woman I worked for discovered that the loss of gold carries a grudge. With her dead, I was out of a job. Three weeks later, I have yet to find another job and my coin is spent."

After listening to Quinn's story, he made notes on a piece of paper, dumped a bit of wax on it, and pressed his ring against it as a seal.

He then looked at Brandt. "What's your name?"

"Brandon Tallister."

Killian wrote the name on a sheet of paper. "What about you? Do you have any experience with a weapon?"

Brandt grinned. "Does sparring with sticks against my older brother count?"

"No, it does not."

"Well, I guess I don't have experience, then."

The man wrote a few more notes while saying, "Don't worry about it. We'll train you to use a musket." He poured a bit of wax on the paper and pressed his ring into it.

"A musket?" Brandt asked in a manner Quinn found quite convincing. "What's a musket?"

"You'll see." Killian grinned as he extended the paper toward Brandt. "Take the papers and head north, out of the city. Take a right at the first intersection, and the road will bring you to the training compound. If anyone tries to stop you, show them the seal."

One of the guards beside Killian announced, "Next."

Sensing they were dismissed, Quinn and Brandt turned from the table and crossed the square, each reading the paper in their hand.

Quinn's listed the name she had given, along with the word *harrier* beside it.

She frowned, unfamiliar with the word. "What's harrier mean?"

Brandt shrugged. "I have no idea. Mine is less confusing."

"What's it say?"

"I'm going to be a musketeer."

With Brandt at her side, Quinn stepped into the training compound. They both paused, their gazes scanning sprawling grounds covered by a row of buildings and hundreds of tents. The nearest camps consisted of dark green tents while tents of light green, brown, and blue could be seen in the distance. A tall palisade built of logs, sharpened to points at the top, surrounded the compound. Everywhere Quinn looked, she found activity as thousands of troops trained for war.

Quinn cast one last glance toward Brandt as he headed toward his camp. She stifled a sigh, pressed her lips together, and proceeded toward the blue tents as she had been directed.

She was forced to pause as an officer jogged past, the man trailed by a regiment dressed in brown leather, each armed with a musket. The squad altered course toward the same cluster of brown tents as where Brandt was headed.

Resuming her journey, Quinn watched warriors sparring with wooden swords, the steady clacking from them a familiar sound. Another squad took turns running forward and tossing blocks of wood toward empty barrels aligned near the palisade wall. Rather than wearing armor, the men throwing the wood were covered in black save for a blue Order rune on their chest.

As Quinn drew close to the blue tents, she noticed that the warriors in the area were all women. Their outfits were padded leather, dyed a deep blue. They stood and sat in clusters, conversing quietly and ignoring her passing. She headed directly toward a tent at the center, marked by a flag waving gently in the breeze – a flag marked with a blue Order rune on a field of white. Standing outside the tent was an armed soldier – tall with broad shoulders, oversized facial features, and long brown hair pulled back in a tail. The towering guard shifted to block Quinn.

"Hold." It was a woman's voice, startling Quinn. "Nobody sees the commander without seeing me first."

"I have orders from Lieutenant Killian," Quinn held the note toward the tall guard.

The woman pressed her lips together and read the paper. "Wait here." She then ducked into the tent.

A moment later, she reappeared, holding the tent flap aside as a stern brunette stepped out. With faint lines around her mouth and angular, brown eyes, she appeared about ten years older than Quinn. Her dark blue leather included a white stripe on each shoulder. She wore a long, curved sword on her hip.

"I am Commander Luon. I run this unit. What's your name, soldier?"

"Jacquinn Mor."

The woman scrutinized Quinn with narrowed eyes. "You appear fit. I assume you know how to use a sword?"

Quinn nodded. "Yes, Commander. I have some training in that area."

"How are you with a shield?"

"My training focused on using two swords."

Luon snorted. "Dual blades? Those won't do you any good here."

"But if you just give me a chance…"

Luon poked Quinn in the chest. "Listen! You might think you have skills, but that matters little to me. Dual blade fighting is appropriate for dueling, but we are going to war. You are now a soldier in the Imperial Army. You will set aside your pride and selfish needs and dedicate yourself to your squadmates, or I will see you in shackles."

Quinn bristled and fought her desire to break the woman's finger. Finding restraint, she responded between clenched teeth. "Yes, Commander."

Luon grinned. "Good. You have spirit and can temper it with self-restraint. I can work with that." Her gaze flicked toward Quinn's sword. "Since you have experience with two blades, I assume you feel comfortable wielding a sword left handed?"

"Yes. Of course."

"Good. *That*, is of use." She turned toward the tall woman. "Liziele, please escort Jacquinn to the armory and have them issue her a uniform, practice sword, and shield. Once outfitted, I want her assigned to squad three. Tell Cleffa to have her prepared. Today's drills begin in an hour."

The commander spun about and stepped into her tent. Liziele put a man-sized hand on Quinn's shoulder, her grip like a vice. "Welcome to the Harriers, Jacquinn. Come with me. You have little time to get outfitted before today's drill."

With a wooden shield strapped to her right arm and a wooden practice sword in her left hand, Quinn followed Liziele back to the Harriers camp. The new uniform Quinn wore chafed in places, the stiff leather not yet broken in. She found herself wondering what was used to dye the leather blue. When she lifted her shield, she noted the three white triangles on her right bicep and wondered what they might mean.

They passed four clusters of dark blue tents before Liziele led Quinn into a camp encircled by eight tents. A woman with dark hair tied in a tail stood and watched Quinn and Liziele enter the camp. Quinn noted the brunette as the only soldier in the group with yellow triangles rather than white.

"Cleffa," Liziele said as she approached the woman. "We have a replacement for Juvi." She gestured with her thumb toward Quinn. "Meet Jacquinn, your new squadmate."

Cleffa was roughly Quinn's size, with a similarly lean, muscular figure. The woman's posture and dark complexion reminded Quinn of her training sergeant from the Torreco Academy of Combat and Tactics. Quinn realized she hadn't once thought of Jasmine during the year since she left the academy. *I wonder if Jasmine knows I was recruited to ICON. Does she even know about the organization? What has Goren shared with her?*

A horn blew, a deep, reverberating sound blaring throughout the compound. The women dressed in blue leather all began shuffling about, entering their tents and exiting with wooden swords and shields.

"Drill time, soldier," Cleffa said to Quinn. "Time to move out."

"Wait," Quinn grabbed the woman's arm, stopping her. Cleffa glared down at Quinn's hand on her forearm. "I don't know what I'm supposed to do."

"First, you are to remove your hand," Cleffa growled. Quinn did it and the woman looked Quinn in the eye. "I have no time for instruction right now. Assuming you know how to swing a sword, all you need to do is watch the squads before us and mimic their action when our turn comes." She turned away, stopping two steps later and looking back. "And don't embarrass me." Bending to scoop up her sword and shield, Cleffa lifted them up and pounded the shield with the wooden sword three times, sending a *clack, clack, clack* that drew everyone's attention.

"Listen up, Squad Three!" Cleffa yelled while slowly spinning about. "Time to dance. Watch me, keep your rhythm, and maintain your position." She then jogged toward an open field, followed by the rest of the squad.

Still confused by what was happening, Quinn joined the group as they circled tents and fell in with other similar squads. Each woman dressed in blue had white triangles on their bicep, some on the left, others on the right, ranging from one triangle to four. She located a cluster with three triangles all gathering around Cleffa and joined them.

"Line up, one stride apart!" Cleffa called out, her voice fighting with other squad leaders. In moments, the chaos settled into order.

Two rows of forty Harriers stood in front of Quinn's squad, all dressed in dark blue leather. Like Quinn, each soldier had a wooden shield strapped to her right arm and held a wooden sword in her left hand. Across the field, rows of armed women waited – all similarly armed but with swords in their right hands. The scene gave Quinn the impression of looking into a mirror.

Sergeant Luon strode across the open ground between the opposing groups and began to shout out orders. "Harriers, prepare to attack! When the horn blows, squads one and five will begin. Maintain the three count and listen to your squad leader! You will continue until the horn blows a second time, and then you will retreat!"

The instructions from Luon did little to clear things up for Quinn, who remained unsure of what exactly was about to transpire. She glanced toward the center of the Squad Three row, where Cleffa was standing. The woman's words replayed in Quinn's head: *Watch the squads before us and mimic their action.*

A horn blew and Squad One burst into a run as did Squad Five, the two rushing toward each other. Just before they collided, the ranks slowed and began exchanging strikes, the clacking of wood on wood filling the air. During this process, the squad two leader was counting aloud. When she reached three, the squad sprinted toward the battlefield, as did Squad Six from the far side. Squads One and Five peeled away, spun about, and ran through the gaps between the charging squads.

Cleffa counted aloud, reaching the count of three when Squad One ran past. Quinn's squadmates then rushed forward and she scrambled to follow. As her squad approached the middle of the field, Squad Two spun about and darted toward them. Two girls ran past Quinn, one slipping through the gap to her left, the other to her right.

Suddenly, the opposing squad was there. Quinn raised her shield urgently and blocked an attacking strike. She swung her sword, the woman facing her blocking it before she swung again. Quinn blocked with her shield, feinted with a high swing, and ducked below the other soldier's strike. Still crouching, Quinn came around fast, her wooden sword delivering a crunching blow to her opponent's knee. The woman cried out and fell as her teammates turned and ran away. Quinn stood over the downed woman, who held her knee and writhed in pain. Another squad rushed in, and she turned to find her own squad halfway across the field. A horn blew and everyone stopped.

Everywhere Quinn looked, women were staring in her direction. She turned and found Commander Luon stalking in her direction, the woman's face a scowl. Luon glared down at Quinn's injured opponent and took a deep breath before shouting. "Squad Seven! I need two soldiers to assist this woman to the healer's tent."

After a brief command from the Squad Seven leader, two women rushed forward and lifted the injured woman upright. Luon turned toward Quinn and grimaced.

"Cleffa!" Luon shouted.

The Squad Three leader rushed over, stopped beside Quinn, and thumped her shield hand to her chest. "Yes, Commander!"

"What happened here? Didn't you provide this soldier the proper instruction?"

Cleffa stammered. "There was little time…"

"It's my fault!" Quinn blurted. Luon turned toward her with a raised brow. "I'm sorry, Commander. Cleffa told me what to do, but I got caught up in the moment. My dueling experience kicked in and I…I guess I went for the kill without even realizing it."

Luon stared at Quinn for a long moment before turning toward Cleffa. "Is this true, soldier?"

Cleffa blinked, her gaze flicking toward Quinn as she nodded. "Yes. Commander."

The sergeant snorted and turned her attention back toward Quinn. "If so, what exactly were you told to do?"

Quinn's mind raced as she considered what she had seen from the others. "Maintain a three count, stay with my team, rush the opposing squad, strike three times, retreat, and repeat with the next wave." She paused briefly, then added, "Only exchange blows, do not take out your opponent."

Tension held Quinn's breath captive while Luon stared at her with narrowed eyes. A long moment of silence passed as the other Harriers waited in anticipation.

Finally, Luon said. "Don't let it happen again." The commander spun about and bellowed, "Reform ranks! We will go again. I want to see ten flawless waves at full speed!"

Quinn emerged from her tent and stretched, happy to be out of her stiff leather armor. Similar to her squadmates, she wore the simple tunic, breeches, and cloak provided by the Imperial army.

The gray skies above were dark to the east, the clouds masking any stars that might have appeared. A fire illuminated the camp, fighting the approaching night. A dozen of her squadmates sat on the logs encircling the fire, the girls eating from wooden bowls and chatting.

Quinn spotted others returning with bowls and followed their path to find four lines waiting near another fire. She stood at the end of a line that inched forward over the next few minutes. The aroma of beef stew caused her to realize the depth of her hunger. When the woman in front of her moved away, Quinn stepped forward and accepted a steaming bowl, a spoon, and a hard roll before turning back to her camp.

The logs around the fire were now full, leaving no place for Quinn to sit. Instead, she stood near her tent and ate in quiet while listening to conversations between various groups of girls, catching bits and pieces of chatter ranging from speculation about the war to which men were the most handsome in other regiments. In her head, she mentally recited the names of the girls who shared her tent.

The tall woman with short hair and tilted eyes was named Bernice. The brunette with a braid and broad shoulders, Evian. Tilly was the short red-head. Last was Ilsa, who matched Quinn's height with an average build and dirty blond hair tied in a tail. When introduced to them, the girls had been cordial but showed little warmth toward Quinn. In fact, she had found little welcome from anyone in the squad. She wondered if their behavior toward her was a result of her mistake during drills or something else.

The crunch of footsteps on dirt drew Quinn's attention and she found Cleffa emerging from the darkness. The squad leader stopped beside Quinn and stared at the fire.

"You lied today," Cleffa said it as fact.

"Yes."

Cleffa narrowed her eyes at Quinn. "Why did you cover for me?"

Quinn shrugged. "It seemed the right thing to do. I'm new and was less likely to receive harsh discipline – at least for my first offense. You might not have the luxury."

The woman sighed. "I shouldn't have allowed my anger toward Juvi influence how I treat you."

"I heard the name mentioned before. Who is Juvi?"

Cleffa's lips pressed together as she stared at the fire. A beat later, she responded. "Juvi was among the more skilled girls in Squad Three. She was even our best duelist. However, she disgraced us, and we still carry that shame."

"What did she do?"

"Deserted."

Quinn's brow furrowed. "She left your squad?"

"Worse. She abandoned her duty – her commitment. They caught her south of Yarth and brought her back here for a public trial. The procedure was brief with Rorrick declaring her guilty as a deserter and for treason. He claimed that anyone deserting would be treated as if they intended to sell secrets to the enemy.

"Juvi was stripped down to her small clothes, as was the entire squad. We each received three lashings with a whip. She received far more than that. They then hanged her blood-covered body from a noose and left it in the middle of camp for three days for everyone to see. I suspect any soldier who had been present will think twice before attempting to run from his or her duty."

Quinn continued to stare at Cleffa, as she had done during the entire story. "Why did the rest of the squad receive lashings? You had done nothing wrong."

Cleffa nodded. "It's because Rorrick is clever. He wants us to know we are responsible for the behavior of our squadmates. If we all risk punishment for the act of one, we have cause to ensure that others obey orders."

Quinn turned toward the fire where other Harriers were sharing stories. The sight left her feeling singled out. She realized that the others blamed Juvi and Quinn was now the subject of their anger as Juvi's replacement. The mistake Quinn made during drills had only made things worse. She needed to do something to gain their trust.

"Do you really have dueling experience?" Cleffa asked. "You mentioned it on the field today."

"Yes."

"Are you skilled?"

"Some might say I am."

"Good," Cleffa said. "Our weekly inter-squad duels happen in six days. I'd like to have you represent Squad Three. While Juvi wasn't able to defeat the champion, she had come close. In the weeks since Juvi's offense, we have fared quite poorly. In all honesty, it has been embarrassing. Perhaps you can change our luck."

Quinn remained silent, knowing this was her chance.

8

THE GIBBET

A creak from the dungeon door stirred Parker from his sleep. The night had been long and restless, filled with troubled dreams spurred by the knowledge of what was to come.

"Wake up, you slime!" Jerrick the jailor shouted.

Normally, Parker would exchange quips with the man. Today, he lacked the fire to play that game or any other.

He rolled off his pallet and stood, groaning at the aches in his joints. When he peered through the bars in his cell door, he saw six armed guards surrounding the big jailor. Jerrick unlocked the door to Hex's cell and scrambled backward. The door swung open and Hex charged out with a roar.

At a height exceeding six feet with broad shoulders, thick arms, and a barrel chest, Hex often caused other men to fear him. In this case, the big sailor rushing out sent the armed guards backward with terror on their faces. He dodged the first blade, grabbed the man holding it, and lifted him into the air. With a howl and wild eyes, Hex tossed the guard into three of his cohorts, smashing them into the wall before they crumpled to the floor.

Hex turned toward the next guard as the man thrust his sword, the blade slicing through Hex's stomach until the tip emerged from his back. A deep grunt came from the big man's mouth and he swung his meaty fist, backhanding the soldier with a solid *crunch*. As the guard fell to the floor, the jailor leaped forward and swung his cudgel, striking Hex in the head with a *crack* Parker felt from his cell. Hex fell to the floor with the sword still stuck in his midriff.

Jerrick turned toward the cells as the guards climbed to their feet – all except the man who had run Hex through. The guard remained on the floor, out cold.

"Does anyone else want to try an escape?" The jailor asked. "I highly recommend it. Not only will you feel the pain of my cudgel, but we will heal you and still send you to the gallows."

Neither Parker nor Pretencia responded. The jailor knelt and held Hex's wrists together behind his back, shackling the big man. He then stood and unlocked Pretencia's cell.

Dalwin emerged wearing a frown. "This is wrong, Jerrick, and you know it."

"Right or wrong isn't for me to decide," Jerrick said. "Our betters give us orders. We follow them. It's as simple as that."

The man shackled Dalwin's wrists behind his back and turned toward Parker's cell.

"Don't make this difficult, Parker. I'm just doing my job, as are these men. It's nothing personal."

"I know, Jerrick," Parker said. "Let's just get this over with."

The man unlocked the door, opening it for Parker.

Jerrick gave Parker a nod. "That's the spirit."

Parker spun about, holding his wrists together behind his back. "I'm looking forward to seeing the sun again, Jerrick. If I must die, then I just want to see the sun, and, perhaps, the aqua waters of Wayport bay."

"Aye, Parker." There was an undeniable affection in Jerrick's voice. "That, I can offer."

With Jerrick's hand on his shoulder to guide him, Parker walked out of his cell, through the dungeon doorway and down the dark corridor. The clanking of armor trailed behind him as a guard walked Pretencia and the others carried the unconscious Hex.

Climbing the stairs, Parker turned at the landing and found welcome light ahead. He emerged into the receiving hall where Captain Sharene waited with a dozen armed guards. The woman watched the others emerge, her brow rising when she spotted four men carrying Hex with a blade still sticking from his stomach and a trail of blood dripping on the floor.

"So, the big man resisted. I'm not surprised." She turned to the side. "Dryfus."

A short man in a purple cloak stepped out from behind the cluster of guards. The man's eyes were round with fear, and he refused to look at Sharene, even as he spoke to her. "Yes, Captain?"

"Please heal the prisoner. He is to be publicly hanged. We can't have him dying before his performance."

"Yes, Captain."

The man scurried over to Hex as the guards set the big man on the tiled floor. One guard put a foot against Hex's chest and pulled the sword from his stomach. Blood gurgled from the wound. Kneeling beside him, Dryfus put his hand on Hex's bald head and closed his eyes. A moment later, the bleeding stopped, and a massive shiver shook the big man. His eyes flickered open, and he gasped for air. Panting, he turned his head and his eyes met Parker's.

"Sorry, Hex," Parker said softly. "There's no way out of this one."

"Rex, Turk, Hammond, Yuli, Fern, get him up and keep him in line," Sharene commanded.

The five guards scrambled around Hex, lifted him to his feet and took position as the two biggest guards each took one of Hex's bound arms and the other three leveled blades at his back. One glance at Hex's downcast eyes made it obvious he lacked the fire for further resistance.

"Chadwick is a traitor, Sharene," Parker said. "Why do you follow him?"

The tall woman scowled at Parker for a moment before a smile crossed her face. "A rising tide floats all ships. You know that. With Chadwick's advancement comes opportunity for the rest of us."

"Is that all you care about, Sharene? How you might benefit, regardless of how it impacts others?"

She sneered. "Don't get righteous with me, Parker. Everyone puts themselves first, and if they say otherwise, they lie."

He shook his head. "I'm saddened to hear you say such a thing."

The sound of horns arose outside the castle, blaring the song meant for a king. The horns settled and Chadwick's voice arose, calling out to the crowd.

"That's our cue." Sharene said in a firm voice. "Let's go."

A shove in the back spurred Parker toward the door. When he reached it, Chadwick's speech became understandable.

"...Empire will bring a new age to Wayport, to Kantaria, and to all of Issalia. Without Chaos magic to threaten our lives, we will thrive and prosper. Your taxes will be lower, and the healing abilities of the Ministry will be available to everyone while those who can channel Chaos are executed – the same fate awaiting anyone who betrays the Empire."

Chadwick turned as Parker, Pretencia, and Hex strode onto the landing atop the stairs. Below, the plaza was packed with people surrounding a newly constructed wooden platform.

"Behold!" Chadwick said in a loud voice. "A trio of traitors who resist our cause!"

A roar arose from the crowd, cheers and jeers that drowned out whatever Chadwick said next. The duke's gaze shifted to Parker, meeting his glare. *I would skewer you before all these people if I could,* Parker thought. Chadwick blinked, his grin dropping away as if he had heard the threat. The guards pushed Parker forward, ending the silent confrontation.

Down the stairs Parker went, toward the hungry, angry crowd. If not for the line of armed guards standing at the bottom of the steps, Parker suspected the mob would have stormed the stairs to get to him.

A narrow wooden ramp ran to the wooden platform. Parker led the way across the ramp, trailed by guards and his two cellmates. Atop the platform were three nooses, dangling from a wooden frame ten feet above. A trap door ran the length of the platform, and the lever for the door waited at the far end.

Two guards gripped Parker's upper arms and forced him toward the first noose. One guard held him in place while the other pulled the rope over his head and cinched it below his chin.

Parker's armpits were damp with sweat, and his breaths came in rapid gasps. The crowd shrieked curses and words of hatred as if he were the reason for every malady inflicted upon them. *They know nothing about me, but they despise me. I have done nothing to deserve their hatred, yet they thirst for my blood.* The realization left Parker doubting his faith in humanity. *Would they even care if they knew about my role in the Battle at the Brink – an event that saved every one of their lives?*

Turning his head, Parker saw Dalwin staring toward the crowd with defiance in his eyes despite the rope about his neck. Beyond Dalwin was Hex, wearing a deep grimace. Beyond Hex, Sharene shifted to stand beside the trapdoor lever.

The crowd quieted and Chadwick's voice arose, drawing their attention.

"These three men have been found guilty of treason, sentenced to a gruesome, painful death. Let this be a message to any who seek to betray my rule or the Empire. This or a worse death will await any who dare to defy me."

As Chadwick spoke, his voice had drawn closer and closer. He then appeared at Parker's left, standing atop the gallows platform opposite from the lever where Sharene waited.

"For the glory of Wayport, Kantaria, and the Empire, I condemn these three men to death." Chadwick turned toward Sharene. "On my word, let them hang…"

The thump of his own pulse hammered in Parker's ears, joined by his own rapid, desperate breaths as they drowned out Chadwick's voice. He closed his eyes and thought of Tenzi, wishing he could see her one last time.

As Chadwick's speech ended, the crowd cheered, the noise drawing Parker's attention. He opened his eyes to fists pumping in the air, the bloodthirsty crowd cheering for his death.

A flash of movement caught Parker's eye, followed by the glint of sunlight off a thrown blade. Sharene jerked backward, and she stumbled with a dagger hilt sticking from her chest. The woman gripped the tall lever beside her as another blade slammed through her left eye. She slid to her knees, twitching as blood ran down her face. Her arm wrapped about the trapdoor lever, using it to hold her upright until she collapsed, pulling the lever with her. The floor panel fell open, and Parker fell with it, knowing he had reached his final moment.

9

TRAITOR

Despite the Kantarian helmet and armor she wore, Tenzi Thanes resisted the urge to turn around, fearing Chadwick or Sharene might recognize her.

Keeping her back to them took everything Tenzi had, knowing Parker stood behind her with a noose around his neck. She had caught a glimpse of him when they brought him out. The image remained in her mind – his clothing soiled, his hair ragged, and a full, scraggily beard on his face. Parker had lost some weight, but he was in better shape than Pretencia. The former king was in poor condition before Chadwick arrested him. Now…

Come on, Brock, Tenzi thought. *We don't have much time.*

Beyond the crowded plaza were the guard towers, square structures that stood three stories tall. Upon each, five guards holding crossbows watched the crowd below while the gate between them stood open to welcome the people of Wayport to the public execution. If Tenzi had her way, it would be Chadwick on the gibbet with Sharene beside him.

Tenzi peered down the line of guards to her left, all dressed in Kantarian armor – Black leather with gold and red trim, the metal plates on their chests and shoulders tinted with a golden hue to match the bracers on their arms. She wondered if their loyalty was to Chadwick or to the crown. The answer would come soon.

Movement atop one of the towers drew Tenzi's attention. A scuffle ensued, but lasted mere seconds. The same occurred atop the other tower. It was time to act.

She drew the daggers strapped to her thighs, spun, and launched the first, the knife plunging into Sharene's chest. The second dagger followed, piercing the hateful woman's eye. Sharene fell to her knees. A *thump* drew Tenzi's attention as a cloaked figure landed atop the far end of the platform, sending Chadwick scrambling away. Tenzi then panicked when she spied Sharene hugging the gallows lever, pulling it down as she collapsed to the floor. Quick as lightning, Tenzi reached behind her back, grabbed the dagger secured between shoulder blades, and made a desperate throw just before the nearest guard tackled her and drove her to the ground.

Broland and seven soldiers waited in the alley, all dressed in Kantarian armor, each with a red ribbon tied around his or her left bicep. Eight arcanists, including Stein, waited with them.

When cheers arose from within the nearby citadel, Broland turned toward Stein and nodded. "It is time."

Stein and the other arcanists closed their eyes as Broland's stomach fluttered in anticipation. Chaos gave them an edge, but the plan to spare the Wayport guards' lives put him and the others at risk. While a Power augmentation might make him super human, death remained just a well-placed arrow or sword point away.

The arcanists began opening their eyes, their irises filled with crackling red energy. The rune on Broland's hand began to glow, as did the symbol marking each of his fellow soldiers. His vision whited out, and he stumbled as a surge of energy wracked his body. The spots fell away and he stood tall, feeling as if he could take on the world.

"Arcanists, you head back to Gulley's and wait. If all goes well, the city will soon be ours."

The four men and three women spun about and scurried down the alley, toward the city center, leaving Stein, Broland, and the guards behind. Broland turned toward his team and the fluttering in his stomach returned. As a prince, he was used to others obeying his orders. However, the lives of these soldiers depended on him.

Broland flexed his arm, tested his shield straps, and confidence stirred inside him. The shield felt solid and familiar, reminding him of countless hours he had spent training. With surprise on their side, this was a fight they could win.

"Remember to watch your strength. Our goal is to overwhelm, capture, and interrogate, not to kill." He gestured toward the three men and woman to his left. "You four take the north tower. The others are with me as we take the south tower. Send two swordsmen to the top. The other two go through the door and disable anyone inside." He turned toward Stein. "Trail discreetly and be prepared to heal in case any of us is wounded."

"Try not to get killed, Broland," Stein said. "I'd rather not be on Brock's bad side."

"I don't blame you." Broland had never seen his father so focused, so intent on something. "The Duke of Wayport is about to find out what that is like. I almost feel sorry for Chadwick. He is about to have a miserable day."

Without another word, he jogged down the alley, darted out into the open, and sprinted toward the south tower at super-human speed. The group behind him split apart as four soldiers drove toward the north tower. As he ran, Broland watched the guards atop the towers. One turned toward him and fired a bolt, taking out the soldier on his left – the other man who was to help take the top of the tower. *It's up to me, now.* Gauging the height and distance, he leaped.

The rush was incredible as he rose up in an arc exceeding fifty feet at its apex. He braced himself and landed on the square tower, bending his knees with the impact and stumbling forward before bowling over the retreating guard who had fired the first shot. The man smashed into the low wall surrounding the tower and lay still, unconscious.

The other four guards atop the tower spun as one. The first fired a crossbow bolt, blocked by Broland's shield. A swipe of the same shield knocked the crossbows from the hands of two others as launched bolts went flying. Crossbows pieces sprayed out from the tower and rained on the crowd below.

When the last guard drew his sword, Broland kicked the man's hand with a crushing blow, shattering bones and sending the sword sailing toward the sea. The man screamed and held his destroyed arm close as he fell to his knees.

Another man reached for his blade, but Broland caught his arm, his grip causing the man's eyes to bulge and his knees to buckle. Broland released the man, drew his sword, and faced his combatants.

"I am Prince Broland, come to reclaim Wayport. Surrender and you will live. Declare your allegiance to my father, and you will remain free men."

The guards who remained conscious blinked in confusion, one asking, "Prince? You still live?"

"Yes, as does my father. Turn around, and you will see for yourself."

Brock remained wrapped in his cloak, his face shadowed by his hood. He listened as Chadwick spewed words laced with lies. The surrounding crowd was too hungry to care. Chadwick placed the problems of Wayport upon the three men on the gibbet. The citizens took his words as truth, and they wanted blood. Brock suspected they would have accepted anyone atop the platform, but his tenure as king had given him insight. The source of these people's problems would most likely be found in a mirror.

He turned toward the south guard tower, a shadowy pillar in the midday sun. From the top, five guards watched the crowd below. *Where are you, Broland? The man is nearing the end of his speech.*

A *crack* sounded from atop the tower as splintered crossbow parts sprayed over the crowd. *Finally!*

With Power-augmented strength, Brock turned toward the gallows and leaped, his long, gray cloak fluttering as he sailed through the air. An audible gasp came from the crowd when he drew a sword and fell toward the gallows platform. Chadwick scrambled away, toward the stairs. Sharene stumbled to her knees with a knife in her throat and another in her eye. With a solid thump, Brock landed upon the platform and spun around with his arm extended, the sword slicing through the ropes tied to Pretencia and Hex. The floor on which the prisoners stood fell away before Brock could reach Parker's rope. The noose snapped tight as a thrown knife sliced through Parker's noose. Parker, Hex, and Pretencia disappeared in the gloom below the platform.

Brock turned toward Chadwick, who was halfway up the stairs.

"Kill him! Kill the attacker!" Chadwick shrieked.

Brock took a deep breath and added Power to his voice, the anger he felt coming through his shout. "Stop!"

Everyone froze, even Chadwick.

With a flourish, Brock tore his cloak free and tossed it aside. He wore his most renowned outfit, a black doublet with gold buttons, gold trim, and a red Chaos symbol on his chest. The gold crown on his head with the ruby encrusted Chaos rune shone in the mid-day sun. Despite the beard on his face, anyone who lived in Kantaria would know him by description. Everyone had heard tales of King Brock.

"I, King Brock of Kantaria, declare Duke Chadwick Von Durran as a traitor." Brock spun about as he spoke, his voice reverberating off the citadel walls. "His actions have made him an enemy of Kantaria. Anyone who supports him or obeys any command from his lips from this moment will also been seen as a traitor and a criminal."

Nobody moved. For a few seconds, nobody breathed. The guards dressed in black stared in shock, including the one holding Tenzi on the ground.

"Release that woman, soldier," Brock commanded, pointing at the man.

The guard scrambled to his feet and Tenzi did the same. She then rushed toward the stairs and began climbing them. Brock turned and his gaze landed on Chadwick, whose eyes grew round just before he turned and bolted.

Brock turned toward the guards lined before the gallows, placed there to protect the duke and to keep the crowd at bay. "Send the crowd home and keep things under control. We don't need any more casualties today."

Tenzi ran past Brock, in pursuit of the fleeing duke.

"Tenzi!"

She slowed and turned toward him. A shadow eclipsed the sun and Brock looked up to find Broland sailing over him to land on the castle stairs beside Tenzi. Brock looked back at the tower where Broland had been standing, a hundred fifty feet away and four stories high.

When Broland turned toward him, Brock shook his head. "That was a risky jump, even with your augmentation."

Broland stepped forward, "Sorry, Father. I figured a healer was required."

Reluctantly, Brock nodded. "I understand. Start with Parker. His rope was cut late." He turned toward the castle, knowing what he must do. "You two need to handle things here. I will deal with Chadwick and Illiri. It's time for them to discover the price of betrayal."

An armed squad emerged from the building and blocked the door – undoubtedly sent by Chadwick. Rather than attacking, Brock fled, racing across the stairs and leaping off, landing fifty feet away in the grass of the tree-covered courtyard between the castle and the outer wall. He looked up at the arched, stained-glass window above, the bright metal frame a telling sign it had recently been replaced. *Ironically, it is about to break again.*

Backed by super strength, Brock threw his sword pommel-first at the window and jumped to follow it. The window shattered, the glass spraying inward with Brock following. He landed inside as glass shards rained upon the tiled floor, benches, and the throne where Illiri sat. The stunned duchess wore a red, shoulderless gown, cut low at the front. Chadwick stood before the throne, covering his head with his arms. When he lowered them, he stared at Brock with frightened eyes.

"Please, Brock…"

"Do you not possess a conscience, Chadwick?" Brock's gaze shifted to Illiri, who glowered back at him while pulling a shard of orange glass from her bared shoulder, leaving a crimson trail down her arm. "Or, perhaps, it is a backbone you lack."

Illiri stood, her shoulder dripping blood. The woman sneered, "Do what you will with us, Brock. It doesn't matter. The Empire has weapons you lack and the backing of those who would rather see Chaos magic gone for good. We are sick of arcanists holding the rest of us hostage with fear."

Brock frowned, moving closer to scoop his sword off the floor. "When have I threatened you with my magic?"

The duchess tilted her head and raised a brow. "You do so right now."

"Only after you betrayed Kantaria," Brock growled. "Treason cannot be suffered, Illiri. If I don't make an example of you two, I risk others betraying me as well. With what we face, I cannot have a kingdom divided."

Chadwick remained silent, his eyes flicking from Brock to Illiri, and back, all the while kneading his hands.

Illiri sneered at Chadwick. "Really, Chadwick? Brock was right. You have no spine."

"What...what would you have me do?" Chadwick whined.

The woman shook her head. "Nothing I suppose. You have always been a disappointment, Chadwick." She turned toward Brock. "Our king, on the other hand...he has a strength and determination you lack."

Illiri strode toward Brock, her hips swaying overtly in her tight gown. Brock remained still, watching as she approached him and put her hand on his chest.

"Perhaps, we can come to an arrangement, Brock." Illiri ran her hand down his torso. When she caught his inadvertent glance toward her exposed chest, she followed his gaze and looked at him with a knowing smile. "See anything you like, Brock? Ashland doesn't need to know."

Brock didn't respond.

Yes, Illiri was pretty on the outside, gorgeous even. However, he knew her well enough that her rotten core spoiled anything his eyes might find pleasing. It wasn't the first time he found himself wishing Chadwick had never married the conniving wench. Besides, he loved Ashland and nothing would make him betray her.

Illiri's other hand suddenly flashed from behind her back, lunging toward him with a dagger. Blessed with exceptional quickness, Brock leaped backward, the blade grazing one of the gold buttons on his doublet and tearing it free. That's when he noticed the black on the blade.

Brock raised his sword toward Illiri. "You'll hang for this, Illiri. The public will watch while you kick and twitch and wet yourself. And then, you will die."

The woman's face solidified into a scowl, laced with determination. "You are wrong, Brock. I control my own destiny. I retain my dignity."

She turned the dagger hilt around and drove the blade into her stomach. Her face twisted in pain as Brock and Chadwick stood in stunned silence.

Stumbling, Illiri fell to her knees, looked up at Brock, and smiled. "You lose."

With a jolt, Illiri's back arched and she fell on her side, twitching and foaming at the mouth as the poison did its work. Three breaths later, she settled, her eyes staring into nothing.

10

SCOUT

Percilus Mebane watched in silence as the sun eased over the ridgeline to the east. His palms rested on two boulders as he squatted between them.

The narrow view of the canyon below revealed Kantarian troops in black and gold armor. Some paced along the wall – at least the intact portion of it. Others moved about the prison, emerging from tents and bunkhouses, entering the mess hall and exiting the latrine. Minutes passed and more soldiers appeared, bringing his count beyond four hundred but less than five hundred.

He had heard stories about the prison from his uncle – the man who had raised him since he was thirteen, the same man who trained him to hunt and shoot. His uncle and many others had spent more than a decade working the mines and living like animals in this very canyon. Percy wanted nothing more than to destroy the place. *Now would be the perfect time*, he thought. *Crush this little army and wipe out the prison all at once.*

Having seen enough, Percy backed out of his hiding spot in a crouch, making sure the boulders remained between him and the canyon floor as he climbed along the narrow trail. A few hundred feet up, the incline began to level. He looked back and found the canyon fully obscured, which meant nobody would see him. Breaking into an easy jog, he crossed the top of the ridge and soon spied another ridge to the south.

He continued jogging downhill, watching where he placed each step as he sank into the shadow-covered ravine. At the bottom, he slowed to a walk and began climbing the next hill. The sun rose higher, chasing the shadows and the lingering chill away. While Percy continued south, he considered what he had seen.

There was only one way to get an army or war machines close to the prison: through the opening at the western end of the narrow canyon. The march from Hipoint was more than twenty miles. Pressed, an army could make it in two days, but it would probably leave them exhausted. Even so, the Imperial force greatly outnumbered the Kantarian soldiers. And, then, there were the flashbombs.

Percy crested the next rise and found the view far more expansive.

The morning sun reflected off the Sea of Fates a few miles to the south. Like much of the coastline between Wayport and Yarth, sheer cliffs hugged the sea, defining the shoreline and limiting where one might land a ship. A gravel road ran along the top of those cliffs, stretching west and then curving south toward Wayport. In the other direction, the road would take Percy to Hipoint, where the Imperial Army waited. With the thought of a hot meal in mind, Percy broke into a run, hopping over rocks and navigating twists and turns as the trail took him toward the road below.

The sun was well beyond its apex when Percy arrived at camp – a camp that had grown noticeably in the three days since he had departed. Tents now lined the road for a mile, and thousands of soldiers milled about the area, most in white tabards, some in the brown of musketeers. Wagons waited along the other side of the road, not far from the cliff edge. A glance toward the sea revealed the town of Hipoint, built in tiers along the hillside. The sea was calm today, the water in Hipoint Bay a deep blue. A single pier split the bay, and workers were busily unloading cargo from one of the two vessels moored there. The activity level was a far cry from when Percy had first arrived at Hipoint two weeks earlier.

He spotted a white tent with a listing flag beside it. The banner included a blue Order rune on a field of white – the emblem for the Empire. That tent was the officers tent – Percy's destination. He briefly considered getting a meal before visiting the tent but thought better of it. Mollis, assuming he remained in charge, was a hothead and might take offense if Percy didn't report immediately. The man was still stewing about the losses he took in the capture of Hipoint, along with the subsequent desertion of his remaining mercenaries.

He approached the pavilion and addressed the two guards standing near the entry.

"Percilus Mebane here to report to the commander."

One of the two guards ducked inside while the other eyed Percy. *My bow is still on my shoulder*, Percy thought, imagining the conversation he might have with the two men. *You needn't worry. Of course, if it were in my hands, you would be dead before you could cry for help.*

The guard reappeared from the tent. "Commander Mollis will see you now."

"Thanks," Percy ducked inside.

The tent was expansive – as big as the chamber Percy and Iko shared in Sol Polis. Two blanket-covered pallets sat on one side of the space, the rest filled by three tables and a dozen chairs. Mollis stood over one table, looking over a map while, Jorgan, his second in command, stood beside him. Both men looked up when Percy entered.

"So, our scout has returned," Mollis said as he stepped away from the table. The man had black hair, a black, bushy mustache, and a stern expression. Percy didn't care much for Mollis, who always seemed more arrogant and self-assured than was justified. "What did you find?"

"It took some searching, but I located the Kantarian force twenty miles west of our location."

"If they are so close, why was it not easy to find them?"

"Someone who knows what they are about hid their tracks, and I spent time searching further out before doubling back. You see, their position is away from the sea, in a hidden canyon. You may have heard of it." Percy glanced at Jorgan and found the big, blond man staring at him intently. "A secret prison is located there."

Mollis' eyes grew wide. "The same prison that held Kardan and Archon Varius?"

Percy nodded. "The same."

The man's fist smacked his palm, his eyes alight as he grinned. "We could crush them and destroy the prison all at once! This is my chance for redemption after…after what happened here."

Hearing a rustle behind him, Percy turned to find a man wearing a blue officer's uniform entering. The man stood six feet tall and was bald despite a face with few wrinkles. Behind the officer was a woman not much older than Percy. She was fit with short, dark hair and hawk-like eyes.

"Commander Brillens," Mollis said. "Your timing is perfect."

Brillens glanced at Percy and turned toward Mollis. "What do you mean, Sergeant?"

Mollis visibly bristled. "It's Commander, now. Same as you, Orville."

The grimace on Brillens' face made his unhappiness clear. Percy was unsure if it were a result of the man's dislike for Mollis or for the use of his first name. Perhaps both.

"Fine. You requested me, Mollis. What is this about?"

"Very well. I had originally requested you join me so we could go over the daily ration plan. With your added troops, we must ensure we don't run out of food." Mollis moved back to his table and swept aside paperwork marked with tables and figures to reveal a map underneath. "My scout just returned with important news." The man looked at Percy. "Come and point out the enemy's position."

Percy and the others approached the table, everyone looking down at a large map of the south-central region of Issalia. Hipoint, their current position, was near the center.

Percy put his finger on Hipoint and ran it along the coast, imagining his journey and how it aligned with the mapped terrain. When he reached a low spot in the ridgeline, he ran it up and back east, pointing at an unmarked spot among the hills.

"They are here, in a box canyon that terminates at the eastern end. There is a narrow, difficult trail allowing you to enter from the south at about here." He tapped on the spot where he had been while spying. "However, the only way to get an army, wagons, and catapults in or out is through the mouth of the canyon to the west. Right about here." He tapped on the map and lifted his head to find the others studying it.

"They are trapped, Brillens," Mollis said. "We could advance and take them out with ease."

Brillens frowned. "Sculdin said we are to remain here until further notice."

"Yes, but that was based on the information he possessed at the time." Mollis sounded confident. "If he knew of the Kantarian Army's position, he would strike."

"What happened last time, Mollis?"

Mollis shook as if he might burst, his face turning red. "That was not my fault. We were tricked by their magic."

"How will this be different?" Brillens' tone was cold, lacking the heat coming from Mollis. "How many squads would you sacrifice to take a worthless prison?"

"I'll not take the enemy lightly this time. Nor will I send soldiers in without ensuring their safety." Mollis tapped his finger against the map. "We now possess two dozen catapults with flash bombs for ammunition – firepower I am not afraid to unleash. My men will ensure the war machines safe passage. Once in position, we will rain Issal's fury down on them."

11

JUST HIDE

Chuli Ultermane crouched as she peered through a gap between two boulders. A few strides to her side, Thiron waited in silence. Like her, he was immobile, watching.

"He is good," Chuli whispered. "I haven't seen more than a glimpse of him."

"Good, yes," Thiron said, his voice hushed. "Yet, we were able to spot him, and that was a failure on his part."

"True."

She and Thiron hid on the ridge overlooking their camp. Five hundred feet away, someone lurked among a pile of boulders on the same ridge. They assumed the man was an Imperial scout. It only made sense. The Empire had likely anticipated that taking the Hipoint Garrison would be quick work. It was. However, Chuli doubted the enemy expected the cost would be so high. Even setting vengeance aside, the enemy couldn't afford to make the same mistake twice.

Time ticked by slowly and her thighs began to cramp. She saw nothing of the scout and began to wonder if he had slipped away. Just when she considered standing, a flicker of movement darted between two rocks. Moments passed and another flash of movement appeared higher up the ridge. *He is leaving, taking the trail back to the road.* It was the same trail she and Jonah had taken after fleeing the destroyed garrison.

The scouting Chuli and Thiron had done over the previous weeks revealed the trail as the only way to enter the narrow canyon other than the canyon mouth to the west. Once known, the two rangers had tasked themselves with watching the trail, waking each morning before sunrise, scaling the cliff, and settling into position as they waited for the rising sun. Days and days passed without seeing anything of note. Until today.

Chuli turned and gazed upon the complex below – the former prison, now a Kantarian army camp.

Tucked into the east end of a canyon and surrounded by tall, steep cliff walls, the prison was protected by a man-made wall that crossed the canyon, connecting the cliff walls to the north and south. Six years past, a portion of the wall had been destroyed during a prison break. It had never been repaired. After abandoning the Hipoint garrison, retreating here had become a natural decision – offering a defensible position with shelter and fresh water.

"He is gone," Thiron said. "Let's descend and alert Marcella."

The man spun about and headed east, crouching the entire time. Chuli followed, her thighs still sore. Just before they rounded the bend in the ridge, they reached a narrow cleft. Thiron climbed down the gap while Chuli waited above.

Twenty-feet down, he came to the spike they had driven into a fissure. A thick rope was tied to the spike – a rope he gripped firmly with gloved hands before facing the cliff side and stepping backward. He rappelled the remaining seventy feet, moving down the cliffside with ease until he reached the ground. Chuli then climbed down the cleft, grabbed the rope, and stepped out into air.

Her heart fluttered as she dropped eight feet, her gloved hands gripping the rope while her feet found a small ledge. Again, and again, she lowered herself in leaps, sliding down the rope until she joined Thiron on the canyon floor. The sun had not yet crested the ridge, and the shadow-covered area was still cold.

Thiron led Chuli toward the buildings and tents housing the four hundred eighty five soldiers who survived the battle at Hipoint.

It had been dark when Thiron and Chuli had left camp for their scouting mission. At the time, the only others who had been awake were the guards on watch, some on top of the wall and others roaming the grounds. Now, however, the entire camp had come to life.

A regiment of a hundred infantry followed along as Sergeant Rios ran them through drills. Others poured from the mess hall, having finished breakfast and waiting their turn to run drills. Thiron ignored it all as he headed toward the old guard barracks, which now served as the officers quarters and as camp headquarters.

The building interior was noticeably warmer than the camp outside. However, once the sun crested the ridge, it would grow much warmer outside, making the building a pleasant shelter from the dry heat.

Captain Marcella was seated at the old table they had found, looking over notes and maps spread out before her. In her thirties, the woman was tall and intense with red hair and green eyes. The other person in the room shared her hair color, eye color, and pale complexion, but his personality could not have been more different.

"What's with the grim face, Thiron?" Jonah smiled. "Oh. Wait. That's how you always look."

Thiron glared at Jonah momentarily before turning to Marcella, who sat back in her chair.

"Did you have anything to report?" the captain asked.

"Unfortunately, yes," Thiron said as he pulled a chair out and sat across from her. "An Imperial scout was on the ridge trail. He left, heading south. Without a doubt, he will return to Hipoint with a full report."

A grimace pulled on Marcella's mouth as she sat in silence, clearly considering the impact of Thiron's report. "What would you do if you were in charge of the men stationed in Hipoint?"

Thiron's hawk-like eyes narrowed in thought. "From our scouting trip, we know they outnumber us six to one, perhaps worse if they have added troops. They likely know this as well. In addition, they have two dozen catapults at their disposal and undoubtedly are well stocked with flashbombs.

"Knowing all this, they are sure to attack our compound. They will eventually march west to attack Wayport or to advance on Fallbrandt. When they do, they cannot afford to have us harry them from behind."

"My thought as well," Marcella nodded. "They know our position and also know they possess the superior force."

"They had the same advantages at Hipoint," Jonah said. "Yet, we lost a few dozen soldiers and they lost over a thousand."

"Do you believe they will fall for a trap again?"

"Well, no. I guess not."

Thiron suggested, "Perhaps we should run, stay out in front of them?"

Marcella nodded. "That makes sense. We would lose our defensible position, but what defense can we muster against their weapons? Once their flashbombs destroy the wall, they would rush us, and we would be trapped with nowhere to go except the mining tunnels. It would be a death sentence." A knock came from the door and Marcella replied, "Come in."

A young man entered and thumped his fist to his chest. Chuli recognized the soldier who Marcella had sent to Wayport with a message for Duke Chadwick.

"I apologize about the interruption, Captain."

"Don't worry about it, soldier. What news do you have to share?"

His gaze swept the room, briefly eyeing each of them. The behavior seemed odd, as if he were deciding how openly he should speak. Finally, he faced Marcella and told his story.

"After leaving here, I rode straight for Wayport. When I arrived, it was late so I chose to stay at an inn for a night. In truth, I longed for a hot meal, a pint of ale, and a soft bed. My decision turned out to be fortuitous.

"As often happens in taprooms, whispered rumors joined the stories and laughter of the patrons. More than once, I overheard people mentioning Wayport as part of the Empire, and they wondered what the future held for the city. I casually asked the barkeep and received a similar response, albeit a brief one. After a few attempts of striking conversations with others, there was little more I learned. My sleep that night was troubled. When I rose the next day, I decided to investigate further rather than attempt to meet with the duke. I soon discovered it was worse than I feared.

"Chadwick has turned traitor, pledging his forces and the city to the Empire. In addition, he has King Pretencia and others held captive. They were to be publicly executed as traitors the day after I left the city – two days ago."

Everyone in the room stared at the soldier, stunned.

"That eliminates the option of running to Wayport," Jonah said, breaking the silence.

Marcella smoothed her red hair, her brow furrowed in thought. "Chadwick is executing a king in public. Clearly, there is motive behind it, likely to inspire others to his cause while instilling fear of anyone turning against him." She nodded to herself. "Jonah is correct. We cannot go to Wayport."

"Do we head north, into the mountains?" Chuli asked.

Thiron shook his head. "Winter lingers there, as does snow, even in the Greenway valley floor. We are ill equipped for those conditions."

Chuli imagined the death and destruction the Imperial Army would bring upon them. Even with Jonah's magic, the only arcanist in camp, there was little hope of surviving or even causing the opposition enough pain to make a difference. The scenario left her wishing she could just hide. She gasped as the idea clicked into place.

"What if we remain here?"

"What?" Jonah was incredulous. "We'll be dead for sure."

"If running before they can organize an attack is the logical thing to do, isn't that also what they might expect?"

Marcella crossed her arms while she stared at Chuli. "I suppose, but what is your point, soldier?"

Chuli explained her plan. It was risky, but if things worked out, it would give them an advantage. Outnumbered and facing superior weapons, they would need any help they could get. The thought stirred another idea, one she was well suited to execute.

12

TRUTH AND LIES

An unarmed man from the city watch stood before Queen Ashland, replying to each question as she interrogated him. Curan DeSanus remained wary during the entire process, ready in case any falsehood was spoken or undetected weapons emerged. Both had occurred with other guards over the past three days. None who had pulled a weapon survived. The orders from Wharton were clear: protect the queen at all costs.

With each response from the man, Curan felt a pleasant wave of rightness wash over him. Of this, he was thankful. A false answer before a charged Truth rune was distasteful at best, and some of the lies had been strong enough to cause Curan to vomit. Once finished with questioning the guard, the Queen dismissed the man, and Wharton escorted him out through a door where two armed guards waited.

They were finally nearing the end of the ordeal, having first examined every guard assigned to the citadel before moving on to those who worked the Kantar city watch. The process had been interesting at first, but Curan now found it taxing. Not only did lies taste vile, the guilty might attack rather than run.

Curan glanced toward the throne where Ashland sat. She seemed weary but determined. She leaned forward and exposed the long tear down the padded back of the throne – a reminder of Magistrate Filbert's attempted coup. The man's poisoned blade had narrowly missed the queen during the skirmish. Filbert's failed attempt to kill Ashland had cost him his life and the lives of the two dozen guards who had aligned with his agenda. It had been a close thing, a traumatic moment for Curan, giving him his first taste of battle. Worse, Wharton had almost died in the process.

As the thought crossed Curan's mind, Wharton reappeared, escorting a tall, lanky guard down the throne room's center aisle. Like the others, the man was dressed in black leather with gold and red trim, the metal plates on his shoulders, chest, and bracers tinted with a golden hue. Curan wore a similar uniform, as did any Kantarian soldier. However, the guard's helmet had been confiscated, along with his weapons.

When Wharton drew close, he stopped just before the red carpet ended. A six-foot section of carpet had been removed, creating a gap between where the man stood and the dais. A painted rune eight feet in diameter occupied the gap. The man warily eyed the rune.

"Step a bit closer," Ashland said.

Hesitating a moment, he did as asked, stopping in the center of the Truth rune before giving her a shallow bow. "Yes, my Queen."

Ashland studied the man for a moment before speaking. "Please, state your name."

"My name is Malik Shurig."

A wave of pleasure ran through Curan. As expected, Malik blinked and looked around in confusion after he undoubtedly experienced the same feeling.

Ashland smiled. "Good. You feel the truth of your statement. I understand that you are assigned to the city watch."

The man nodded.

"I'm sorry, but I require a verbal response."

"Yes, my queen," Malik replied. "I work the city watch."

"Thank you." She folded her hands on her lap, her smile fading. "Are you loyal to me, and to the crown of Kantaria?"

He stammered. "Yes…Of course."

Revulsion roiled in Curan's stomach, and a red hue briefly darkened the room. The man winced.

"Your lie tastes of bile, Malik." Ashland leaned forward, her glare intense. "I must know, do you seek to betray your queen?"

Malik's eyes flicked around the room and sweat began to bead on his forehead. "I...I would never do such a thing."

The sickness hit again, so intense Curan thought he might vomit. Malik clutched his stomach and doubled-over.

"What are you doing to me?" the man asked between clenched teeth.

Ashland sat back with a sneer on her face. "You do this to yourself, Malik. Lies in the presence of a Truth rune are as revolting as discovering a traitor masked as a supporter."

Malik's stubble-covered face paled, his eyes growing wild. "But, I would never betray you..."

The man's hand clenched his stomach as he doubled over again. Suddenly, he bolted toward the door at the side of the room. Curan was ready. He lunged forward and swept a long leg, hooking the man's foot and sending him sprawling. Without pause, Curan landed with a knee on Malik's back, driving the wind from the guard and pinning him to the floor. Curan then clamped a shackle to Malik's right wrist, pulling the man's arm back to meet the other. Once shackled, he climbed off the man and hoisted him to his feet. The other castle guards ran in, grabbed the man, and escorted him from the room.

When the doors closed behind them, the Queen sat back in her throne. "That was the last of them?"

Wharton drew closer, nodding. "Yes, my Queen."

Her face was a grimace. "I find it quite disturbing to discover these vermin in our midst. How many have we found?"

Wharton ran his hand through is long dark hair and sighed. "Malik brings the total to seven traitors among the city watch, in addition to the three we found in the citadel itself. Of those ten, four are dead."

Wharton glanced at Curan as he ended the sentence. Those four traitors had attempted to kill the queen when exposed. As a result, those men had discovered how quick Curan was with his blade. Their faces lingered in his nightmares.

"Ten, and that's after the lot who died in the attack led by Filbert." She stared into space with a frown. "I wish I had considered using the Truth rune and interrogating every guard before the attack. Perhaps Ned would still be alive."

"He was a good man. Honest, reliable, and skilled." Wharton rubbed his goatee. "If only I had two dozen more like him."

"You'll need half that number to fill the recent openings. We can use the same process to sort through candidates to find ones we can trust."

Wharton nodded. "Yes, my Queen."

"In addition, I must consider what to do with the guards we just imprisoned. I hesitate to execute them when they have done nothing wrong other than *think* traitorous thoughts. On the other hand, if we banish them, they might return under another identity and cause trouble."

"As King Brock often said, the crown is a burden few would wish to carry."

"So true," Ashland said with a sigh. She then turned toward Curan, her eyes narrowing. "I am thankful Cassie sent you here, Curan. If not for your help, Wharton and I would both be dead and Filbert would sit in my place."

"I merely followed my training and did my best, your Majesty," Curan said. "Your magic is what made it possible."

"Nonsense. You deserve my thanks and more." She rose from the throne and stood before him, her head tilted up to meet his gaze. "I believe that Wharton and I now have things well in hand. Since those with betrayal in their hearts have been removed, extra protection is unwarranted. In addition, Kantar resides far from the true threat, one that could extend its reach even this far if not thwarted.

"I, again, thank you, but it is time for you to return to the Ward."

Curan frowned. "You are sending me away?"

"Yes. You are too valuable an asset to remain here. War is coming, and every able body will help, especially a warrior trained to fight when augmented by magic." She turned and returned to her seat on the throne. "Pack your things, get a good night of sleep, and depart for Fallbrandt in the morning."

13

MORE THAN A DREAM

Cassilyn Talenz willed herself toward the glowing blue Order symbol and beyond, into the realm of dreams as she had come to call it. Bubbles surrounded her in every direction, near and distant, appearing like so many stars in the black void of the realm. She focused her thoughts toward Elias Firellus, hoping to replicate the success she had when searching for her mother's dream. The world around her warped and settled, leaving her surrounded by another set of bubbles.

She gazed into the nearest bubble, its surface swirling with dark blues, aquas, and a hint of pink. Fingers first, Cassie slid her hands into the bubble as if parting waters in a pool, and stuck her head inside.

Long corridors ran in every direction, lined by alternating doors and glowlamps on the walls. A girl roughly Cassie's age stood at an intersection, dressed in the uniform of a student at the academy of magic and engineering. The girl seemed anxious and confused, her head on a swivel. She looked up and saw Cassie, who must have appeared like a floating head and arms.

The girl jumped with a start, her hand going to her chest. "Oh, my. You startled me." The girl immediately recovered, as if Cassie's appearance were normal. "Do you know which way I take to get to Master Alridge's classroom?" She asked in panic while spinning about. "I'm late for Chaos Theory."

"It's all right," Cassie said. "This is just a dream."

The girl turned back toward her. "A dream?"

"Yes. This is all in your mind. Wake up and it will all go away."

The bubbled popped, the girl disappearing and leaving Cassie back in the void. She turned toward the next bubble and hesitated as she recalled numerous times where she had entered dreams involving either private or lewd moments. Sometimes both.

"You won't find him if you don't try, Cassie." The words sounded hollow, the sound deadened in the void.

She closed her eyes and thought of Firellus – the man's grim expression, secretive nature, and mysterious past. When Cassie opened her eyes, she had again shifted, and a new bubble hovered before her. Dark reds and midnight blues swirled in the surface and gave Cassie the impression of a nightmare. Gathering her will, she told herself it would only be a dream. *I have my magic if I need it.* She pushed her hands and head through the surface and found another world.

Elias was there but a younger version of himself. His hair was tied in a tail, as usual, but it was completely black and lacked the gray that defined it today. He sat on a rock on an open hilltop while staring toward a red glow in the distance. A blanket of low, dark clouds hid the sky.

Cassie stepped through the bubble and dropped to the ground behind the man. He turned and she gasped. His eyes glowed red, as if he were channeling Chaos.

"Who are you? What are you doing here?" Elias stood with ease. There was no cane in sight. His clothes were old, the frayed edges billowing in the breeze. "Better yet, tell me how you got here."

"Where are we?" Cassie asked.

Elias crossed his arms, his eyes narrowing. Fearsome howls arose in the distance. Cassie looked around and found the land barren, as if a massive fire had destroyed everything. The sky was dark save for the direction of the red glow on the horizon, hidden beyond a line of black mountain peaks.

"You had better answer my questions," Elias warned. "I called out to my army and they will return soon. You won't wish to meet them."

Cassie had always considered Elias mysterious and somewhat intimidating. Something about him had always given her pause, but she had never been able to define it. Such ambiguity did not exist with this version of the man. Instead, Cassie found herself terrified.

"I...my name is Cassie. You know me, Elias."

Elias shook his head. "There are no females here." He looked about, frowning. "This place is afflicted – the animals twisted, overgrown abominations. The plants are no better." His eyes landed back on Cassie. "How did you know my name?"

"I told you. We know each other. You know my parents, Brock and Ashland."

The man's eyes narrowed, the screams growing nearer. Cassie searched her surroundings and tried to discern their origin, but a forest of twisted trees obstructed the hillsides below from her view.

"Those names are familiar, as if from a dream."

Cassie found her gaze drawn toward the red horizon. "What is that glow?"

Elias turned toward it and sighed. "It marks the boundary. We cannot pass it, for it corrupts us more than we already are. Even we arcanists cannot control so much Chaos."

The trees below began to shake, the twisted, dead branches becoming a wave rushing toward the hilltop. When the wave hit the last row of trees, monsters emerged. Like Elias, their eyes glowed red. That is where the likeness ended.

Pale white skin contrasted their long, black matted hair. Each monster appeared like a man, but stood ten feet tall. Tattered rags covered their bodies, and long, dark talons shone like onyx blades at the end of each finger.

"Banshees," Cassie mumbled as terror forced her backward.

"Yes." Elias sounded sad as he waited for the hulking beasts to reach the hilltop. "This is my army – my affliction. I made a mistake and find myself unable to escape the trap I unknowingly created."

"This a dream, Elias," Cassie blurted. The banshees were drawing close, and she had no place to run. "Please, wake up! It's only a dream!"

Elias shook his head. "I don't deserve to wake. This nightmare is my penance."

Panic drove Cassie as she used a fingernail to carve a rune in her hand. She reached out for Chaos and was thunderstruck. The magic raged into her like never before, taking her breath with it as the energy threatened to tear her apart. She pushed it out, eager to be free of it before it was too late. The rune glowed brightly before pulsing and fading.

Cassie staggered and fell, the world gone white. She gasped for air, her vision slowly returning. She was on her hands and knees. The banshees were mere strides away. One blasted a blood-curdling scream that was returned by the others, the sound forcing Cassie to cover her ears. The entire time, Elias stared at his feet in resignation.

Hurriedly, Cassie got her feet under her in a squat, and she leaped.

Cassie had experimented with a Power rune numerous times. She knew what to expect and how to handle it. After all, it was easy to hurt yourself or someone else while you were twenty times stronger than normal. In this case, she must have been a thousand times stronger.

Up, she flew. High above the hilltop with the monsters and Elias falling away until they appeared as ants. At this height, she could better see the glow on the horizon – a distant peaked mountain of glowing red crystal, the land around it glowing similarly and appearing like a massive field of crimson ice.

And still, she continued rising until dark clouds engulfed her, blinding her from the twisted world. A pop sounded, the nightmare disappearing as she emerged in the void with Elias' dream bubble now gone.

Cassie withdrew from the dream realm, back through the rune gateway and opened her eyes. Her room was dark and silent save for the rapid thumping of her pulse and her rasping breath. Covered in sweat, she sat up and turned toward the Atrium window. It was still dark and morning was likely hours away, but she knew she couldn't sleep after the harrowing experience. Despite the bizarre nature of what she had witnessed, she felt there was more to the dream than a simple nightmare. It had seemed more like a memory in the way Elias framed it, in the way he held onto it as a form a self-punishment. *Enough, Cassie, or you'll have nightmares about it yourself.*

With slippers on her feet, she grabbed her robe from the hook beside her door and padded across her dark apartment, pausing to gaze into Rena's empty room. *I pray she is alive.* Rena seemed unwell before she left on her mission – a mission Cassie knew little about.

Pale blue light from glowing floor tiles and ceiling beams illuminated the corridor outside Cassie's apartment. She descended three levels and headed toward the kitchen.

The kitchen fell dark when the door closed, save a sliver of blue light leaking beneath it. Another slice of light came from the closed door across the room where Irma, the head cook, lived. Cassie had discovered that Irma was protective of the kitchen and paid close attention to the food stores. It would be unwise to be caught digging for food in the middle of the night.

With soft steps, Cassie crept across the room, toward one of the metal cabinets opposite from Irma's room. She opened the door carefully and swirls of white came out, giving her a chill. The cold boxes were still a marvel to Cassie, able to keep meat and other perishables fresh for extended periods. It was an example of Infusion she thought should be shared with the world. A few businesses in Fallbrandt possessed a cold box or an enchanted oven, but it was rare to see Chaos-infused creations elsewhere in Issalia.

Digging, she found a bowl and smelled it. *Beans,* she thought as she put the bowl back. The next item she found was more interesting. She closed the door and began to unwrap the sausage, eager to eat after her exhausting evening. *Who knew dream walking was so much work?*

The sliver of light across the room became a beam as the door opened. Cassie ducked and hid behind a counter. The door closed, taking the light with it.

Someone was in the room, and Cassie feared her pounding heart would draw their attention. She sought her center and focused on the Order rune within herself, seeking calm in meditation. Her pulse slowed and her breathing calmed.

She opened her eyes and peered around the counter. Although she heard no sound, she spotted a shadow slinking to the storage room door. The door opened, the shadow disappearing into it. Moments later, the shadow emerged and closed the door, the latch barely making a sound.

The shadow moved across the room and a rune appeared to Cassie, bright red and floating in midair. She gasped, the sound barely audible. Yet, the shadow froze. Neither Cassie nor the intruder moved as one waited for the other. The rune remained between them – a rune Cassie had never before seen. She stared hard at the symbol, memorizing the curves, the lines, the pattern.

Finally, the door opened, casting just enough light for Cassie to identify the man before he slipped out and disappeared. Darkness reclaimed the room.

Cassie remained there alone for a long moment, wondering why Delvin was sneaking into the storage room. More importantly, she wondered if the rune she discovered meant what she suspected – what she hoped.

A new use for Chaos, she thought. *I must find a way to test it.*

14

SHOCK

Wincing from the pain in his ribs, Iko slid his practice sword into an open slot in the weapon rack and turned toward his opponent. The man's face was covered in blood, his arm hanging limp.

"Thanks for the match, Tarvick," Iko said. "You tagged me pretty good."

Tarvick grunted. "A glancing blow. Not enough to win."

Berd called from the side of the sparring yard. "You should be proud, Tarvick. You're the first to hit anything but his shield, sword, or empty air."

The comment elicited another grunt from the muscular guard as he turned and headed toward the barracks. Iko watched him retreat and imagined what would have happened if the match were one of life and death, with true blades in hand. Iko would have a slice across his ribs – one that would require healing or at the very least a bandage. Tarvick would have a bloodied face, much like he did now, but he also would be missing an arm and would have a hole through his stomach. The thought left Iko wondering how many healers their army would include. People sufficiently skilled with Order were rare. His mother had the gift, but Iko did not. *I failed you in that regard, Mother.* She never said it, but he knew she was disappointed by his inability to manipulate Order.

Iko removed his helmet and ran a hand through his damp hair. It felt good to let the chill morning air cool the sweat. Crossing the yard, he opened the door and climbed the stairs. The door to Sculdin's office stood open. Inside the doorway was a travel-worn man, waiting while Sculdin read over a report.

Sculdin's gaze flicked from the man in the doorway, to Iko, and back. "Thank you, Beadles. Go get some food and rest. I will share this news with the Archon."

The messenger bowed and slipped past Iko.

"Your timing is good, Ikonis," Sculdin said as he exited the room. "Follow me."

Iko did as requested, following the captain while still clutching his sparring helmet under one arm. "What is this about?"

"You will find out in a moment."

The man took a stairwell down to the main hall and approached the closed Council Chamber door, where two guards waited.

"Hello, Tarshall, Vlick," Sculdin gave the guards a nod. "Is the Archon still in there with the Council?"

Tarshall nodded. "Yes, Captain. Both she and General Kardan."

"Good. I have news to share with them all."

Vlick glanced toward Tarshall and cleared his throat. "The Archon demanded they not be disturbed."

Sculdin patted the man on the shoulder. "They will make an exception in this case." Without waiting for a reply, Sculdin opened the door and led Iko in.

The Council Chamber was a rectangular room with arched windows along one side. Sunlight streamed in, the beams shining on the back of the four thrones nearest to the windows. On the room's other side, four more thrones faced the windows. Each of those eight thrones was occupied by a wizened man dressed in a white cloak with blue trim. At the far end of the room, on a throne standing higher than the others, was Iko's mother. As usual, she wore the white and gold marking her station. Opposite her, with his back to the door, was General Kardan in his dark blue uniform. Unlike the others, he sat in a simple chair with wooden arms and midnight blue cushions. The floor was a mosaic of blue tiles with a white Order rune at the room's center.

The sound of the door opening stopped Councilman Vildardi in mid-sentence. All faces turned toward Sculdin as he strolled into the room, passed Kardan, and stopped atop the order rune.

"What's the meaning of this?" Council member Ruelin demanded in outrage, his tone matching his expression.

"Give me a moment and I will explain." Sculdin bowed toward Iko's mother. "I apologize for the interruption, Archon. However, I have news most urgent to share with you and the Council."

"I trust your judgement, Captain Sculdin," Iko's mother said. "Please continue."

The captain, turned slowly, his eyes shifting from one face to another. All attention was focused on him. Scowls remained on some faces while others appeared intrigued to hear what the man had to say. None were prepared for what came next.

"We have lost Wayport." The words hung in the air, lingering like the scent of spoiled meat. "A trio of my spies just arrived with the news. Chadwick is dead, and Wayport is again in the charge of our enemies."

"What happened? Was there an assault by sea?" Kardan asked.

"There was no assault. The city was retaken by subterfuge. Chadwick was publicly hanged as a traitor, clearly an act intended as a message to any who might side with the Empire."

"No assault? No siege?"

Sculdin shook his head. "None. In fact, my men believe Captain Sharene was the only casualty other than the duke and duchess."

Iko's mother spoke, drawing everyone's attention. "Who could have pulled off such a gambit? It would require unspoken loyalty from the Wayport guard."

The captain nodded. "You see to the heart of the issue, Archon. That brings me to my next piece of news, something perhaps more dire than losing Wayport." Again, a heavy silence claimed the room and held it hostage.

With his jaw set firm, as if he were gathering resolve, Sculdin said, "King Brock lives. He now holds Wayport and the troops stationed there."

Captain Jamison Sculdin knew his statement had taken the Empire leaders by surprise. Even Kardan's face reflected shock at news. The plans the general had made counted on King Brock's death and holding Wayport.

Sculdin's noticed that Iko's face had gone pale. After being sent to Kantar with the task of killing Brock, Iko had returned and reported his mission a success. In all the years Sculdin had known Iko, he had never known him to lie to his mother. He suspected Iko had honestly believed the king and prince dead.

Archon Varius leaned forward in her throne, her knuckles white as she gripped the ornately carved chair arms. "You know this for sure, Sculdin?"

"All three of my men reported the same thing, Archon. King Brock and his men disrupted a public hanging with thousands present. The men on the gibbet were King Dalwin and Parker Thanes." His face darkened when he considered his next statement. "Brock and others were charged by Chaos."

At the mention of the forbidden magic, the room fell silent.

Varius narrowed her eyes and leaned back in her throne. "Brock faked his death and waited to make his move." Her nails continuously tapped the chair arm as she spoke, reasoning through the scenario. "The timing was perfect. He foiled a hanging but appeased the blood-thirsty crowd with another, all the while making it clear he would suffer no traitors."

Unexpectedly, Iko asked, "What of Prince Broland? Is he alive as well?"

"Yes."

Sculdin noticed a flicker of something cross Iko's face, the expression seemingly one of relief.

"This changes everything." Everyone turned toward Kardan as he stood and began to pace. "We were counting on holding Wayport to protect our army's rear flank during our campaign to capture Fallbrandt. We dare not head north while Brock holds the city."

The conclusion was the same Sculdin had come to when receiving the news. "Yes, General. We must alter our strategy. Wayport is critical to our success."

Kardan said, "I have already sent word to Olvaria. While she is to continue patrolling the west coast, additional Ri Starian longships should arrive soon. With their help, we can plan a sea attack. If we time it right, a strike from land could overwhelm the city. With our superior numbers, Brock's troops won't be able to stand against a two-fronted assault backed by flash powder." His face twisted, as if the words he was about to say were sour. "Not even with their dark magic."

The room settled as the Council members looked at one another, most seeming unsure.

Varius spoke, her voice firm. "I agree."

"Wait," Councilmember Brighton stood and held his palms out in appeal. "Perhaps we should reconsider our course. Having Wayport fall into our laps was a huge stroke of luck and paved the way for a much less complex campaign."

"True," Council member Dorlan said. "We agreed to support this war based on our possession of superior weapons, a superior force, and a clear path to capturing Fallbrandt. Since then, much has changed." The old man stood, wincing with his palm against his lower back as he straightened. "A quarter of our force was lost in taking Hipoint. Then, we discovered Corvichi destroyed, which sapped our flash powder reserves. Now, Wayport slips from our hands and into those of our arch-enemy." He shook his head. "We must rethink this conquest."

Varius stood with fists clenched at her sides, appearing ready to spit fire. "Do you think this is a game? Should we just walk away and forget that Chaos runs amok throughout Issalia? Do you believe Brock will be satisfied with Wayport after we tried to kill him?" The glare she aimed at Dorlan made the old man shrivel. "Despite a few setbacks, the Empire retains the upper hand. We will take Wayport back, and when we do, I'll see Brock's head on a pike."

She stepped down from the dais and walked past Sculdin, not stopping until she was beside Kardan's chair. "It is time for action, Leo. Send the troops. We must take Wayport back, and we must do so as soon as possible."

Varius exited the room with Ikonis at her side, while the Council members frowned in concern. Dorlan glared at Brighton, both men appearing livid. Kardan, however, reflected resolve. He stood and motioned for Sculdin to follow. They had much to plan, more to do, and little time to waste.

As Sculdin exited the room, his hand went to his torso, his palm caressing the book hidden beneath his coat. The Council did not know of Budakis' journal. Sculdin had made Iko promise to keep it a secret, even from his mother. Within the journal were the plans that would lead the Empire to victory. More importantly, the Empire's victory would seal King Brock's fate.

Iko hurried to keep pace with his mother. They soon arrived in her private chambers. The moment Iko closed the door, she began to swear. Iko said nothing.

He knew his mother well and expected her anger to cool rapidly. When it did, she sat heavily in her desk chair and held her hand to her forehead with her eyes closed. The silence was even more uncomfortable than her rant.

Iko cleared his throat. "I'm sorry I failed you, Mother."

She lowered her hand and shook her head. "Do you really believe that is what I am angry about?"

"You gave me a task. I failed."

"We have multiple reports that the royal quarters were destroyed in the explosion. You planted the bomb. You were with the king, the queen, and the prince in the room before you escaped. Everything you did conforms to your mission objective." Her mouth twisted as if she tasted something sour. "However, Brock and Ashland…they are both sly and talented. Worse, they possess a magic we barely understand. You are not at fault in this. It was I who failed by not following through to verify the man's death."

Iko sighed in relief at not having her anger directed toward him. The feeling was compounded by the relief he felt from Broland surviving the blast. The prince's death – his friend's death – had been a crushing weight on Iko's soul. Discovering Broland alive removed Iko's shackles of guilt.

His mother turned toward the window, her expression contemplative. "Knowing Brock lives creates new questions, such as: Where was the man these past weeks? What will he do next?" She spoke softly, as if to herself. "His recapture of Wayport appears to have cost him nothing.

That brings him closer to our borders and greatly alters his ability to defend both Kantaria and Fallbrandt."

"I agree, Mother." Iko didn't know what else to say. He wasn't even sure she was speaking to him.

She spun about. "Enough about Brock. I will worry about him. You have your own role in this endeavor."

"What do you wish of me, Mother?"

"I will remain in my chamber, or next door in Kardan's office, for the remainder of the day. The floor is guarded, so there is little need for you to be held captive here." She reclaimed the seat behind her desk. "Go see Sculdin. He has much to do and will likely have tasks for you." The Archon dipped a pen into her inkwell and began drafting a letter.

Iko walked down the long corridor, passing Ydith, the guard on duty. She gave him the briefest of nods and continued in the opposite direction. He passed Quinn's room and thought, *Where are you, Quinn? Are you truly chasing a spy or have you abandoned us?* Distracted by thoughts of Quinn, he soon stood before Sculdin's door. His knock was met by silence. After waiting a minute, he lifted his fist to knock again when the door opened.

"Kardan." Iko said, surprised to see the man in the doorway. "I'm sorry if I am interrupting. I came by to see if Sculdin needs anything from me."

"Come in, Ikonis," Kardan stepped aside. "I was just leaving."

Iko entered to Sculdin bent over his table, writing notes on a map. The door closed, leaving Iko and Sculdin alone. Sculdin stood with a pen still in his hand. A drop of ink fell from it and landed on the tile floor in an oddly silent moment.

"The time for planning is over, Ikonis. We make our move immediately."

"What do you need from me, Scully?"

"Prepare your things; you will soon hit the road." The man set the pen down, circled the table, and stopped a stride away. "Commander Korbath and our cavalry are due to arrive from Sol Gier in a few days. You will join them and ride to the garrison outside Yarth with new orders from Kardan."

"New orders?"

"Yes. Kardan is sending Captain Rorrick and the entire garrison west.

They will begin a hard march to catch Mollis and Brillens, who are marching from Hipoint. We will take Wayport and then push north to Fallbrandt."

When a tinge of fear arose, Iko swallowed it, set his jaw, and asked, "What about you?"

"Don't worry about me." Sculdin clapped a hand on Iko's shoulder. "I have a part to play, but it's better kept secret."

"Yes, Captain."

Iko turned to the door and left the room. He walked the corridor lost in thought, worried about the impending war while wondering how it had come to this end. Memories of his time at the Torreco Academy of Combat and Tactics resurfaced. A year had passed since he left the school – a year of growth and struggle and change. Things were simple and life was enjoyable back then – back when he had Quinn at his side. He longed for those days. *Where have you gone, Quinn?*

15

MUSKETEERS

B randt waited as Sergeant Ferdinand issued orders, repeating the same exact instructions Brandt had heard during the previous week. He and the other musketeers practiced the same process every day, multiple times a day. In between, they ran and performed calisthenics to remain fit. However, today was different. Today, they would actually use their muskets. Twice.

"Remember, this might be your last chance to fire your weapon until you are in an actual battle. We have limited flash powder and cannot afford to waste it." Ferdinand stopped and glared at his regiment. "And, for Issal's sake, do not shoot anyone and do not spill any flash powder. I don't have to explain why."

Ferdinand strolled along the line as he spoke, his stride stiff as if he were made of wood rather than of flesh and bone. "Each squad will fire upon my command. After your first volley, you will shift to the rear and reload your weapon. When you reach the front line, you will again fire on my command and then return to the rear. After all ten squads have fired twice, you will remain at attention and wait for further instruction."

As the man strolled toward the far end of the ranks, Brandt glanced to the side, meeting Roy's gaze.

A year older than Brandt, Roy was of a similar height and build. In fact, within the first hour of meeting Roy, Brandt had felt a kinship. All it took was a simple prank Roy pulled on Tonda, the tallest of their tent-mates. When Tonda shrieked and bolted from their tent, Roy rolled in laughter before producing the source of Tonda's terror. Roy held the empty snake skin toward Tonda when he tried to reenter, producing another shriek before Tonda realized it was harmless. The memory of the moment brought a smile to Brandt's face.

Roy leaned toward Brandt and whispered, "When we are finished here, do you want to watch the duels?"

"Duels?"

"Yeah," Jorreck stood to Brandt's other side. Short and thin, the teen had a narrow face reminding Brandt of a weasel. "Today's dueling day."

Brandt shrugged. He had nothing better to do, and he actually enjoyed spending time with his tent mates. "Sure. Let's do it."

The commander's gruff voice emerged in a shout. "Squad One, ready your weapon!" A series of clicks marked the moment as flints were cocked into place. "Squad One, take aim!" The hundred musketeers in the front row raised their weapons. "Squad One, fire!"

A rapid concussion of blasts came from the muskets, joined by a flash of green flame and a puff of smoke. The bales of hay along the palisade wall jumped and twitched as slugs buried inside them.

The Squad One musketeers spun around, slipped through the ranks, and fell in line behind Squad Ten. Brandt and his fellow squadmates advanced two strides and waited while the next squad fired a volley. A minute later, Brandt and the other Squad Five musketeers stood at the front with nothing but two hundred feet of open dirt between them and the hay.

Ferdinand called out for them to ready their weapons. Brandt cocked the flint and suddenly became acutely aware he was about to discharge a small explosion. The sergeant commanded him to take aim and he did, pinching one eye shut while staring down the long metal barrel in his hands. His pulse thumped in his chest, his breath rasping as the anticipation built higher and higher.

"Fire!" the commander shouted, the word causing Brandt to flinch. He pulled the trigger, heard a deep bang, and felt a thump of pain in his shoulder, nearly causing him to drop the musket.

Grimacing, Brandt lowered the weapon, spun around, and hurried toward the back of the line. His shoulder stung mightily, his arm hanging limp as he winced in pain.

"What are you doing?" Roy asked as he pulled a cartridge from the long pouch across his chest.

"I forgot to hold the musket tight to my shoulder," Brandt said between clenched teeth.

The comment caused Jorreck to snicker and shake his head. "The sergeant warned us about that. Many times."

"I know." Brandt opened his pouch and removed a cartridge. "I guess this is a learning moment."

Roy smiled. "Some people have to learn the hard way. I'm not surprised you fall into that group."

Despite his pounding shoulder, Brandt grinned in return. "You have no idea."

Brandt bit the end off his cartridge, tearing the paper away and spitting it out. He then half-cocked the flint on his musket and tilted the strike plate open. With care, he poured a bit of flash powder from the cartridge into the opening behind the strike plate. He slowly uncocked the flint and tipped the musket up with barrel aimed toward the gray sky. The cartridge, which included more flash powder and a metal slug wrapped by paper, was stuffed into the barrel. He detached the ramrod from the barrel and used it to shove the cartridge down, thumping it four times to make sure the load was well packed. By the time he was reconnecting the ramrod, Roy and his fellow squadmates were doing the same.

Kenten, Brandt's squad leader, shouted "Squad Five take position!"

They scrambled forward and formed a straight row two strides behind Squad Four. Shots rang out and the squad moved forward, again and again until it was Squad Five's turn. Brandt cocked his weapon, aimed, and fired. He then scrambled to the rear and waited for the remaining squads to complete their second volley.

During the wait, thoughts of Quinn invaded. Brandt missed her, not having seen her even once since they had joined the Imperial Army. *I wonder how she is faring.* Memories of their time together in Yarth had him oblivious to his surroundings until Roy elbowed him.

—✦—

Friendly barbs and laughter surrounded Brandt as he and his four tent mates passed the camps of other musketeer squads. As the target of Jorreck's jokes, Lewin did his best to counter, but he lacked the quick wit of his opponent. When Lewin had had enough, he tried to grab Jorreck, but the squirrely teen ducked, weaved, and scurried away, leaving the heavy-set Lewin frowning in frustration.

A crowd had gathered – a variety of soldiers wearing the colors of their regiments. Brandt and his companions wore brown coats cinched at the waist by black belts. There were women wearing dark blue, some in tunics and breeches; others wore leather. He also saw men dressed in black, all with their heads shaven, their expressions grim. Among the uniforms and armor was the familiar sight of standard infantry wearing white tabards over chain mail.

Jorreck reached the crowd first and began to wiggle through. Roy, Brandt, and Tonda did their best to follow, the three continuously apologizing as they jostled the people they passed. Lewin trailed behind, requiring a path twice the width of the others.

At the heart of the crowd was a dirt field separated by ropes tied to four stakes. The spectators pressed against the rope, a meager barrier between them and the sparring ring.

A man dressed in a black uniform stepped onto the field and spun about as he reached the center. Gold stripes marked the man's shoulders, and an Order rune of the same color was stamped on his left breast. The man raised his arms and the crowd cheered. Moving his hands in a lowering motion, the crowd quieted.

When the noise subsided, the man shouted to the crowd. "Welcome to this week's contest. I am Sergeant Aladar, leader of the Infiltrators. My regiment prides itself on being the bravest, toughest, most dangerous element of the Imperial Army."

The statement caused a stir and raised more than a few jeers.

Roy poked Brandt. "Maybe they should have stuck you with him."

"What are Infiltrators?"

Jorreck leaned toward Brandt and said, "I hear they are armed with bombs. Their job is to infiltrate and destroy enemy strongholds even if they die in the process."

Brandt blinked at the idea. Having seen flashbombs in action, he was well aware of the destruction they could render.

Aladar roared. "Quiet!" The crowd simmered and he resumed. "Each week, a warrior within my ranks steps forward in the hope of claiming the title of best Infiltrator duelist. This week is no different." He spun and pointed. "First, I give you Harron Buddig, our current champion."

A tall man with a shorn scalp stepped forward, lifting his arms high. He had muscular shoulders and a barrel chest. When Buddig flexed his thick arms, Brandt envisioned the man snapping a tree in half with his bare hands.

The cheering fell away and Aladar announced, "Welcome this week's challenger, Sandar Grange."

A combination of cheers and jeers greeted the soldier as he entered the ring. Also with shorn hair and dressed in black leather, Sandar Grange was neither as tall as his opponent, nor as muscular. At roughly ten years younger than Buddig, Grange's movements were fluid and effortless, his body lean and athletic.

"That Buddig guy is a monster," Brandt said aloud. "Do you think Grange is good enough to beat him?"

Roy shook his head. "I doubt it. Buddig has throttled every opponent thus far. Most don't last more than a minute."

Aladar led the two men to the weapon rack at the far side of the sparring field. Buddig chose a massive wooden great sword. Grange stepped back with a longsword in one hand and a shield on the other arm. The trio returned to the middle of the field with Aladar standing between them.

"When I give the word and vacate, you will begin. The duel ends when I call it and not before. Got it?"

Both men nodded. The crowd stilled in anticipation. Aladar backed away and shouted, "Duel!"

With a roar, Buddig drove forward, swinging his massive great sword with both hands. Grange lifted his shield to block the strike. A loud clack sent Grange stumbling sideways. Another swing followed and Grange opted to scramble away. Buddig advanced with a dark scowl as Grange backed away in a circle.

Apparently having enough of the cat and mouse, Buddig burst forward with another massive swing. In a blink, Grange ducked beneath the strike, his shield protecting his head as he lunged with his longsword extended.

The thrust took Buddig in the stomach, resulting in a grunt. However, Grange was too close and couldn't avoid Buddig's backhand swing. The smaller man hastily raised his blade to block it and was able to redirect the strike enough for a glancing blow off his helmet. Grange rolled with the impact and rose to his feet. He shook his head and blinked repeatedly.

Perhaps sensing his advantage, Buddig charged his smaller opponent. Grange blocked a swing with his shield and stumbled from the impact. Altering the angle of the next swing, Buddig chopped down at this opponent hard enough to drive Grange to his knees when he tried to block the overhand stroke. Buddig kicked, his boot striking Grange in the chin. The result was immediate.

With his face toward the sky, Grange fell backward, his sword tumbling to the ground as he fell to the dirt. There, he lay still with his eyes rolled back and blood running from his mouth and chin.

Buddig raised his sword to the sky and spun toward the crowd, who cheered his name as a small woman in a blue cloak ran in and knelt beside his vanquished challenger. A moment later, Grange opened his eyes and sat up, wiping the blood from his chin. The woman offered Grange a hand, but he shook his head and stood on his own. He shot a frown toward Buddig and stomped toward the sidelines before slipping into the crowd.

Commander Aladar stood beside Buddig and lifted the man's hand. "Once again, Harron Buddig is our champion!"

The cheers continued as the sergeant and the victor walked toward the gap in the rope. There, Aladar spoke briefly with a woman dressed in blue leather armor. The woman had short, dark hair and angular eyes. Like the man she spoke with, stripes marked the woman's shoulders as a notation of her rank. She then walked into the sparring ring and held her hands high.

"Greeting, members of the Imperial Army. I am Commander Luon, leader of the Harrier regiment, the fastest and fiercest warriors in Issalia." The statement stirred the crowd, but the woman continued, refusing to be influenced. "I present to you the current Harrier champion, Liziele Mray."

The crowd roared even louder than when Buddig won his duel. A tall figure stepped out onto the field, standing nearly as tall as the previous champion. Liziele had thick shoulders, muscular arms, and powerful thighs. At first glance, Brandt thought a man had entered the dueling grounds, but he then realized Liziele was actually a big, powerful woman. Her dark blue armor left her biceps bare, her forearms covered by blue-tinted bracers. She stopped beside Luon, standing more than a head taller than the commander, and crossed her arms.

The crowd quieted and Luon bellowed, "This week, we bring a new challenger to the field, one who hopes to make Squad Three proud. Please welcome Jacquinn Mor."

Brandt's mouth dropped open at the name. His eyes then found her, moving through the crowd, ducking under the rope, and striding onto the field. *No, no, no.* He shook his head. *We are supposed to blend in and observe.*

He was not surprised. He knew Quinn well enough by now. She would never be satisfied as a subservient soldier. Quinn's spirit was among the things he loved about her. He just hoped her spirit wouldn't find them trouble. *Not now. Not here.*

Quinn stopped near the center of the sparring ring, and her stance mirrored her opponent's with her arms crossed over chest with a glare challenging anyone who dared to meet it. However, Liziele stood a foot taller than Quinn and outweighed her by a hundred pounds. The memory of Grange losing to Buddig stood fresh in Brandt's mind, and the physical differences between Quinn and her opponent were even more significant than the previous bout. *I hope you know what you're doing, Quinn.*

16

DUEL

Quinn emerged from her tent dressed in her full armor. A week of training had broken in the leather. Twice, a healer had come by and healed Quinn's blisters despite her insistence that she did not require healing. Apparently, it was standard practice.

Her helmet rested in the crook of her arm, the pale blue plume that ran down the center fluttering in the breeze. Ilsa, one of her tent mates, stood and walked over.

"So, you are actually going through with this?"

Quinn turned toward her and nodded. "I said I would. I make a habit of following through on my commitments."

"Juvi was much bigger than you. Strong and brash, too. She was skilled and almost bested Liziele. However, I believe that loss was why she deserted." Ilsa's eyes drifted toward the ground. "I don't think she had ever lost before and being beaten like that...in front of everyone. Well, it created a crack of doubt in her confidence. The woman just sort of crawled into her shell, refusing to talk to any of us. And, then, she was gone."

"I heard about the lashings. I'm sorry you had to endure such torture."

Ilsa shook her head. "The whip hurt, but the pain faded." Her voice dropped to a whisper. "The shame of it all...being stripped to your smallclothes and driven to tears in front of your fellow soldiers. It lingers."

Quinn put her hand on Ilsa's shoulder. The girl lifted her head and met Quinn's gaze. "I'll not break so easy, Ilsa. Whatever happens today, win or lose, I will remain steadfast. You can trust me."

Ilsa smiled, the first smile Quinn had seen directed toward her since joining the Harriers. In fact, Ilsa had initiated a real conversation with Quinn. Another first, despite Quinn spending most of her waking hours with the girl. With the barrier between Quinn and Ilsa crumbling, perhaps the other girls might begin to accept her.

Quinn knew her own faults. She tended toward isolation and kept others from getting too close. However, having others relentlessly treating her as an outsider had left her lonelier than she wanted to admit. *Perhaps my relationship with Brandt has changed me.* She sighed. *I miss him.* Another thing she hated to admit.

Cleffa strolled over with a raised brow. "You trying to talk her out of it, Ilsa?"

Ilsa shook her head. "Not at all. I just wanted to let Jacquinn know that Squad Three is with her. She will hear no cheer for Liziele from us, right?"

Cleffa gazed at Quinn with narrowed eyes. "Do you actually think you can win?"

"I once knew someone like Liziele," Quinn said. "While not quite as big, she was fast, strong, and a natural athlete. This girl had everything you might wish for in a warrior except for one. If Liziele lacks that one thing, I might have a chance."

A snort came from the squad leader. "What thing do you mean?"

All the girls from Squad Three had gathered during the exchange and now surrounded Quinn and Cleffa. With an intense glare, Quinn moved closer until her nose almost met Cleffa's.

All fell quiet in a moment of tension, the silence broken when Quinn whispered, "The will."

Cleffa's brow furrowed as Quinn backed up a step. "What?"

"I have the will. Does she?" Quinn spun about, her squadmates parting to create a path as she marched through camp and headed toward the sparring grounds.

"The will?" Cleffa yelled from behind Quinn, "The will to do what?"

Without stopping, Quinn spoke over her shoulder. "Whatever it takes."

Quinn left the words behind her as a lingering testament for all who heard them. Quinn was determined to gain the faith of the girls in her squad. While she could not say exactly why it was so important, she wanted them to know she was nothing like Juvi. She would not break. She would not shame them nor betray them.

The crowd had already gathered around the sparring grounds, leaving Quinn on the outside. Rather than fighting her way to the front, she stood alone and considered how to defeat a taller, stronger opponent.

The training Quinn had received at the Arcane Ward focused on quickness and worked best when combined with an element of surprise. In her duel with Darnya, Quinn was powered by a personal grudge, but she held no such grudge against Liziele. Without vengeance to drive her, Quinn needed something else.

Girls from the Harriers filtered into the crowd, some giving her a nod as if to offer her a bit of courage. Others ignored her. It didn't matter. She would make her mark in the ring.

The Infiltrator commander walked past Quinn. He was tall, muscular, and impressive. However, the man trailing him was even more imposing – a walking giant who caused the crowd to shy away as he passed them. The man's height, build, and obvious arrogance reminded Quinn of Wyck.

When Quinn interrupted Wyck's assassination of Archon Varius, she had faced a much larger, stronger opponent. In addition, Wyck was wearing armor and wielding a sword while Quinn had nothing but a knife. If not for Everson's Chaos trap, Quinn would have died that day. *I wish I had one now*, she thought. *Although, using Chaos magic when surrounded by an army whose mission is to end Chaos forever might not be the best idea.*

A handsome young man dressed in Infiltrator armor passed by. Standing six feet tall with broad shoulders and dark hair, the man reminded Quinn of Iko. Her thoughts turned again and she wondered what role Iko might play in the struggle to come. His unexpected appearance in Sol Polis had nearly spoiled everything. However, she did find some solace in the memory of beating him. Her fist clenched at the thought of doing it again.

Shouts and cheers came from the crowd, joined by the distinctive clacks of wooden weapons colliding. Hearing the ruckus made Quinn's stomach tremble with anxiety. The match continued for no more than a minute before the cheering reached a crescendo. As it died down, the crowd parted before Quinn. Two Infiltrators walked through the gap, each holding an arm of the handsome man in black. He was unconscious, his drooping head flopping with each step. A string of red spit swayed from his lips and his toes left trails in the dirt as the soldiers dragged him by.

When Quinn turned back to the sparring ring, Commander Luon was entering with a confident gait. She welcomed the crowd and announced Liziele as the current champion. Liziele stepped into the ring with one fist raised, bringing a round of enthusiastic cheers. Quinn knew she was next. There was no turning back, so she took a deep breath and walked through the gap. She crossed the rope barrier and found a thousand pairs of eyes watching, measuring her, underestimating her.

"Today's challenger for the Harrier sparring crown is Jacquinn Mor."

The cheers at her name were few and lacked spirit. The only thing Quinn heard was those who laughed. Her opponent, Liziele, towered over Luon, who was slightly taller than Quinn. *They expect me to fail and fail badly*, Quinn thought. *I might feel the same way if I were them.* She slipped her helmet on and pressed her lips together in determination.

"Warriors, choose your weapons." Luon gestured toward the weapon rack.

Liziele strode toward it, covering the ground in three easy strides. A moment later, she turned from the rack with a longsword in one hand, a shield in the other.

As I suspected, Quinn thought as she moved to the rack and considered a strategy. Quarterstaffs, shields, bucklers, and swords of different lengths were among the options. A shield and sword would provide the best defense, and she had grown used to the combination over the past week. However, she needed every advantage she could gain in this bout, something Liziele might have had less experience facing. That left only one choice – the same choice Quinn had made over a year earlier when she was at the military academy. With two short swords in hand, she turned and faced her opponent.

"When I give the word, you will begin. The duel ends when I say it's over and not before then."

Liziele nodded, as did Quinn. The crowd grew quiet, the thumping of Quinn's heart filling her own ears.

Luon backed away and shouted, "Duel!"

The duel ends when I say it's over. The words replayed in Quinn's head. *Broken bones won't end this fight, nor will someone stepping outside the ring.* Something occurred to Quinn, a thing she had never considered before a duel. *What if I die?*

Liziele snarled and attacked, her sword slicing for Quinn's torso. Quinn raised a sword to block the strike. A clack sounded and Quinn staggered. Another strike from Liziele fell at an angle and Quinn raised both swords, crossing them to block it. Even then, the impact was tremendous and sent a shock through Quinn's shoulders. Again and again, Liziele attacked, forcing Quinn backward with her powerful swings. The woman's long reach and longer sword made it impossible for Quinn to get near enough for a counterstrike.

When Quinn felt the rope at her back, she blocked a swing and then dove, rolled, and came to her feet as Liziele spun to face her. Quinn made a quick thrust and pelted the woman in the hip before she could get her shield around. Liziele's longsword followed and Quinn ducked, but the glancing blow off her helmet sent her staggering.

The ringing in Quinn's ears and spots before her eyes forced her to blink and back away. Her vision cleared just in time to respond to another swing. Liziele then charged forward and thrust her shield out, smashing it into her face. Pain exploded, and all went black.

Brandt held his breath while Quinn fought.

Her oversized opponent was relentless, driving Quinn backward and keeping her on the defensive. Even when Quinn dodged a blow and was able to tag Liziele with a thrust, the woman seemed unaffected and only attacked harder.

Liziele charged Quinn, her shield smashing Quinn in the face and lifting her off her feet. Brandt gasped as Quinn landed hard, three strides away. He pressed against the rope but, somehow, was able to restrain himself from running out to heal her.

He squeezed the rope and stared at Quinn, praying she was all right. After a moment, she rolled onto her side and pushed herself off the ground.

Blood covered her face, running from a gash in her forehead and from her swollen nose. She staggered, but still held both swords.

Luon stepped between the two warriors, facing Quinn. "Do you yield, Jacquinn?"

Quinn shook her head and Brandt noticed the look in her eyes as they shifted from blue to steely gray. "Never."

"Your nose is broken," Luon said. "Are you sure you wish to continue?"

"Yes. Unless Liziele is afraid." Quinn's grin, with her teeth bloody and blood tracking down the side of her face, was perhaps the scariest thing Brandt had ever seen.

"Liziele is in trouble," Brandt said aloud.

"What?" Jorreck was incredulous. "Look at that girl. She's getting killed out there."

"Jorreck's right," Roy agreed. "One more hit and the new girl is finished."

"Want to bet?" Brandt asked.

"Sure. I could use another silver." Roy grinned.

"Done."

Luon turned to Liziele, who nodded without removing her eyes from Quinn. The commander then backed away and shouted, "Resume!"

Liziele appeared fresh, balanced, and ready. Quinn was a mess, her face covered in blood, her breathing ragged, her stance wobbling. Liziele advanced, and attacked. Quinn ducked below the blow, spun, and smacked the taller woman's knee. A grunt came from Liziele as she took a backhand swing toward Quinn who blocked the strike with both swords. When Liziele thrust her blade out, Quinn twisted, and it slid past her. Quinn then launched an overhand strike. Brandt gasped. With Liziele's reach and height, the woman was too far from Quinn for the blade to connect.

He didn't expect her to throw it.

The wooden sword sailed over Liziele's shield and smashed into the woman's nose. She lifted the shield to cover her face as she stumbled backward. Quinn charged.

Leaping high, Quinn drove both heels into the taller woman's chest. The impact added to Liezieles' momentum, taking the tall woman off her feet. She landed on her back and slid across the dirt. Quinn stood, collected her sword, and took a ready stance.

Liziele sat up, wincing in pain with one hand on her ribs. The woman's face was even worse than Quinn's – the skin torn away from the side of her nose to her cheek while blood oozed from her nostrils. She kept her hand on her ribs as she stood, wincing mightily.

Luon stepped between them. "Do either of you forfeit?"

Liziele shook her head. "I do not."

Quinn grit her teeth. "Never."

Brandt shook his head, but couldn't stop a grin from forming. *That's the girl I love.*

Quinn glared at her opponent. From her behavior, she knew the kick had hurt Liziele's ribs – a pain Quinn knew well. This time, Liziele advanced cautiously with her shield held in front of her torso for protection.

Switching tactics, Quinn darted forward and slashed low. Liziele parried the strike, and Quinn's other sword followed with a thrust that met Liziele's shield. When Liziele countered with a backhand swing, Quinn ducked and spun, her sword connecting with the same knee she had hit earlier. Liziele grunted and staggered back. Quinn went for the kill.

With a flurry of crossing attacks that Liziele blocked with her sword and shield, Quinn pressed her backward. Quinn then paused, gasping for air, seemingly out of breath. Liziele took the bait and drove at Quinn with a thrust. Quinn twisted around it and thrust her sword past her opponent's shield, striking Liziele's sore ribs with full force. The sickening cracking of bones carried up the length of Quinn's wooden sword, the gasping cry from Liziele the last sound before she collapsed.

Liziele lay on her side, gasping for air, her bloodied face twisted in agony. The area had fallen to stunned silence save for the whimpers from

Quinn's downed opponent. Luon moved in and bent over Liziele. After a brief word, the commander waved and called for a healer.

As the healer ran in, Luon turned toward Quinn. "Now, that was a duel to remember." Luon then grabbed Quinn's hand, lifting it high and facing the crowd. "I present to you, Jacquinn Mor, our new Harrier champion."

The crowd erupted with shouts and cheers. Money began exchanging hands, but even the losers seemed impressed.

The Harriers from Squad Three pushed through the crowd, ducked under the rope, and encircled Quinn, patting her back, hugging her, and congratulating her. Suddenly, the girls hoisted Quinn upon their shoulders, carried her through the crowd, and paraded her back toward the Harrier camp. The mob of girls surrounding Quinn cheered her name the entire way.

Euphoria lifted Quinn even higher, leaving the pain of her injuries behind.

17

SUBTERFUGE

The night was still, as were Percy and the archers in his party. A distant, warbling call of a jackaroo echoed in the pre-dawn twilight at the eastern horizon. Time passed, and the dark outline of the ridge materialized as the sky behind it slowly grew brighter. He was positioned between the same two boulders on the same trail as he had been three mornings prior.

Four pale glowlamps gave faint illumination to the prison wall below. Curiously, the lamps had not been charged for many hours, the glow-stone powder settled at the bottom. Near the lamps, Percy could just make out the guards on duty. He stared hard at one guard for some time, but there was no movement. *Perhaps he fell asleep. Just as well. There is no escape now.*

It had been a long night. At Percy's suggestion, the army had advanced the last few miles during the night and without the use of steam carriages to pull the catapults. Mollis had resisted the idea, but Brillens insisted and refused to bring his musketeers unless Mollis took precautions, among which included sending scouts ahead to sweep for traps.

The army had advanced eight miles during each of the first two days before camping for a night. On the third evening, Percy and a woman named Riva Lorric led a small squad of rangers ahead of the primary force. Percy took the group along the narrow trail to their destination. Covered in darkness, the rangers then descended to the canyon floor and swept the area from the trail to the canyon mouth, leaving only the thousand feet nearest to the prison wall unscouted. They then marked the safe zone with a long line that ran across the road and beyond before sneaking back to the narrow trail where they now waited. Percy, Riva, and the other rangers remained ready with bows to make sure nobody escaped by taking the trail.

Percy heard the creaking of approaching catapults as they were pushed into place. Soon he spotted the nearly imperceptible silhouettes of the Imperial army filling the canyon.

Another jackaroo call echoed from the east end of the canyon, and the sky grew brighter as sunrise approached. The plan was to strike at first light. However, Mollis was not a patient person.

Shouts echoed from the Imperial Army's position, followed by the unmistakable thuds of catapults launching. Percy stood for a better view since stealth was no longer necessary.

A dozen thumping explosions of green fire lit the night as sections of the wall blasted apart and shook the ground. Some bombs landed beyond the wall, one hitting a building inside the compound. The fires turned orange, the bloom making it easier to see.

One section of the wall remained, the guard posted on top of it now leaning to one side but not moving. Percy frowned as he stared at it. Moments later, more flashbombs detonated, destroying the last of the wall in a flash of green.

That was a dummy, Percy realized. *Why post dummies on the wall?* The moment he thought it, he burst into a run down the trail, toward the canyon floor. As he ran, soldiers pushed catapults forward, reloaded them, and fired again. This time, every bomb landed inside the compound, destroying buildings and whatever else might remain within.

As Percy reached the bottom, the sun edged over the horizon, lighting the surrounding ridgeline but was still too low to shine upon the canyon floor. He ran toward the road where Mollis and Brillens waited on horseback, the commanders calling out orders as the men on foot prepared to attack.

Waving his arms to get their attention, Percy shouted, "Stop! Stop! Don't fire! Don't attack!"

Finally, Brillens noticed Percy running toward them. He said something to Mollis and both turned toward Percy as he slowed, panting for air.

"Don't waste any more bombs," Percy said as he came to a stop. "Hold the attack."

Mollis scowled. "We have them right where we want them. Why stop?"

Percy shook his head. "No, you don't. They aren't here."

Mollis was about to retort but was interrupted by Brillens. "Explain yourself, soldier."

"I see no movement inside. I hear no screams or shouts of panic." He pointed east. "On top of the wall, they had dummies posted to make us think the wall was guarded. I caught a clear view of one guard just before the last explosion. It was nothing but straw on a stick, wearing armor."

With a contemplative expression, Brillens stared at the prison, its walls now only burning rubble. The other man glowered, as if Percy had been the one who tricked him.

"Have Riva and the rangers scout the place," Brillens said. "Make sure it is empty and free from traps."

Percy was prepared to retort, but thought better of it. Instead, he ran back to the trail and waved the rangers down. Led by Riva, they hurried to the canyon floor and surrounded him. When the last man was there, Percy turned to Riva.

"I suspect the prison is abandoned but Brillens and Mollis ordered us to scout the complex for enemies and for traps. Let's split into two groups. Half go with Riva, the other half with me."

He waited for Riva to reply. The woman was a decade older and outranked him. Dressed in green leathers, with short-cropped hair and eyes like a bird of prey, she looked every bit a ranger. The bow in her hand and knives at her hips didn't hurt.

"My group will take the north side; Percy will take the south," she said. "Everyone remain wary with an arrow nocked."

Riva called the names of four rangers and took off toward the north end of the wall. With a wave, Percy spun and jogged toward the south end of the wall with his squad close behind.

The sections of the wall that had been intact before the assault were now piles of burning rubble. Thankfully, the portion of the wall that had been destroyed years ago had not been targeted and lacked the flames that burned elsewhere. Percy climbed the old, dusty debris while watching the compound interior.

Smoke swirled and fires still burned from the closest buildings, or what remained of them. There was no movement inside. The scouts advanced carefully, running to each new building before peeking around the corner and advancing to the next. It wasn't until they were deep into the compound, beyond the last building, when Percy spotted someone moving about. He lowered his bow and approached her.

"Did you see anyone?" Percy asked Riva.

"No. We searched the bunkhouses. They are empty. This entire place appears abandoned."

He peered toward the dark tunnel openings cut in the cliff wall. "We should check the tunnels, but I doubt we will find anything." The air rang as his short sword slipped free from its scabbard. "We will need some light. I'm sure it will be dark in there."

—+ ϕ +—

Mollis paced before his horse with his fists clenched. Between the man and the ruined wall were hundreds of footprints, all leading from the prison to the canyon mouth. In the dark of night, it had been impossible to see the tracks left by the Kantarian Army. With the sun now shining on the canyon floor, the same footprints were impossible to miss.

"You checked the mining tunnels?" Brillens asked while Mollis paced.

"Yes, Commander," Riva said. "They are a bit of a maze, some becoming loops, others dead ends, and a few collapsed, but we found nobody inside."

"They must have run east, to Wayport." Mollis said in a heated voice. "We hold the city, so they will find no shelter there. If we continue, we will catch them and grind them to dust outside the city walls."

Brillens narrowed his eyes in thought. "While I agree with your assessment, advancing to Wayport is outside of our current orders. We were to wait for word from Captain Sculdin or General Kardan." He gestured west, toward the waiting Imperial Army. "These troops are our responsibility. What if Kardan has other plans? Taking them down to Wayport could ruin everything."

Mollis thrust his chest out and drew close to Brillens. "What other plans? Where else would we go? Fallbrandt? With winter still holding the valley hostage?"

The distinctive sound of a galloping horse arose and drew everyone's attention. Turning to look west, Percy spied a rider coming toward them at a fast clip. The rider slowed to a trot upon reaching the soldiers, their gazes following as the man passed by.

Just short of where Mollis and Brillens stood, the man stopped his horse and wiped his brow. "I'm seeking Commanders Mollis and Brillens."

"I am Brillens."

"Commander Mollis, here," the man puffed up as he spoke.

The rider nodded. "I thought so. When I reached Hipoint and discovered you broke camp, I was worried. Thankfully, an army with war machines leaves a trail difficult to miss."

"Yes, yes. Now, what is this about?" Mollis demanded.

"I come from Sol Polis with new orders." The man drew a folded parchment from his saddlebag and handed it to Mollis.

The commander examined the wax seal, opened it, and read to himself. His grimace deepened as he squinted in concern. A grin then replaced his frown, and he handed the message to Brillens. "It turns out our decision has been made. We are to march to Wayport immediately. When we arrive, we attack at Sculdin's signal."

"Attack?" Percy exclaimed. "But Chadwick is on our side."

"Yes, he was. However, dead men have no allegiance."

"Oh, no," Brillens groaned as he read the missive. "King Brock lives. He has executed Chadwick and reclaimed the city. We are to attack four days from now and take it back."

Mollis climbed onto his horse. "We have sixty miles to travel and little time to do so. We had best march. Now."

18

HIDING

Jonah and Thiron squatted in silence in the same location Thiron and Chuli had occupied in previous mornings. They would typically return to camp and report seeing nothing of interest. Today was different. Today, the Imperial Army occupied the canyon.

After a rain of flashbombs, the prison wall had become rubble. The officer's quarters and two of the bunkhouses still burned, evidenced by the black smoke rising from the destroyed buildings. When the bombs stopped falling, enemy scouts had stormed the complex to find it abandoned.

All had gone as planned until the scouts entered the mines. Twenty minutes later, those scouts emerged and returned to meet with the Imperial commanders who huddled between a line of catapults and the waiting army.

"I wonder what they are discussing," Jonah said aloud.

Thiron's remained focused on watching the distant conversation "I suspect they are guessing at where Marcella's troops have gone. Unless they believe we have fled north to join the Tantarri, they will assume we are heading toward Wayport."

In the distance, a trail of dust emerged, stirred by a rider moving at a gallop. The rider slowed and stopped when reaching the officers. Two minutes later, one of the officers rode down the middle of the army, waving and shouting orders. Crews began spinning the catapults about while others formed ranks. The army was leaving. In an orderly fashion, the march resumed and they headed west. Minutes passed and Jonah grew anxious.

"How long do we have to wait?"

Thiron snorted. "Do not allow your impatience to rule prudence."

Jonah gave Thiron a look. "Since when have I ever been prudent?"

"Thank you."

"For what?"

"Reinforcing the point I was making." Thiron smiled, a rarity.

"You still didn't answer the question."

The man sighed. "When they are out of sight and cannot see us, we will descend."

"I was afraid you would say that."

The army slowly faded into the distance. At the far end of the canyon, miles away, the army turned south and disappeared.

Thiron stood and began picking his way along the boulders on the ridgetop. When he reached the cleft, he lowered himself down and gathered the coil of rope he had pulled up the evening prior. He tossed the rope down, gripped it with gloved hands, and began his descent.

While Jonah was anxious to reach the tunnels, he was nervous about rappelling down the cliff side. As he lowered himself down toward the waiting spike and rope, he recalled his discussion about the process with Chuli. She had explained the method to him and assured him he was capable, but his doubt remained – not that he would ever allow Thiron to know.

Fear brought cold sweat to his armpits and left him gasping as he gripped the rope and began to back down the sheer cliff wall. While Thiron had made the descent in less than a minute, it took Jonah far longer. Ten minutes later, he stepped onto the canyon floor and silently thanked Issal.

Jonah gave Thiron a weak grin. "No problem."

Other than raising one brow, Thiron said nothing. Instead, he drew a glowstone from his pack and entered the nearest tunnel with Jonah following. The man took a right branch and then a left before the tunnel opened to a cavern where the only other exit was now collapsed.

Thiron cupped his hand to his mouth and shouted. "They are gone! We are going to free you, now."

The man removed one glove and held out his hand. "All right, magic boy. Do it."

"Magic boy?" Jonah asked as he began drawing a Power rune on Thiron's hand. "I guess it's better than some of other names you have called me."

Powered by the augmentation, moving the wall of boulders would be short work, as it had been the day before when the man had built it. While Thiron worked, Jonah imagined what Marcella might have done if something had happened to him. If not for Jonah's magic, how long would it take her army to remove the boulders? How long would they survive, trapped? The idea gave him a shiver.

With the camp now destroyed, they would leave and follow in the wake of the enemy army, sure to remain distant enough to avoid discovery.

Jonah's thoughts shifted to Chuli, who had departed alone the day prior. He prayed her mission would be a success.

19

STEALTH

The sound of a hammer and the scent of burnt metal greeted Cassie as she stepped into the Forge. The room was occupied by gadgeteers crafting components and a few of the older arcanists, busily infusing Chaos into those pieces. The sight was common during waking hours, particularly late morning as it was now.

Thankfully, she didn't see Master Firellus, nor did she expect to see him in the Forge. He rarely ventured there, which was good. She had thus far evaded him since stepping into his nightmare. The memory gave her a chill.

When she spotted Everson, she crossed the room, circling benches and piles of scrap metal before stopping near a hot forge. With a pair of tongs in one hand, he pressed a thin sheet of hot metal against an anvil, shaping it into half a cylinder. Standing this close, the ring of the hammer made Cassie's head ring along with it.

Ivy sat nearby, working on something far more delicate. A pair of magnifying goggles covered half her face. Seeing anyone wearing those goggles made Cassie think of a bug. *I would hate to meet a bug that size,* she thought with another shiver.

Everson set the hammer aside and wiped his brow. "Hi, Cassie," he said in a loud voice as a drip of sweat ran down his temple. "What brings you here?"

"You don't have to shout," she grinned at him. "I can hear you just fine."

He lowered his voice. "Sorry. My ears are still ringing from the hammer." He frowned. "I really should plug them before I do this, but I usually forget."

Ivy lifted her goggles. "Hello, Cassie." She pulled a glob of blue wax from each ear. "That's better," she said as she set the earplugs on the workbench.

"Perhaps you should have Ivy remind you, Ev," Cassie suggested. "She seems to remember to wear them."

He nodded. "She is more organized than I am. It's one reason I love having her around."

Ivy narrowed her eyes. "I certainly hope there are other, better reasons."

Everson blinked. "Um. Yes. Of course."

Standing, Ivy smiled and reached for Everson's hand. "Don't worry. I was only joking."

He grinned sheepishly and glanced at Cassie. "Yes. I should have known."

Cassie chuckled, "Don't ever change, Everson. I find it refreshing to have someone honest and innocent around."

"Yes. I do like you just the way you are." Ivy slipped her arm around him and then pulled away. "Well, perhaps when you are less sweaty."

He winced. "Sorry about that. Pounding steel is hard work."

Ivy grabbed his upper arm. "I've noticed how good you look when your shirt is off." She flashed a devious smile as her hand moved to his chest, where his tunic was damp with sweat. "All this hard work is paying off."

"Well, that's not why I do it. However…"

"I came to ask for help," Cassie blurted, deciding it was time to change the subject. When they looked at her, she said, "I may have discovered a new use for Chaos."

Everson's eyes lit up. "What is it? How does it work?"

"I'm not exactly sure. That's why I came to you."

His brow furrowed in thought before he nodded to himself. "To be sure we don't destroy anything if the rune proves false, we should test it outside."

Cassie nodded. "I expected as much. Go grab some warmer clothing, and I'll meet you two near the stables."

—·◆·—

The sun was out, the weather surprisingly mild. Water dripped from long icicles hanging off the stable roof, each drop disappearing into narrow holes that had formed in the snow beside the building.

Cassie wore her gray wool cloak, but kept the hood down since there was little wind. The bright reflection of sunlight off the snow-covered ground forced her to squint while Everson and Ivy crossed the gravel stable yard.

"Sorry it took so long," Everson said as they drew near. He turned to Ivy as he spoke. "Someone made me wash up and change shirts."

"Some of us are sensitive to bad smells," Ivy noted. "Something for which you certainly qualified."

"Thank you for not offending our sense of smell, Everson," Cassie said with a smile.

He sighed. "Enough of that. What can you tell me about the new rune?"

Cassie looked around to ensure they were alone. "Two nights back, I couldn't sleep so I went to the kitchen to scrounge up some food."

"Ooo. Don't let Irma catch you in there."

"I know. That's why I was trying to do it quietly. While I was in there, the door opened, casting light into the room. I hid, thinking it might be Irma. Instead, it was Delvin. Without making a sound, he crossed the room, went into the supply closet, and slipped away. As I studied him, I was amazed by his silent, fluid manner – the epitome of stealth. That's when the rune appeared."

"You were holding tight to Order during this event?" Everson asked.

"Yes. I...It has become a bit of a habit. Besides, I had woken from a nightmare." Cassie shivered as she recalled Elias' dream. "Meditation helps when I am upset."

Everson said, "With the last rune you discovered, you had been focused on Brandt's speed and quickness and that's when the Speed rune came to you?"

"Yes."

"And this time, you were focused on Delvin's sneaking skills – his stealth. That is the augmentation you suspect?"

Cassie nodded.

"That makes sense to me," Ivy said.

Everson rubbed his chin. "Inanimate objects acquiring stealth would only make them hard to notice. We need to test this with something that moves to measure the effect of the augmentation."

Cassie looked at Ivy with a raised brow. "Does it ever bother you when he talks this way?"

Ivy's brow furrowed. "What do you mean?"

"Never mind."

Everson's eyes brightened. "I've got it!"

"What exactly do you have?" Ivy asked.

"I know how we can test this new rune. Follow me."

He walked toward the open side of the stable yard and followed a trail of tracks that ran around the building.

"That's what we will use."

"Our snowman?" Ivy said.

The thing Everson had indicated was made of snow, wide at the base and narrow at the top. It had sticks for arms, buttons for eyes, and a carrot for a nose.

"Why did you make a man from snow?" Cassie asked as she stared at the odd-looking creation.

"Because it's fun." Ivy sidled close to Everson and hooked her arm in his.

"You haven't built a snowman before?" Everson asked.

"No," Cassie shook he head. "I never even experienced snow before this winter, remember?"

"Oh. Yeah." Everson tugged Ivy forward and the two walked toward the snowman. "Growing up in Cinti Mor, we used to build one every winter. Quinn would often name them, as if each had its own personality."

"I used to do the same in Selbin," Ivy added. "Except for naming them. I never thought to do that."

They stopped in front of it, all three looking at the misshapen man made from snow. Everson produced a charcoal stick from his pocket and began to draw a symbol on the snowman. When finished, he handed the coal to Cassie.

"Draw your new rune right here." He tapped a blank spot above his rune.

Cassie did so, closing her eyes twice as she recalled the symbol. Getting it wrong would be disaster, but at least it would be outside where little harm would follow. She stood back and handed the coal to Everson.

"Let's back up and stand beside the stable," Everson said. "Then, you can charge both runes. Just be sure to charge mine first."

The trio retreated and stood in the shadow of the stable with their backs to it. Cassie closed her eyes, embraced Chaos, and drew it in. Raw power surged through her, filling her with life – too much life. She opened her eyes and released a portion of it into the Animate rune before channeling the rest into the new rune. In turn, each rune glowed, pulsed, and faded.

The snowman began to shake, the base breaking apart to form legs made of snow. It stood, the stick arms moving and flexing. And then, it disappeared.

"Where did it go?" Cassie spun around, searching for the snowman.

Something white flashed in her peripheral vision, but when Cassie turned toward it, nothing was there. She turned again and saw it in the edge of her vision, this time closer, but it was again gone when she turned and looked directly where she thought she saw it.

Furrows appeared in the snow beside her and she gasped. Tentatively, she reached out and felt the snowman, but she couldn't see it. Everson and Ivy were both wide-eyed. Again, a faint white shape hovered at the edge of her vision, right over the tracks.

"The thing is right here beside me," Cassie said. "Odd, but I can't see it unless I look away."

Everson turned his head and grunted. "You're right." He reached his arm across Cassie and patted the near invisible snowman. "I can feel it and see a shadow of it in my peripheral vision." He turned toward it. "But when I stare directly at it...nothing."

"I did it," Cassie smiled. "I discovered another rune. We should go in so I can draw it for you. We will need to record it with the others." Her grin stretched. "I can't wait to share this with Brandt."

"There is one thing you are forgetting," Ivy said.

"What's that?"

"You animated the snowman. The thing is going to follow you around like a pet until the augmentation fades."

Everson chuckled. "This should be interesting. I wonder how long it will take to melt once we are inside."

After recording the new rune on paper and helping Everson and Ivy mop up the melted remains of the snowman, Cassie left the study and climbed the stairs while imagining how the new Stealth augmentation might be used.

Magic-enhanced stealth would be an incredible tool for an espion like her brother. She considered reaching out to him but recalled his current mission and decided to wait.

She reached the fifth floor and followed the corridor to her apartment. Using the key she kept on a cord around her neck, she unlocked the door, stepped inside, and closed it.

"I was wondering when you would return."

Cassie gasped in alarm. She spun around to find Master Firellus seated on her sofa. As usual, the man was dressed in clothing of one color – his tunic, trousers, and cloak all black. Unlike the dream, the gray had returned to his hair and the wrinkles to his face.

"Master Firellus. I...I wasn't expecting you. How did you get in?"

"I did not pick the lock, if that's what you think." He reached into his pocket and produced a gold key, eyeing it as he spun the key around. "Some of us have keys that open every door in the Ward." He repocketed the key. "Of course, we did not give one to Master Garber." A grimace crossed his face. "Delvin wouldn't use a key anyway. The man prefers to use other means of entry and sees it as some sort of challenge."

Cassie's brow furrowed. She crossed the room and sat across from him. "You don't like Delvin much, do you?"

He snorted. "I don't need to like him. Delvin has a role, as do I. So long as he plays his part, we will continue to work together as required." The grimace returned. "I just wish I knew where he went off to this time."

The mention of Delvin disappearing caused Cassie to reflect on her encounter with him in the kitchen. She had not seen him since that night.

"Never mind, Master Garber." Elias leaned forward. "I am here to speak with you."

Cassie swallowed and looked away, trying to find something to focus on beside the intimidating man who sat across from her. Her gaze settled on the Ratio Bellicus table between them.

"What about, Sir?"

"Have you been abusing your abilities?"

"Abusing? What abilities? If you refer to Infusing a living thing, I would never..."

"I refer to your ability to visit the dreams of others."

He knows. "Well, I don't know how to improve my skill without actually entering the dream realm."

"Did you visit my dream two nights back?"

"I...I'm sorry if I did something wrong."

He sat back, but she continued to look at the table, refusing to meet his glare. "The past is the past, Cassie. What's done is done, both for you and for me." Something in the man's tone changed, ringing of regret. "I have made many poor choices in my life – more than good ones. I am doing my best to rectify that imbalance. You must know this."

She met his eyes with a frown. "I don't understand. What was that place?"

"It was a place of horrors – a past I wish to forget but cannot. The man in the dream, he is not me." Anger returned to his voice as it rose in volume. "I have changed and am no longer that man!"

Cassie jumped at the outburst, her gaze meeting his. She gasped. "Elias. Your eyes..."

His eyes were red, but not his irises as was normal when someone held Chaos. Only his pupils glowed, as if something burned deep inside them.

"What?" he said, alarmed.

"They...they are red."

He closed them, his body shaking as he took long, deep breaths. After a moment, he opened them and the red glow was gone.

"Since you have a hint of my past, it will do little harm for you to know the rest." He held his hand toward her. "You must heal me, Cassie.

It has been too long, and I may not control it long enough to see Master Alridge."

Cassie looked at his hand. "What am I healing, Sir?"

"You must heal the Chaos trapped inside my body before it claims me again."

20

RESPECT

The rain persisted. At first, the patter of the drops striking his metal helmet had irritated Iko. Hours later, he had grown used to the noise, and he now only longed to shed his armor for dry clothing.

As he had grown numb to the falling rain, he had also lost himself to the rhythm of his galloping horse. A column of five hundred cavalry trailed him – men he did not know.

Many of Commander Korbath's soldiers had experience. Those who didn't had been training down in Sol Gier for months. Before leaving Sol Polis, Iko had briefly met with Korbath on two different occasions, during visits with Captain Sculdin. Iko had the distinct impression that Korbath only abided his presence because of Sculdin's orders. The nature of their conversations since their morning departure only reinforced the feeling. When interacting with Iko, Korbath would bite off each word as if even speaking to Iko were beneath him.

Iko's gaze shifted past Korbath, toward the sea to the west. White-caps were plentiful along the rough water, stirred by the storm. Moored vessels lined the docks, rolling as if they were far out at sea. With the rain and failing light, it was difficult to see much beyond the harbor.

Just east of the road was Yarth's western wall. The ramparts were barren save the guard towers at the corners and over the gates along the north and south walls. Puddles dotted the gravel road they traveled, some areas thick with mud. Iko did his best to guide his steed around the worst of it, yet his backside was covered in mud splatter. He suspected that the riders at the rear of the column had the worst of it.

After circling the walled city of Yarth, they turned and followed a road into the forest. With the trees hugging the road and the gray skies turning black, visibility became an issue, so the riders slowed to a trot.

The trees soon parted and the wooden palisades of the Yarth Garrison came into view. As the cavalry drew close, guards with pikes formed ranks three rows deep to block the gate. A tower stood to each side of the gate and archers waited atop each platform, watching the approaching cavalry with bows ready.

When Korbath raised a hand and slowed his horse to a stop, Iko did likewise. He looked back at the trail of riders dressed in blue tabards, their weapons sheathed. Iko gazed down at his own armor. The metal plates over brown leather made him feel out of place, the odd man out among the unit. Like Korbath's, the strip of white plumes on his helmet marked Iko as an officer. *An officer without soldiers to lead*, Iko thought. *What is my role, Sculdin?* The man's response echoed in Iko's head. *Your rank will force others to listen. You are smart, have training, and might offer insight that will save lives. Besides, when the fighting begins and action is required, I know you will do what must be done. That includes stepping in, should another officer fall.*

"Ho!" Korbath shouted, removed his helmet, and shook his head. Dark curls from his shoulder-length hair clung to his forehead, his mouth and goatee drawn into a frown. "I am Commander Korbath, leader of the Sol Gier cavalry unit. We have come with orders from General Kardan."

A woman stepped forward, staring at Korbath as she approached. "It *is* you, Korbath."

"Sergeant Halle," Korbath nodded. "How are things at the garrison?"

"Restless." She shook her head. "Your arrival wouldn't by chance indicate a change in plans?"

"Sorry, Sergeant. That news is for Captain Rorrick to share."

Halle sighed, "I thought you might respond that way, but I would like to know if I should prepare my squads for a march."

"Would you mind having them move aside? The ride from Sol Polis has been unpleasant. Food, shelter, and a bed would be most welcome once I have met with Rorrick."

"As you wish." She turned toward the pikemen and issued orders. "Move aside. Let the commander and his troops through!"

The pikemen split down the middle, half moving to each side of the road.

"Thank you, Sergeant," Korbath nudged his horse into a walk. More quietly, he added, "If you have anything to address here, I would do it now. Your stay at the garrison is nearing an end."

Halle smiled, "Thank you, Commander."

Iko and the other cavalry followed Korbath through the gate. Inside, Iko spotted a row of buildings along the wall to his right and hundreds of tents to his left. The tents were arranged in clusters and grouped by color. In the center was a field of mud, littered with footprints. Soldiers moved about in squads, many with hooded cloaks shielding them from the weather. Wagons rolled about, following gravel roads that encircled the camp. The garrison felt something like a city – a temporary, primitive city. He had known that thousands were stationed within the garrison walls, but the truth did not strike him until he witnessed it himself.

Following a road down the center of the garrison, they headed toward the first building – a structure hundreds of feet long and half as deep with a peaked roof running its length. With Korbath at his side and the cavalry unit at his back, Iko rode through an open barn door. Blessedly, the patter of rain fell away. *Dry. It will be nice to dry off.*

He pulled his helmet away and shook the water from his hair. Four stable hands sat on hay bales just inside the entrance, rolling dice beside a glowlamp. The four men looked up, their eyes widening before they scrambled to their feet and stood ready.

"Take care of our horses." Korbath said as he dismounted. "They need food and water, but should remain saddled. We will be leaving soon. Where can I find Captain Rorrick?"

The commander handed the reins to a man who replied, "Rorrick is in the officer quarters, three buildings down. Look for the building with the flag posted beside it."

"What about the mess hall?"

"It's the big building in the middle. Just look for the green doors."

Korbath nodded and turned to his cavalrymen, who were still dismounting. He raised his voice for all to hear. "You heard the man. Head to the mess hall and eat. I will report to Rorrick and inquire about lodging for the night. Don't drink too much or stay up too late. Tomorrow will be a long day." The commander then waved toward Iko. "Come along, kid."

Iko frowned at Korbath's back as he walked out, into the rain. *I knew it. He doesn't respect me.* A sigh slipped out as he followed Korbath, hoping he wouldn't face the same issue with Rorrick.

They crossed the open grounds and passed another building. With each step, Iko felt the ground squishing beneath his boots. He thought of the tents and expected they would remain a mess once packed, the mud carried to another location for the next camp. A building with a flagpole beside it came into view, the flag at the top white and blue. Iko followed Korbath to the front door. There, they both did their best to stomp off the mud on the porch before entering.

A buzz of conversation and the aroma of mutton greeted them, the latter causing Iko's mouth to water. Since breakfast, he had eaten nothing but trail rations. Warm, dry conditions and a hot meal would be most welcome. But first, they had to find Rorrick. He scanned the surroundings, searching for the man as described by Sculdin.

The building interior was lit by glowlamp sconces mounted along the walls and on posts that ran down the middle. A grid of thick beams hovered over the room, the beams casting shadows across the vaulted ceiling. Four long tables occupied the space, the tables filled with men and women dressed in a variety of armor. At the end of the farthest table, Iko spotted a middle-aged man, his head shaved clean, his beard thick and brown and curly. The man wore a uniform identical to Sculdin's.

Iko leaned close to Korbath, "Is that Rorrick?"

"Yes." Korbath headed toward Rorrick with his helmet still beneath his arm. When he reached the captain, he stood at attention and thumped his chest. "Captain Rorrick. Commander Korbath of the Sol Gier Cavalry reporting."

Rorrick sat back, his gaze shifting from Korbath to Iko and back, "Welcome to my garrison, Commander. Would you like to join us for dinner?"

"Very much, so, Captain. However, General Kardan requested that I brief you immediately upon arrival."

Rorrick's face turned to a scowl, but he stood and nodded anyway. "I should have known. Duty often toys with my stomach, sometimes forgetting it altogether. Follow me."

Iko studied Rorrick as the man led them toward a door at the side of the room. Six feet tall with square shoulders, a barrel chest, and a confident gait, the man was the image of the quintessential soldier. With lines on his forehead and near his eyes, he was older than Sculdin, but younger than Kardan. *I bet he was in the Holy Army,* Iko thought.

Rorrick led them into a small room, holding the door until Iko and Korbath were inside. A table along one wall, a desk in the middle, and four chairs were the only furnishings. Orange coals lingered in the small fireplace at the side of the room, offering warmth.

"Now," Rorrick said as he circled the desk and sat. "What is this about?"

Korbath reached into the satchel on his hip and withdrew a piece of folded paper. "We departed from Sol Polis this morning with orders from General Kardan." The commander handed the paper to Rorrick, who examined the seal.

"This may take a minute." Rorrick said as he broke the seal. "You may sit if you like."

"If it's all the same, Sir," Iko said. "We've been in the saddle all day and standing is a welcome change."

The man unfolded the note and nodded. "Suit yourself."

Iko noticed Korbath watching Rorrick intently. *I'm sure he would like to read it himself,* Iko thought. The commander knew the army was ordered to march, but that was only one aspect of the message in Rorrick's hands. Iko knew the entirety of what the letter contained. Kardan had forced him to memorize every word should something happen to Korbath or the letter.

Once finished, Rorrick stood, approached the fireplace, and began stirring coals with a poker. He then tossed the message in and watched it burn.

Rorrick turned toward Korbath. "You are dismissed, Commander. Get some food, then go next door and ask for Soreen, the camp outfitter. She will find lodging for you and your men."

Korbath thumped his fist against his chest and turned to the door. When Iko moved to follow, Rorrick said, "You are not dismissed, Lieutenant."

With a backward glance at Iko, Korbath opened the door and left the room. Rorrick reclaimed his chair and stared at Iko for a long, uncomfortable moment.

"Kardan and Sculdin seem to think you will be of use to me. I have no idea what that entails, but I see I am saddled with you." The man leaned forward, his dark eyes intense. "You had better realize you'll receive no special treatment from me. My job is to take the field, defeat the enemy, and protect the lives of my soldiers in the process. Archon's whelp or not, you are just another officer – worse, an officer without a squad to lead. Do you even have any battle experience?"

"No, Sir. However, I am well trained with the sword and spent time at TACT."

Rorrick snorted. "Military school? Do you think tactics study in a classroom can replace experience?" He stood and circled around the desk to stop a half-stride away. The man glowered at Iko and made him want to back away. "If we are in the heat of battle and you freeze, don't think I will try to help you. I'll not allow your presence to distract me and cost the lives of my soldiers. I suggest you keep quiet and stay out of the way. If I need something from you, I will let you know. Understood?"

Iko bit off a retort, swallowed his pride, and nodded. "Yes, Sir."

"Good. You are dismissed."

Iko turned and left the room. He would eat and think of a way to get into the man's good graces. *Why did you send me here, Scully?*

—✦—

With a full stomach and his head abuzz from ale, Iko stepped out of the officers' hall with his helmet under his arm. The rain had stopped, but the ground remained a muddy mess. He was reluctant to even step off the porch. His boots had only dried an hour earlier.

The door opened and Commander Luon walked out, the woman thumping him on the back as she stepped from the porch into the mud.

"Good night, Ikonis. It was good to meet you." She turned toward him. "Perhaps we will dine together again while on the march."

"Thank you, Luon. I look forward to it." He smiled. "Have a good night."

When she turned and faded into the darkness, he reflected on his evening with the officers. He had found Luon and many others friendly. Telling stories while drinking ale tended to whittle down barriers, and tonight was no different. While Korbath had slipped away early and Rorrick had retired to his office, the remaining officers seemed to welcome and accept Iko.

The group had remained in the building for two or three hours before they began to head back to their individual camps. By that time, the ale barrel was empty and everyone present was deep into his or her cups. It had only seemed fitting to drink it before leaving the garrison. After all, who knows when the opportunity would arise next? For some, it would be their final chance to drink. Ever. As officers, they were experienced enough to know the next battle might be the last.

Iko took a deep breath and noticed stars winking through the thinning clouds. It was a good sign, the rain likely behind them. However, he still wore his armor and longed for more comfortable clothing. With that thought in mind, he headed back toward the stables.

When he arrived, he pulled the barn door open and found two stable hands back on the hay bales. One was dozing while the other strummed a lute. The man set the lute aside and approached Iko.

"What can I do for you, sir?"

"I rode in with the cavalry unit a few hours ago. I wanted to find my horse and get something from my saddlebag."

"Yessir," The man said. "We have eight large pens and split the horses between them." He turned back to the hay bale, lifted one of the two lanterns, and handed it to Iko. "Go back that way and find your mount. Just return the lantern when you're finished."

"Thank you."

Iko headed toward the end of the stables, passing four small pens before he found the larger ones. The smell of manure was strong, forcing him to breathe through his mouth. He opened the gate and meandered among the horses, searching for the piebald he had ridden, thankful he had not ridden a brown steed as had the majority of the cavalry unit. In the poor light, picking one out among all the others would be far more difficult.

Not finding his horse, he exited the pen and moved to the next one. The door at the end of the building opened, and a blond girl dressed in blue entered. She stopped and stared at him, her eyes going wide.

"Quinn?" Iko said in shock. "What are you doing here?"

21

TRAITOR

With long, smooth strokes, Quinn ran her blade across the oiled whetstone. She sat on a crate beside the tent entrance. Outside, the rain continued, as it had all day. A lantern hung from the post in the entrance and provided sufficient light for the interior.

Tilly lay on her bedroll, reciting a tale involving her older sister and a boy she grew up with in Port Hurns. Evian sat beside Tilly with a needle and thick thread, attempting to repair a tear in the shoulder of her leather armor. Bernice was sharpening her own sword – a sabre with a long, curved blade. Ilsa lay on her stomach, listening to Tilly's tale.

"...and so, my sister told him she wouldn't give him what he wanted unless he licked the metal gazing ball in the duke's garden to prove his adoration. When he agreed, they met up later that night, snuck into the Duke's estate, and made their way to the garden. There, under the starlight, was a statue of a man holding a shiny metal ball with reflected starlight twinkling from it. So, this boy approaches the statue, sticks out his tongue, and does the deed.

"Mind you, it was a chilly winter evening. Some folks know about frost and wet things. Others don't. Some believe it a myth. I can tell you it is not. Sure as water is wet, the boy's tongue stuck to the gazing ball. Try as he might, he couldn't pull it away. My sister laughed at the trick and fled, leaving the distraught boy behind."

As laughter filled the tent, Quinn grinned at the image of a sixteen-year-old boy's tongue stuck to a metal ball in a private garden.

"The next morning, one of the duke's men came to our door. With him was this boy, the same boy who had been pursuing my sister for weeks, teary-eyed with his bandaged tongue sticking from his mouth. His mother stood beside him, her face like a thundercloud.

"My sister confessed to putting the boy up to the task. When his mother heard the reason behind the trick, she gripped his ear and hauled him away. Rumor has it, she made him wait a full day before taking him to the temple healer."

Ilsa sat up, facing Tilly. "I bet that stunt gained your sister a bit of respect."

"It sure did. The boys in town all took her more seriously afterward. That particular boy didn't speak with her for weeks, but she never liked him much anyway. Besides, my sister is pretty and always had boys fawning at her. She hoped future advances would include motivation other than just them wishing to lift her skirts."

Quinn held up her blade, gleaming in the lamplight. "While her trick was clever, there are more direct ways to command a bit of respect."

"Would you threaten them with your sword, Jacquinn?" Ilsa chided. "Perhaps suggest they might lose an appendage?"

"Perhaps," Quinn chuckled. "However, I don't need weapons to intimidate a boy."

Evian grunted. "That's true. A knee to the groin would have them thinking twice about laying a hand on me."

"I doubt you have to worry about it, Evian," Bernice said. "I don't exactly see boys lining up outside the tent, waiting for their turn."

The comment stirred another round of laughter, save for Evian, whose face turned to a grimace.

A head poked in through the tent flap. "Time for dinner," Cleffa announced. "See you in the mess hall."

Quinn stored her sword whetstone while the other girls got ready. With boots and cloaks on, they exited the tent and crossed the mud-covered grounds, slowing while the Harriers ahead of them slowly filtered into the mess hall.

As Quinn stood in the food line, she heard hushed whispers from other girls – talk of them marching in the morning to begin a march west.

It wasn't just one group, but many who whispered the same rumor. Marching west was not part of the mission, and she wondered how she and Brandt should proceed.

Men dressed in brown began to clear the benches as women dressed in blue replaced them. When Quinn reached the front, she accepted a plate of mutton and potatoes before grabbing a hard roll and heading toward an open table. She sat, knowing that her squadmates would join her.

A hand touched her shoulder and someone leaned close, his breath tickling her neck.

"I have missed you."

She smiled, but didn't turn her head. "I have missed you as well."

"Meet me tonight. We have business..."

Her heart fluttered at the thought. "Where?"

"The stables, in two hours. Enter through the eastern door."

She couldn't restrain a smile. "I will be there."

The hand slipped away, the memory of his touch lingering.

Ilsa sat down across from Quinn. "Why are you smiling like that?"

Quinn shrugged. "Just a pleasant memory."

Tilly, Evian, Bernice, and others from their squad soon joined them. There was conversation and laughter as the group ate, but Quinn didn't hear it. Weeks had passed since she was last alone with Brandt. In two hours, her wait would be over.

The area was quiet, as were the camps she had passed on her way to the stables. When she slipped inside, a soldier with a glowlamp stepped out of a stall. Her heart skipped a beat when she recognized him.

"Quinn? What are you doing here?" Iko asked, appearing as shocked as she felt.

"I..." Quinn struggled with a response, mentally grasping for something that might sound plausible. "I followed the spy to Yarth and then here. He has been eluding me for days."

Iko stepped closer and lowered the lamp. Quinn shifted to the side, feeling as if he were attempting to corner her. Before he could ask another question, she tried to shift the tide.

"What are you doing here?" she asked. "Why aren't you in Sol Polis?"

He blinked, visibly taken aback. His lips pressed together in a frown. "I cannot say. I...I don't trust you, Quinn. Something isn't right here."

She sighed and tried to appear nonchalant as she leaned against a pen wall. "Things are rarely as they seem, Iko. That's why I am here. I'm trying to get to the root of the plot. I believe someone in the Imperial Army is behind it all."

He jerked as if he had been punched, but his frown remained. Finally, he grunted. "If that were true..." His brow furrowed and he stared into space. "What if it is someone in our own ranks? What if someone seeking power is attempting to displace my mother and the other leaders? I never considered..."

Quinn found hope in his statement and hurried to feed the fire she had started. "Exactly. Imagine if they had an ear in the palace yet had control of a force significant enough to take Sol Polis when the time was right."

In a hushed voice, he asked, "You suspect Rorrick?"

Quinn shrugged, happy for the suggestion. "Who is in a better position? What loyalty does he owe to your mother? You have known Kardan and Sculdin for years. What do you know of Rorrick?"

Iko's brow furrowed and his frown deepened. "I only just met the man."

"And?"

"I don't like him one bit, nor does he wish me here."

"Interesting. Why does your presence trouble him?" Quinn moved closer and put her hand on his arm. "What does your heart tell you, Iko? Consider the puzzle before you and how the pieces fit."

He stared at her for a long moment before he relaxed. When he shook his head, she knew she had him.

"It makes too much sense. Who else would know Pretencia was held in the Sol Polis dungeon? Who else would have the means to slip a spy into the palace, a seasoned soldier nonetheless?" Iko's face contorted in anger. "He tried to have my mother killed. That traitor!"

"Shh..." She rubbed his arm, hoping to quiet him. The last thing she needed was more attention. "Listen, I only came in here to see if the rumors are true. Word is we will break camp tomorrow and begin our march. I figured the horses would need to be saddled and ready for morning if it were true."

He nodded. "Yes. It's true. We are to break camp tomorrow. That's why I am here."

The door behind Iko opened – the same door Quinn had used.

A whispering voice said, "Quinn," as someone stepped in.

Iko turned toward the door and pale light from the glowlamp lit Brandt's face. "You!" Iko exclaimed. "You're the spy Quinn was chasing!"

In a desperate move, Quinn tore the helmet from beneath Iko's arm and smashed it over his head with all her might. The clang from the impact was tremendous, the result immediate as Iko collapsed in a heap, his lantern rolling across the dirt before stopping against Brandt's boots.

"Remind me not to turn my back on you," Brandt said as he stepped closer. "What is *he* doing here?"

"What's going on back there?" A voice called out from the middle of the stable.

Quinn dropped the helmet, grabbed Brandt's hand, and pulled him toward the door. "Let's go!" she whispered as she hurried out the door with Brandt on her heels.

She immediately started toward her camp, walking as fast as she dared. She didn't want to attract attention.

Brandt caught up to her, his hand gripping her arm and pulling her to a stop. "What is happening?"

"We have to leave, Brandt," She looked back at the building, eager to be away. "Come on. I'll explain when we get further from the stables."

She resumed her long, fast strides while her mind raced and he attempted to keep up.

Iko now knew she and Brandt were together. With Brandt pinned as a spy, she would earn the same label. Rorrick was sure to use the situation to his advantage. If caught, she and Brant would become examples to the army as a deterrent against treason. Juvi's offense had been nothing compared to this. Images of nooses and whips and chopping blocks flashed before Quinn's eyes, solidifying her resolve. *We must escape, and we must do it now.*

22

FLIGHT

B randt passed through the musketeer camp, walking as quietly as possible. With mud squishing beneath his boots, his footsteps weren't as muted as he would have liked. The area was still with only a single waning glowlamp hanging in each cluster of tents.

He reached his tent and ducked inside. Lewin was snoring, as usual, the soft rumble masking Brandt's movements. Moments later, he had his pack in one arm, his cloak in the other, and he was slipping outside.

"Going somewhere?"

Brandt turned to find Commander Ferdinand glaring at him. The man's hand rested on the pommel of his sword, still in its scabbard. Before Brandt could reply, the man interrupted.

"I saw you sneak off earlier. Now you come back for your cloak and pack?" He arched a brow. "You do know what they do to deserters, right?"

"I…I wasn't deserting. I'm just…um…going to meet a girl." *That much is true.*

"A girl?"

"Yes. One of the Harriers."

"Why your pack?"

Brandt looked down at the pack in his hand. "I made something for her. A gift."

The man stared hard at Brandt, his curled mustache twitching as his mouth twisted in thought. "While I understand the lure of the opposite sex, and I do remember what it was like to be your age, I must insist you return to your tent for the evening."

The pained expression on Brandt's face was legitimate. He needed to leave and he had little time. Quinn was waiting.

Turning, as if to head back into his tent, Brandt suddenly swung around, his pack striking Ferdinand in the head. The man staggered and Brandt hit him again. With the commander bent over, Brandt kicked hard, his boot striking Ferdinand's temple and sending him sprawling in the mud. When the man did not move, Brandt ran.

Since the ground was wet and slippery, he had to run at a controlled pace. He circled to avoid another camp and split the gap between it and the next camp. When the palisade wall came into view, he slowed, frantically searching for Quinn. Thoughts of her running into trouble surfaced. He couldn't leave without her.

"Quinn," he said in a hushed voice.

"Over here."

Hearing her call from the right, he angled toward the voice and soon spotted her waiting near the wall.

"I was growing worried," she said as he slowed to a stop.

"So was I." He said between breaths. "My commander caught me leaving. I had to hit him."

"Oh, dear Issal. You didn't kill him, did you?"

"No. I don't think so. He was unconscious when I left."

"Well, if they weren't after us for knocking Iko out, they will be now."

"What can I say?" Brandt grinned. "I'm an overachiever."

Even though it was dark and he couldn't see it, Brandt imagined Quinn rolling her eyes.

"Enough stories," Quinn said. "Let's get out of here before they catch us."

"Right."

Brandt dug in his pack, dug out a chunk of glowstone, and began drawing a rune on the back of his hand.

"Why do you always get the augmentation?" Quinn asked. "I know how to handle myself with a Power rune, you know."

"You want to carry me?"

"Sure. Why not?"

Brandt sighed. "Is now really the time to argue about this?'

"No. It's not. That's why you should just do your magic on me, and let me do the rest."

He stared at her, slack jawed, unsure of what to say. Finally, he sighed. "Give me your hand."

"I thought you would never ask." Quinn's smile shone in the starlight.

He sketched a Power rune and closed his eyes. Chaos was there, as always, surrounding him and everything else. He drew in the energy – something that once required great effort but was now easy. Yet, holding the magic still felt as if he had eaten a storm.

Staring at the symbol on Quinn's hand, he poured the energy into it, setting the rune aglow with crimson light. The rune pulsed, faded, and Quinn stumbled.

Brandt caught her. "Easy, Quinn."

She nodded and stood upright. "I'm fine now. I forgot how hard it hits you at first."

Brandt stuffed both the glowstone and his cloak into his pack. With it clutched to his chest, he nodded. "I'm ready. Let's jump the wall."

Quinn scooped him up, throwing him slightly in the process before catching him in her arms.

"My, you are light," Quinn noted with a grin. "Have you been skipping meals?"

"Why are you suddenly so glib?"

"Perhaps I'm just happy to be the one in control. Besides, you act this way all the time. How does it feel to be on the receiving end?" Before he could respond, her grin fell away and she lifted her gaze to the wall. "Now, hold on."

Quinn took three steps and leaped.

The acceleration pinned Brandt against her as they sailed over the wall. A burst of butterflies emerged in his stomach, tickling him as they plummeted toward the ground on the other side. When she landed, the force again drove him into her arms. Quinn whooped in surprise when her feet kicked out, slipping in the mud as she tried desperately to right herself, but it was too late. Her back smacked against the ground and drove a grunt from her lungs while mud splattered everywhere. The fall sent Brandt rolling off her and into the slimy muck, it covering half his body. When he sat up, he looked at her and was about to speak until she interrupted him.

"Don't say a word, Brandt. Not one word."

With his eyes closed, Brandt lay back in the copper tub, enjoying a moment of peace. While it was nice to be back at the Jolted Jackaroo Inn, he knew their stay would be brief. Yarth was far too close to the garrison for them to remain there more than one night.

The bathwater had cooled considerably but remained warmer than the air in the room. Despite attempts to do otherwise, his thoughts continually drifted back to the events leading to their latest predicament. He decided it was time to alert the Ward.

Cassie, he closed his eyes and called to her. *Cassie. Are you awake?*

He knew it was late, but he had to try.

Yes, but I'm a bit busy, she replied.

Sorry. Things have gone badly here, and I thought it best if I let you know.

What happened? Her concern carried through their bond.

Quinn and I were discovered by the Archon's son. We had to desert the Imperial Army. They are bound to come after us, so our true flight has just begun. Would you please wake Delvin and find out which direction we should head?

Delvin's gone.

Gone? Gone where?

Nobody knows. He left a week ago.

Brandt frowned, wishing it were otherwise. *In that case, please meet with the other leaders first thing in the morning. We will do our best to evade pursuit while we wait for orders.*

I will, but you should know I am considering leaving the ward.

Why?

War is coming, and it's time for the rest of us wardens to do something about it.

Please don't do anything stupid.

Why? Are you afraid I'll steal your thunder?

He laughed. *Perhaps.*

Be safe, Brandt.
I'll do my best, so long as you do the same.
I will.
I…I miss you, Cass.
I miss you as well.

Opening his eyes, he gathered resolve and climbed out of the tub, the bathwater now tinted brown from the mud that had covered him. He dug out clothing that had been in the pack – the same clothing he had worn on the day he and Quinn had first entered the garrison. Once dressed, he scooped up the pack and his boots and padded out into the hallway.

The washroom door beside his stood open, the room empty save for a tub of dirty water and a damp towel hanging from the knob. *Quinn must already be in our room.*

Exiting the hallway, he passed the taproom where Bula was wiping down the bar while her maid, Jelsie, swept the empty room. *Past closing time,* Brandt thought. *I should get some sleep.*

He hurried up the stairs and stopped at the third door on the right – the same room he had shared with Quinn during their previous stay. The rapping of his knuckles on the door earned him a reply to enter. Quinn was lying in bed, her hair damp, and her clothes on the floor. A dim glowlamp on the nightstand lit the small, familiar room.

"I'm surprised you took so long," Quinn said.

"You were right. The bath was a great idea. I only climbed out because the water was growing cold." He pulled his shirt over his head and tossed it aside. "I reached out to my sister. I thought it best if the Ward knew what has happened."

Quinn sat up and leaned on an elbow, the covers falling away to reveal her torso – or at least, the parts her shift didn't cover. "What did Delvin say?"

"Nothing. He isn't there. Cassie says he left over a week ago and nobody knows where he is."

A frown crossed her face. "While he leaves often, this is a strange time to do so."

"I thought so as well." He pulled his breeches down and sat on the bed to free his legs. Looking down at the floor with Quinn to his back, he shared something he knew was meant only for him to know. "Cassie told me she left the Ward."

"How come?"

"It sounds as if she is seeking a bit of danger herself. She wishes to help fight the Empire."

"I hope she doesn't drag Everson with her."

He shook his head. "That doesn't sound like Cassie."

"Good." Quinn put her hand on his back. Her palm felt warm and comforting. "Now that Iko knows, he will be driven to capture us. We must be away at first light."

Now wearing only his smallclothes, Brandt tossed the breeches aside. "I know." He slid under the covers and put an arm around her. "Which direction should we go?"

"I...I don't know." Quinn dropped her head to the pillow as he gazed down at her. "The army is to break camp tomorrow and begin a march west."

He considered what that meant. "It will take some time to break camp and get everyone organized. Unless the cavalry rides ahead of the infantry, it will take a couple days for the army to reach Hipoint, even at a hard march. Even then, organizing hundreds of horses and riders will take a good hour or so."

"Alone, we could ride ahead of them."

"True, but we will need a horse."

"A horse would be best," she agreed. "I'd rather not steal one, but it might be necessary in this instance."

Brandt grinned. "You wish to break the law?"

She smiled in return. "Clearly, you are a bad influence, you scoundrel."

He reached over to the table, lifted the cloth lying there, and covered the lamp, plunging the room to darkness.

"I'll show you a scoundrel," he said.

His lips found hers – warm and soft and inviting as was the rest of her. Brandt suddenly felt quite warm and thoughts of sleep fell away.

23

A BOLD MOVE

E verson hummed to himself as he connected an actuator to the linkage. Beside him, Ivy worked quietly. She never complained when he hummed. It was another thing about her he adored. He noticed Ivy's long dark hair partially obscuring her face as she focused on her own assembly. Happiness bubbled up inside him.

Ivy finished and her eyes met Everson's. "Why are you staring at me?"

"I was just thinking of how lucky I am to spend time with such an intelligent, pretty, and thoughtful girl."

Ivy's cheeks flushed and she smiled shyly, her eyes looking away in embarrassment. "Everson...that is very sweet of you."

He smiled, his heart racing when her gaze again met his.

"You are certainly getting better," Ivy said.

"I am trying."

He was truly trying. Ivy had requested that he try to focus more on the feelings of the people around him rather than physics and calculations and his next great discovery. It wasn't that Everson was insensitive – far from it. He just tended to miss social cues while focusing on other, more pragmatic issues.

Everson noticed Ivy looking beyond him. He turned and saw Cassie approaching. The expression on her face alarmed him.

"What happened?"

Cassie looked around, making sure they were alone.

"I just spoke with my brother." Cassie said in a hushed voice. "He and Quinn were discovered and had to flee the Imperial Army last night."

Everson gasped. "Are they all right?"

"Yes. They are both safe…for now." She frowned. "They stole a horse this morning and are heading west, ahead of the army."

"What do you mean ahead of the army?" Ivy asked.

"The enemy is breaking camp and leaving the garrison to march west. War is coming, sooner than expected."

The words sank in, and Everson turned to Ivy with a silent question in his eyes. She replied with a nod.

Cassie's brow furrowed. "What is it? Are you two up to something?"

"Are we that obvious?" Everson asked, worried.

"To me, yes," Cassie said. "However, my brother and I were raised by some of the best tutors in the world. They taught us to study others and guess at their intentions – to watch for words unsaid. I sometimes notice things others miss." Cassie put her hands on the bench and leaned closer. "Now, out with it."

Ivy glanced at him before replying, "Everson and I plan to leave the Ward."

"What? Why?"

Everson realized that telling Cassie would be necessary. He needed her help. "We built Colossus for a reason. If the Empire is marching toward us, we intend to stop them."

"Alone?"

"Well, not alone. Kingdom forces are sure to meet the Imperial Army. Jonah, Chuli, Thiron, and Torney are out there somewhere as well. We intend to find them and lend a hand." Everson put his hand on Cassie's. "We could use your help."

"What?" There was a heat in Ivy's voice. "Don't guilt her into coming with us. She doesn't have to risk her life just because we are willing to do so."

He turned toward her. "I'm not asking her to join us. However, we need supplies, and we lack the skill to get them. With my legs, I can't exactly sneak anywhere. And, you – I adore you, Ivy, but you aren't exactly athletic or fluid."

"The Stealth rune?" Cassie asked and he nodded in reply. The thought struck a chord and gave her something she had been missing. "It would be fun to test it." She smiled. "I'm in. However, that's not the end of it."

"What do you mean?" Everson asked.

"I'll get you your supplies, and then we leave."

"You wish to come with us?"

"Yes."

Ivy shook her head. "The leaders won't like that much."

"That's why sneaking out is the only way." Cassie grabbed a stool and sat beside the bench. "Now, what's the plan?"

"Amazing," Everson said in awe. "I can't see you."

He stared toward where Cassie had been a moment earlier, but she was invisible despite the glowlamp he held in his hand. A flicker of movement danced at the edge of his vision and was gone.

Cassie's voice arose from behind him. "Oddly, everything is brighter, more vivid to my eyes. My steps make no sound, not even to myself."

He spun about and looked toward where he thought she might be. "Try the door. See if your augmentation extends to objects you affect."

Another flicker in the periphery was followed by the doorknob turning, the door opening to reveal the illuminated hallway. The entire process was silent.

He shook his head in wonder. "Outstanding. Your discovery is a revelation, Cassie."

"The corridor is empty," Cassie said. "I'm heading to the kitchen. I'll meet you as planned."

"Agreed. Just don't try anything exotic," He said. "Get the supplies we need and get out."

"Of course. I am not my brother. I actually try to avoid danger when possible."

Silence followed and Everson assumed she was gone. He gave his apartment one last long look, recalling various moments of his stay since becoming a warden.

Similar to his time at FAME, he and Jonah had shared the apartment since the beginning. However, many weeks had passed since Jonah departed on a dangerous mission. Everson wondered how his roommate and the other wardens fared. He missed Jonah and his wry sense of humor. Somehow, their time together had helped Everson grow into a more confident person. The combination of Jonah and Ivy brought out the best in him.

With a sigh, Everson picked up his and Cassie's packs and stepped into the hallway. After locking the door, he headed toward the stairwell as quietly as possible, which was still quite noisy – a negative aspect of his mechanical legs. *I wonder if I can infuse them with a Stealth augmentation.* The concept took hold and stirred excitement. Focused on the thought, he was downstairs and in the Forge before he remembered needing to be cautious.

Glowstone pillars lit the room, as always, in addition to the amber hue of glowing coals in nearby forges. However, all was quiet and nobody was in sight. Everson crossed the room and headed toward the barn doors at the back. He stepped through the utility door beside the larger ones, into the room called the Dock.

Metal scraps and rods stood along the walls to each side, along with bins of coal. The far wall had an oversized door similar to the one leading from the Dock to the Forge. The center of the room held Colossus, his latest creation. *Our latest creation*, he corrected himself as Ivy stepped from the machine.

"It's about time," she said as she held the door for him. "My pack is already in here. I checked, and the water tank we added is still full."

"Good." He walked to the machine and slid the two packs through the door. "I feared it might leak."

"Did you doubt my skills?"

"No," he said hurriedly. "It's just that things leak all the time."

She shrugged. "What took you so long, anyway?"

"I went over the list of items with Cassie to make sure she gets everything we need. Once I was confident she had it memorized, I watched her perform the augmentation."

"And?"'

Everson grinned and shook his head. "It's wonderful. I have some ideas on things I would like to test, but I'm confident this discovery is even more important than the Speed rune."

A voice arose behind him. "I believe so as well."

He jumped with a start and turned toward the voice, but saw nothing. "Did you get the items?"

"Of course."

A grin crossed his face. "I can't even see what you are carrying. I was hoping the augmentation would extend in that manner."

A flash at the edge of his vision preceded her voice coming from inside the machine. "Open the exterior doors, and let's get out of here."

"Right." Everson turned toward Ivy. "You open the doors while I get it started. After I pull through, close them and we'll be off."

He climbed into the machine and up into the pilot position. Looking through the front window, he waited while Ivy unlocked the doors and pushed one open to reveal the starlit, snow-covered yard behind the Ward, the walls surrounding it too distant to see in the darkness. When she pushed the other door open, he gripped the two drive levers and pushed them forward one notch. The machine lurched into motion and rolled outside. Once clear of the doors, he stopped Colossus and waited while Ivy closed the doors. Moments later, she climbed back into the machine.

"Let's go."

"What about the guards outside the gate?" Cassie asked.

"That's where you come in," Everson replied.

"What do you mean?"

He pushed the levers into drive. "When we draw close, you will slip out, distract the guards, and we will drive out. Once we are out, this thing is too fast for them to catch, not without a horse. By then, we will be long gone."

To remain as quiet as possible, Everson advanced Colossus slowly – the only noise the crunch of frozen gravel beneath the wheels. As they rolled toward the gate, his pulse began to race in anticipation. For months, he had prepared for this venture. It was finally happening. He would test his magic-powered invention against an army backed by fire-powered weapons. *I wonder what they will do when they see their own weapons used against them.* He only prayed they would arrive in time.

24

AWE STRIKING

"I am sorry, Hinn," Quinn said as Brandt tied the boy's hands behind his back. "If it weren't a life or death situation, we wouldn't be doing this."

Brandt finished and patted Hinn on the shoulder. "Don't let Mason give you a hard time about this, either. You've seen how dangerous Quinn is with a wooden sword in her hand. Just imagine how she handles the real thing."

The boy moaned and said something unintelligible, a result that was expected. After all, that was the purpose of the gag in his mouth. With Hinn bound, Quinn sheathed her blade and considered how he would be treated once discovered.

"Tell the owner you defended his horse the best you could, but we knocked you out. The cut on your forehead should be enough to sell the story." Quinn reached out and touched the boy atop the head. "I'm sorry about that as well."

She turned to find Brandt climbing on the horse, a chestnut mare with a black mane. He extended his hand, so she gripped it, put her foot in the stirrup, and climbed into the saddle behind him.

"Be well, Hinn. Today, we are off to save lives. Perhaps thousands." She wrapped her arms about Brandt. "Perhaps that knowledge will offer this horse's owner a bit of solace. Then again, I am sure he will be quite upset. Horses like this are expensive."

With a kick, Brandt urged the horse into motion. The rising sun was pushing the darkness aside, the sky above turning pale blue. At an easy trot, Brandt guided the horse down the streets of Yarth, toward the north gate. Here and there, shopkeepers appeared, opening doors, lifting blinds, and sweeping front steps.

When the riders emerged into the square near the gate, the bell tolled, marking the start of a new day. Brandt pulled the horse to a stop, and Quinn gazed up at the tower they had climbed weeks earlier. Typical of most moments Quinn had spent with Brandt, she recalled the event fondly. Even the memory of their muddy escape the night prior offered a shade of sentimentality Quinn's life had lacked before meeting Brandt – especially their evening alone in their room at the inn. The memory made Quinn blush and brought a smile to her face.

She squeezed him and whispered in his ear. "The gate is open. Let's be off, my Prince."

"As you wish, Milady." Although she couldn't see his smile, she heard it in his tone.

The horse resumed at a trot, and they rode past guards who were busy watching the farmers and travelers entering the city.

—+ φ +—

Quinn climbed off the horse and stretched. It had been a long but uneventful day. The miles had passed far more quickly than walking, but not as fast as she wished. Brandt handed her the reins and crept forward.

Again, Quinn thought about the friends she had made in the Harriers. She had grown fond of many of the girls. They might be in the Imperial Army, but they hardly seemed enemies. In fact, most didn't even know why they were fighting.

She waited while Brandt squatted near the edge of the wood and stared through a gap in the trees. A full minute passed before he turned and rejoined her.

"I don't see any activity."

"What do you think it is?"

"It appears to be some sort of barrier, but it now looks abandoned."

"Why would they do such a thing?"

His brow furrowed in thought as he examined the distant barrier. "This was the edge of Empire lands before they captured Hipoint. Perhaps the barricade no longer has a use since they have established a new front further west."

"That makes sense to me."

"Still, I think it best for us to proceed with caution. With the bluff on the inland side and a distant drop to the sea on the other, the location acts as a chokepoint – a narrow piece of land we must cross if we wish to continue west. If we roll through and hit an ambush, it will be difficult to escape."

"I am with you so far. What do you suggest?"

"We leave the horse here and sneak in on foot. If there are guards inside the building, we take them out and then advance."

She considered the idea and had nothing better to offer. "Fine. Let's go."

He tied their mount to a tree, leaving the tether loose so the horse could continue to nibble on the long grass that covered much of the forest floor. They then scurried out of the woods and crossed the open ground between the trees and the cliff wall.

Once the cliff and rocks were between them and the barrier, they crept around the bend. The barrier reappeared but much closer – no more than three hundred feet away. The wall was easily twice the height of a man with a scaffold along the visible side. A small building stood to the north side of the road. The area seemed abandoned.

Brandt signaled for her to follow and the two of them hurried toward the building, crouching the entire time. They crept along it, and he peeked around the corner.

"Draw your sword," he whispered. "Quietly."

With a nod, she did as he requested, pulling the short sword from the scabbard ever so slowly.

He then extended his open hand and whispered, "Give it to me."

"What? Why?"

With an eye roll, "Why are you always so difficult? I need it to knock out whoever answers the door."

"Why can't I knock them out?"

"Because. You are the pretty one. You knock, the guard will open the door, and I'll whack him."

"What if the guard is a girl?"

His lips drew a thin line as he glared at her and grabbed the sword from her hand. "Then, I'll kiss her to distract her, and you can hit her over the head."

She smiled, in spite of the situation. "Oh, now I really hope it *is* a girl."

With an eye roll, he slipped around the corner and hid behind the door. As she drew close, he knocked.

Silence.

Impatient, Quinn knocked, louder. After a moment, a rustling came from inside.

The door opened. "Why can't I just get a moment of peace?" The man in the doorway had long, dark hair that was a complete mess. Standing a head taller than Quinn, he was in his late twenties and was overweight. He stared at Quinn with his lids at half-mast. "What? Who are you?"

Quinn imagined Jeshica when she was first pulled from the Sol Polis dungeon. With that image in her mind, she did her best to appear a whimpering, pleading, wretch. "I'm alone and am traveling from Sol Polis to visit my uncle in Hipoint. My horse lost a shoe and came up lame. He's tied up just over there," She held one hand to her chest, the other pointed toward the woods, "I don't know what to do. I would be most thankful if you could help me."

The man smoothed his hair and puffed out his chest as his eyes traveled the length of Quinn's body. She knew how tight her breeches and jerkin fit and suspected he had not seen a woman in some time. While he gathered his thoughts, she peered past him into a small unoccupied room.

The guard smiled, "Well, just how appreciative might you be if I were to help you?"

She pressed her hand against his chest and ran it down his torso. "Very, very appreciative."

His grin widened and he stepped out, closing the door behind him. Brandt lunged, the hilt of Quinn's sword striking the man in the back of the head. Hard. Like a felled tree, he tipped to land face first in the gravel and did not move.

Quinn shook her head. "You knocking people out has become a disturbing habit of late."

He glared down at the man with a frown. "I didn't care for the way he spoke to you."

She smiled. "Are you jealous?"

"No. Not jealous…maybe protective is a better word."

"I can take care of myself."

He snorted. "Nobody knows that better than me. Now, did you see anyone else inside?"

She shook her head. "No. It appeared empty."

"Good." He opened the door and stepped in with the sword ready.

As Quinn had seen, nobody else was inside. She counted eight bunks, one missing a pillow, which was on the floor beside it. A round table sat in the middle of the room and a closed wardrobe was at one end of the building while a wooden chest waited beside the door.

Brandt crossed the room, his eyes searching. He opened the wardrobe and poked through the contents.

"What are you doing?" Quinn asked.

"I'm checking to see if there is anything we can use."

Deciding it was a good idea, she bent and opened the chest. She gasped and stepped back.

"What is it?" He asked.

"Flashbombs."

"Wow," he said as he stopped beside her. "That would make a very big explosion."

Scenes of Castile Corvichi blowing up in a ball of flame flashed before Quinn's eyes. She hated to admit it, but flashbombs scared her – made her feel powerless. *How can I fight something like that? How can anyone?*

Brandt turned and pulled a sheet from one of the bunks.

"What are you doing now?"

"I am going to tie the guard up before he wakes." He walked out before she could respond.

Quinn's considered the flashbombs as she thought of her friends in the Harriers. Flashbombs would kill anyone nearby, leaving the Harriers as much at risk as Kingdom soldiers.

The thought made her want to destroy the bombs, but doing so here might cause more damage than intended. She gasped as an idea came into her head. When combined with magic, the idea had the potential to do something awestriking, but very, very dangerous.

The barricade was located where the tall bluff to the north and the cliff edge to the sea were no more than two hundred feet apart. The road split that gap while the barricade ran from bluff wall to cliff edge.

Brandt, Quinn, and their horse had moved beyond the barricade to a location five hundred feet to the west. She stood in the road and stared at the chest of bombs sitting beside the barricade, imagining what might happen. She began reconsidering her plan.

"Wait," She put her hand on Brandt's wrist. "Perhaps this isn't a good idea. Perhaps we are too close."

He looked back at the barricade while lifting the flashbomb resting in his palm. "I can only throw so far, Quinn. Even from here, I will need to get much closer before I throw the bomb and run for my life."

"That's what I mean," she said. He turned toward her and she stared into his eyes. "I…don't want to lose you."

He smiled. "You won't get rid of me that easily."

"How long until your magic recharges?"

He shrugged. "Soon, I think. Regardless, I must try before the other augmentation expires."

"What about the weakness that follows? Remember what happened last time?"

He put his free hand on her upper arm, his tone shifting toward compassion. "I know what happened. Yes, it's a risk. However, I have you to watch out for me. As long as we can get someplace safe while I recover, all will be fine."

She glanced westward. "Are you sure there's a safe place between here and Hipoint?"

"I am sure we will figure it out. Besides, you said it yourself. The risk is worth the reward."

"You could try using the horse," she suggested. "That's what any sane person would do."

Brandt shook his head. "Horses are fast, but not fast enough to clear the area in time. That's why you will ride from here, and I will catch up." He stared into her eyes. "Why all the concern now? This was your idea, remember?"

"True, but I was allowing my feelings for my friends in the Imperial Army to cloud my judgement."

"I have friends in that army as well. This is for all of them – your friends, my friends, and anyone else who became caught up in the Empire's plans." His jaw set firmly as he turned east and stared at the barricade. "We *have* to do this, Quinn. Besides, imagine if this plan is successful. It will outdo *any* mission ICON might have assigned to us."

She reached out, taking his hand while staring at the rune drawn on it – a rune he had used only once before. When her gaze lifted, he was staring at her, waiting for a response.

"You are right," Quinn said. "We must do this."

He gave her hand a squeeze before letting it drop.

"Hey!" A shout came from behind them. "What are you two doing?"

Quinn spun about to find seven Imperial soldiers rounding the bend to the west, all dressed in mail and white tabards. Anxiety twisted her innards and sent her pulse racing. She looked at Brandt, unsure of what to do.

"Oh, no," he said under his breath before speaking louder. "Never mind us," he yelled loud enough to be heard over the distance. "We are just two lovers out for a ride." He turned toward Quinn, hugged her, and whispered in her ear. "When I release you, run. Don't stop until you are well clear of the barricade."

"What about the horse?" Her eyes flicked from the horse to the approaching men. Two had a bows ready, arrows nocked and in range.

"We have no choice but to leave the horse behind. If we try to mount it, we'll be easy targets." He squeezed her tightly, a squeeze she returned. When he let go, she turned and ran.

The barricade somehow seemed farther away, the distance closing agonizingly slow. In the periphery, she saw Brandt running a step behind and two strides to her side. Shouts came from behind her, but she did not turn around. An arrow struck the ground between them, but neither slowed. Eventually, the wall drew closer, as did the chest of bombs beside it. Quinn glanced down at the rune drawn in the road beside the chest and wondered just how effective it might be. *Should we run more softly? How far does it extend?* Questions ran through her mind as she passed through the barricade, crossed another hundred feet, and turned to look backward.

Brandt stood in the road, steps away from the chest. His eyes were closed with one hand held before him, a bomb gripped in the other. Beyond him, the attacking soldiers were approaching in a rush. Quinn froze, fearful for Brandt. The men drew closer and closer while she prayed to Issal that Brandt would succeed.

As Quinn ran through the open barricade gate, Brandt slowed to a stop and looked back toward his pursuers. Of course, the soldiers were chasing them. He knew they would. It didn't matter. One way or another, he would succeed. The only question was if he would live or die. With that thought in mind, he closed his eyes and sought Chaos.

It was there, surrounding him as it always had. He reached for it, but the energy slipped away. When he tried to draw it in, he found resistance, as if he were attempting to roll a boulder uphill. Still, he tried, but it continued to pull away from him. *It's too soon*, he thought. *Only twenty minutes have passed since I applied the Brittle augmentation to the road.*

He opened his eyes and found the soldiers only a couple hundred feet away. With urgency, he squeezed them shut and –using every bit of will he could muster – grappled with Chaos. The magic fought against him as he tried to draw it in until, all at once, the resistance fell away.

A storm of energy filled him. Brandt's eyes flashed open and he pushed the Chaos into the Speed rune on his hand, knowing he had little time. The rune glowed red and began to pulse. He turned to find the lead soldier with his sword drawn, mere strides away.

From somewhere behind, Brandt heard Quinn scream his name. The man wound back and swung, the blade coming around, certain to cleave Brandt in two.

It struck.

Not the blade, but the augmentation.

Brandt lurched, his body convulsing, his muscles twitching as the magic took over. All sound ceased: Quinn's scream, the charging soldier's roar, the rush of waves far below – everything fell quiet as if he had gone deaf.

Opening his eyes, Brandt discovered the attacking soldier's blade no more than a foot away, seemingly frozen as it moved toward him at an unperceivable pace. Stepping to the side, beyond the arc of the blade, Brandt held the bomb out over the chest.

"Farewell, good soldier," he said to his attacker, the man's face locked in a nasty snarl, his eyes thirsting for blood. "Sorry about this, but you are simply in the wrong place at the wrong time."

He released his grip and the bomb held in the air. Gravity would take hold of the canister and draw it toward the bombs below. By that time, Brandt would be far away. With the thought in mind, he turned and ran.

Quinn stood a hundred feet beyond the barricade, a distance he covered as quick as thought. He stopped beside her and turned toward the barricade, beyond which the Imperial soldiers remained locked mid-step in their mad rush, the man in front still frozen in mid-swing. He noticed Quinn staring toward the barricade – her eyes wide, her mouth gaping as she screamed in horror.

"I knew you cared for me," he said, knowing she couldn't hear him. After all, the words came out in the fraction of a second. "Don't worry, I'm fine. However, I told you to continue running. This is far too close for what's about to happen."

Gently, he scooped her over his shoulder, and darted away. A breath later and he had covered the quarter mile to the forest edge. Another breath and he was a half mile from the barricade – far enough to be safe, regardless of what happened.

He set Quinn down, turned around, and prepared himself for the exhaustion he knew would come. Time passed, slowly for him, racing for everyone else. Green light flashed behind the barricade as the world lurched.

Noise rushed in, and a bloom of green flame erupted from the barricade, joined by the rapid thump of numerous explosions.

Another lurch and silence filled Brandt's ears. In the distance, the blast was frozen in time with parts of the barricade floating in the air amid flames hundreds of feet high.

The world lurched again, all sound returning as the destruction morphed into something beyond imagining.

An enormous *crack* shook the ground, carrying a shockwave that passed beneath Brandt's feet. The road, from the towering bluff to the cliff edge, crumbled and began pouring into the sea. Rocks, both massive and small, fell hundreds of feet to splash into the rough waters. The landslide brought the burning remains of the barricade and guardhouse down with it. Dust and smoke billowed into the air, the fires snuffed out by rock and water.

When things finally settled, a massive gap remained – a quarter mile across, steep, and impassable.

As expected, Brandt felt exhausted, as if he had run many miles and had not slept for days. He leaned forward with his hands on his knees, partly to remain standing, partly to catch his breath. An arm wrapped about him.

"Are you all right?"

He nodded. "I'll be fine." He wavered and fell to his knees, his head slumping. "I just need rest. Lots of it."

A sound emerged as things quieted – a rumbling from behind him. He frowned and realized it was drawing closer. With an immense effort, he turned toward riders approaching at a gallop.

"Oh, no," Quinn said, bending and tugging on his arm. "We must leave."

Something part laugh, part sigh, and part guffaw came from Brandt's lips. "They are too close, Quinn. I can barely stand, and they are on horseback."

She turned toward the horses as they slowed and the lead rider commanded, "Stay where you are or you die!"

Brandt shook his head, knowing this was the end. He could barely move, so flight was out of the question. Without the use of his magic and him incapacitated, there was little hope of fighting them. In the distance, another force emerged – hundreds of Imperial cavalry who would reach their location in mere minutes.

He croaked, "We must surrender."

Quinn glared down at him, her eyes gray like steel. "Never."

With an effort, he put his arm about her waist and used her to keep himself from falling over. "Please, Quinn. If we surrender, we might live to fight another day. Don't die for nothing." He gazed up at her, pleading. "Please, I don't want to lose you."

The riders stopped and half dismounted. Four of those still on horseback held arrows nocked, ready, and aimed at Brandt and Quinn. The approaching men drew swords, all save for their leader.

"Why did you betray me, Quinn?" Iko asked.

"You fight for the wrong side, Iko." If Quinn's gaze was steely before, it was molten hot iron now. "I am trying to save lives. The Empire is trying to destroy them."

Iko set his jaw and glared back at her, not flinching or backing down. After a moment, his gaze shifted further west, toward the destroyed road.

"What have you done?"

"I told you. I am trying to save lives. If the army marching from Yarth cannot reach the battle, they cannot die."

Iko's frown deepened. "Please. You don't care about the lives of Imperial soldiers. You only care about your precious kingdoms and the use of Chaos."

Quinn shook her head. "I am saddened you believe that, Iko. I thought you knew me better than that. Regardless of where they live, all people have hopes and dreams and wish to live long, fruitful lives. Why would I want anyone dead just because of the armor they wear or because of their beliefs? There is room enough in Issalia for us all to live as we like so long as we don't prey on others."

She stepped forward, and Brandt fell onto his hands.

Quinn poked Iko in the chest. Hard. "Regardless of what you believe, the kingdoms of Issalia experienced years of peace and prosperity before the Empire came along. You and your Empire are like bullies who did not get their way, using flash powder to threaten, burn, and destroy until others think and live the way you believe is best. Who made your mother God, Iko? Why does she get to dictate how we are to live?"

Iko stared at Quinn the entire time, his face a scowl, his jaw trembling. Finally, he turned away.

"Bind their wrists. Gag them so I don't have to hear any more of this nonsense."

The men approached with rope and strips of cloth, a few still pointing swords at Quinn and Brandt. Iko climbed on his horse and stared at Quinn, his anger gone, replaced by quiet contemplation.

She did it, Brandt thought as two men hauled him to his feet and began tying his wrists behind his back. *She planted a seed a doubt in his mind. If only we knew how to make it grow.*

25

JOURNEY

Gorgant slowed to a stop and snorted, the horse sending a puff of swirling steam into the chill air. The village of Sarville waited just ahead.

Curan's memories of his first visit to the small mountain village a season ago remained fresh. Though he longed for a warm room and a soft bed, he decided to ride through town and camp somewhere beyond it.

A nudge sent Gorgant into a trot along the snow-covered road. A snowstorm had passed through earlier in the day, slowing his progress with a blanket of fresh powder covering everything, the snow depth ranging from a few inches to over three feet deep where the drifts gathered.

Smoke rose from the chimneys in Sarville, spilling out and drifting to the east. As he passed through town, Curan came across only three people, none of whom paid him any attention. Soon, he passed the last inn, and the road continued north amidst snow-covered pines. As he rode, Curan cast his mind back on the past few days.

The first part of his journey from Kantar had been uneventful, and he was thankful for it. His trek began with a long, arduous day through the Brimstone Mountains. He had pushed Gorgant hard to make it to Fenrick's Crossing to take advantage of the pleasant weather, fearing what the lingering winter might bring. The village also offered the benefit of shelter for him and the horse for a night.

Rising early the following day, he pushed Gorgant until they made it across the Malloram desert. Although the desert could be dangerously hot in the summer, winter was milder, with moderate days and cold nights.

The ground rose as he entered the Skyspike Mountains. That's when the storm struck, forcing him and Gorgant to hide in a narrow cleft in the mountain pass. He waited all night and well into the next day, while snow fell and the wind whistled through the pass. It was midday before the blizzard finally passed, the snowfall stopped, and the wind settled to normal levels. The resulting drifts and poor footing forced him to travel at a slow walk, sometimes while riding Gorgant and other times leading the horse on foot. It wasn't until he reached the valley floor that he felt comfortable to ride at a trot.

Gorgant rounded a bend, and the horse slowed as he came across a particularly deep drift. An odd sound came from ahead, causing Curan to frown. Curan stopped the horse and sought the source of the noise.

Something moved beyond the snowy pines. Something big. It drew closer, rounding the bend in the road and rolling into sight.

It was an imposing machine, vaguely resembling a steam carriage. However, no steam rose from it, and the machine was much bulkier than a carriage. A metal wedge at the front of the vehicle cut a path through the snow, pushing it aside and creating a bank on each side of the road. The machine had three sets of wheels and something mounted on the back.

Curan urged Gorgant to the side of the road, not wishing to get run over by the approaching behemoth. As it drew even with him, the machine came to a stop. The door opened and someone in a wool cloak stuck a head out.

"Curan? What are you doing out here?"

He recognized the girl's voice just before she lowered her hood. "Greetings, Cassie. I am returning to the Ward."

"You are supposed to be in Kantar, protecting my mother."

"Yes." He nodded. "I was, but she sent me away."

"She is well, then?"

"Yes. Of course." He frowned at the machine. "What is this thing?"

Everson peeked from behind Cassie. "This is a weapon, Curan."

Curan then noticed the multi-armed catapult on the back of the vehicle. He had heard of Everson's brilliance during his brief stay at the Ward. The machine was surely one of his creations.

"Where are you going?" Curan asked.

Cassie glanced at Everson, who nodded. She then turned to Curan. "War is coming, and we head south to join the fight."

The news was not surprising. Even before becoming a warden, Curan had known war was likely. His gaze shifted north as he considered his plan to return to the Ward. Other than continuing his training, he could accomplish nothing from within the building. His decision was easy.

Curan looked back at them. "I am coming with you."

"We will be happy to have you with us," Cassie said.

Curan rode at a trot, following the trail left by Colossus. Only two or three inches of snow remained after the big machine plowed through the deep drifts, making the journey far easier than it had been earlier. The cloudy sky darkened further, and it soon became difficult to see anything beyond a hundred feet away. Colossus turned from the road and entered a small snow-covered grove before stopping. Gorgant settled beside the machine as Cassie climbed out. Everson and Ivy followed, the three of them tromping through the deep snow as they circled the machine.

"Where are you going?" Curan asked.

Everson stopped and turned toward him. "It's cold, even inside this thing. We plan to build a fire and warm up a bit."

Curan frowned in confusion. Rather than ask additional questions, he climbed off the horse and followed. When he rounded Colossus, he found Cassie nearing a boulder thirty feet away from the machine. She traced a symbol on the rock and returned to join Everson and Ivy, who stood huddled in their cloaks beside Colossus.

Moments later, Cassie's eyes opened, her irises flaring bright red in the purple light of dusk. The rune on the rock bloomed with light, pulsed, faded, and the rock burst into white flames. The heat hit Curan in a wave, the fire burning fifteen feet high and rapidly melting everything in the surrounding area.

"That is useful," Curan noted.

Cassie laughed.

The heat from the burning rock soon thawed the chill that had settled deep inside Curan. As the snow in the area melted, steam rose while fallen branches and trunks emerged from the blanket of white that had been covering them. By the time the fire began to die down, nightfall had darkened the forest around them. They gathered wood scraps and tossed them toward the burning rock, starting a fire that would continue well after the augmentation failed. Everson emerged from Colossus with an arm full of food and began to hand it out to everyone.

A downed tree too big to move became a bench where they sat while eating. Curan shared news of his stay in Kantar, including Filbert's failed coup. Of course, Cassie asked many questions, and he reassured Cassie of her mother's safety, particularly after weeding through the guards with the Truth rune.

Cassie, Ivy, and Everson then shared events from the Ward in addition to the information passed to them through Cassie's brother. The news painted a clear picture: War was coming, and it would hit soon.

Cassie froze. Curan turned to Everson and Ivy with a cocked brow.

"It must be Brandt," Everson said in a hushed voice. "Wait and see what she has to say."

They waited a bit, while concern reflected in Cassie's eyes. Finally, she looked at Everson and said, "My brother and your sister are in trouble."

Everson's eyes filled with alarm. "What happened?"

"They used a combination of Chaos magic and flash bombs to collapse a portion of the cliffs south of Hipoint. The result left the road impassible and trapped the bulk of the Imperial army on the other side, unable to advance."

"How is that trouble?" Everson said. "It sounds like an ingenious plan and an extreme stroke of luck."

"True," Cassie said, her tone shifting toward sadness. "However, they were captured in the process. It sounds like the Archon's son is holding them hostage. They are returning to Sol Polis to be tried and executed as traitors."

26

MADNESS

Rena was cold. Everything was cold. When snowflakes found their way inside her hood and melted on her neck, she pulled her cloak together, gripping it at the front. She and her companions slogged through the fresh snow, her mind as numb as her toes and fingers. The world was going mad. She feared the madness, felt its tentacles slithering around her, searching for a way to burrow inside. She was weary from holding the madness at bay.

With each step, her footsteps fell into the tracks left by Nalah. She had tried to follow Bilchard, but his strides were longer and required too much effort. Kirk's footsteps were worse, sometimes longer strides, sometimes shorter, often weaving, always erratic. Nalah paused and Rena ran into her. Rena shook her head in an attempt to clear the haze.

"Finally," Kirk muttered. "I was wondering if we would ever reach the Ward."

Through the haze of falling snow, the dark silhouette of the tower loomed ahead, just beyond FAME academy. A blanket of white covered the buildings and surrounding grounds, smothering them, holding them captive. To Rena, it seemed as if winter had claimed the land for all eternity.

They resumed their journey and Rena's mind slipped back into oblivion, not resurfacing until she was inside the Ward. The others stomped their boots and shook snow from their cloaks. Rena did the same. It seemed like the thing to do.

"I am looking forward to a hot meal," Bilchard said.

"You are always looking forward to a meal," Kirk retorted. "I remain shocked that we were able to talk you out of stopping in Fallbrandt."

Nalah snickered at the comment while Bilchard shrugged.

"Before we eat, we had best report." Kirk said as he began up the stairs.

The others followed with Rena trailing. Kirk knocked on the Briefing Room door and entered when bid to do so. Again, Rena was last, entering the dimly lit room where Masters Firellus, Nindlerod, and Hedgewick waited at the table.

"I'm glad you returned safely," Hedgewick said. "Where's Kwai-Lan?"

Kirk glanced at the others before replying. "Kwai-Lan is dead." Since the man's death, Kirk had assumed the role of leader without argument. None of the others wanted the job anyway.

"What happened?"

Kirk began to recite the tale, and Rena's gaze drifted downward, settling on the small puddles near the man's feet. The trip to Vallerton had been a nightmare she did not wish to relive, yet it remained fixed in her mind. The madness.

"What of the people from Vallerton?" Nindlerod asked.

"The journey was slow, but we brought the survivors to Selbin and met with Duke Harper. He promised them food and shelter until they could earn their keep and pay for a place to live. Based on what happened, he agreed that returning to Vallerton would not be an option until it was safe."

Hedgewick looked at Firellus, who had a scowl on his face. The man had always left Rena uneasy. Now, she backed away in terror. *He knows. He sees into my soul.*

"Do we have a rogue arcanist?" Hedgewick asked.

"It seems so, but with what motive? A stag seven years ago, a badger this past summer, and now, rabbits?" Firellus shook his head. "Why such odd time gaps? Why do it in the first place?"

"Regardless, the Red Towers remain unsafe until the issue is resolved."

"Yes," Kirk agreed. "Duke Harper decided the same thing. He said he would approach King Cassius about the issue and suggested blocking off the road running through the forest and scheduling armed guards to patrol the road to the north. Other than keeping everyone out of the tainted forest, there seems little he can do."

"True, but what more can *we* do?" Nindlerod said.

Firellus leaned back, his eyes narrowed as he surveyed the room. "We have no other trained wardens we can send and even if we did, it wouldn't be safe. We have no idea what we face here."

"Madness," Rena murmured.

"What was that, Rena?" Hedgewick asked.

She looked up at him, "It's as if the world has gone mad. Oversized, evil animals roaming the land. Pure madness."

Hedgewick turned to Kirk. "Is she all right?"

The man shrugged. "I don't know. She was behaving oddly before we even reached Vallerton. And then…she was there when Kwai-Lan died. In fact, we thought her dead as well."

Nalah put her hand on Rena's arm. "Rena, how are you feeling? Will you tell us now?"

Rena shrugged. "I…I don't know."

Kirk grunted. "See. You'll get nothing out of her."

"Perhaps Cassie would fare better," Bilchard suggested. "They are roommates and Rena is closer to her."

"Unfortunately, Cassie is not here," there was anger in Firellus' voice.

"What?" Rena blinked. "Where is she?"

"Gone. She, Everson, and Ivy left in the dark of night. We believe they have gone south."

"Why," Kirk asked.

"A conflict with the Empire now appears inevitable. We believe they intend to join this conflict."

"War?"

"I'm afraid so."

Rena swallowed hard and forced a question out, one she feared to have answered. "What of Torney? Have you heard anything?"

The three masters at the table exchanged sad glances. A terror stirred inside Rena, like an evening shadow creeping across her heart.

Hedgewick stood and approached her with sadness in his eyes. He opened his mouth and she shook her head. *Don't say it. Please don't say it.*

"I am sorry, Rena," Hedgewick grabbed her hands and looked down at them, his voice dropping to a whisper. "Torney is dead."

The darkness inside her reared up and blotted the light as horror, pain, and madness washed over Rena, seeping into the cracks in her mind until everything shattered.

Somewhere distant, someone shrieked. "No!"

That someone might have been Rena, but Rena was lost. Gone. Forever.

Only madness remained.

27

PREPARATIONS

The farm was similar to the others – a cluster of buildings, split rail fences, and fields recently plowed over, ready for planting come spring. Broland's horse rode along the gravel drive, toward the stable. A squad of Kantarian cavalry trailed him, riding at ease, but ever vigilant. The Empire's leaders had proven their guile and, as Broland's father warned, he should never assume anything was as it seemed. Not even here, in the woods north of Wayport.

A modest farmhouse waited in the center of the buildings. A brown barn, a grass-covered mound, and a shed encircled the house. The barn door was open, revealing an empty wagon and plow inside. A workhorse stood in the pen beside the building, gnawing on a mouthful of hay.

Broland spotted a stairwell in the mound leading down to a dark, open doorway. This wasn't the first farm he had visited with an underground cellar. After the first such sighting, he had inquired about it to the guards in his escort. A man raised on a farm explained how underground food stores were less likely to spoil, particularly in warm climates. Broland recalled the basement storage rooms in Kantar and how they remained cool even on hot days. *Makes sense,* he thought.

A boy in his early teens emerged from the cellar, his eyes going wide when he spotted the approaching riders. He bolted toward the house, tore open the door, and closed it behind him.

Broland reined in his horse and dismounted. Two soldiers climbed down to join him while the others fanned out in a half-circle facing the farmhouse. Removing his helmet, Broland shook his head to free the sweat-slicked hair from his forehead.

The sun emerged from behind a cloud to reveal it now well past its apex. By all accounts, the day was beautiful – mild weather lacking the oppressive humidity he had heard about during warmer months. This far south and near the sea, winter's touch was light with chilly nights and pleasant days. To the north, up in the mountains, he was sure things were different.

Without a word, Broland walked toward the farmhouse while two guards shadowed him. He lifted his hand, his knuckles rapping on the door with authority.

"Please come out. We mean no harm," he said in a loud voice.

He waited. Nothing new. His other visits had been met with fear and doubt. The people didn't understand what was coming. If they did, their fear would have made sense.

The door opened to reveal a middle-aged man holding a scythe. Behind him, the boy gripped a crossbow, the bolt loaded and aimed toward the door. A woman stood beside the boy, kneading her hands as if they were dough.

"Good afternoon," Broland said, bowing his head slightly. His helmet remained tucked under an arm, his other hand resting easily on the pommel of his longsword. "Please put your weapons down. I would hate for anyone to get hurt."

"Who are you, and why are you on my land?" The man asked, his eyes flicking from Broland to the guards and back. The scythe remained ready as did the boy's crossbow.

"My name is Broland Talenz, Crown Prince of Kantaria. I represent my father, King Brock." The man's eyes widened as Broland spoke, his jaw dropping. "I am sorry to disturb you, but I come with a warning and to make an offer." His tone grew more firm. "Put your weapons aside."

The man blinked, nodded, and set his scythe down, leaning it against the wall. He turned and waved at the boy in an urgent, jerking motion.

"Put it away, Yuri. Now." When the crossbow was lowered, the man turned back toward Broland. "I apologize, your Grace. Um...your Highness. My Prince. We are simple folk and unused to armed men on our land."

"Completely understandable." Broland reached inside the pouch on his hip and withdrew a folded piece of paper. He found the last name and read it aloud. "Gilbert Forness?"

The man nodded. "That's me."

Broland replaced the paper with a nod. "Wonderful." *The list is complete after this stop.* "Master Forness, I am here to ask you and your family a question."

"A question? Um. Of course. What is it?"

"Would you prefer to live or to die?"

The woman gasped and grabbed the boy, the man backing away a step as he struggled to reply.

"Before you jump to conclusions," Broland said. "I reiterate, we mean you no harm. However, an army will soon arrive. I can't say exactly when, but they will come. When they do, you will die. They come from the east with a thirst for blood and distaste for citizens loyal to the Kantarian crown." Broland gave the man a heavy look. "You are loyal to the crown, right?"

The man's eyes flicked to Broland's sword. He nodded eagerly. "Yes. Of course. We have always supported King Brock."

"Very good." Broland reached into the pouch and withdrew a small sack, tied at the top. He held it toward the man, the sack dangling between two of his fingers. Despite the small size, it had a good weight to it. "Take this."

The man reached out, and Broland dropped it into the man's palm. "There is gold and a writ inside. Show this writ when you get to Wayport, and they will let you in. You may stay at the shelters inside the citadel walls or use the gold for passage to Kantar."

"Wait. What?" the man appeared confused.

The woman rushed forward, dragging the boy with her. "You are taking our farm?"

Broland shook his head. "I am not taking your farm. I am doing what I can to spare your lives. When this army comes, your farm and every-thing within is at risk. They bring death and destruction backed by a lust for conquest. Your King, my father, wishes you to avoid such a fate."

"This farm has been in our family for generations," the man said, his voice thick with sadness. "If it is destroyed, what will we do? Where will we live?"

"We cannot protect your home, nor can we protect you unless you are within the walls of Wayport. Even there, the risk will be great." Broland reached out, his hand landing on the man's shoulder. "If you remain, you are unlikely to survive. When the threat is gone, you may return and rebuild if necessary – something you cannot do if you are dead."

The man put his arm around his wife and nodded. "Thank you for the warning. We will take heed, but we must discuss this…as a family."

"There is one more thing I must request."

"Yes?"

"Your food stores, whatever you can take when you leave, deliver them to Wayport. We may face a siege and will lack the means to bring in food once it begins. Consider the coin pouch as payment for the people you will feed." Broland held the man's gaze, ensuring he understood the gravity of what he was about to say. "Be sure to decide soon. When the army comes, we will destroy Gramble Bridge and crossing the Gramble River to the west bank will become far more difficult."

"Why would you destroy the bridge?"

"It is but one among many precautions we must take to protect the city." Broland stepped back and gave the family a nod. "May Issal watch over you. Good day."

He turned and walked back to his horse, hearing the door close behind him. Placing one foot in a stirrup, Broland climbed into the saddle and slid his helmet on.

"That was the last farm on the list. Let's return to Wayport."

They rode down the narrow drive at a trot. When they reached the road, Broland kicked his horse into a gallop. It felt good to have the wind in his face, the trees slipping past in a blur as his stallion stretched its legs. The miles passed quickly and the river appeared to the west, running parallel to the road as they approached Gramble Bridge.

The bridge was built of brick and mortar, supported by a series of arches large enough for small craft to pass beneath. Broland led his horse onto the bridge and slowed to a trot as he surveyed the view – a view that had changed much over recent days.

The river flowed south, skirting the eastern city wall and expanding as it approached the bay. Spires from the Wayport citadel jutted above the wall, overlooking the river. The area along the west bank had been cleared of trees and was now a field of trampled yellowed grass amid the remaining stumps. At the western edge of the new field, soldiers were stripping the felled trees to bare trunks and planting them into the ground, creating a twenty-foot high palisade that ran from the city wall to the woods, bounding what would become the battlefield. *Those Torinlanders know how to clear away trees*, Broland thought, as men in the brown and green of Torinland chopped down the last of the designated trees.

At an intersection, Broland turned south toward Wayport. Here and there, he found people dressed in civilian clothing, sitting near freshly cut stumps. Other stumps that had already been infused now glowed with a faint blue hue, even in the sunlight. At night, those stumps would light the battlefield and prevent any surprises in the dark.

Near the midpoint of the new field, Broland passed a rock formation bigger than a house. Locals called the massive rock pile Irongrip's Rock, named after a famous pirate who had frequented Wayport centuries earlier. That rock formation would be the only obstacle north of the city by the time the enemy arrived.

When the horses approached the north gate, Broland slowed to a stop and his escort gathered behind him.

"Ho, the gate!" he shouted. "It is Prince Broland, returning to the city."

Two guards stepped forward. "The password, your Highness?"

"Tipper," Broland replied.

Using the name as a password had been Broland's father's idea. It was part of the plan to retain control of the city, requiring it for anyone armed or dressed as a soldier.

"Welcome back, your Highness. You and your escort may enter."

Broland rode through the gates and into the city. He was greeted with an unlikely sight.

All normal activity of Kantarian citizens had been relocated to the heart of the city, leaving only a military presence along the north wall. The houses in the area had even been evacuated, some of the residents moving to the city temple while others camped in the citadel square. With the citizens removed, soldiers now lived in those houses – at least until the fighting began.

At a walk, Broland and the other riders crossed the square, passing ranks of soldiers before entering the narrow streets. They passed shops – a butcher, a baker, and citizens standing to the side, all staring nervously at the procession. It was no secret that Kantaria was at war – a war they expected to come to the city. The situation had created a high level of anxiety despite his father's promise to do everything possible to protect the people of Wayport – everything short of surrender to the Empire.

The city center was busy, filled with wagons being emptied for food stores, all paid for and controlled by the Kantarian Army. *You will not starve,* King Brock had said in his speech. *We will feed and protect you, Issal willing.* Broland doubted a siege could last long, not with the weapons involved. No. His fears were in a different direction as he imagined flash-bombs destroying the city, setting it ablaze, and leaving nothing but charred rubble in the aftermath.

Turning, he rode toward the castle overlooking the city, built on top of the hill in the southeast corner. Another wall surrounded the citadel, divided by two square lookout towers with the gate between them. He passed through the gate and crossed the tent-filled square as he rode toward the stables situated between the castle proper and the north wall. There, he dismounted and removed his helmet.

"Thank you," he said to his escort. "Get yourselves some food and rest. Morning will come soon, and I'm sure my father has another task planned for tomorrow."

Handing the reins to the stable hand, Broland headed into the castle, nodding to the guard as he entered the dark halls. He passed through corridors adorned by tapestries and paintings, some beautiful, some elaborate, some obnoxious – all worth more than the farm he had just visited. The collection gave him added insight as to what kind of ruler Chadwick had been. *I begin to understand why the people had little love toward the man or his wife.*

He climbed the stairs and emerged into the expansive hall outside the throne room. Two guards, a man and a woman, stood beside the door, both nodding to him as he approached.

"I would report to my father. Is he inside?"

"Yes, your Highness," the female guard said. "King Pretencia is with him."

"Very well," Broland pushed the door open, not waiting for approval.

The throne room was empty save for two men seated beside a table near the front. They spoke quietly to each other, the sound muffled by the distance. Light from the late afternoon sun shone through the stained glass windows, casting beams of red, green, yellow, and blue upon the rows of benches that filled half the room. Upon a dais at the fore, stood two empty thrones. Broland imagined the peacock, Chadwick, and his pretty, conceited wife, Illiri, sitting there, as they had done for years.

The former duke and duchess were now nothing but a memory, both having discovered the steep price of betrayal. While Illiri's suicide had been out of Brock's control, Chadwick's execution still surprised Broland. Carrying out the act was out of character for his father. *The crown is heaviest at times like this,* his father had said. *However, treachery requires the harshest of responses, if only to discourage others from taking the same path.* The image of Chadwick swinging from the gibbet resurfaced as it had in more than one nightmare in the nights since his execution. Broland prayed he had the strength to make the hard decisions should he become king.

Reaching the front of the room, Broland's gaze swept across the three tables his father had added, each covered with a different map, every map marked with arrows and notations.

King Brock, looked up and asked, "What news do you bring?"

"It is done, father. I visited the last six farms today, including the one at the eastern edge of the wood."

"Good. The city is already receiving some of the farmers. The food stores will soon be overflowing – a problem I am willing to accept."

"Yes. I passed wagons being unloaded when I rode through Central Square."

"How do you intend to bring down the bridge?" Pretencia asked. "We don't have any flash powder and the bridge was well built – made of brick and mortar if memory serves me."

Brock sat back. "Don't worry, Dalwin. I have a plan."

Pretencia chuckled. "You never change."

A snort preceded Brock's reply. "I wouldn't say that. When I first took the crown, I doubt I would have handled some of the less savory decisions the same way. However, time brings wisdom and alters one's perspective."

Broland, again, recalled the execution – the hard look on his father's face as he denounced Chadwick and then called for the platform to drop. He wondered if the scene haunted his father as well.

"True words, Brock." Pretencia said.

Broland cleared his throat, reclaiming their attention. "If you have nothing else for me, I could use a hot meal, warm bath, and a soft bed."

"Nothing else today, son." Brock stood and looked Broland in the eye. "Meet me in my room at first light. I have another task for you. We must continue to prepare, right up until scouts return with word of the enemy's advance. Additional steps are required to complete the defense General Budakis and I planned, all those weeks ago." Sorrow reflected in his eyes. "I wish Gunther were still here with us."

Sadness washed over Broland as he recalled discovering Budakis murdered in his bed – an act of betrayal. The fact that his friend had killed the man still caused Broland's insides to twist in discomfort. He closed his eyes, banished the painful memory, and focused on the present.

"I still don't understand why you are so sure the Empire will attack Wayport." Broland muttered. *It would almost be a shame to prepare so hard and not have the enemy attack. Almost.*

Brock turned toward the window, a window that had been recently replaced – the same window Tenzi had broken during her escape weeks earlier and then, again, by Broland's father while capturing Chadwick. In the light coming through the window, his father glowed as if he were some heroic legend of old, risen from the pages of a book.

"I know these enemies, son. I know Varius. I know Kardan. I know The Hand. They cannot suffer my survival, nor will they accept losing Wayport. The city is too important. Without it, they dare not press north and take Fallbrandt, for it leaves their south flank undefended. They also need Wayport before they attempt taking Kantar. The ports in between matter little, but Wayport is the gateway to the west and among the busiest ports in Issalia." He shook his head. "No, they cannot allow me to hold the city. They will attack."

"And you are sure they know what happened here?" Broland asked.

Brock nodded while still staring out the window. "They are aware. Of that, I am sure. Our takeover was a very public act as was the subsequent execution. The Empire undoubtedly had spies in the city to watch Chadwick – to ensure his loyalty to their cause. Word of what transpired here has likely reached Sol Polis by now." He spun about. "They will surely attack. *When* is the only question. I believe the answer is *soon*, for the more time we get, the stronger our position will become. The Empire knows this." He picked up a letter from the table. "Besides, a scout arrived with news late last night."

Broland glanced at Pretencia, who was sitting back, watching Brock. "What news?"

"Additional troops and war machines have arrived at Hipoint. The messenger estimates over four thousand infantry, dozens of catapults, and at least thirty wagons filled with supplies now occupy the area. Undoubtedly, flashbombs are among those supplies."

"No cavalry?"

"Not yet. They are likely coming up the coast. Perhaps that is why the troops linger at Hipoint."

There was a knock at the door. "Come in," Brock said loudly.

A guard opened the door and admitted a woman dressed in brown riding gear.

"Sorry to interrupt, Your Majesty," the guard said. "But she says it is urgent."

"Don't worry about it, Dillard," Brock replied

The guard nodded and pulled the door closed, leaving the woman alone. She crossed the length of the room, glancing at Broland before facing his father.

"What news do you have, Shilla?"

"It is as you suspected, my King. An army comes this way, down the coastal road from Hipoint."

"Where are they now?"

"I left them late this afternoon and rode hard. At the rate they travel, the army won't reach the river until tomorrow evening, the next day at the latest."

"Thank you, Shilla. Get yourself a hot meal and relax. I need you back out in the morning to rejoin Ronald. I want to keep eyes on the enemy to limit surprises."

"Yes, Sire," with a bow, she turned and walked toward the exit.

With her gone, Pretencia said, "So, it begins."

"Yes," Brock reclaimed his seat with a sigh. "One day. We have one day left to prepare. I pray we haven't missed anything."

28

DOUBT

Iko rode in silence, lost in thought.

The dozen cavalrymen lent by Commander Korbath were also quiet. None had spoken to him since the capture of the two spies.

The first night, the cavalry had camped at the edge of the wood just east of the destroyed road. The next morning, Korbath and the main force began searching for an alternate route west while Iko and his entourage began the long ride back to Yarth.

During the journey, Iko encountered Rorrick and his army. As Iko had expected, the man did not take the news of the destroyed road well, nor did he believe it impassible. *Of course. Why would he listen to me anyway?*

Still, Rorrick did not try to stop Iko from returning to Sol Polis with the two captives. He suspected the captain was happy to be rid of Iko and considered twelve soldiers a small price to be rid of him.

With the army continuing westward, Iko and his party rode back to the garrison for a night of rest. The garrison felt empty with just a skeleton crew remaining to hold it. Also present were two dozen wagon drivers who would deliver food and supplies to the army. After planning sessions with Sculdin, Iko had developed an appreciation of the logistic complexities involved in feeding an army of thousands.

The next morning, they were again off and away early. As they rode south, the clouds thickened, the sky threatening. By the time the white walls of Sol Polis were in sight, everything had darkened – partly from the clouds and partly from the sun setting somewhere beyond the storm.

As he approached the north gate of Sol Polis, Iko brought his party to a halt. Two halberd-bearing guards wearing Imperial armor stepped forward, crossing their weapons to block Iko's path.

One called out, "State your name and business in Sol Polis."

Iko frowned, his mood surly. "Look at my armor, the plume on my helmet – you can see I'm an officer."

"Listen," the other man said. "We don't know you, so why don't you introduce yourself."

"Fine." Iko glared at the man. "I am Lieutenant Ikonis Eldarro."

The first guard nodded. "I've heard of you. The Archon's son."

"Yes."

"What about them?" he shifted his halberd and nodded toward Iko's right, toward the horse tethered to his own.

Iko glanced toward the horse and the two people in the saddle. Rope bound them together and to the horse, their wrists tied and mouths gagged.

"These two are spies I have captured – spies whom the Archon will wish to interrogate."

"While you look the part, we cannot take your word and allow armed warriors to enter without papers."

"I thought you might say that," Iko said as he dug into his saddlebag.

A moment later, he removed a sealed note and handed it to the guard. The guard examined the seal before breaking it and reading the letter. A moment later, he handed it back to Iko.

"Let them pass," the guard said as he stepped aside.

Without another word, Iko nudged his horse to an easy walk, guiding it and the trailing horse through the gate.

The streets of Sol Polis were busy, filled with people about their every-day business. Farmers with carts filled the square, selling fresh produce. Shop owners along the streets sold food and wares. Traffic, on foot, horseback, and on wheels, passed by as citizens went about their business. The narrow street opened as they approached the heart of the city where the citadel waited.

Iko nodded to Sergeant Marissa, the ruddy-faced woman in charge of the rear gate. With a wave of her hand, the gate opened. His gaze shifted to the towers near the stables as the patter of rain drops began to strike his helmet.

Two towers remained intact, tall and white and majestic. The third tower was broken half way up, its shell blackened by a fire. *Why do I feel more like the broken tower? Much is wrong in my life, yet I can't see what is right.*

After passing his steed to the stable boy, Iko and two others unstrapped Quinn and her companion from their horse and pulled them down. The remaining riders were dismissed while the trio led the prisoners toward the door to the main building. Iko nodded to Berd, who guarded the door. Berd did not notice since his gaze was focused on Quinn.

"What did she do, Iko?" the big man asked.

Iko looked at Quinn and frowned in thought.

Some of Quinn's hair had come loose from its tail, frizzy as if she had just woken. Her wrists were bound together behind her back, and the gag tied around her head kept her from talking. However, the fire had not left her eyes. The glare she gave him was filled with loathing. Ebran – if that truly was his name – stood beside her, also bound and gagged but lacking her spirit.

"She lied, Berd. To you, to me, to my mother. Everything was a lie."

Berd raised one brow. "A spy?"

Iko nodded as the rain shifted from sprinkles to something more. "It appears so."

To escape the rain, Berd backed up to the door and hid under the eave as Iko grabbed Quinn's arm and pulled her through the door. The other two soldiers pushed Quinn's accomplice along, the five of them following a corridor to the receiving hall.

The hall was empty and quiet as if it were the middle of the night rather than late afternoon. The only people in the hall were the two guards standing beside the closed Council Room doors. Recognizing the guards, Iko removed his helmet and slid it beneath his arm.

"Tarshall, Ydith," he said, nodding to each. "Is my mother in with the Council?"

"Aren't you supposed to be off fighting a war?" Tarshall asked.

"Yes, but things have changed." Iko glowered at Quinn. "I have something important to present to my mother and Kardan."

"What did she do?" Ydith smirked as she stared at Quinn.

Iko growled. "Is my mother in there or not?"

The door opened and a servant stepped out with an empty tray. Iko did not recognize the man, but he expected there were many servants he would not recognize. In his late twenties, the man was clean shaven with dark hair and of average height.

The servant bowed to Tarshall. "Dinner has been served, but the Archon requested more wine."

Iko frowned. *Wine? My mother barely drinks the stuff. Why would she ask for more?*

"Why are you telling me?" Tarshall waved him along. "Go on and get more wine."

"Yes, Sir." The servant bowed again his gaze flashing from Iko to the prisoners. His eyes grew wide. "Oh, my. What happened to them?"

Iko rolled his eyes, his frustration flaring to anger. "Why does everyone keep asking? They are my prisoners and are part of official state business! You are a servant, for Issal's sake! Why would I tell you anything?"

Ydith snickered, which earned her a stern glare from Iko.

The servant bowed again. "Yes. Well, then." His eyes flicked about nervously as if he sought escape. "I had best be off for the wine."

As the man slipped away, Iko turned toward the guards. "These prisoners are important. My mother, General Kardan, and the Council will wish to hear what I have to say. I'm going in."

Tarshall shrugged at Ydith. "Go on. If they get upset, I'll claim you left us no choice."

Iko pushed past them and put his hand on the knob. "That's fine because it's true."

He opened it, stepped into the room, and froze.

His breath caught in his throat mid-gasp. The scene before him was from a nightmare.

29

SUBTLETIES

A light, airy tune filled the small room – the type of song that rang of contentment. Delvin Garber finished combing his hair back and then rubbed his chin while staring at his warped reflection.

"I do miss my goatee," he said to no one but himself. "Without it, I appear too young. The others already seldom take me seriously." He grinned. "Of course, I am rarely serious and that might have something to do with it."

He straightened his dark blue coat and adjusted the collar. Satisfied by his appearance, he scooped up the vial of black liquid from his nightstand, slipped it into the band hidden in his sleeve, and left his small room in the servant's quarters.

A curvy blonde was storming down the hall while looking over her shoulder. He put his hands up, catching her upper arms to stop her from running into him.

"Excuse me, Jeshica." Delvin smiled his best smile as she looked at him with a start. "What's the rush?"

She frowned up at him. "It's the Archon, Helman. She assigned me a list of tasks to complete before she returns to her chamber, some of them quite time consuming. I have much yet to do and am on my way to get new sheets for her bed. I just hope Mavis has them ready, but I know she is quite understaffed right now."

"Since Varius is locked away with Kardan and the Council, I'm sure she will be occupied for hours yet. In fact, Sheen has requested I help serve them dinner."

Her brow furrowed. "Are the others still sick?"

"Yes," he nodded. "This sickness has now stricken much of the citadel staff, guards and servants. Many have been healed multiple times, yet they continue to grow ill again and again." *That's what happens when you drink from cups cast in pewter and arsenic.* "The Ecclesiasts fear it is a disease they cannot control."

Worry filled her eyes. "I pray to Issal I don't become sick as well."

"Well, the afflicted were sequestered this morning and are being held in the towers, away from those who are not ill. We can hope that keeps us free from this plague."

The fear became more obvious as she bit her lip. "You don't believe it's actually the plague, do you?"

Delvin shrugged. "I am neither a healer nor a medicus, so I'll not speculate." *Don't worry, honey. Your cup was not among those I switched out.* "Regardless, it is best to remain cautious."

Jeshica nodded. "Yes. Of course." Her eyes found the floor. "Now, if you will excuse me, I have much to do."

He stepped aside and held his arm out. "Please continue. Just try not to run anyone over."

Jeshica continued past him, and Delvin eyed her swaying backside until she faded into the laundry room.

He shook his head. *Too bad I don't have time for another conquest. Quinn was right, the girl has changed for the better, her personality no longer spoiling her appearance.*

With a sigh, he continued down the corridor and climbed the stairs, not stopping until he was on the second level. He stepped into the kitchen and found Master Sheen doling out instructions. A male and a female servant were nodding to Sheen while cooks, the two who had not become ill, were busily filling bowls with steaming soup and arranging them on wooden trays.

Sheen turned toward Delvin as he entered, the man huffing aloud. "There you are!"

Delvin nodded, "Yes. I believe you are correct, Sir."

The man's mouth turned to a frown. "I see your time away has not changed you other than the loss of that dreadful goatee. Someday, your mouth is going to get you into trouble."

Someday? Try most days. "You are likely correct, Sir."

"More importantly, keep your hands off the other serving girls. You already cost one girl her job, and you were lucky that you were only suspended."

"This is the third time you have reminded me this week, Sir."

Sheen's fists rested on his hips, his face a scowl. "How many more will it take for it to register?"

"None, sir. I am quite finished with serving girls."

"Good. As it is, you are lucky to have reappeared just when I needed help after Ebran disappeared." He gestured toward the trays. "Now, take two trays. Poul will take the third and a bottle of wine. Marnie will take the water and goblets."

"What about you, Sir?"

"I have other things to attend to at the moment," His grimace deepened. "I pray this illness is short lived. I am exhausted from running this place with a skeleton crew."

With a small bow, Delvin turned from Sheen and picked up two trays with four bowls on each. Poul claimed the third tray – the one holding two bowls, a pile of spoons, and a plate of rolls – before grabbing a carafe of red wine. They headed toward the door where Marnie waited with a tray filled with goblets and a pitcher of water.

Departing the kitchen, the trio hurried to the stairwell and descended to the ground floor. The hall was quiet with magistrates, guards, and palace staff all ill or afraid of becoming ill. Two guards outside the closed Council Chamber doors were the only people to be found.

Poul led them toward the guards where he stopped and bobbed his head. "Hello Tarshall, Ydith. We are here to serve dinner."

Ydith shrugged. "Go on in, but you might find yourself scolded. They were expecting it some time ago."

She knocked three times, waited a moment, and opened the door for the servants to enter. Led by Poul, Delvin and Marnie stepped inside before Ydith pulled the heavy door closed.

The nine thrones in the room were occupied as was the chair Kardan used when present. Many of the faces turned toward the servants, and some Council members commented about the food being late. Delvin ignored the comments as he set the two trays on a long table near the door. He and Poul then moved small tables from along the wall, placing one before each person. Once each table was in place, Poul and Marnie began placing and filling goblets with wine or water while Delvin returned to the bowls of clam chowder.

With his back to the room, Delvin removed the vial from his sleeve while humming an easy tune to mask any noise he made. He uncorked the vial and carefully poured a few drops of black ichor into each bowl. After recorking the vial, he slid it back into his sleeve and placed a spoon into each bowl, stirring the poison into the cloudy soup.

Poul arrived at his side and took a tray as he did the same. In moments, they had passed bowls of chowder to each person in the room. The trio of servants then returned to stand near the serving table as they waited on further instruction.

"Thank you," Archon Varius said. "You three may leave."

"Very well," Poul said as he bowed.

Delvin, who was not yet prepared to leave, cleared his throat to draw attention. "Pardon me, Archon. As you are aware, much of the staff remains ill, including our best cooks. Before we depart, I wish to ensure you are satisfied with the food."

Varius sighed. "Very well."

Most of the Council members had already consumed one or more spoonfuls of chowder. Varius and Kardan each took a bite, completing the process.

"The soup is fine," Varius said. "You may go."

Delvin frowned. "Fine?" He shook his head. "Fine will not do."

Some of the Council members began to cough and choke, drawing a frown from Varius. Mouths began to foam as they shook and twitched. The Archon's eyes filled with alarm and she gasped. Kardan tried to stand, spilling his chowder in the process, the bowl rolling across the floor and creating a trail of pale liquid. The general stumbled and fell to his hands and knees as he tried to vomit.

The entire time, Poul and Marnie gaped. Finally, Poul looked at Delvin with wide eyes. "Poison!"

Delvin shook his head. "Sorry, Poul."

In a fluid move, Delvin drew the dagger hidden under the back of his jacket, gripped Poul's shirt, and pulled the man close. After slicing the man's throat, he tossed him aside. Marnie spun toward the door, but was still too close. Delvin snagged the back of her dress and yanked. She stumbled backward with a yelp. His arm looped around her front and sliced her throat. Marnie fell to her knees, choking as blood seeped from the wound. Delvin's gaze swept the room with his knife ready just in case the poison hadn't finished the job.

The men of the Council were all clearly dead, as was Varius, who was facing him with a lifeless stare. Kardan was sprawled on his stomach, still twitching. Delvin knelt and wiped his blade clean on Poul's jacket before returning it to the hidden sheath. He then straightened his coat and picked up the carafe of wine, which was still half full.

"This will not do," he said as he poured the remaining wine into the pitcher of water, turning it to the color of blood. "My, how fitting."

He then approached the door with carafe in hand. A backward glance toward the room revealed everything as it should be – motionless and lifeless. Opening the door, he slipped outside.

30

AN UGLY OUTCOME

The Council Chamber door closed behind them – a thud echoing in the silent room. Quinn stared in shock, the scene before her one of horror.

Blood pooled on the floor beside two servants, wide-eyed, staring at nothing. The gashes across their throats made it clear those stares were permanent as if they witnessed their next life waiting. This one had certainly ended.

General Kardan lay near the two servants, his tongue swollen and black, his eyes also locked in a death stare. The man's chair sat behind him, empty. His soup was spilled on the floor, the spoon still in the man's hand.

Council members occupied the eight thrones along the length of the room, many of the men slouching with their necks bent in an odd manner. All their tongues were black and swollen like the general's. Two of the men had spilled their chowder, one on his lap, the other on the floor where the man's spoon rested. Quinn processed all of this in a moment but was unable to tear her gaze from the throne at the far end of the room.

Varius stared at her with a face twisted in pain. A blackened tongue stuck out from her lips, her skin pallid. Like many of the others, foam and spittle covered the front of her shirt. Quinn stared hard, waiting for the woman to move.

Quinn's gaze shifted toward Brandt, their eyes meeting. She knew he was thinking the same thing. *What did you do, Delvin?*

Iko cried out, "Mother!" and ran across the room.

He knelt beside Varius and held her hand with a spoon still in its grip. His hand ran through her hair as tears tracked down his cheeks. Despite Quinn's anger toward him for how she had been treated since her capture, a tear of sympathy slipped down her cheek.

"Mother, please," Iko begged. "Please don't be dead."

Wiping his face with the back of his sleeve, he looked across the room toward where Quinn stood, along with Brandt and the two cavalrymen who had escorted them from Yarth.

"You," Iko growled as he stood upright and glared at Quinn. "You had something to do with this."

He stomped across the room, drawing his sword in the process, his glare seething. Leveling his blade at Quinn's heart, he held it inches away.

"Remove their gags."

The two soldiers responded instantly and began to untie the cloth from the two prisoners. With her mouth free, Quinn gasped and spit and worked her jaw. Her throat was dry from having it forced open for hours with little water to quench it.

"What do you know about this?" Iko demanded.

Quinn looked at Varius and shook her head. "I am sorry, Iko. I had no idea."

"Lies!"

He extended the sword until the tip pressed against her sternum. She refused to flinch or acknowledge the pain although she felt blood track down her stomach.

His face twisted in a snarl. "I am through with your lies!"

Quinn shook her head. "This is not a lie, Iko," she said in earnest. "Not this time. I did not know, and if I had, I would have stopped it."

Iko's entire body shook, his jaw clenching. With a flick, he ran the sword point across Quinn's tunic, slicing the fabric and her skin as he focused on a new target.

With his blade leveled at Brandt's throat, Iko asked again. "What do you know?"

Brandt's eyes flicked toward Quinn and back to Iko. "I...I don't know anything. Not about this."

Iko closed his eyes, clearly frustrated. A long moment passed before he opened them, spun, and slid his sword into the scabbard.

"Fetch the guards outside the door." Iko's voice sounded cold – emotionless. "We will lock down the citadel and find the assassin. When we do, I'll make him wish he had never been born."

As commanded, the man hurried to the door, opened it and lurched back as a sword emerged from his back. As the blade was withdrawn, the man crumpled to the floor to reveal Delvin standing in the doorway. Delvin's thrown knife buried deep into the throat of the other soldier, who fell to his knees and clawed at it as blood gurgled from his mouth.

"Assassin!" Iko shrieked his eyes flaming with hatred.

Iko drew his sword and launched himself toward the door. Desperate but still bound, Quinn swung her leg out, kicking Iko's shin hard and hooking his ankle as he passed by. With a grunt, he crashed to the floor and slid across the tiles. Brandt scrambled toward Iko and kicked his hand, knocking the sword free. As Iko's blade spun toward the open door, Delvin leaped over it and then lunged out with a kick. The toe of his boot connected with Iko's face, the force snapping his head backward and likely shattering an eye socket. Delvin raised his sword, ready to deliver the killing blow.

"No!" Quinn shouted. "Delvin! Don't kill him!"

Delvin held his blade ready as he glared down at Iko, who stared up at the sword while blood ran down his face, his brow and cheek torn open.

"What good can come of allowing him to live?" Delvin asked. "This is the Archon's son."

Quinn walked toward her mentor, pleading. "I know him well enough to know there is good in him." She glanced toward the dead leaders, slumped over in their thrones. "Thus far, he has been a pawn to his mother and the Empire. Varius and the Council will pull his strings no longer." She turned back toward Delvin, meeting his gaze for a moment. "You have seen to that."

Delvin frowned, his eyes shifting from Iko to Quinn and back. "What do you suggest we do with him?"

She moved closer and gazed down at Iko, who glared at Delvin with unmasked hatred in his eyes, one of which was blood red. "We tie him up and gag him, as he has done to us." *You deserve that much, Iko,* Quinn thought. *We'll see how you like it.* "And leave him here until he is found."

After a moment of consideration, Delvin grimaced at Iko and shook his head. "Sorry about this."

With a hard kick, Delvin's boot slammed into Iko's face. Iko rolled onto his side and held his head as he groaned in pain.

"Turn around," Delvin said as he gestured toward Quinn.

As requested, Quinn turned her back to him, felt a blade slip between her wrists, and the rope fell away. Quinn rubbed at her raw wrists and rotated her arms to loosen her sore shoulders. She turned to see Delvin with his sword ready and a dagger in his other hand. *I wonder where he keeps those knives.* The tear across Iko's forehead was twice as bad as before, the lump beneath it an angry red. His eye was bloody, purple and swollen.

"Use the rope to bind him. There should be enough remaining from what I cut away," Delvin said.

Quinn knelt and tied the rope around Iko's wrist before tying it to the other. When she finished, Delvin moved to Brandt and cut his wrists free.

As Quinn had done, Brandt rubbed his wrists and nodded to Delvin. "It feels great to be freed. Thanks."

"Why, Delvin?" Quinn asked.

Delvin squatted and pulled his dagger from the dead guard's throat before wiping it and the sword on the man's clothing. "You know why."

"Did you have to kill them all?"

He inspected the blades in his hands as he stood. "Don't be so naïve, Quinn. Did you really believe there was any other outcome? These people wanted anyone like your boyfriend dead." Delvin pointed his dagger toward Brandt. "Every single one. They would commit genocide for no reason other than their fear of magic and the power it holds. In the end, it was us or them. I saw an opening, so I took a shortcut. We are now free of their thirst for conquest and their desire to control our lives. In the end, the world will be better for it."

Delvin's statement hit upon the very conundrum Quinn had been facing for months. She had desperately sought another outcome, but the solution had eluded her. Despite despising the ideals the Empire stood for, Quinn did not wish Varius and the others dead, so she had made every effort to stop them without reaching this end. Those efforts had only delayed what Delvin declared as inevitable. *Perhaps it was,* she admitted to herself.

Delvin extended the sword toward Quinn. "If your conscience is satisfied, tie his ankles, gag him, and let's be off."

Quinn accepted the sword without another word. Brandt gagged and bound Iko as she looked on with troubled thoughts. Despite how angry she had been with Iko during the journey to Sol Polis, she now found herself feeling sorry for him.

"I need a favor, Brandt," she said. "Are you able to heal right now?"

He shrugged. "Sure. Give me your hand."

Quinn shook her head. "Not me." She pointed toward Iko. "Him."

Brandt frowned. "Why?"

Quinn growled. "Just do it, Brandt."

"Will you two hurry?" Delvin peered out into the receiving hall while standing over the dead soldier in the doorway. "There's no telling when someone will find the mess out here."

Brandt reached for Iko, who flinched and jerked away. Grimacing, Brandt grabbed Iko's wrist and closed his eyes. The magic took hold, healing the wounds on Iko's forehead and eye, leaving only dried blood on his face. Iko's body shook with a chill and Brandt stood.

"He'll be crazy hungry, but I consider it poetic justice since he didn't feed us all day."

"Enough chat. We leave. Now." Delvin darted out of the room.

Quinn and Brandt exited to the main hall, where two more corpses waited. Ydith had an ugly gash across her hand, the surrounding skin blackened. Her tongue was black and swollen as was Tarshall's, who had a similar cut across his thigh. *Blackbane, same as the others,* Quinn thought. *Delvin poisoned his blade before he attacked them. A scratch is all it took for them to die.*

The three of them ran for the side door, into a long corridor, and stopped at the door that led outside. Before Delvin could open the door, Quinn gripped his wrist.

"There is a guard just outside."

Delvin's brow furrowed and then he smiled. "Step into the doorway when you hear the signal." Without another word, he burst out the door, panting hysterically. "They broke free and they're after me!"

"What?" Quinn heard Berd reply, "Who is after you?"

"The spies! They killed everyone! Look out, here they come!"

Quinn glanced at Brandt, who shrugged and jumped into the doorway in a menacing manner. With her sword in the lead, Quinn stood beside him.

The rain had become a downpour. Berd stood two strides outside the door with his back to Delvin. The big man's eyes grew wide when Quinn appeared. He drew his sword, stiffened, and fell to his knees. Delvin put one foot against Berd's back and yanked the dagger from the guard's neck. The man toppled over and twitched briefly before falling still.

"Did you have to kill him, too?" Quinn asked while staring down at the dying guard.

"Oh, please, Quinn. This is us or them. Escape or die."

Delvin spun and ran through the rain toward the gate with Quinn and Brandt close behind.

Sergeant Marissa and two male guards Quinn didn't know stood just outside the bars, both facing away from her as they attempted to huddle beneath wet cloaks. Delvin slowed to a creep as Quinn and Brandt did the same. He then gestured toward Marissa and the guard on the left while he snuck up behind the guard on the right.

Quinn gathered her will, knowing she had little choice. *Escape or die,* she told herself. She imagined thrusting her sword between the bars, the blade skewering Marissa in the back. Repulsed, Quinn lifted the sword high and slammed down hard, the pommel striking the woman's helmet with a loud clang. Marissa collapsed to the cobblestones.

Brandt had one arm around a guard's neck, the man struggling until Delvin stabbed him. The guard then slid down the gate bars until he was sitting. Brandt let the man go before he and Delvin turned toward Quinn.

"That was loud," Brandt noted.

"Exactly." Delvin growled. "It will be a miracle if nobody heard you." Anger was thick in Delvin's voice. "What were you thinking? The woman's back was facing you. Why not just stab her and be done with it?"

Quinn glared back in defiance. "I'll not murder an innocent person. Killing her was not my mission."

Delvin turned to Brandt. "Is she serious?"

"Yeah." Brandt put his arm around her and grinned as rain ran down his face. "Makes you love her even more, doesn't it?"

With the shake of his head, Delvin opened the gate. "You two will be the death of me."

He led them out into the quiet square, past the glowlamp at the corner, and down a dark city street. At the first intersection, they joined a group of sailors returning to the docks, melting in with the cluster at a nonchalant pace.

Quinn knew Delvin. He had a plan and would get them out of Sol Polis. Her time in Kalimar was finished, and it was time to go home.

I'll see you soon, Everson, she thought. *Please stay safe.*

31

POSITIONING

The sun was a glowing ball to the west, partially blocked by tree trunks. With the tight clustering of trees in the wet earth, the forest canopy grew high above. That's how it was on the east side of the Gramble River as it neared the sea – low swampland unfit for buildings or travel.

Percy advanced carefully, seeking solid ground for each step as he crept toward the sunlight. Beyond the trees, the river flowed south. A single rowboat sat in the middle of the river, creating a wake of ripples as the flowing water slipped past it. Two fishing poles dangled over the water, the lines trailing toward the sea. Percy knelt just inside the first line of trees and surveyed the situation.

Gramble Bridge was north of the boat, far enough to make the boat appear innocuous but close enough for an easy view. Five people occupied the boat, three of whom wore leather armor hidden beneath grey cloaks. He could also see the runes drawn on two of the bridge's brick arch supports. *This is just as Budakis recorded in his notes. The fishing poles are just for show. When the army reaches the bridge, the magic-wielders plan to destroy it.*

His task, as outlined in the plans supplied by Sculdin, was simple in concept but nearly impossible to execute. Having trained for years with a seasoned ranger, Percy was an expert in hunting, tracking, and wood-craft, but his skill with the bow easily eclipsed his other talents.

He eased his bow over his head and drew three arrows. The sun dipped lower, half hidden by the mountains far to the west. Percy waited patiently, praying that Mollis had the same sense.

Noise to the north informed him of the Imperial Army's approach. Through the tree trunks, he spotted the vanguard rounding the bend and heading toward the bridge.

Led by Mollis, who sat proudly on his horse, the army began cross-ing. The people in the boat took notice and stared toward the bridge, waiting.

Oh, you pig-headed man, Percy thought.

He moved forward, emerging from the woods as the last of the sun faded. In the dusk, the boat and its occupants became silhouettes hundreds of feet away.

Percy stood at the edge of the bank and measured the wind coming from the sea. He lifted his bow and focused on his target. Calm filled him, his target seemingly enlarging as he stared the man down, pulled the bowstring back, and loosed the arrow. Without waiting, he drew another arrow, and loosed again. The first arrow struck, his target jerking in reaction. The others in the boat turned toward the dying man in surprise as the second arrow struck. Shouts came from the boat, men standing, rocking the boat as they drew their own bows. Percy drew and fired three rapid arrows before retreating to the woods. He didn't care if the last three arrows found their targets. The remaining guards were irrelevant. He had killed the two who lacked armor – the two enemies who could truly cause damage.

Jogging through the woods, Percy soon emerged to join the army as they marched across the bridge. In the middle of the pack, Brillens was on his horse with a messenger riding beside him. Mollis, Brillens, and the messenger, Kerns, had the only horses in the army since they were still waiting for the cavalry to catch up. *Where are you, Iko? We need that cavalry.*

Iko and Commander Korbath should have arrived by the time Mollis reached Wayport, moving at a far faster pace than the foot soldiers. Where the cavalry might have been, there was only a train of steam carriages towing war machines and wagons filled with weapons, tents, and food.

Percy hopped up onto the bridge wall and ran, passing the soldiers as they crossed the river. He glanced toward the rowboat. A single soldier feverishly rowed south, pushed along by the current while the others in the boat remained unmoving, likely dead.

Over a quarter-mile to the south, Wayport waited. Fresh tree stumps filled the area between the bridge and the city – now an open field split by the gravel road as it turned and ran south toward the city gate. A few hundred feet to the north side of the road was the newly established forest edge. The only break in the trees was the road that led north, toward Fallbrandt.

Incredible, Percy thought. *Everything is exactly how it was outlined in the journal Iko stole from General Budakis.* Possessing the journal provided the Imperial Army an immense advantage. The attack plan Kardan and Sculdin had hatched was designed specifically to counter the strategy Budakis had outlined.

Percy slowed as he drew even with Mollis. The man looked down from his steed and nodded.

"Good work, soldier. I knew you would ensure our safety."

Percy wanted to lash out, but he kept his tone even. "It was a close thing. I had to wait until the sun set so the glare wouldn't affect my shot."

The man nodded. "The timing was perfect then."

Sighing inwardly, Percy shook his head. *There is no point in pressing. He is too arrogant to understand how close his impatience nearly caused disaster.*

"What now, Commander?" Percy asked as he gazed over the field of stumps. In the failing light, many of them glowed as if made of glow-stone. *Smart. Lighting the field will prevent us from sneaking close to the city.*

"Our orders are to prepare and wait until the signal," Mollis said as if he religiously followed his orders. "While I would love to attack now, we will remain away from the city and wait. I just hope whatever Sculdin is planning happens soon."

32

SURPRISES

Tenzi strolled Razor's deck, staring up at the stars emerging in a sky still pale purple to the west. Shuttered glowlamps hanging from each mast provided just enough light to navigate the ship's deck, moored alone in a narrow cove. To the east, across an open bay, was the city of Wayport.

Glowlamps at the end of the city piers gave her perspective, as did the dotted line of blue lamps beyond the piers – lights mounted on the masts of the ships moored there. The blockade was a key component to Brock's plan and was the reason he brought a fleet of fifteen vessels with him to the city. Of course, the three hundred soldiers and ninety-six arcanists the ships delivered to Wayport were part of the plan as well.

A shadow moved near the prow, joined by a familiar voice. "I was wondering if you had forgotten."

"That's fair," Tenzi admitted. "I do get distracted sometimes."

Parker shifted closer, meeting her as his arms wrapped about her waist. "Since we are stuck here waiting, there is less to distract you."

"True. Still, the report delivered this morning has me disturbed."

"Why? The Imperial Army marches toward Wayport. Brock suspected that would happen."

"Exactly," she said. "I've seen enough to know things don't go as you suspect. Surprises are the most likely outcome."

He laughed.

"I hate surprises."

He laughed harder. "Of that, I am well aware."

"I also despise doing nothing. Just sitting here, waiting for something to happen."

"You have made that clear. I might agree, but I am still feeling a thrill each day I wake outside a dungeon cell."

She reached up and touched his cheek, recalling Parker with a noose about his neck. "I was afraid I might lose you."

"And I, you," he said softly. "When I stood on the gallows, I feared I would never see you again. More than death, that thought brought me to despair."

"We have had close calls before," she said.

"Yet, somehow, we persevere."

"I pray Issal will see us through this trial as well."

"As long as we are together, the outcome is irrelevant."

She smiled. "You are smooth, Parker Thanes, but I know you better than that." Her finger ran down his chest. "You have too much good in you to stand aside when oppression bares its fangs to feast on the innocent."

He stared into her eyes, his hand running through her hair. "Nobody knows me as you do."

As their lips met, Tenzi felt his warmth, his strength as passion took hold. She responded, her hands running up the back of his tunic while her body pressed against his. An explosion rang in her ears, sparks she continued experiencing after two decades together.

Another boom sounded, and her eyes opened in surprise. Parker pulled back and looked over her shoulder.

"Oh no," he said as a distant blast came from across the bay.

She turned as a crashing noise came from the direction of the blockade. Flashes of green came from further out and a staccato of thumping booms followed. The lights from the blockade began to fade, some sinking into the sea, others disappearing in an instant.

"They are attacking," Parker said.

"At night," Tenzi added. "They actually attacked at night."

"Who does that?"

"Ri Starian sailors." She cupped her hands to her mouth as she strode toward the quarterdeck. "Sound the alarm! All hands on deck! Wayport is under attack!"

The throne room was quiet, dark save for a single lantern on one of the tables, its pale blue light shining on the maps lying there. Brock stood alone, staring out the window toward the lights of the blockade. Dalwin had retired for the evening, off to rest while they waited for the enemy to tip the first tile – tiles Brock and his general had prepared months earlier.

"I miss you, Gunther," Brock muttered to himself. "I could use your mind right now. I fear I have overlooked something – something that could lead to disaster."

The words echoed faintly in the chamber, large enough to hold hundreds.

His thoughts turned to Broland, manning the north wall with a skeleton crew of archers and arcanists. Once the enemy advanced within range, Broland would initiate the shockwaves. If things went as planned, those waves of earth would reduce their numbers and would buy more time as Brock prepared for the next phase. *If things go as planned,* Brock thought. *That didn't happen with the bridge.*

It disgusted him that the enemy would attack a seemingly innocent fishing boat. Only one soldier survived the ordeal, the man reporting they were ambushed by an archer. Based on the distance to shore, the unknown archer must have been quite skilled. *They couldn't have known it was a trap, could they?* Brock wondered. Only a few had known about it, just three people other than those in the boat. A list including only himself, Broland, and Dalwin, none of whom were capable of treachery.

Brock? Are you awake?

He smiled. *Yes, my love.*

Are you well? Is Broland safe? Ashland asked.

I am well, but nobody here is safe. The enemy is on our doorstep, threatening to break in.

He felt her concern through their connection. *I will pray for your safety.*

Shifting subjects, he asked. *How fare things in Kantar?*

All is as it should be now that I have replaced the guards with people I can trust.

And Curan?

I sent him back to Fallbrandt a few days ago. His presence here was a gift, but one I dare not keep. He has much of his father in him, and I suspect he will be needed elsewhere, soon.

I wish he were here. His father as well.

As do I, she agreed.

A flash of green appeared in the dark of the harbor. A thump followed. Brock put his hands on the window, staring out with alarm. Other blasts followed, shaking the blockade.

We are under attack. I must focus. I will speak with you later, Issal willing.

Be well, Brock. I love you.

And I, you.

The door to the throne room burst open and two guards ran in.

"King Brock! We are under attack. An enemy fleet is in the harbor!"

Brock walked toward the door, contemplating the next move. The arcanists among the blockade knew what to do in this event. He had to trust them to succeed. The thought of what might happen if the enemy came up the river made him shudder.

"Gather everyone and meet in the square. We may have to jump to phase three."

The men thumped their fists to their chests. "Yes, Sire!"

As the men ran off, Brock reached behind one of the doors and grabbed his metal-reinforced staff, gripping it as he gathered himself. *People will die tonight. It is us or them. We will not bend to tyranny.* The words gave him strength.

The window behind him shattered in a spray of glass. A bomb hit the floor, exploding in a flash of green flames and blasting Brock through the open doorway before all went black.

—⊹ ⟡ ⟡—

From his position on top of the city wall, Broland watched the Imperial Army. They had arranged themselves along the woods a half-mile north of the city walls, just as his father had anticipated. Although night had fallen, the pale blue glow from the Chaos-Infused tree stumps provided ample light to monitor the field between the city walls and the Imperial army, even at this distance.

The army's arrival had come earlier than planned. Somehow, the enemy had known to target the arcanists waiting in the fishing boat, killing them both along with two guards. With the arcanists dead before they could use their magic, Gramble Bridge remained intact and allowed the enemy a direct route rather than forcing them through the tiny village of Elmbridge, eighteen miles to the north. That blunder had eliminated two days of preparation time in addition to sparing the enemy warriors who would have died in the bridge explosion.

The Imperial Army stretched along the battlefield perimeter from the bridge to the northeast to the new palisades to the west. Broland wondered if the enemy would wait until morning or if they would attack at night. *At least we can see them*, he thought.

He strolled along the parapet, running his hand along the waist-high outer wall. Inside the wall, the city waited. The area along the wall where the army had camped was now deserted, the buildings dark and dormant. Newly-constructed catwalks connected the city wall to the nearest rooftops with more catwalks crossing the streets beyond, creating an escape route. He wondered how much time remained before their escape was required.

An archer patrolling the wall approached, nodding to Broland as he passed by. Although night had fallen only an hour earlier, the city was unnaturally quiet – as if everyone inside were holding their breath in anticipation of an attack. It would come. Of that, Broland now had no doubt. The only question was when.

Broland stopped when he noticed movement in the distance and heard the faint crunching of gravel. A catapult emerged as a crew of Imperial soldiers pushed it down the road and toward the city. Another followed, both siege engines advancing slowly as the city defenders looked on in concern.

"Do you think there is any chance they will come within bow range?" the archer asked.

The man stood a few strides to Broland's side with his hands on the wall as he stared into the night.

"I highly doubt it," Broland replied. "Catapults can launch as far as a thousand feet. How far can you shoot?"

"With a longbow? Five hundred feet, perhaps six with a tailwind, but not accurately in either case."

Broland nodded to himself, filing the information away.

When the enemy catapults were about a thousand feet away, they stopped with each positioned to opposite sides of the road. Some of the men then jogged back to the main force while others waited beside the war machines.

"What are they planning?" Broland mumbled. "And, why advance only two catapults? The scouts reported twenty or more."

"I can't guess at what they are doing, but I fear it will happen soon," the archer added.

"Just remember the plan," Broland said. "We need to keep the arcanists alive."

He leaned forward and eyed the runes drawn in the ground outside the walls. The symbols were still intact. Turning, he spied clusters of arcanists on nearby rooftops, sitting in wait.

A series of thumps came from the south. Brandt turned with a grimace. "Those explosions are from the harbor."

Another soldier jogged toward Broland. "There is an attack. What do we do, Your Highness?"

"We remain at our post and pray that others will respond. Our job is protect the city from the enemy camped outside it."

More explosions sounded as distant flashes of green and orange came from the harbor. As time went on, Broland grew nervous.

The Imperial soldiers lined up across the field and began advancing at an easy pace. The army stopped a few hundred feet beyond the two catapults. A man on horseback rode down the middle, pausing when positioned between the enemy force and the two catapults. There, he waited.

"Arcanists!" Broland bellowed. "Prepare yourselves!"

A thump came from behind and Broland spun about to find a burst of green flame coming from the castle. Shouts came from across the battlefield and the officer on horseback waved his sword over his head. The catapults fired.

"Run!" Broland screamed as he bolted across the catwalk, toward the nearest rooftops.

Explosions came from behind, the concussion causing Broland to stumble and nearly fall from the catwalk. The archer trailing him wasn't so lucky, the man landing hard on the cobblestones three stories below.

Broland turned to find a portion of the wall beside the city gate destroyed and the remaining bricks on fire.

Rising to his feet, Broland shouted, "Arcanists! To the wall, now!"

The four arcanists on the nearest rooftop followed as he returned to the wall. A glance to each side revealed others crossing catwalks. Looking out when he stepped onto the wall, Broland found the enemy army waiting as soldiers hurried to reload the two catapults. The man on the horse issued orders and the army charged forward.

"Hurry!" Broland shouted. "Charge the runes!"

Moments passed as the enemy rushed forward. Between the army and wall, the soldiers wound back the arms of two catapults. Below the wall, the runes began to glow red, pulse, and fade.

In rapid bursts, shockwaves launched from the runes, fanning out as the tidal waves of earth raced toward the invaders. The leader turned his horse, waved his arms, and raced away from the city. The surrounding army turned with him and ran the other direction as shockwaves chased them. One of the catapults fired, the launch arm flinging a bomb into the air just before a shockwave pounded through it and the other machine. Blasts of green flame and sprays of dirt came from the area as the catapults popped up, flipped, and fell.

Broland grabbed the arcanist to his left, tugged on her tunic, and shouted, "Run, Libby!"

He sprinted east, away from the gate, trailing the woman and two other arcanists who ran ahead of him. The flashbomb struck, the explosion launching him forward. Broland crashed into the woman, who stumbled into the man in front of her. She fell to the side and slid over the interior edge of the wall. Broland gripped her forearm, but her weight pulled him over the edge until he clung to the top by one hand while she dangled from the other. He tried to pull himself up, but she was too heavy.

"Let me fall," the woman said.

He looked down at her and the cobblestones below. "We are too high up. You'll break your leg or worse."

"You are too important." Libby's large, brown eyes locked with his. "I'm sorry, my Prince. I must do this. This is my time. Tipper is waiting for me."

The woman kicked and jerked her arm from his grip, her eyes

remaining locked with his as she fell. She landed on her back, her head striking the stones with a sickening crack. There, she remained, unmoving.

With an effort, Broland swung his other hand up, gripped the wall, and the man above helped him up. Rising to his feet, he found the army now far across the battlefield, beyond the reach of the shockwaves. Other than the two catapults and the people manning them, he saw no casualties among the enemy.

"They knew what we had planned," he said to himself aloud. "How did they know?"

An explosion to his right forced him to raise his hand and shield the heat. When he lowered it, he found a hole in the ground where one of the shockwave runes had been. The result left an unprotected gap in their defenses.

"What? Where did that come…"

Broland then spotted men in black sneaking along the outer base of the wall. The infiltrators began tossing flashbombs, striking the Shockwave runes, each blast sending a burst of green flame and splattered earth into the air.

Realizing their intent, he shouted, "Below the wall! Shoot them!"

It was too late. The enemy had been able to sneak men inside the shockwaves and were taking them out, one by one. Without the shockwaves to guard the north wall, the invaders would attack. Catapults armed with flashbombs would destroy the wall, and the enemy would enter the city far more easily than anticipated.

Broland was now certain the Empire had known their defense plan the entire time. *Kony*, he thought. *You had something to do with this. I know it.*

33

INFILTRATORS

Captain Blaine Sculdin stood at the prow of the longship with the wind in his face and his cloak flapping in the breeze. A Ri Starian sailor stood beside him, a rough looking man who peered intently into the darkness. Sculdin wondered if the man could see or if he were just pretending. Other than the occasional whitecaps on waves, Sculdin saw nothing but blackness, heard nothing but the sea lapping against the hull and the oars cutting through the water. Still, Ri Starians were famous for their skills on the sea. Having no other choice, he put his faith in their reputation. In fact, the campaign he and Kardan had conceived hinged heavily on the skills of this ally from the north.

After two decades, tonight Sculdin would strike back at Chaos – the magic that had destroyed his family. He still missed his sister, Tegan. With her red hair, fierce determination, and fiery spirit, she was difficult to forget. Her talents as a duelist had her destined for greatness, sure to become a senior officer in the Holy Army. More importantly, if she were still alive, she would surely be among the leaders within The Hand.

However, her destiny was denied when Cameron DeSanus dragged her and the other paladin trainees from Fallbrandt to fight in a war they had no business fighting. Like so many others, Tegan never returned. *She was so young*, Sculdin thought. *Her whole life waited for her, only to have it crushed by Chaos.*

After learning of Tegan's death, his mother became withdrawn, barely able to get out of bed. Three months passed before Sculdin returned to find her dead – poisoned by her own hand. His father died two years later. The medicus couldn't pin the cause for the man's death. Sculdin remained convinced it was from grief.

It took Sculdin years to discern the truth of what had happened to his sister. It took even longer to find a way to right the wrongs committed against her. The destruction of his family left him seeking answers at the bottom of a bottle – an indulgence he repeated often. Drinking ended up costing him dearly, and he lost his position working for Duke Gort of Sol Gier after a failed assignment. He then drifted for weeks before finding a new line of work. As a lifelong military man, accepting a position as a prison guard was beneath his skills, but the choice had changed everything.

There, he had discovered the missing members of The Hand, imprisoned for their belief that Chaos was evil. Vandermark and many of the older leaders had already died during their years of incarceration. Yet, the brightest minds still lived. With them, Sculdin plotted in secret. During a leave of absence, he located Karl Jarlish, and a plan fell into place.

Jarlish as an ally made the prison break a success. The flash powder obtained from the mines, along with Karl Jarlish's brilliant mind, became the foundation upon which a new empire would be built. *Like so many others, Chaos has claimed Jarlish – now just another name on the list of those who deserve vengeance.* The thought of Corvichi's destruction still irritated Sculdin. Flash powder weapons had since become precious commodities.

The man beside Sculdin raised a white flag, pointing starboard, and the ship began to turn. By the time the man lowered it, the lights of Wayport had become visible to the north. Methodically, the longship drew closer to the city, and Sculdin was able to make out the string of lights running from the pier to the eastern portion of the harbor.

"Just as Budakis planned," he noted.

Knowing the plans of the Kantarian defense provided an immense advantage, and Sculdin was glad to use such knowledge.

Nine Ri Starian longboats trailed behind, sailing in a V formation. All had their sails tucked away, moving with the use of oars alone.

He climbed the stairs to the quarterdeck and nodded to the woman at the helm. Like many of the Ri Starian's, Hiaga had blond hair and light eyes. Her hair was tied into a long braid, exposing ears with large hoops dangling from them. Despite the chill, the woman wore a leather vest, her muscular arms bare to the shoulders.

"Remember the plan," Sculdin said.

Her face was masked in shadow, but even in the dark, he sensed the woman's scowl. "Don't tell me how to run my fleet."

He pressed his lips together and held back a retort. A moment passed and then Hiaga turned toward a man standing to her other side.

"Now, Challo."

The man lifted a lantern from the deck and removed the cover. It glowed blue from one side as mirrors shrouded the other three sides. Holding it up high with the light directed toward the trailing fleet, the man waved a panel in front of the lantern in an altering rhythm. The other ships saw it as a series of blinking lights. Sculdin didn't understand the odd language, but he knew the message they were sending.

Hiaga put her mouth near the long tube sticking above the deck and said, "Quarter-speed."

Moments later, the longship began to slow, and two other longships passed them, heading toward the blockade. The vessels appeared as faint shadows slipping across the water.

Hiaga called out again, and the oars of her ship fell still. The man with the light flashed another signal. One more vessel sailed past them as Hiaga's longship and the rest of the fleet settled. Sculdin leaned against the rail and stared toward the string of blue lights dividing the eastern bay from the city.

He was eager for it to begin. His wait was short.

Blasts of green flared from the flash cannons onboard the lead crafts. The resounding thumps were met by crashes as the cannonballs crashed into the blockade. Distant shouts arose, only to be drowned out by another volley from the cannons. Some lights blinked out. Others began to sink. Fires arose on one blockade ship, the orange flames lighting the night and reflecting off the water, making it easy to see the silhouettes ahead.

The third longship passed the first two Ri Starian vessels, navigating between them at full speed. Without stopping, the beam at the prow of the longship smashed into the bow of the blockade ship adjacent to one that was sinking. The Kantarian ship rocked and shifted, creating a gap between it and the sinking ship. The oars of the longship continued turning, slowly pushing the blockade ship aside until the longship squeezed through the gap.

"They breached the blockade!" Sculdin said with a clenched fist. "Once my Infiltrators destroy their magic defenses, Brock will have no choice but to react. When he does, we will have them!"

The other two longships began to fire again, launching cannonballs at the blockade while the Kantarian soldiers and sailors aboard scrambled to respond.

"I got your men through, Sculdin. What now?" Hiaga asked.

"Now, we wait."

"For what?"

"First, watch the castle." He pointed toward the tallest building, towering above the southeast corner of the city. A flash of green emerged from the rear of the building, turning orange as the thump of the explosion reached his ears. "Perfect."

"That's why you mounted a catapult to one of my longships?"

"Yes."

"To fire one flashbomb at the castle?"

"Consider it a signal of sorts."

"A signal for what?"

"For our army to attack, which will force the defenders on the north wall to react."

A loud crack sounded, followed by another.

"What was that?"

Sculdin pointed toward the blockade. "Look!" He chuckled in glee. "It worked."

"Is that...ice?"

"Yes. The blockade is frozen in place. They cannot break free to stop us from landing on shore!"

"So, I can tell my fleet to begin the assault?"

"Yes." He rubbed his hands together. "And while my team sneaks in from the south, our troops on land will strike from the north."

Hiaga called for the oars to resume at full speed, the man with the lamp signaling the fleet to follow.

She turned toward Sculdin. "Why did you place all those men on the lead ship if you knew it would became trapped in ice before reaching the river?"

He stared at the frozen bay, lit by two burning kingdom ships, the onboard fires now raging. In the distance was the longship that had broken through the blockade, now trapped in ice near the river mouth. His Infiltrators on board were descending a rope ladder and running across the ice, toward the west riverbank. Those men had volunteered for a role that would make them heroes, but it was a suicide mission. If any survived, it would require a massive stroke of luck.

"Those soldiers are the final piece of the puzzle. If they can negate the magic that is undoubtedly keeping our infantry at bay, the city will soon be ours."

34

TWISTING WINDS

A haze of pain masked all else. Within the void, there was nothing but agony and smoke, masked beneath a red-tinted haze.

A pale blue glow appeared, flaring brighter and brighter, turning everything to frigid cold.

Brock gasped, a shiver wracking his body as his back arched. His eyes opened to the light, and a face hovered over him. It was an old face. A kind face, the man's eyes full of relief.

"It is done," Minister Dryfus sighed.

"Thank Issal," Dalwin said, crouching lower as he patted Brock with a blanket. "We had feared the worst."

A half circle of guards stood over him, all staring down in concern. Brock sat, up, his stomach yearning for food, his muscles shaking as if he hadn't eaten in days. Pain came from his chest. He looked down at the gaping holes in his still smoldering doublet.

"Ouch!" He grabbed the shirt and pulled, tearing it open as he yanked it off.

"Your burns were bad, your Majesty," Minister Dryfus said as Brock tossed the ruined doublet aside. "The lump on your head was also quite serious. You should rest."

Remembering the explosion, Brock turned toward the throne room.

The doors had blown off, the interior still burning, and black smoke filled the room. Everything smelled of soot.

"How long was I out?"

"The explosion occurred just a couple minutes ago, Brock," Dalwin replied. "We rushed in and found you on the floor."

All eyes were focused on him, waiting.

"Thank you for the healing, Minister Dryfus." Brock said to the old man as he pulled his feet beneath him and rose on shaky legs. He set his jaw, his anger boiling inside. "They made a mistake."

Dalwin's brow furrowed as he glanced toward the fire. "What do you mean?"

"They didn't kill me." He turned to the guards, his voice growing louder. "Pretencia is in charge of the Citadel defenses while I am out. You will obey his orders as if they were my own. And for Issal's sake, set up a bucket line and put out this fire before it spreads."

The guards thumped fists to their chests, turned, and ran out to fetch buckets and water.

Dalwin gripped Brock's shoulder. "Where are you going?"

"To lead my army. Wayport is a Kantarian duchy, and I'll not allow the Empire to take it as long as I still breathe."

Bending, he picked up his staff and stood. A hand gripped his wrist.

"Please, Sire," Dryfus pleaded. "You must at least eat something. The healing taxes the body...you need your strength."

He nodded. "I will stop by the kitchen on my way out. Besides, I need a different shirt."

Without another word, he ran to his quarters. After donning a black sleeveless jerkin with a red Chaos starburst on the chest, he stopped by the kitchen. A quick meal had him recharged, the cavernous hunger in his stomach sated.

When he reached the front entrance to the castle, he found guards waiting.

"I suppose you two plan to escort me?"

Grim nods answered the question. Rather than argue, he ran outside with the guards a step behind. Explosions shook the city, and a burst of green flame lit the night sky over the north wall. Flashbombs rained down, detonating again and again, causing massive damage. In the citadel square, thousands of people huddled in fear, hoping this would not be their end.

Please be safe, Broland, thought Brock as he sprinted down the steps, through the crowd, and out the citadel gate.

Broland ran along the wall, shouting for everyone to retreat. Arcanists and archers ran along the catwalks and across the rooftops, fleeing toward the city center. By the time the walls were cleared, the enemy catapults were in position. One launched and Broland ran toward the nearest catwalk. As he reached it, the flashbomb hit, striking the ground outside the walls and destroying the last intact Shockwave rune in an eruption of green flames and chunks of earth. Rather than damaging the invading army, the arcanists had wasted their ability on nothing. It would be an hour or longer before those people could again wield their magic. By then, it would be too late.

Broland sprinted across as another bomb struck the wall. A wave of heat washed over him, and the catwalk began to fall. He made a desperate dive, his upper body landing on the nearest rooftop. The foot-bridge crashed to the street below while he held on to the clay roof tiles.

Dragging himself up in short, effort-filled bursts, he lay on the roof for a breath before rising to his feet and breaking into a run. Behind him, flashbombs began raining down. A tower of flames lit the night and made navigating the rooftops easy as he reached the next catwalk and scurried across. A number of buildings later, a scaffold waited at a gap that was too broad to jump. He climbed down the scaffold and was soon in an alley with a twelve-foot tall wall blocking the north route.

When he reached the city center, the arcanists and archers who had fled the wall were there, many hunched over with hands on their knees, gasping for air. Those men and woman had joined the core of the city's defense – an army exceeding a thousand. Even then, their force was a quarter of what waited outside the city walls – walls that would soon be nothing but dust.

Broland pushed his way through the crowd, toward the fountain at the center. Glowlamps lit the area, many on posts, some held by the soldiers gathered there. The last of the crowd parted and he stopped.

A man stood there, alone. His head was bald and his arms bared to the shoulders, dressed in a black leather jerkin with breeches and boots to match. A red starburst marked the left breast of the jerkin, matching a bigger symbol marking the man's back. Even without hair, Broland would know the man anywhere just by his stance.

"Father! What happened to your hair?"

Brock turned toward him. "Thank Issal." He looked toward the fires to the north. "I hoped you had the sense to retreat before it was too late."

Another bomb ignited to the north. "In truth, it was a close thing." Broland stepped closer, his voice dropping to a whisper. "I fear we were betrayed. They knew our plans and how to counter them."

A deep grimace crossed Brock's face as he stared toward the destruction. In that moment of silence, in the reflection of flames from his father's eyes, Broland feared the man. He had seen that look once before when Chadwick swung from the gibbet. For the second time, he understood what it was to be king.

"Budakis."

"What?" Broland said in shock. "He would never betray you."

Brock shook his head. "Not intentionally. However, he used to keep a journal. I wonder if he kept notes on our defense plans and those notes fell into the wrong hands."

"Kony," Broland nodded as he said it, knowing it was true.

"We must change our plans."

"And do what?"

"Attack."

Tenzi stood at the helm, watching distant explosions light the night. Wayport was under attack – a violent assault meant to cause destruction and draw the defenders toward the north wall, which was surely about to fall. The shadowy ships sailing into the unprotected harbor were the true threat. If successful, they would infiltrate the city and strike the defenders from behind. Tenzi could not allow that to happen.

She glanced up at the sails, stretched full by the westerly breeze. *At least something has gone right tonight,* she thought. With a stare like an animal stalking its prey, she watched the other boats, gauging their speed to hers. It would be a close thing, but she had surprise on her side so long as nobody spotted her ship too soon.

"You were a good ship, Razor." She slid her palm along the wheel, feeling the polished wood and the pulse of the vessel for the last time. "All things must end. Perhaps we will go down together."

A man climbed upon the quarterdeck, interrupting her moment. "You wished to see me, Captain?"

"Yes, Stein. I wanted to thank you for our years together. We have had a good run."

He stepped closer, lowering his voice. "What's this about, Tenzi?"

"We are about to engage with the enemy, but they outnumber us seven ships to one. You are the only arcanist onboard. Do you have any ideas?" She pointed toward her quarry, a half-mile away. "They seek to breach the city walls and they possess flashpowder. You know what that means."

"Their sails are down. How are they moving?" he asked as he stared at the enemy fleet.

"Ri Starian. They have oars, driven by a crew down in the hull."

"If we can stop them from rowing?

"That would work."

"Why not smoke them out?"

She shook her head. "No good. The oar openings are too tight. Not even Parker can get a flaming arrow in there."

Stein stared at the ships for a moment before speaking, his tone grim. "Permission to call for the ballistae, Captain."

"Do it but hurry."

Stein leaped to the main deck and gathered six crew members who rushed to the storage room. With an arm full of bolts and a glowlamp in the other hand, Stein led the sailors carrying the three ballistae toward the bow. The ballistae were cranked into launch position while Stein sketched runes on the bolts.

In the meantime, the Ri Starian longships drew nearer, now close enough that Tenzi was able to see silhouettes moving amid the dim light of the shuttered lamps on deck.

Parker returned to the quarterdeck and settled beside Tenzi. "I wish we had a larger crew. Those vessels are filled with soldiers and we have, what? Ten sailors on board?"

"It wouldn't matter; they have flashbombs," Tenzi said. "Besides, we aren't going to board them."

"What?"

"I have other plans," she said, firm in her resolve. "Ready the longboat and prepare to jump ship on my signal."

He put his hand on her shoulder. "You intend to ram them?"

"Well, one of them."

"The others?"

"Stein is doing what he can."

Parker stared at her for a moment and then nodded. "As will I."

He turned and bolted down the stairs as Tenzi's gaze shifted to the bow. Each of the three ballistae were resting on the rail while the sailors holding them braced themselves. Stein stood between the ballistae, waiting. Finally, the man's eyes began to glow bright red as he gathered Chaos. The first bolt began to glow red and the ballistae fired, launching the heavy metal projectile toward an enemy longship. It struck with a tremendous crack, the bolt turning a hot white and setting the hull ablaze. In sequence, the other two bolts fired, each striking a different longship and setting it on fire.

Shouts and screams rang through the night.

"Abandon ship!" Tenzi bellowed. "To the long boat!"

The sailors onboard Razor hurried toward the lifeboat hanging over the port rail. However, she remained behind the wheel, staring down her target.

Motion to the starboard drew Tenzi's attention, and she found an enemy craft bearing down on Razor. A flash of green lit the night, and a cannonball hit Razor mid-deck, blasting a spray of planks and rail pieces across the deck. Tenzi ducked behind the wheel as shards rained on the quarterdeck. The dust cleared to reveal a chunk of the ship missing and a body lying on the deck, dead.

Panic struck. She leaned forward and stared at the shadowy corpse, trying to determine if it were Parker. *No. Not him. Please.*

A flaming arrow arced from the bow, followed by another, and another, all landing on the deck of the craft ahead of them. The arrows hit enemy sailors, setting their clothing ablaze and creating havoc as the flailing, burning men stumbled about. Others on board the longship scrambled to avoid the flames.

Parker appeared in the night, running toward the quarterdeck with his bow still in hand. He swiped his knife through the lifeboat rope and it fell into the bay, taking the sailors onboard with it. Circling the hole in the deck, he reached the stairs just as the Razor collided with the enemy longship.

Crashing, cracking wood and grinding hulls joined the screams that rang in the night. The force of the collision drove Tenzi into the wheel and to her knees. Pulling herself upright, she found Parker lying on the deck. He rose to his feet and ran toward her.

"What are you doing?" she exclaimed. "You were supposed to get off the ship!"

He stumbled up the stairs and grabbed her hand. "I'll not leave without you."

An explosion of green flames took the Razor, the force of the blast knocking Tenzi and Parker to the quarterdeck and sending debris raining down upon them. As it settled, she uncovered her head and looked around. Parker's shirt was on fire. She urgently patted at it, burning her hand as she smothered the flame.

"Thanks," he groaned, taking her hand and helping her up. "Now, let's jump ship."

"Good idea. On three." She turned toward the stern. "One. Two. Three."

As the pair ran toward the rail, the other flashbomb struck. A blast of green flame surged around them, propelling them off the ship and into the darkness.

35

ATTACK

The longship circled the sheet of ice, the oars cutting through water mere feet from the frozen edge. Two trapped ships fired on the blockade, the third ship now abandoned, the soldiers and sailors either gone or dead.

Fires burned on the blockade vessels even as archers stationed upon them loosed volleys upon the longships. Yes, the sailors on the two longships trapped outside the blockade had been sent to die, same as those aboard the ship that broke through the blockade. As planned, the distraction also trapped the kingdom fleet when the arcanists used their dark magic to freeze the area where the river poured into the bay. The remaining longships headed toward shore unchallenged.

Explosions sent bursts of green and orange flames into the sky over the city. *King Brock has little choice but to respond,* Sculdin thought, *assuming he survived the bomb that struck the throne room.* The north wall had likely turned to rubble, as had anything located near it. If allowed to continue, the assault would destroy Wayport and everyone inside. *By now, the Kantarians will be preparing to meet the army. I wonder if they know about our muskets.*

Turning, Sculdin strolled toward the quarterdeck. Soldiers on deck moved aside for him. He patted a few on the shoulder as he passed by, offering words of courage. Armed with flashbombs, muskets, and swords, they carried weaponry that required little additional confidence, but it never hurt for soldiers to feel supported by their senior officer.

As he reached the steps to the quarterdeck, Sculdin heard a crack from a nearby longship, followed by shouts and screams. He ran up and stood beside the helm, peering out to see a longship on fire, the raging flames taking the thing as if it were doused in naphtha.

Another crack sounded, and another longship went up in flames. By the time the third Ri Starian vessel ignited, he spotted the source.

"There," he pointed into the dark, off the port side and toward a faint light coming off shimmering sails, like a ghost in the night. "Sink that ship. Now!"

Haiga called out, and a flashcannon was turned to the port rail. A call was issued, the cannon blasting a flash of green flame. The cannonball struck, rocking the enemy ship as a massive hole opened at the midpoint of the main deck.

He ran to the nearest rail and shouted. "Bombers! Strike that ship as soon as we draw close enough!"

Infiltrators ran through the crowd on deck with slings ready. The first began swinging his sling, the whirling sound of it cutting through the air rising above the din. A crash came from the night as the kingdom craft collided with a longship, the prow driving through the hull near the stern.

The bomber released his sling, the bomb arcing through the air to strike the opposing ship mid-deck. A bloom of green lit the night, the fire turning orange, and Sculdin caught a good view of the damage.

Three Ri Starrian longships were burning, listing and sinking. They would not make it to shore. The kingdom ship was in the same condition if not worse, its prow firmly locked into the side of a longship that was taking on water. Another explosion blasted the kingdom ship, this one turning the quarterdeck into a ball of flames.

He turned away and stomped over to Hiaga.

"My men are dying!" he growled.

"As are my sailors!" Hiaga yelled.

"Get us to shore before anything else happens. As it stands, I will have little more than three hundred soldiers...unless your sailors will join us."

"Join you? This has been a disaster!" Hiaga got in his face, snarling.

"You said this mission would cost me three vessels, but I've already lost seven!" She turned back to the wheel. "We are sailors, not fighters. I'll get you to shore, but we are not storming this blasted city. You do what you must, but I plan to take my last three ships and retreat as soon as I am rid of you."

Percy strolled along the rear ranks, the area illuminated by glowing stumps. *It's convenient to have this light,* he thought, knowing it had been the enemy's way to limit surprises. He had read the plans himself, even before sharing them with Kardan and Sculdin. Yet, seeing it all unfold just as planned gave him a chill. *It cannot be this easy,* he thought. *We are missing something.*

Ranks of soldiers stood between him and the catapults, positioned a thousand feet from the city wall. Brillens' thousand musketeers stood in front while Mollis and his infantry waited behind them. At the rear was Mollis and his own, much smaller, regiment of musketeers. Everything appeared as it should, the plan progressing as intended.

A thud came from a catapult as another flashbomb was launched toward Wayport. By the time it landed, the launch arm was already being cranked back for another round. The war machines were pushed forward a few strides between each round as they slowly ate away at the city. Each time the war machines moved forward, Brillens' musketeers would follow, creating a gap between them and the rest of the army.

As Percy reached the men on horseback, he shouted. "Commander!" Both Mollis and Brillens turned toward him, the latter frowning at the back of the former's head. Percy knew what Brillens thought of his fellow commander. *I agree, Brillens. Mollis is a pig-headed idiot.* "When are you going to send the army in?"

"According to the plan," Mollis said in a haughty tone, "King Brock will eventually decide he has no choice but to attack. When he does, Brillens' musketeers will take their turn." Mollis grinned at Brillens. "Not even magic can prevent dying from a musket shot. I'd like to see Brock try healing someone with a lump of lead in them."

"My musketeers are ready, Mollis." Brillens gestured toward the front line. "The moment the kingdom forces emerge, they will do their job. It's up to your squads to clean up the mess afterward."

Mollis chortled. "A job my soldiers are well suited to perform."

Percy turned from them and climbed atop a particularly tall stump. Shielding his eyes from the fires burning in Wayport, he gazed over the field.

The river to one side of the city prevented anyone from sweeping the Imperial army's eastern flank unless they came across the bridge. Even then, Brock's army was in Wayport and would need to cross the river, travel through the bogs south of the bridge, and then attack through that narrow funnel. The move would be suicide with the army positioned as it was.

His gaze shifted to look west of the city where the palisade of stripped tree trunks had divided the field. Sections of the wall were missing, creating gaps with fires still burning on the neighboring logs. *That is where we must focus,* Percy thought. *With the fires burning as they are, it is Brock's only choice.*

A flicker of movement appeared beyond a gap in the palisades, followed by another.

"They come!" Percy warned. "The enemy is attacking from the western flank!"

"Finally!" Mollis laughed and then shouted. "Cease the catapults! Take aim for the palisade!"

Brillens rode forward down the road, through the gap in the ranks and roared, "Musketeers, prepare to attack!"

36

FIGHT LIKE A WARDEN

B rock stood outside the wall and considered his plan. He and eighty-seven others had received a Power augmentation. While it was a small portion of his army, each augmented soldier was worth dozens of standard warriors.

Those soldiers leaped over the west wall, returning to the city side. Moments later, they jumped back carrying another soldier. Without a gate to that side of the city, over the wall was the only way out. Soon, seven hundred warriors stood outside the city wall, waiting alongside his Power augmented super-soldiers.

Four sizeable gaps now existed in the half-mile-long palisade connecting the city wall to the forest edge. Fires burned on the flash-bomb-blasted logs adjacent to the gaps.

Brock used Power to augment his voice. "It is time to make our stand!" His voice was loud and clear, over the thumping explosions from the northeast. "The augmented soldiers are to lead the way and break the enemy front. The others will clean up. Take out the war machines first and keep moving to make yourself a difficult target. This is a fight to the death, so take no quarter!" He raised his arm high. "Attack!"

He spun about, ran toward the palisade wall, and leaped over it.

A flashbomb exploded below him, the force of the blast knocking him off balance and sending him falling face-first toward the ground, fifty feet below.

Broland stood in the center square along with two hundred soldiers. Those men and women stared at him, waiting for his command. Somewhere to the west, his father was forming a counterattack while he stood here doing nothing. Explosions continued in the north quarter of the city as fires raged. The blasts were slowly growing closer.

He turned toward the citadel where the citizens huddled in fear – thousands of people who wondered if they would survive the night. *I cannot allow the enemy to reach the citadel,* Broland thought. *Those people… we promised them protection.* The hundred guards within the citadel walls were the last line of defense, something he hoped would not be needed.

Another explosion rocked the night, and Broland frowned, turning to look south. "Did that come from the harbor?"

The next blast left little doubt as a tower of flames and dust filled the sky over the gate. Broland climbed on top of the fountain edge and turned toward the troops assigned to him.

"Listen! My father is dealing with our threat to the north, but the south gate is locked and unguarded. They seek to surprise us by capturing the city while we fight to the north!" A thousand eyes were staring at him, relying on him for direction. "We cannot allow Imperial forces into the citadel. Here is what we must do!"

Brock got his hands beneath him and pushed himself to his knees. His body hurt, but was whole. The Power augmentation had saved him from a fall that would otherwise shatter bones.

His Chaos-charged squad ran past him as a staccato of bangs came from the Imperial Army. Many of the men and women lurched, staggered, and fell. One landed beside him with a hole in his forehead, eyes staring vacantly into nothing.

"We must be more evasive!" He climbed to his feet and released a Power-augmented shout. "Jump! Don't let them take aim at you!"

With a massive leap, he flew toward the nearest catapult. Two more leaps carried him over the enemy's front line – soldiers armed with long weapons made of wood and metal. *Those must be muskets,* he thought. Many tried to shoot at him but missed.

Brock landed beside a catapult, dropped his staff, and grabbed ahold of the frame. Lifting it with a furious jerk, he spun about. The catapult – a thousand pounds of wood and metal – swung in a circle and smashed through every Imperial soldier within a twelve-foot radius of where he stood. One rotation later, he released his grip and sent the machine sailing through the air to land thirty feet away, crushing dozens of enemy soldiers before crashing into another catapult. A flashbomb fell from the second catapult's launch basket and ignited. An explosion erupted, the blast killing a score of the enemy.

Around Brock, Chaos-charged soldiers tore into the invaders, cutting through them as if they were straw before a scythe. More explosions followed as the battlefield became a killing ground.

Everson stared out the window as Colossus raced down the hill, toward the distant fires lighting the night.

They had camped just five miles north of Wayport. The first explosion had woken Curan, the second bringing Cassie awake as well. By the time Everson and Ivy had stirred, Curan was preparing Gorgant to ride. There was little doubt as to what was occurring, and they had no time to waste.

Rounding a bend, Everson turned a tad too late and Colossus ran over the shrubs beside the road before careening off a tree. The machine returned to the road, leveled, and came upon another bend, this one more gradual and easier to navigate – even at a high speed.

Ahead, the fires became visible through the trees. A hand clamped on Everson's shoulder and he jumped, pulling the drive levers backward, Colossus slowing as he looked backward.

"Stop the machine, Ev," Cassie said.

He disengaged the drive levers and pulled the break, bringing them to a stop.

"What's this about?" He turned back to find Cassie at the door with their only Chaos trap in her hand.

"I'm getting out."

"You needn't worry," Ivy said. "Remember the augmentations we did to this thing? It should be fairly safe."

Cassie arched a brow. "Should be?" Ivy glanced at Everson, but before he could reply, Cassie said, "Never mind. That's not why I'm getting out." She opened the door as Curan and Gorgant settled on the road beside them. "I'm joining Curan. It is time to use my magic for something that matters."

"What?" Ivy said with alarm.

"What about us, and why did you take the Chaos trap?" Everson asked.

Cassie turned toward him. "Do what you came to do. This is the chance for all of us to make a difference. The trap is for me. I'll need it after I use my magic on Curan."

With that, she closed the door. The thump of explosions arose from ahead, the flames flickering in gaps through the trees.

"She's right." Ivy said as she settled in beside him. "We only need two of us to make this thing lethal."

He nodded, taking a breath to firm his resolve. "Right. It is time to behave like a warden."

When the drive levers moved forward, the Chaos-Conduction engine whirred and the machine lurched into motion. The machine rounded a bend and slowed as the battle came into view.

A wall of wagons and steam carriages blocked the road, the vehicles stacked three rows deep. Well beyond the blockade, thousands of Imperial soldiers stood on an open field staring toward a burning city. Catapults at the front of the army were aimed at the city, firing bombs and bringing destruction to the innocents who lived within. The sight stirred anger within Everson as he found himself facing another bully, intent on their own agenda regardless of how it impacted others.

"Hold tight!"

He slammed both drive levers forward, the acceleration pinning him to the rear wall of the cockpit. When Colossus crashed into the narrow gap between the first two wagons, he stumbled forward, watching as the plow blades lifted the wagons, tipped them up, and pushed them aside before colliding into the second row. Again, Colossus shoved the obstacles aside and then crashed directly into a steam carriage. Colossus slowed, but the wheels continued to spin, pushing the metal carriage forward until it turned and tipped over.

Suddenly, they were in the open.

"Ready the weapon!" Everson pulled back on the drive levers, slowing Colossus to a stop while he located his first target.

Ivy stood and opened a drawer where the bronze-encased flash-bombs were stored. Everson moved Colossus forward, turning it slightly until the crosshairs he had etched into the windshield aligned with his target.

"Ready," Ivy said.

"Fire!"

The moment the catapult fired, he pushed one lever forward, pulling it to neutral when properly aligned. The first bomb struck, demolishing the enemy catapult.

"Fire!"

Another launch resulted in another catapult destroyed. The duo repeated the process, again and again, destroying the Imperial war machines and anything near them.

Cassie watched Everson drive away and turned toward Curan with a chunk of glowstone in one hand, the Chaos trap in another. The trap was bulky, larger and more powerful than the ones Everson had made for Quinn.

"Show me your rune."

Curan tossed his cloak aside and pulled up a sleeve to expose his arm. He frowned at her while she drew a rune on her own hand. "What are you doing?"

"I'm making a difference."

She lifted the glowstone, giving enough light for her to see his rune. With a belly full of determination and backed by fear, she grappled with Chaos and drew it in, absorbing as much as she had ever held. Her body trembled with the energy as it threatened to destroy its host. She poured Chaos into the symbol on Curan's arm. It glowed red, pulsed, and faded, bringing a wave of exhaustion with her magic expended.

She then pressed the Chaos trap against the rune on her hand. Pain seared her skin as raw, electric energy poured into the rune. With her teeth gritted, Cassie held the Chaos trap in place until the magic was spent. Tossing the Chaos trap aside, she waited as the rune pulsed and began to fade.

A gasp escaped as the augmentation took hold, the intake of her breath sounding louder, more distinct than normal. The darkness receded, the forest growing lighter as if it were midday.

"Be well, Curan," She said before slipping away.

When Cassie used her magic on the symbol marking his arm, Curan's vision turned white, and he feared he might fall from the saddle. His sight returned, but Cassie was gone.

"Be well, Curan." He heard her voice, but she was nowhere to be seen.

Where'd she go? He wondered. Pushing the thought aside, he dismounted. "This fight is not for you, Gorgant. Stay here where it is safe. I will return if I survive."

He turned and ran, moving faster than humanly possible, powered by the augmentation. A leap took him beyond the pile of wagons and steam carriages at the edge of the wood. He landed north of the battle-field, not far from where Colossus stood. The machine was firing flash-bombs toward Imperial war machines, across a sea of soldiers waiting for slaughter. With his shield leading, he slammed into the rear ranks, driving a particularly imposing soldier forward with enough force to knock down dozens of others.

Curan drew his sword. Enemies to the left and right drew weapons in response. Cries of rage rang out from hundreds of warriors intent on murder.

These soldiers had never fought a man under a Power augmentation. If they had, they would have run rather than fight.

Blood began to rain upon the battlefield.

Jonah ran, as did the hundreds of Kantarian soldiers with him. Captain Marcella, on her horse, led them at a trot with Thiron riding beside her. Even in the dark, it was easy to imagine the scowls imprinted on their faces.

Thumps came from ahead as fire lit the evening sky. Wayport was dying. With that much firepower, the city had to be dying. An invading army of thousands had attacked at night, something that surprised even Marcella.

Her army had trailed the enemy since leaving the prison, never approaching closer than four or five miles. When the attack began, Marcella stirred them into a hurried march. Despite a much smaller force with a single arcanist, she demanded they try to save the city. Fed with her fierce words of inspiration, that force now ran toward the enemy, banking on the advantage of surprise. Jonah just hoped they didn't die from exhaustion.

They rounded a corner, and a bridge came into view. Beyond the bridge, pandemonium.

Explosions rocked the field as the Imperial Army waited for the battle to reach them. Behind the army was a massive metal machine unlike anything Jonah had ever seen.

The Kantarian Army raced across the bridge and crashed into the east flank, swords slashing and blood-soaked as they roared. The Imperial enemy turned to receive them. Marcella hacked at surrounding enemies, and her horse trampled any who fell before her. Thiron fired arrow after arrow from the saddle, taking out Imperial soldiers at will. The flank went from calm to chaos in a moment as soldiers began to die.

Jonah avoided the melee and settled on the empty road as he considered what he should do.

He spied a tall Kantarian soldier tearing through the invaders as if they were paper dolls, his sword whirling as an unstoppable deliverer of death. It was as if he were a legend come alive. A trail of bodies lay behind him as he relentlessly marched along the army's rear flank. Then, he leaped impossibly high and landed closer to Jonah before charging into the fray, his sword swinging left and right in broad, deadly strokes that left corpses and body parts in his wake. *Power augmentation,* Jonah thought. *This is why wildcats are so dangerous.*

The Power-augmented soldier lurched when an arrow pierced his back. He lurched again and again and again as other arrows pelted him. Someone's sword thrust in and buried deep enough to emerge from his back. This grand warrior, this force of nature, crumpled to his knees.

Thunder shook the ground, and Jonah turned toward the sound. His eyes grew wide, and he cried out in fright.

Chuli rode low on Rhychue, hugging the horse as she sped down the road. Her uncle, Cameron, rode beside her on his white stallion, wearing his helm and full armor. She, he, and the Tantarri warriors were riding to war.

Four hundred warriors rode with them – all with dark topknots trailing shaved heads, dressed in leather, and armed with swords, spears, or bows. Those men and women were trained to fight from a young age, raised to be the protectors of the Tantarri nation. This fight may not be theirs, but old grudges held fast. It had been two decades since the Empire had warred with the Tantarri, yet everyone remembered. The rise of their old enemy would not be suffered, so they rode to support Cam's friend, King Brock.

As they approached the bridge, the battlefield came into view. Cam drew his sword and raised it high while he issued a battle cry, immediately returned by the riders behind him.

Marcella's troops were engaged with the invader's eastern flank, just south of the road, so Cam and the Tantarri circled around the Kantarian army and struck the enemy from behind. Chuli broke off from the group, slowing as someone standing in the road scrambled out of the way – someone familiar.

The horse drew to a stop and Chuli turned toward him. "Jonah?"

"Thank Issal you arrived!"

"Yes," She surveyed the battlefield.

"One of ours just fell, right there," He pointed toward the downed soldier. "A tall guy, charged by Chaos, fighting alone. A wildcat, I think."

"A wildcat?" Chuli spotted the man, not far from where the Tantarri were fighting.

Jonah put his hand on her leg. "Clear the path, Chuli. Perhaps I can heal him."

A surge of pride ran through Chuli. "You are a good person, Jonah." Raising her bow, she reached into her quiver, nocked an arrow, and began to fire, loosing arrow after arrow.

37

UNPREDICTABLE

Percy remained in the shadows, watching. Riva and the other scouts were with him, spread out along the edge of the forest where they had retreated to monitor the battle.

To the south, the Imperial Army continued its advance, led by the line of catapults firing on the city. The Kantarian defenders had emerged from the broken palisades and the Imperial musketeers met them, taking dozens of the Kantarians in a flash. *Things continue as planned*, Percy thought. *It cannot continue. War is too unpredictable.*

A moment later, he spotted another force in Kantarian armor racing across the bridge, led by a female soldier on horseback. Hundreds poured onto the battlefield and attacked the Imperial Army's eastern flank.

Percy was not concerned. Though unexpected, a few hundred additional soldiers would not change the outcome, not when the Imperial force still greatly outnumbered them.

He then heard a rumbling sound that gave him pause.

"What is that?"

A metal vehicle with thick wheels and a plow at the front smashed into the barricade blocking the north road, pushing wagons and steam carriages aside as if they weighed nothing. The oversized steam-carriage stopped and fired, launching two metal balls from a catapult mounted to it. A moment later, a distant Imperial catapult exploded.

"Flashbombs!" Percy hissed. "They have flashbombs!"

He took a step toward the machine and froze, still in the shadow of the trees. Someone in Kantarian armor stormed past, moving faster than humanly possible. Percy watched in awe as the man slammed into the Imperial Army, creating a dent in the rear flank as soldiers tumbled to the ground as if they were tiles lined in a row. The soldier then began laying about him with a longsword, sweeping through the Imperial force at will, leaving nothing but blood and body parts in his wake as men screamed and died.

Percy loosed an arrow at the man, but it took an Imperial soldier in the chest when his target leaped high and landed fifty feet away. There, the super-charged soldier resumed his assault, tearing through the Imperial ranks.

"Riva!" Percy said as he ran toward her. "We have to take that man out. He is using some dark magic."

She nodded, her eyes wild. "He is like death walking among us."

Thunder coming from the east had Percy turning in that direction.

Tantarri cavalry, two hundred strong, raced across the bridge and attacked the rear flank between his position and where the Kantarian army fought. The magic-imbued Kantarian soldier leaped again, changing his position before delivering death to those around him.

Percy set his jaw and issued a command, taking over for Riva, who appeared shaken. "We kill the man first and then we begin taking out those on horseback."

He ran along the woods, leading the other scouts. When he had a clear view, he loosed an arrow and then another, both striking his target. Three other arrows joined his, all five jutting from the man's back. A daring Imperial soldier thrust his sword, piercing the man and sending him to his knees. Percy drew another arrow and took aim at the man's throat.

Something slammed into him, sending the arrow astray to strike an Imperial soldier. Percy looked for his attacker and found nothing but shadows. Something flashed past the edge of his vision and Riva stumbled, her arrow striking another scout in the ribs, the man crying out as he fell to his knees. Another archer loosed an arrow when a gash appeared across his hand, killing a fellow archer by piercing his eye.

Again, Percy looked around but saw no enemy nearby.

"What sorcery is this?"

Sculdin waded through waist-deep water toward the rocky shore with his gaze fixed on the dark city walls. Not far to the east, glowlamps lit the closed south gate. In the distance, explosions continued as Wayport died.

He climbed the rocks and moved into the shadow of the wall while his squad climbed onto shore. The longships backed away with Hiaga and her crew eager to be far from Wayport. *Blazing Ri Starians*, he thought. *They honor our pact but will do nothing more.*

When the soldiers were all on shore, Sculdin waved for them to gather. They huddled in close, and he began issuing orders. Moments later, a pair of Infiltrators scurried off, hugging the wall as they ran toward the gate.

Somewhere to the north, men and women were dying. The battlefield was surely a bloody mess. By now, the northern end of the city was rubble and the populace was huddled in the citadel, praying for relief. None would come. Once Sculdin's squad captured the citadel, the fight would be over. King Brock, assuming he survived that long, would never risk the lives of those people. With the populace held hostage, Brock – or whoever led the Kantarian forces at that time – would be forced to surrender.

A series of explosions came from the gate and created a tower of fire that lit the docks.

"Let's take the city!" Sculdin roared as he broke into a run.

His force trailed him as they ran along the wall. All that remained of the gate was a pile of burning rubble and bent, twisted iron. Bricks were still burning where the wall still stood, but the gap in the middle was easy to navigate.

Once past the rubble, they advanced with caution – shields up with flashbombs, swords, and bows held ready. The streets were empty, the city eerily quiet. The bombs had stopped dropping on the city, but distant explosions continued to the north where the battle raged.

The street opened as they reached the city center. The square was empty save for a few dozen bloody, dead soldiers propped against the fountain and surrounding buildings. Sculdin paused in the square and scanned the rooftops for archers but found none. To the east, the citadel waited on a hilltop, looming above the city.

"We must take the citadel," he said to his troops. "Hold your shields high in case they have archers posted above us. Advance slowly and watch for trouble. Remain quiet and listen for my orders."

Taking the lead with his shield high, Sculdin marched down the dark road. Glowlamps waited at the far end, marking the plaza that stood outside the citadel walls. As they drew closer, the citadel gate became visible.

A squad of Kantarian guards stood before the gate, armed with swords and shields. On top of the two towers straddling the gate, archers waited.

"The last line of resistance," Sculdin said, grinning. "Infiltrators!"

His last five Infiltrators slipped in beside him, their faces locked in grim masks.

"The citadel gate must fall at any cost."

The men nodded and each removed a bomb from his pack, holding it ready.

Sculdin called out, "I need twenty soldiers to shield these men and get them within range of the gate. Just remember, once we take the citadel, Wayport will be ours."

Grouped tightly with a wedge of soldiers shielding them, the bombers advanced toward the plaza and the gate waiting on the far side. Sculdin found himself wondering what waited inside the citadel walls and how many guards Brock had left behind while mounting his counterattack.

Possessing the plans outlining the defense of the city had proven a massive advantage. The only thing that had gone wrong was the surprise sea attack and the subsequent loss of the soldiers on board the sunken longships. *Four hundred men, lost so quickly. Such a shame.*

His face drew a frown, his stomach twisting. *Something is wrong.*

A thin shimmer at the end of the road, no more than a foot above the cobblestones, reflected pale light from a nearby glowlamp, Sculdin gasped when he realized what it was. The lead soldiers stumbled…

"Trip wire!" Sculdin shrieked.

Some of the men stopped, but others stumbled into them. Along with a half-dozen soldiers holding shields, one bomber tripped, and the bomb he was holding struck the street.

38

DESPERATE MEASURES

Cassie slipped through the edge of the wood unseen, past the wagons and steam carriages blocking the road. Curan streaked past, leaped over the blockade, and attacked, bringing his fury upon the invaders. At first, Cassie gawked at the terrifying display. Then, she turned away, sickened by the brutality. Never before had she seen so much blood and violence, and it all stemmed from one person – a person who was gentle and kind-hearted despite his stature.

Yet, the situation demanded action. Cassie's parents had taught her violence was sometimes necessary to protect the innocent. The Ward had taught her how to use weapons and how to convert others into weapons themselves. Her magic ran through Curan's veins, forging him into a warrior of legend. The deaths he caused were hers as much as his. The thought forced her to stop and vomit.

With her stomach emptied, she noticed archers tucked into the woods to the east. They might be standing in dark shadows, but to her magic-infused senses, they were easy to see.

The closest in the group, a young man, issued instructions to the others. Cassie gasped when she realized what they planned. When Curan leaped to a new location further east, the archers ran along the wood to follow. She ran after them.

The archers caught up to Curan, stopped, and began firing at him, their arrows striking him in the back. Cassie launched herself at the nearest archer, the one who appeared as their leader, shoving him hard and sending his arrow astray. She kicked the next archer's arm, making her arrow hit a fellow bowman. Drawing her knife, Cassie slashed one bowman's hand, causing his arrow to strike another in the eye.

"What sorcery is this?" the leader cried as he searched for Cassie, unable to see her while she was under the Stealth augmentation.

Cassie kicked him in the crotch. When he doubled over, she kicked again, smashing his face and sending him sprawling to the ground.

"Where are you?" the female archer cried as she dropped her bow and drew a dagger.

"Who?" another archer asked.

Carefully, Cassie snuck around the perimeter of the group.

"Someone is here."

"I don't see anyone." The man sounded doubtful.

Cassie slipped in, steeling herself as she drove her dagger into the man's kidney. As he fell, she removed the blade.

The female archer backed away, her eyes filled with fear as she held her dagger out and backed away . "Show yourself!"

Cassie rushed past the woman, slicing her bowstring before the blade slid across her neck. Four archers were on the ground, two dying, one dead, the fourth unconscious. The only one standing was attempting to bandage his shooting hand.

She turned and sought Curan.

Chuli fired arrow after arrow, each striking a target with lethal accuracy as she feverishly cleared the area around the fallen Kantarian soldier until he was lying amid a pile of bodies and dying soldiers. Jonah bolted past her, climbed over the dead and knelt beside the wounded warrior. When Jonah pulled the helmet off the man, Chuli gasped.

"Curan!"

Chuli dropped off her horse and raced to kneel beside Jonah. Curan lay on his side with six arrows in his back. Blood was everywhere. Putting a foot on Curan's back, Jonah pulled an arrow free. Chuli joined in, removing two arrows while Jonah finished the others. Jonah then knelt and closed his eyes with his hand on Curan's sweat-covered brow. The fight continued around them with Tantarri warriors on horseback, Kantarian soldiers on foot, and Imperial forces all around.

An enemy soldier broke from the melee and slashed down, his blade digging into Jonah's lower back, sending blood splattering onto Chuli as she gasped in horror. Jonah's eyes popped open and his mouth moved, but no words came out. The soldier lifted his sword high, ready for a blow Chuli knew was meant to kill her. Another sword swept past and took the Imperial soldier's head off clean, his body crumpling to the ground. She looked up and saw Cam on his horse, the man's blade and armor bloodstained. He jumped down and knelt beside Curan.

"My son!" He lifted Curan off the ground and held him to his chest. "Please, no! Please, Issal," Cam cried. "Do not take him."

Chuli remained in shock, as if she were an impotent bystander to some distant nightmare, viewing a horror story and unable to change it. Jonah was dying in her lap, the gash across his lower back deep and bloody with his spine showing through. He did not move, but his chest still rose and fell with shallow, weak breaths. With no one to heal him, he would be dead in moments. She kissed the top of his head.

"I'm sorry, Jonah. Your bravery will be remembered, my dear, dear friend." Tears ran down her cheek and disappeared into his red hair.

There, the four people remained – Cam holding Curan, Chuli holding Jonah. All the while, men and women died around them, fighting over differing ideals. The irony left her wondering how it had come to such a disastrous end.

No matter who won, the dead on the battlefield would remain dead. People elsewhere would go on, living their lives regardless of the outcome. Only those who could touch Chaos were at risk should the Empire win. Yet, she couldn't deny those people the right to carry out their lives to the fullest. *Whether slavery or genocide, it is wrong to condemn others for who they are or for what they believe. Our actions alone should determine the sentence we are to serve.*

Something struck Chuli's shoulder, stirring her from her reverie. She saw nothing but a flicker in the corner of her eye. Curan stirred and Cam relaxed his embrace.

"Son?"

Curan's eyes flickered open and he groaned. "I feel like a pincushion."

Cam laughed as he hugged his son tightly.

Jonah shook with a violent shudder in Chuli's arms. She watched in amazement as the gash across his back wove shut, the rip in his tunic revealing smooth, pale skin surrounded by blood-soaked cloth.

"What?" She gasped. "How?"

A familiar female voice came from nowhere. "I healed him. It was a near thing – an extremely difficult thing. I only hope he can still walk."

"Cassie?" said Chuli. When she reached out toward where the voice came from, she found nothing but empty air.

Everson called for Ivy to launch again. He dared not tell her what was coming, not while they could still impact the battle. An Imperial officer on horseback rode toward them, his eyes alight with a fiery rage. He pulled his horse short and threw something.

"Get down!" Everson crouched low.

The bomb struck, the sound blasting in Everson's ears and rocking Colossus enough to send him to the floor. He looked up and found receding flames outside the windows.

"It held! Colossus survived a flashbomb!" He and Ivy climbed to their feet. "Flip the lever and crank those launch arms back again."

She nodded, despite appearing shaken.

Everson peered out the window and saw the man on horseback shouting orders. Turning Colossus, Everson called for another launch. Hundreds of musketeers ran up alongside the man on the horse and began to shoot at the machine. Thuds and tings came from the slugs striking the magic-augmented metal body, but Colossus held steady.

Again, Everson turned the machine as he set his sights. "Fire!" he shouted, feeling more confident as Ivy sent two more bronze flashbombs toward the Imperial war machines.

A group of five soldiers in black ran forward, tossed bombs at Colossus, and ran away.

"Get down!" Everson squatted and held to the wall.

The blast was more significant, the explosion strong enough to tip

Colossus up where it balanced for a moment and then fell on its side. Everson and Ivy slammed against the wall. Luckily, their remaining flashbombs held tight in the padded storage compartments.

Everson slowly got to his feet. His shoulder throbbed and his neck was sore. A few feet away, Ivy's forehead was bloody, her eyes closed, her body still.

"Ivy!" He knelt beside her and found her breathing.

They were on a battlefield and tipped up like a turtle on its back. Helpless, the enemy would soon have the door open. Panic began to squeeze Everson's throat and he wheezed for air, panting. He heard his sister's voice in his head. *Calm down, Everson. Use your brilliant mind. You'll think of something.*

With conscious effort, he slowed his breathing and then spotted a bronze ball still clutched in Ivy's hand. He grew alarmed. If it had gone off...

He took the bomb from her and looked up at the cab door and the starry sky beyond it. An idea formed, but it would require perfect timing. He gathered Ivy into his arms and squatted on the floor while staring up at the door. Holding the squat was easy – nothing more than allowing his mechanical legs to remain in position. However, it wasn't just any position. It was a position of potential – a position of power waiting to be unleashed.

A face appeared in the window above him, grinning like a reaper come to take him. Everson waited. The face disappeared. Moments later, the door opened. When it did, Everson released the power in his legs. The result was a Chaos-charged leap that sent him through the opening in a flash.

Up and up Everson sailed. As he rose, he dropped the bomb in his hand. The bomb tumbled past the surprised enemies who surrounded Colossus and fell into the cab. It detonated, igniting the other bombs inside to create a massive explosion that consumed everything nearby and launched the officer off his horse. A burst of hot air arose beneath Everson and lifted him even higher, but he held tight to Ivy and remained upright.

Everson's momentum died, his arc peaking at eighty feet before he began to fall as the inferno below billowed and receded. Thirty feet from Colossus, his metal legs landed amid burning grass, his knees bending as the compressed air released from his legs and absorbed the impact. He then burst into a run, carrying Ivy toward the road and away from the fighting.

Broland lay still, taking slow, even breaths, doing his best to keep his chest from rising. Led by a man in a gold tabard, the invaders crossed the square and circled the fountain. The soldiers moved slowly, warily eyeing their surroundings.

Stopping just a few strides from where Broland sat, the leader held his hand up and said, "We must take the citadel. Hold your shields high in case they have archers posted above. Advance slowly and watch for trouble. Remain quiet and listen for my orders."

The enemy resumed their careful advance, some of the invaders actually stepping over Broland and the others who lay against the fountain.

His neck ached from the odd position he maintained, doing his best to appear dead. The pig's blood on his neck and arm was wet and disgusting. Rather than dwell on the blood, he prayed none of the Imperial soldiers chose to be thorough and use their swords to poke him or the other "dead" Kantarian soldiers. When the last soldier passed on, an exhale of relief slipped out.

Moving with care to remain silent, he and the other dead men climbed to their feet. He slid his hand into the cold fountain water and grasped the hilt of his sword, drawing it out slowly.

With soft steps, Broland crept toward the nearest building, placing him out of the sightline of the enemy. He dried his palm on his breeches and adjusted his shield as a force of sixty guards gathered around him. Blood-smeared and grim-faced, they were a frightening sight.

"Get ready," Broland said in a hushed voice. "We must strike them from behind before they see us. If the trip wire doesn't work, the archers on the tower will blow the horn. Either signal and we attack."

Moments later, he heard a shout, followed by the rapid thumps of multiple explosions.

"Now!"

He turned the corner and found a billowing tower of fire blocking the far end of the street. The Imperial soldiers had their shields raised, their backs facing Broland and his squad. Broland reached the rear flank and sliced low, sweeping his blade across the hamstrings of three enemy fighters. The men cried out as they fell to the street, and he leaped forward to strike again.

The other Kantarian fighters attacked with blades slashing and thrusting in a melee of blood, shouts, and screams. The invaders turned to counter the attack but faltered when doors along the lane opened and Kantarian soldiers leaped out with blades flashing.

In a minute, half the Imperial force was down. Broland pressed forward at the head of a wedge with his blade slashing repeatedly, his shield deflecting blows as the enemy faltered and tried to retreat but were unable to do so with the fire behind them and attacks coming from all sides.

Suddenly, the man in the gold tabard was there – the Imperial captain.

The man came at Broland, his sword flicking in. Broland knocked it away, but not quick enough as the blade slashed across his stomach, cutting through his leather armor in a streak of blood. The wound was shallow, but it burned.

Broland held his shield closer, blocking the next strike before countering with his own. The man's face was as an intense scowl, his eyes a mixture of determination and fury. His blade flicked again and Broland redirected it. The sound of fighting around them was furious, the street slick with blood, but the man would not yield.

Tiring, Broland made a desperate thrust. The man twisted and countered, but his thrust was deflected by Broland's shield. The man's shoulder dipped, and Broland lowered his shield to block an expected low strike but missed when the man swept his sword upward. The sword slid beneath the plates on Broland's shoulder and bit deep enough to lodge into the bone. He cried out, and the man jerked his sword free.

Blood spurted from the gash and Broland's shield suddenly was too heavy to lift. His shoulder throbbed with searing pain as blood seeped down his arm. Sensing the advantage, the man attacked with fury, forcing Broland backward. Broland's heel struck a downed soldier and he stumbled, falling to land on the dead man. His sword slipped from his palm and tumbled away. The enemy captain leaped forward, his sword coming down in a killing thrust. Broland rolled aside, the sword just missing him as it buried deep into the dead soldier.

A lost dagger lay on the street inches from Broland's hand. He grabbed the hilt, rolled again, and made a desperate throw. The blade pierced the enemy captain's eye, burying deep. His head jerked backward and he staggered, swinging his sword blindly. The man fell to one knee and lifted his sword in defiance before tipping sideways. He crashed to the street, dead.

Broland gritted his teeth and sat upright. The slice across his stomach burned, the deep gash in his arm throbbed, and his arm was drenched with blood. A wave a nausea hit him, and the world spun. He fell to his side, his head landing on a dead Imperial soldier. There he lay as the sound of the surrounding fight faded. The fires were dying down while a line of Kantarian guards waited beyond the flames, the heat twisting the image. His eyes drifted closed but he forced them open, fearing he would never wake if he allowed himself to sleep. Everything was blurry, his head lost in a fog of pain. He was losing too much blood, but he lacked the strength to do anything about it. The fog thickened, his eyelids growing too heavy to lift as darkness crept in, consuming him.

Brock's staff whirled, his body constantly moving as he hit one Imperial soldier after another. Backed by the Power rune, his strength, speed, and stamina made him and his squad super human. So long as the enemy couldn't hit him with a musket shot, arrow, or sword, he was unstoppable.

A musket flashed toward him and he smashed it, sending the weapon flipping through the air. A sweep took the musketeer's legs out, breaking them as he collapsed with a scream.

Leaping, Brock landed behind a group of enemies clustered around a squad of Kantarian soldiers. He swept the legs out from five men with one strike, the men falling in a pile of broken bones and dropped weapons. Another swing hit three men in the helmets, knocking them all unconscious. He leaped again and slammed his staff down across three aimed muskets as he landed, knocking the weapons to the ground and breaking the hands, fingers, and wrists of those who held them.

All around, men and women were dying. Hundreds, if not thousands, already lay dead. It was time to stop the killing.

With giant, running leaps, he covered hundreds of feet in the passing of a breath. He leaped again and landed on top of Irongrip's Rock, the towering formation in the middle of the field. To the north, the battle raged. To the south, the city burned.

Brock pulled a chunk of glowstone from his pocket and traced two runes on the rock. He then embraced the surrounding energy of Chaos, drawing it in. He had saved his magic for this moment. The storm raged inside him and, still, he absorbed Chaos, more than he had ever held. Almost blinded by the tempest within, Brock poured the magic into one rune and then the other, falling to one knee and nearly fainting from the wave of exhaustion that followed.

The first rune pulsed and faded. The rock formation flared bright white. Realizing what would happen, Brock leaped away as the other augmentation came to fruition. A massive crack resounded across the battlefield, and bright glowing rock shards sprayed through the air, some pelting him as he sailed away.

39

MAYHEM

I gnoring the pain from his broken cheekbone, Percy ran through the shadows, watching the battle unfold. The sight was total mayhem with the Imperial forces broken into fragmented, disorganized groups. Neither Mollis nor Brillens had considered attacks coming from multiple fronts. The result was disastrous. Little time remained to reorganize before it was too late.

When he came upon the burning, twisted remains of the odd vehicle he had seen earlier, Percy felt relief that something had gone right. It wasn't until he circled the wreckage that he discovered what the explosion had rendered.

Hundreds of Imperial soldiers lay dead, some blown apart, others burnt husks. Among them was a dead horse, impaled by a chunk of metal. Mollis lay beside the horse, the man staring at nothing, his neck twisted in an unnatural position. A healer in a purple cloak was kneeling beside Mollis. She looked up at Percy, their eyes meeting. The woman shook her head. Mollis was dead.

Since Mollis would be no help, Percy ran down the gravel road in search of Brillens.

He passed a cluster of swordsmen who were fighting a single Kantarian soldier. The man's sword sliced, cutting through his attackers without resistance. *Chaos magic*, Percy thought. *He must die.*

Percy slowed, drew three arrows, and loosed them in rapid succession. Each arrow found its mark, two striking the man in the back, the third in the hamstring. The man stumbled to a knee and a sword sliced in, decapitating him. With the soldier dead, Percy ran forward to continue his search.

He finally spotted Brillens shouting orders to his musketeers. A female soldier in Kantarian armor leaped high, sailing into the air with her sword ready. Musketeers fired, shots striking the woman and causing her to jerk in a series of rapid lurches. She fell to the ground, and Imperial forces converged on her.

Percy called out, "Brillens," as he drew near.

The man turned toward him, lifted his hand to acknowledge Percy, and his head jerked backward. An arrow stuck out from the man's cheek, and his eyes widened in horror. Another arrow buried itself in the man's chest. As Brillens fell from the saddle, Percy turned to search out the assailant.

The Kantarian archer was a middle-aged man with dark hair and hawk-like eyes. Percy loosed two arrows before the man could spot him. The first took the man in the shoulder, the second buried in the man's stomach. The Kantarian archer fell to his knees, and Percy rushed him and buried his dagger in the man's temple. He pulled it free and moved along, seeking his next target.

The battlefield bloomed with light, as if the sun had suddenly risen. The roar of battle fell to a hush, the moans of the wounded and dying the only sounds. A massive crack sounded from the direction of the light as bits of brightly glowing rock blasted from it and rained on the battlefield.

When Percy's eyes adjusted, the sight left his jaw slack and his mind struggling to accept.

Somehow, a massive, shining monster of white rock stood before him. On two legs, the rock monster advanced toward the heart of the battle, emitting a grinding rumble with each step. The ground shook, and troops retreated in haste to avoid being crushed by thousands of tons of rock. A boulder-sized first smashed into the ground, sending a spray of dirt into the air. While others retreated in fear, Percy found himself rooted, transfixed as his mind grappled with what his eyes witnessed.

Muskets fired, arrows loosed, all striking the rock monster. None had any effect. Perhaps flashbombs could damage it, but Percy doubted any remained. He hadn't heard an explosion in some time.

At that moment, an explosion came from somewhere deep inside the city. *Sculdin,* Percy thought. *He is taking the citadel.*

Bows and muskets were lowered as everyone realized they could do no damage to the monster. Soldiers backed away from the glowing abomination. The shadow of a man suddenly appeared on top of the white, glowing rock, and the monster halted a mere hundred feet before Percy.

With a staff raised high, the man on the rock monster bellowed, "Stop!"

A heavy silence fell over the battlefield.

"Lay down your weapons. You do not need to die today. Enough have already paid that price."

Silence.

"I will say it one last time. Lay down your weapons. You cannot win, so why die? Is it worth your life so the Empire can further its conquest?"

Imperial troops began throwing down their weapons.

"No!" Percy shouted.

Nobody listened.

Rage built up inside Percy. He would not allow the twisted magic of Chaos to win. Rather than dropping his bow, he fired three arrows at the man on the living rock.

The first shot took the man in the arm, the second in the thigh, the third in the chest. The man staggered, but he did not fall. After cries of shock, a hush fell over the crowd who stared in transfixed shock. And then, they all gasped.

The arrow in the man's arm popped out and fell, leaving a trail of blood. The man lurched and the arrow in his leg came out on its own and flew toward the crowd below. When the last arrow burst from the man's chest, blood bubbled from the wound. The blood stopped, and the three wounds closed on their own as the crowd remained transfixed in stunned silence.

"What in the name of Issal?" Percy exclaimed.

"I, King Brock, demand that you throw down your weapons." The man on the rock commanded. "As you can see, Issal has healed me, for he wishes the killing to end."

The use of Issal's name stirred Percy's rage. *How dare one who wields the evil of Chaos even mention God?*

Percy again drew an arrow, this time aiming for the man's head. Focusing on his target, he pulled the bowstring back, and his arm suddenly lurched forward, his arrow falling short and striking the rock beast. He looked down and found an arrow poking through his forearm.

"What?"

He staggered as pain seared his neck. Falling to one knee, his hand went to his neck and he felt another arrow. Blood bubbled up inside his throat. He coughed and choked. Fear struck him – fear of death, fear he had done something to disappoint Issal, fear he might not be rewarded in the next life.

Someone stepped in front of him – a female form who eclipsed the light.

"You lost, Percy," Chuli said. "The first arrow was for Darnya and Simone, who you murdered. It was also for Quinn, who you betrayed." She stepped closer and snarled, "The last arrow, the one in your throat, that was for Thiron, the archer you killed moments ago."

A choking, blood-filled cough was the only reply Percy could muster before he fell face-down and died.

40

A MIRACLE

Cassie slipped through the battlefield, careful to avoid swinging weapons. Here and there, she would find a wounded Kantarian or Tantarri warrior and heal them before moving along. Each time, the person would look around in shock, likely believing their recovery a miracle. Saving lives felt good, and she knew she was making a difference.

She then spotted Thiron, firing arrows toward an Imperial officer on horseback. An enemy arrow hit Thiron in the shoulder, another in his stomach, sending him to his knees. Before Cassie could react, someone ran in and stabbed Thiron in the temple before hurrying off.

Cassie rushed forward, ducking beneath a sword that almost clipped her, and slid in beside the fallen ranger.

Thiron's angular eyes were open, and blood ran down the side of his face. Cassie put her hand on his forehead, but the man was already dead.

A bright glow flared, the light painful to her heightened senses. Cassie shielded her eyes and willed them to adjust. Moments passed, and she heard a loud crack.

When she looked up again through squinting eyes, a massive, glowing rockpile was advancing toward her. The rock monster slammed a fist into the ground and stopped just over a hundred feet away.

She then heard a man call out, "Stop!"

Cassie gasped as the battlefield fell silent.

"Lay down your weapons," the man said in a voice she knew well. "You do not need to die today. Enough have already paid that price."

"Father?" Cassie gasped in wonder. "You live?"

Her heart soared at hearing his voice, but she struggled to look into the light to confirm it was truly him. Compelled to divine the truth, Cassie moved against the tide of retreating soldiers and, instead, walked toward the animated rock monster.

When her father issued a command for everyone to drop their weapons, all fell silent. He repeated the command and many obeyed, but not everyone. Squinting at the light, Cassie gazed up at the silhouette, but she was still unable to see clearly to confirm it was him.

Steeling herself, she reached the leg of the rock monster and began to climb. The beast neither moved nor acknowledged her presence. When Cassie neared the top, she stood and looked up to find her father standing just a few strides away. *It is him! He lives!*

Brock lurched when an arrow struck his upper arm. He grunted when another pierced his thigh. He staggered when a third buried deep into his chest.

"Father!" Cassie cried as she scrambled up the rock.

"Cassie?" he said between gritted teeth, his eyes still looking over the battlefield.

When Cassie noticed a Power rune drawn on his hand, she knew the augmentation was the only thing keeping him upright.

She put her hand on his arm. "I'm here." Tears blurred her vision. "Hold on."

Gripping the arrow in his arm, she twisted it and pulled it out, drawing a trail of blood. After discarding the arrow, she worked on the one in his thigh, removing it and tossing it aside as he groaned at the pain. The arrow in his chest posed the biggest risk. She would have to heal him even as she removed it so he wouldn't bleed out.

With one fist around the arrow shaft and the other gripping her father's wrist, Cassie found her center, extended her awareness toward him, and pulled the arrow free. The Chaos of the man's wounds raged and she fought to contain it, to smother it with his own Power-augmented source of Order. It was a struggle of nature against her will, a struggle against time. The wounds wove closed, and the bleeding stopped as a shudder shook his body and left him gasping.

"Thank you, Cassie," he said quietly before standing tall and calling out to the crowd. "I, King Brock, demand that you throw down your weapons." He raised his healed arm, lifting his staff high. "As you can see, Issal has healed me, for he wishes the killing to end."

Incredibly, the remaining soldiers began tossing weapons aside, many of them collapsing to the ground.

The battle was over.

—+ φ +—

A shiver shook Broland, and he gasped for air. His eyes opened to find the citadel minister beside him, concern apparent on the man's face.

"Thank Issal," Minister Dryfus said. "I feared I might be too late, but I couldn't reach you until the fires died down."

Broland's stomach rumbled as he sat up. He felt through the gap in his armor and found his gash closed, the wound healed. Blood still covered his arm, but the flesh had been mended.

Rising to his feet, he stumbled and fell to one knee, supporting himself on the dead man beside him.

"Careful, your Highness," Dryfus said. "You lost a lot of blood."

"Yes, Dryfus," he said, glancing down the street. Over a hundred lay dead, the majority in Imperial armor. Along the side of the street, Kantarian guards stood with weapons ready, watching Imperial fighters who stood weaponless with their hands behind their heads. "See if there are others you can help."

The minister hurried off as Broland stood, wavering as the world tilted and spots danced before his eyes. Kantarian soldiers marched in past him with ropes and shackles in hand to bind the prisoners. The city was safe, at least for now. Broland felt relieved, but he shook with hunger.

"Gather them up," he said with as much force as he could muster. "Strip them of weapons and escort them to the dungeons. We will hold them until my father returns."

With the order issued, he turned and staggered down the street. He passed the rubble of the destroyed buildings at the end, walked through the three-foot deep hole from the bombs, and crossed the plaza outside the citadel wall. Archers on the tower cheered as he approached the gate.

Pausing, he waited for the gate to rise, the chain clanking as the guards cranked up the portcullis. When it was locked into position, he entered and joined the frightened citizens of Wayport.

People were huddled in clusters from wall to wall, all turning toward him as he crossed the square. Children stood beside parents while mothers held them close and fathers looked on in concern. The crowd ranged from infants to the elderly – a populace who feared for their lives, fear reflecting from each set of eyes he met.

After climbing halfway up the stairs, Broland turned toward the crowd.

"The immediate threat has passed," he shouted, "but a hostile army remains outside the city. Until my father returns, I beg of you to remain here, where you are safest."

With that said, he sat on the stairs with a sigh, exhausted.

"Can someone please get me something to eat?"

41

AFTERMATH

The days following the battle were busy for everyone. Farmers left the city to return to their homes. The citizens of Wayport did the same, at least those whose homes had not been destroyed. Those who had no other place to live were provided housing within the Citadel with the promise that their homes would soon be rebuilt.

Once stripped of their weapons and having given an oath toward peace, the Imperial soldiers were set free. Their only penance was to help clean up the destroyed north quadrant of the city and to help dispose of the dead. The latter was a concern, requiring haste to ensure the corpses did not fester. Pestilence trailing a battle of this scope was a true danger. With two thousand bodies to bury, there was little choice but to perform a mass funeral.

The dead were stacked around the massive boulder in the heart of the battlefield, which was once again a dull gray inanimate pile of rock. The survivors from both sides gathered in a huge circle with the dead and the rock at the center. Minister Dryfus led the funeral proceedings with a brief, but sorrow-filled prayer. Cassie used a Heat augmentation to set the giant rock ablaze, creating an intense heat easily felt from two hundred feet away. The bodies burned quickly and were reduced to ash. When the fire subsided, the ash was gathered and dumped into the sea.

Late on the second day after the battle, Cassie went in search of her father and brother to convince them to join her for a trip to the docks. She wished the reason for the outing to remain a surprise, which made convincing them difficult. After extended cajoling and promises that the trip would be worth it, her father finally gave in. Pretencia and Captain Marcella had been meeting with Brock and Broland at the time. They decided to join the party after Cassie had sufficiently stirred their curiosity.

She led them from the chamber her father had claimed after the destruction of the throne room and down to the receiving hall. There they met Everson, Ivy, Chuli, Curan and Jonah, who had been waiting at her request.

Jonah rested in Curan's arms like an oversized baby. His legs lacked feeling and function since his injury, and the paralysis had affected him dramatically. Gone were the smiles and jokes Cassie had grown used to, replaced with a melancholy mood. She could not blame him. Though he was lucky to have survived, what would his life be like without the use of his legs?

Everson gave Jonah a hopeful smile. "I understand, Jonah. I lived most of my life burdened with my weak legs. I solved the problem for myself. I can do the same for you."

For the first time since waking from his injury, hope glimmered in Jonah's green eyes. "Thanks, Ev. You have always been a great friend."

"I am simply returning the friendship you have shown to me."

After an uncomfortable moment of quiet, Everson turned toward Cassie. "What's this about, Cassie? Why so cryptic?"

Cassie's father stopped behind Everson, raising a brow and adding, "Yes, Cassie. Tell us."

Everson turned and gasped when he noticed Brock. He bowed and stammered, "I...I'm sorry, your Majesty. I didn't..."

"Don't worry about it, Everson." Brock put a hand on Everson's shoulder. "We are all friends here." He then turned to Cassie. "What is this about?"

She smiled and shook her head. "Sorry. I'll not ruin the surprise."

A woman's voice came from behind her. "What surprise?"

Cassie turned as Tenzi and Parker entered the room. Parker's head was as bald as her father's – the result of escaping their ship during a flashbomb explosion. Tenzi had fared better. Her hair was now shorter, but she had lost her hat in the fire.

"We are taking a stroll down to the docks. Would you like to join us?"

Tenzi glanced at Parker. "I guess. As a pair of sailors without anything to sail, we have little else to do at the moment."

Brock placed his hand on her shoulder. "Patience, Tenzi. I told you I would get you a ship."

She nodded. "I know. It just makes me feel...like I've lost a limb or something." Her eyes landed on Marcella and widened. "Oh, I'm sorry. I need to watch what I say."

Marcella's sword arm ended at the shoulder after losing it in the heat of battle. Despite the apology, she glared at Tenzi as if ready to start a fight.

"Peace, Marcella," Brock said. "Tenzi meant nothing by it."

"Yes, your Majesty," she replied, though her face remained clouded. "I'm sure she didn't intend to remind me of how useless I am now – just a washed-up warrior unable to swing a weapon."

"Put the past behind you, Marcella," Brock said. "You no longer need to swing a sword. Your mind is the weapon that will best serve me moving forward."

Marcella shrugged. "As you have told me."

"You reported to Gunther, and you know the condition he suffered during the years prior to his death. He was less able to take the field than you are now, yet he proved his value time and again as a leader and an advisor. Did you respect him any less just because he couldn't wield a sword?"

The woman blinked. "No, I guess not."

"Good." Brock nodded. "Now, leave your days on the battlefield behind you. I need you to focus on what you can do as my general and advisor."

Cassie cleared her throat to reclaim their attention. "If everyone is ready, we should leave or we will be late."

Broland frowned at her. "Late for what, Cassie?"

She grinned. "You'll see."

With Cassie in the lead, they headed out the front door and down the stairs, gathering an escort of a dozen guards along the way. Once outside the citadel walls, they crossed the plaza and the recently repaired section of the street. The rubble from the destroyed buildings had been removed, but the repairs had not yet begun. The streets were filled with people who moved aside to allow them past, many clapping and cheering. Death had come to their doorstep, and the group passing by had led the defense that preserved the city and saved many lives.

Here and there, shop owners and farmers held food or trinkets toward the group as gifts. Cassie accepted an apple with thanks, and some others accepted food as well. Her father, however, took nothing and said nothing, but rather nodded and shared a forced smile. Cassie knew the deaths and destruction weighed heavily on him. He was the King, and the citizens of Kantaria were his responsibility. Leading the defense of the city only made it more evident.

Cassie put her hand on her father's arm. "You did your best, Father. We survived as did thousands of others who would be dead if you had failed."

Again, he nodded but said nothing.

In the square, farmers stood beside their carts and clusters of people were sharing stories, buying food, and enjoying the afternoon. Everything felt as it should be. A group of young women filling buckets from the fountain paused and stared as the group marched past. The girls held their hands to their heart as they stared at Cassie's older brother with doughy eyes.

Foiling the capture of Wayport had gained Broland a hero's status. As a young, attractive prince, he had also stolen the hearts of many. When Cassie noticed her brother smiling and waving at the girls, she flicked his ear with her finger.

"Ouch. What's that for?"

"Your head was growing a bit big, so I was trying to pop it."

"Funny."

She grinned. "I thought so."

The procession turned south and entered another busy street. Cheers again followed in their wake, along with shouts for King Brock. Hearing those cheers made Cassie proud. The people of Wayport clearly loved her father as the people of Kantar had for years.

They passed through the gap in the wall where the south gate had once stood, and the ocean breeze hit them, blowing Cassie's hair back and forcing her to squint. The western pier remained intact. The far end of the east pier, which stood closer to the river inlet, had collapsed and burned with only broken and charred pilings now jutting above the water. Just beyond the pier, the remains of sunken wrecks dotted the bay with masts and hull sections visible. Further out, a single ship was sailing into port.

Cassie led everyone down the pier, watching the approaching craft as it furled its sails. The ship drew near the pier and met the approaching dock workers who caught thrown lines and guided the vessel in before tying them off. By the time the ship was docked, Cassie and her entourage were approaching the end of the pier.

The boarding plank was extended and lowered to the dock. A sailor crossed the plank and began speaking with the dock workers.

"Cassie," Brock said, sounding annoyed. "I have much to do. Why are we here?"

Her face split in a grin, and she pointed. "That's why."

Brandt, Quinn, and Delvin appeared at the ship's rail. Cassie waved, and Brandt waved back at her.

"Everson!" Quinn blurted as she ran down the plank and hugged her brother.

Brandt followed to hug Cassie, lifting and spinning her, his embrace squeezing her hard enough to force a cough. He set her down and clasped Broland's arm, both smiling broadly. Turning toward his father, Brandt nodded.

"Hello, Father."

A tear ran down Brock's face, and he embraced Brandt with a bear hug. "I feared I might never see you again, Son."

Cassie wiped tears from her eyes as she turned toward Quinn, who had finished hugging Chuli. "I'm glad you kept him alive."

Quinn smirked at Brandt. "It wasn't easy."

Delvin clapped his hands, drawing everyone's attention. "If you are finished with your blabbering, I could really use a hot meal and a soothing bath."

They laughed, turned, and headed back toward the citadel with Cassie feeling better than she had in months.

Broland and the others listened intently as Brandt relayed his tale – a tale that began with the blond girl standing beside him. This girl, Quinn, first arrived in Sol Polis to take a position as a maid at the citadel. With a conniving plan and a bit of luck, she soon finagled her way into the Archon's trust and became the woman's personal bodyguard. The duo then described how they freed King Pretencia from the dungeons and sent him off to Sol Polis on Tenzi's ship. Pretencia, who had joined them in Brock's study, reiterated his thanks to Brandt and Quinn. While the king's escape had been impressive, things only grew more incredible after that.

Stealing a map marking the secret location where flash powder weapons were crafted led to another mission. Brandt and Quinn had journeyed to an old, hidden castle in the Sol Kai Mountains, infiltrated the facility, and destroyed it before fleeing for their lives.

"Hold on, Brandt," Broland's father said. "Where did you learn about this Speed rune?"

Brandt looked at Cassie with an arched brow. She shrugged. "I thought Cassie would have told you by now. She discovered it shortly before I left for Sol Polis. We tested it once on an animated boulder but never on a human until that moment."

Brock stared at Brandt for a long moment. "You do realize how dangerous that was?"

Nodding, Brandt's gaze found the floor. "Yes. I know." He looked back up at the man. "Desperation..."

"Sometimes outweighs risk," Brock finished the sentence. "I know quite well." He then turned to Cassie. "You can visit the dreams of others and discover new uses for Chaos. What else are you not telling me? What other uses have you found?"

"You now know it all, Father," Cassie said. "I already told you about the Stealth augmentation and of how I woke Mother from her coma. The Speed rune was the only other thing of note."

"Stealth augmentation?" Brandt asked, now his turn to arch a brow at Cassie.

She grinned. "It's wonderful, Brandt. Your footsteps and movements are silent, and you are nearly invisible, even in broad daylight."

"Nearly?"

"Apparently, movements are sometimes perceptible from someone's peripheral vision."

"Now *that* is an interesting use of magic," Delvin Garber said, slouching on the sofa, his hand on his belly as if he had overeaten – which was likely after the way the man had attacked his food. "I would very much like to test it out."

Brandt ignored him and focused on his sister. "And, other than peripheral movement, you are undetectable when using this rune?"

"Yes. Well, other than perhaps your odor." Cassie grinned. "You *do* need a bath, you know."

"He does," Quinn agreed. "As do I. It has been a hard week, and I can barely stand my own scent at the moment." Her eyes widened and she looked at Brock. "I apologize if that was inappropriate, your Majesty."

Brock waved her off. "You need not worry. We are all friends here, and we may set the titles aside for now. It's best if I just hear the straight of it, without propriety interfering."

Resuming his tale, Brandt explained how he and Quinn had recovered in Yarth while waiting for a new mission objective. That wait ended when given the task of joining the Imperial Army. The very night they learned that the army was to march west, they were discovered by the Archon's son, Ikonis. Knocking the young man unconscious, they escaped and headed west.

The next revelation was shocking to all, a move of pure brilliance. By destroying the road leading west from Yarth to Hipoint, Brandt and Quinn had effectively cut off half the Imperial Army, including the cavalry unit, leaving them unable to join the attack on Wayport.

Brock stared into space as he considered the news. "As things stood, there were moments where the battle could have gone either way, the gap between victory and loss far too narrow for my liking. I shudder to think what would have happened had we faced four thousand additional soldiers and an expanded supply of flashbombs."

Quinn said, "Winning the battle here was just one reason to prevent the advance of the army."

"What do you mean?" Cassie asked.

"During our time at the Imperial garrison, Brandt and I grew to know the people in our squads. Many had no idea why they were even fighting.

Most turned out to be good, honest people who were forced into service." Anger came through Quinn's voice. "Even to their own people, the Empire was nothing but a bully in disguise, hiding behind their righteous cause."

"What Quinn means is that we didn't want to see those people die merely to further the Empire's agenda. It's why we devised the plan to stop the army's advance in the first place. The benefit to the defense of Wayport was an afterthought."

Pretencia spoke up. "Well, whatever the motive, you two did a wonderful thing."

"Yes, and we are all thankful for it." Brock frowned at Delvin, who was busy examining his fingernails. "That still doesn't explain how you came to arrive here on a ship with your Master Espion."

Brandt nodded. "Right." He turned toward Quinn, who was scowling at Delvin. "The moment after we collapsed the cliffside, and the road fell into the sea, we were captured by the Archon's son and some other riders. The Speed rune I had been forced to use to survive the destruction of the roadway also left me exhausted and unable to do anything but surrender. We were bound and returned to the garrison in Yarth as prisoners. The next day, we arrived in Sol Polis, where the Archon and Council were sure to execute us for treason. Instead of meeting our end, we ran into Delvin and discovered what he had done.

"We entered the chamber where we thought we would hear our death sentence and found Archon Varius, General Kardan, and all eight Council members dead from poison. Of course, this sent the Archon's son into a rage. I have little doubt we would be dead if Delvin had not returned to save us."

Quinn snorted. "Delvin would be dead as well if I hadn't saved him."

"You believe that, don't you?" Delvin said with a smirk on his face.

"I know Ikonis well. His skill with the longsword is unrivaled. He is strong, quick, and would have gutted you on the spot if I hadn't tripped him."

That name, Ikonis. It sounded vaguely familiar. Broland only knew one person who could best him in a duel, and that was the person who had betrayed him.

"Hold on," Broland said a bit too loudly, drawing everyone's attention. "This Ikonis. Is he about this tall?" Broland held his hand a few inches above his own head. "Does he have black hair and amber eyes?"

Brandt shrugged. "Yeah, I guess."

"Don't let those eyes fool you," Quinn added.

"Kony," Broland said. "He told us his name was Kony. He tried to kill me, Mother and Father as well."

Brandt gave Quinn a questioning look.

"After Iko arrived in Sol Polis, I overheard a discussion about it but was afraid to tell you." Quinn reached out and took his hand. "They believed your father and brother to be dead. I...I didn't want to put you through such pain until I knew the truth of it."

With narrowed eyes, Brandt stared at her. "You hid this from me?"

"Yes. I'm sorry, but telling you would have inflicted pain. I...I couldn't bear to do it." She nodded toward Brock and Broland. "When we arrived here and found them alive, I was glad I didn't, even if it was wrong."

"She wasn't the only one," Cassie said, biting her lip as Brandt turned toward her. "I knew..." Her voice trailed off as she stared at him. A long moment of silence followed.

"I guess I should thank you for sparing me the pain. I just...find it irritating to be the last to know."

Brock stood and moved closer to Brandt, looking him in the eye. "Setting your hurt feelings aside, are Varius and the others positively dead?"

"Yes. Very much so."

Brock turned and strolled toward the window with his hands clasped behind his back, lost in thought. Although he stared toward the sea, all was black with the harbor now fully in night's grip. After a long moment of silence, he turned and addressed the room.

"The Empire was driven by the old leaders of The Hand. Those people are now dead. The flashpowder weapons the Imperial Army used are all but gone, the facility where those weapons were crafted now destroyed. A third of their army has been reduced to ash, and many of those who remain have plead fealty to Kantaria. It seems that the threat has passed and, perhaps, we can now live in peace."

Pretencia stood and approached Brock's desk, leaning forward with his hands on it as he spoke. "What of my kingdom, Brock? Kalimar remains under their control."

"Would you risk the lives of your citizens just to take it back, Dalwin?

What of Vinacci and eastern Hurnsdom? Would they be next? How long must we fight? How many more lives must we lose?"

"They stole my kingdom from me, Brock!" Pretencia slammed his fist on the desk.

Brock's face turned red and he shouted back, "And they took Hipoint, killed a thousand of my people, and destroyed much of Wayport!"

The two men glared at each other for a moment before Brock sat with sigh, his fury expended.

"I cannot deny there are those who fear magic, who would prefer to live out their lives away from it. If I try to force my magic down their throats, I am no better than the Empire and their desire to crush Chaos."

"What are you saying, Brock?"

"I'm saying we should allow the Empire to exist as is, in peace. The kingdoms of Issalia will remain a haven for those who can wield Chaos, the Empire will become a refuge for those who wish to avoid it." He sighed. "I'm saying we need to let it go."

"What of me, Brock? I'm a king without a kingdom."

Brock stared at Pretencia for a long moment before replying. "I could use a trustworthy, experienced leader to take over here. How does Duke Dalwin of Wayport sound to you?"

Still leaning over the desk, Pretencia stared into Brock's eyes. After a moment, he nodded. "Very well. Let peace guide our path for now. It won't continue forever, but we can focus on rebuilding what we have until the Empire forces us to do otherwise."

"Thank you, Dalwin," Brock said before turning toward Brandt and Quinn. "What of this Ikonis? Will he be the new leader? If so, will he listen to reason?"

Quinn said, "I don't know if he will lead them or if it will be Rorrick, their last remaining army captain. I believe there is some goodness inside Iko. He was raised to hate Chaos, yet he has exhibited a thoughtful reluctance to follow orders from Varius and Kardan. I believe he will listen, but I cannot guess at what his agenda might be moving forward."

"That," Brock said, "Is more than I could have hoped for under the previous regime."

—+✦+—

Ikonis Eldarro stood in front of the Sol Polis Citadel. The morning sun cast long shadows across the square while a breeze blew in from the sea to the west. Behind him was the entire citadel staff, or at least those who had survived. The dead guards and servants had been laid to rest two days earlier. Today was the final day of funerals. Today, his mother would return to Issal.

Ten funeral pyres stood before him, each laid out on a block of stone. The center pyres were for Kardan and Iko's mother. Upon the others, the eight Council members lay.

After discovering his mother, Kardan, and the Council members poisoned, another type of poison had run through Iko's veins. For days, he had been driven by hatred and revenge, wishing nothing more than to kill anyone related to the incident. Yet, Quinn's words remained in the back of his head, refusing to be discarded. *There is room enough in Issalia for us all to live as we like so long as we don't prey on others.*

Three days after Iko's mother's death, a messenger arrived from Wayport. The assault of the city had failed, leaving thousands dead including Sculdin, Mollis, Brillens, and Iko's friend, Percy. After hearing this news, Iko's anger fell away, leaving him numb and empty.

Minister Derrine from the citadel temple finished the funeral rites, bowed toward the Archon's pyre, and held a torch to it. Orange and yellow flames licked the kindling briefly before setting it ablaze. The woman then moved to Kardan and continued down the line. Iko's focus remained on the flames consuming his mother's body, and he wondered how it had come to this.

Within the feelings that had consumed Iko for much of the previous four days, he found his answer: hatred. The hatred his mother, Kardan, and the Council members had held against Chaos had consumed them until the bitter end. That hatred had led to their own deaths, taking Scully, Percy, and thousands of others with them.

In that moment, while staring at his mother's burning corpse, Iko made a pledge that the Empire would persevere. That could only happen if there was peace. Too much had been lost already to continue down the previous path.

Iko had received word of Rorrick returning to the garrison two days earlier. The man still commanded an army of thousands and held the power to challenge for the seat of Archon. Iko could not allow that to happen. Before Rorrick could return, Iko had to take the seat himself and solidify his position. There was only one way to counter Rorrick's military might: Iko would have to align himself with the local guildmasters here in Sol Polis as well as Sol Gier and Yarth. With their money behind him, he would become the next Archon behind the promise of prosperity in the wake of their recent war.

In time, the Empire might extend itself beyond the current borders. Somewhere out there was the assassin who killed Iko's mother. Somewhere out there was the person or organization behind it all. Someday, when the time was right, Iko would deal with the issue.

42

RETURN

The sea breeze ruffled Brock's tunic as he leaned over the ship's railing. While much had occurred in the world since he had last gazed upon his city, Kantar appeared unchanged. A season had passed – a winter filled with loss balanced by the promise of a better tomorrow. He put his faith in the notion. Duty required him to remain vigilant, but he prayed for a future filled with hope and joy and peace. To that hope, he held firm, gripping it as if he would fall to his death by letting go. Perhaps that was the truth of it.

Morning sunlight reflected off the dark blue waters of the harbor. The docks were busy with sailors, fisherman, and dockworkers, each focused on the task before them and oblivious to the troubles weighing on their king. That was the way of the world – citizens going about their lives and placing their faith in the crown, leaving the greater worries to those who ruled. Many sought the mantle of king as a path to power. Brock treated it as a burden to protect those who could not protect themselves. *Perhaps my ideals make the crown heavier, but it is all I know.*

The ship slipped past the breakers, and the captain called for furled sails. With a course set for the nearest open slip, the crew furiously prepared to dock. Accordingly, Brock turned and went below deck so he wouldn't be in the way.

Knocking at the first door, he waited until he heard "Come in."

Inside, Tenzi rested on a bunk, propped up on one elbow. Parker sat in a chair with his feet on her bed.

"We are arriving," Brock said. "Tell the others to gather their things. I promised the captain the ship would be his again as soon as we landed."

"At least the man has a ship." Tenzi said, her tone conveying her discontent.

"Must we do this again, Tenzi?"

"Just ignore it, Brock," Parker said, his face showing the hint of a smile. "It's nothing personal. She feels incomplete without a ship and will moan about it until the issue is resolved."

"Have you two considered my offer?"

"I spent two decades as an admiral, Brock," Tenzi said as she pushed Parker's feet aside and swung her legs down. "I'm not sure if I want the job again."

"That was then. This is now. After Olvaria threw her lot in with the Empire, we must be doubly wary of our position on the sea. Ri Star appears to have withdrawn, but it may not be the last of them. Until I have assurances from Olvaria, I'd prefer to take precautions."

"You will guarantee spots for my crew if I take this position?"

"Absolutely, on your ship or on another."

Rather than reply, Tenzi stood and stretched. "Hand me my boots, Parker."

"Are you two staying in the citadel?"

Tenzi sat and began pulling her boots on. "No. We'll stay at an inn with the crew, or what's left of them."

The comment brought a sigh to Brock's lips. Only five members of Tenzi's crew remained, the rest lost over the previous months during various battles – just another reminder of the price paid for freedom.

"Very well. I'll see you on the docks."

Brock ducked out and moved to the next room, opening the door and startling Broland awake.

"What?" Broland sat up, rubbing his eyes. "What time is it?"

"Perhaps two hours after sunrise." Brock reached into the wardrobe, pulled out his pack, and began stuffing it with clothing.

"Why did you let me sleep so late?"

"I figured you needed it. The last few nights didn't go well for you." Brock recalled Broland spending the bulk of three days and nights on deck, throwing up anytime his stomach contained anything more than water. Rough seas could affect anyone, and Broland was particularly sensitive to such things. "Eventually, your body needs a long, restful night to catch up."

"You're packing."

"You're observant."

"Have we arrived?"

"We will dock in the next few minutes."

Broland slipped his boots on and began gathering his things. By the time their belongings were collected, the ship had settled. Brock and his son headed up the stairs.

Tenzi, Parker, Joely, Hex, and Shashi were already there, huddled with Captain Thumbolt. The group turned and headed down the plank as Brock and Broland approached the captain.

"Thank you again, Captain."

The man bowed, his fingers absently twisting the tip of his waxed mustache. "It was my pleasure, your Majesty."

"As promised, the quarters are, again, yours. I'll send a courier down this afternoon with payment, so don't be too quick to set sail."

"No worries. I plan to stay the night anyway. I need time to find cargo to bring back to Wayport."

"Do me a favor, Thumbolt," Brock said.

The captain's face drooped with worry. "Sire?"

"Wayport is in dire need of food. The battle, brief as it might have been, was a drain on the resources. Do not overcharge them."

"But, your Majesty, trade is all about supply and demand. Their demand is high, so prices rise with it."

Brock put a hand on the man's shoulder. "I am not asking you to forego a profit; rather, I am telling you to set a discreet price. I will hear of it if greed surpasses your ethics."

The man sighed. "Yes, my King."

With a chuckle, Brock patted his shoulder. "Good man."

He turned and descended the plank to join Broland and Tenzi's crew on the pier.

The walk into the city was quiet, interrupted with only snippets of conversation. Brock drank in the view of the docks, the bay, the city walls, and the bridge to the south. He passed through the gate with the guards watching him and the others as if they were no different from any other visitors. Dressed as he was with his hair far shorter than usual, he appeared nothing like his normal kingly self. Broland had donned a hat, which hid his features. Traveling with Tenzi and the others, the king and prince could easily have been mistaken for common sailors. It had been decades since Brock had experienced anonymity. The feeling was liberating, if even for a short time.

Center Street was busy – a thriving throng of people buying and selling goods. Brock and the others weaved their way among the foot traffic, carts, wagons, and the occasional street performer. The city felt healthy, prosperous, and alive.

The scent of freshly baked bread stirred Brock's hunger as he came to a bakery. Stopping, he bought two loaves of bread. He broke off a chunk for Broland, another for himself, and handed the other loaf and a half to Tenzi, who began tearing off pieces for the others. The bread was warm with a hint of butter, delighting his mouth and surpassing the promise his nose had whispered. Chewing on their delicious prize, the group continued along the street, moving uphill and toward the waiting citadel.

Just before reaching Upper Kantar, Tenzi and her crew departed with the plan to settle down at the Aspen Inn for a few days. Brock and Broland wished them farewell and resumed their journey.

He and Broland passed through Upper Kantar with ease, and it wasn't until they reached the citadel gate that Brock was challenged.

"Stop and state your business at the citadel."

The guard was new, a young face Brock had never before seen.

"I must speak with Captain Wharton."

The guard looked at his companion, who was a few years his senior but also was unknown to Brock.

"What's this about?"

Brock sighed. "Just get the captain. He will know me."

"You expect me to bother the captain of the guard without even a name?"

"Tell him the son of a tanner is at the gate and wishes to speak with him. Unless, you would rather fetch me Queen Ashland?"

The man's eyes flared. "Do you play me for a fool?"

"Not at all. In fact, I'm doing my best to make you not appear a fool." Brock said in earnest. "Just get me Wharton."

After a drawn-out, frowning glare, the man turned toward his companion. "Draw your sword and watch them." Speaking to the archers on the wall, he called, "Shoot these two if either one moves."

The man then whisked off while Brock and Broland waited.

A few minutes later, the man reappeared with an imposing man in a black leather uniform. The man's dark, wavy hair ran to his shoulders, his stern face marked by scars and a dark goatee. As he drew close, the man's mouth turned up in a smile.

"Your Majesty!"

The guards stared at Brock, their mouths gaping, eyes wide. The younger one began backing away as if Brock might bite him.

Brock hugged Wharton as the two thumped each other on the back, Wharton hitting Brock hard enough to force a cough.

"It is good to see you, my King!" Wharton then turned to Broland, hugging him fiercely. "And you as well, my Prince!"

Brock smiled, "While I am happy to see you, Wharton, I miss my wife desperately."

"Oh, yes. She is in court at the moment but will happily retire for the day when she learns of your return."

Wharton turned to lead Brock into the castle, but Brock paused and approached the mouthy guard. He placed his hand on the taller man's shoulder, the man flinching as if the touch burned.

"Do not worry. You were only doing your job. Just try to remain humble and courteous unless the people you deal with force you to do otherwise."

The man nodded. "Yes, Sir...um Sire."

"Good man."

Wharton then led them into the castle, through twisting corridors, and into the great receiving hall. When they approached the throne room, the guards, both unknown to Brock, parted and allowed them in.

Ashland was seated on the lone throne at the front of the room, her brown curls glistening in a beam of sunlight streaming through the high windows. Brock noticed the throne was hers, his nowhere to be seen. A guard stood beside her, armed and ready. A clerk sat to her other side, recording the words from an old man who stood before the dais. When

Ashland's eyes met Brock's she stood, the man stopping mid-sentence and turning to see what had captured the queen's attention.

"Brock!" she whooped, jumping off the dais and flashing past the startled man, her skirts billowing behind.

When Ashland reached him, he wrapped his arms about her and lifted, spinning her as his heart sang with joy. He put her down, their lips meeting in a long, urgent kiss that left his heart racing and both of them gasping. Her eyes gazed into his, bright blue and full of love. *My goodness, I have missed looking into those eyes...*

"Ahem," Wharton said, breaking the spell. "You do realize this is a public forum?"

Brock turned around and found dozens of citizens seated on the benches, all staring toward him with mouths agape, eyes like saucers.

"Yes, it is I, King Brock, returned from battle," Brock bellowed. "You see, the news about my death was premature. Know this: we have soundly defeated the Empire, and they will not threaten Kantaria again for years to come. Wayport took much damage, but the city remains and the citizens there will rebuild. More importantly, the freedoms we value remain intact."

Ashland extended her arm toward Broland who stepped into her embrace. She kissed his cheek and smiled. "Oh, Broland. Thank Issal, you are all right." Broland stepped away, and Ashland looked at Brock. "What of Brandt and Cassie?"

"Both are well. In fact, they are heroes and played key roles in saving many lives. You will be proud to hear of what they have accomplished."

A tear ran down her face. "Yes. I am sure I will." Her gaze lifted higher, her hand running along the short layer of hair on his head. "What happened to your hair?"

"I had a little accident. Nothing worth mentioning." *No need to worry her.* He then said in a loud voice, "Court for today is adjourned, for I would very much like to be with my wife." He kissed her again and stared into her eyes. "In fact, court, and everything else at the citadel, will take a leave of three days. We have more pressing things to address."

"Like what?" Ashland asked with a twinkle in her eye.

"I suspect you know, but I will save that for someplace more private."

She laughed, the sound lifting Brock's spirits even higher and bringing tears of joy to his eyes. He was with Ashland again. He was home.

The carriage hit a bump, sending Everson and the other passengers into the air. Ivy grabbed his hand, and he gave her a smile. Across from him were Jonah and Cassie. Jonah chose to ride in the carriage because he didn't dare ride a horse with his paralysis. Of course, he never enjoyed riding anyway. Cassie chose to ride with Jonah, saying she wanted to avoid the weather. Based on the looks she gave Jonah's unmoving legs, Everson suspected she was concerned for him.

Everson peered up at the mountains, still white with snow although the valley had thawed and was in the process of turning green. Melting snow followed by early spring rain had left ruts in the road, resulting in a rough ride.

The Fallbrandt Academy of Magic and Engineering came into view as they circled to the east. Above it, the Arcane Ward towered over the school, dark and windowless and brooding. Even knowing the truth about the Ward, Everson felt the searing impression as intended. *Fear me,* the building demanded. Most obeyed.

Riders passed the carriage in a gallop – Curan, Chuli, Brandt, and Quinn. Watching his sister ride by with a grin on her face left Everson wondering what it would be like to ride a horse. Fear of falling lest his useless legs betray him had been a deterrent for much of his life. Since he invented his mechanical legs, the opportunity had never presented itself. Perhaps it was time to make it happen. With the war behind them, Everson found his future filled with new possibilities.

The carriage slowed as they passed through the gate and entered the Ward stable yard. When the carriage stopped, Everson turned toward Ivy.

"After you, my dear."

"Everson." She rolled her eyes. "This is one of those times where you should go first and then extend your hand to assist me."

"Oh. Sorry. I'm trying."

"I know. Don't worry about it. Just climb out so we can go inside."

He opened the door, holding it while he helped Ivy and Cassie out.

Curan and Brandt opened the other door and helped Jonah out so Curan could carry him. The eight wardens headed inside. Without discussion, they headed to the second floor and knocked on the Briefing Room door. A moment later, Benny Hedgewick opened it and blinked in surprise.

"You have returned." He stuck his head out and looked around. "Where are the others?"

Quinn responded, "Delvin sent us back and told us he needed time to meet his contacts in Kalimar before he returns."

Benny nodded. "That sounds like him. And Thiron?"

Sadness passed Chuli's face at the mention of Thiron's name.

Everson said in a somber tone, "May we come in? We have much to tell you."

"Yes. Please."

The meeting consumed an hour as Everson and the other wardens relayed the events in Wayport and Kalimar. Telling of the deaths of Torney and Thiron cast a veil of sorrow over the group. Though many others had died, the impact of losing friends had a much stronger impact.

"What of the other wardens? Has Rena returned?" Everson's voice fell to a hush. "Does she know about Torney?"

Benny looked at the other leaders, a look that only increased Everson's concern. "They have returned, all except Master Kwai-Lan. He did not survive."

"And what about Rena? Is she all right?"

"Physically, she is well." Firellus shook his head, his worry apparent. "However, her mental state is...very poor."

Cassie gasped. "Where is she?"

"In her room, I suspect. We meet with her daily, taking turns. However, she remains despondent and will barely eat."

Benny added, "Most days, she won't even get out of bed."

"What happened?"

Nindlerod answered, "The mission in Vallerton did not go well. They saved most of the citizens but were forced to abandon the town. In fact, King Cassius has closed the Red Towers and the entire surrounding region completely, barring anyone from entering. Something is very wrong there."

"When the squad returned, Rena was already in bad shape," Benny said. "Hearing about Torney's death proved to be too much for her fragile state. We don't know what to do. As you are aware, it is not possible to heal mental illness."

Everson thought of Cassie, aware that she and Rena had grown close. Her concern was evident and he wondered what they could do to help.

A long moment of silence was interrupted when Brandt stood. "If that is all, I am beat," he said. "A hot meal and an even hotter bath would both be quite welcome."

"There is one more thing," Nindlerod said. "We approved Henrick's expedition. He departed last week and set off for Vingarri."

Everson frowned. "Why Vingarri?"

"Since it is the oldest city in Issalia, he expected to find the oldest wrecks off shore there. More than anything, the boy seems determined to find keys to our past hidden at the bottom of the ocean."

Everson wondered what it would be like to explore an ancient shipwreck. As the group wandered out of the room, his mind wandered, dreaming of what Henrick might discover.

EPILOGUE

Henrick Churles held tight to the side of the fishing boat, peering over the side as the hired men pulled on the oars. The old fisherman and his son had demanded a full gold mark for the use of their boat, claiming it was compensation for missing a day of fishing. Based on the size of the small boat and the condition of their clothing, Henrick doubted the men earned a gold piece from an entire month of fishing. Still, he had the money. More importantly, he needed a boat and a guide who knew the bay.

A mile to the west, the coastline appeared to rise and fall as the ocean swell rolled beneath the boat. The city of Vingarri was nestled in the bay, built on a hillside with a zig-zagging street leading from the docks to the castle on top. It was not a large city, but it was an old city – the oldest in Issalia. For that alone, Henrick has chosen it for his first expedition.

The oars settled, and Henrick asked, "What is it? Is something wrong?" Despite his desire to explore the ocean depths, he had little experience on boats and was unsure of what to expect.

"The reef you asked about. It's right there." The man nodded toward a post, painted red, sticking three feet above the surface. "There's your marker."

"And you're sure there is a wreck here?"

"There is, but she's sunk deep. The reef is only four or five feet below the water, but it drops off fast, down to forty or fifty feet for sure."

Henrick nodded. It was perfect.

He removed his cloak and coat, undressing to a tunic and breeches. The water would be cold, but a southern current had warmed it noticeably since he had first arrived in Vingarri six days earlier. He pulled on the Heavy-augmented boots and strapped the diving harness to his torso. Pulling some slack from the reel of rope, he had the old man tie it to the loop on his back.

Henrick hung the bell on the reel and said, "Remember, you are to pull me up after I ring the bell twice." Silent nods were his only reply.

He placed the Chaos-conduction air pump on his seat while the curious fishermen looked on. With the pull of a lever, the pump began to run with a steady hum between whistling pumps of air. Henrick placed the metal-framed glass helmet on his head, twisted it, and secured it to the harness. He made sure the coil of tubing was secured on both ends and free to uncoil before giving himself a mental nod.

The reality of the situation struck. His heart began to pound as if it were trying to escape his chest. He sat on the edge of the boat, his armpits damp despite the chill of the wind.

You can do this, Henrick. He looked at the fishermen who were staring at him, waiting. *What if I don't jump in?* The raw embarrassment of failing after everything he had done to get to this point...well, that was enough to overcome his fear.

Henrick pushed off and plunged into the cold, dark water. His chest constricted, and he found himself panting for air as he sank downward, panicking.

Air. I can breathe. His breathing calmed, and he turned to examine his surroundings.

The reef, filled with greens and oranges and whites, slid past as he continued to sink. Fish of various sizes and colors swam past, some with stripes, some solid, some iridescent. Many had their noses buried in the reef and some even darted into dark recesses to hide. All in all, the sight was mesmerizing.

And still, he continued to sink.

Henrick spotted the remains of a ship on the bottom, the hull snapped in half. Both masts were pointing upward at an angle, one toward him, the other away from him. Pale barnacles and green moss covered most of the ship. Where the wood showed, it was now black.

When he finally landed on the sandy ocean floor, he peered up through the rising bubbles emitted from his helmet. His gaze followed the curving trail of the air line and the rope connecting him to the fishing boat, the hull a dark silhouette amid the brightly lit surface.

With slow, floating steps – each covering four to five feet at a time – he moved toward the shipwreck. A shadow moved within the wreck and darted out into the open water. Henrick froze at the sight, his hand gripping the hilt of the dagger on his hip. The fish had visible, pointed teeth, each the size of one of Henrick's fingers. Its mouth was big enough to take a sizable chunk out of him if it decided he was food. The fish was seven or eight feet long and as black as night. Beady eyes seemed to measure him for a moment, and then the fish sped off, chasing a school of shining, silvery fish darting this way and that in unison as if choreographed.

He had been holding his breath, but now Henrick exhaled and continued his advance.

An anchor as big as a man lay beside the wreck, partially buried in the sand. The broken vessel leaned against a huge dark rock. By climbing the rock, Henrick drew even with the tilted deck.

He stepped onto the deck, which was slippery where it was green but provided traction where the pale barnacles resided. After a moment of consideration, he angled toward the open door of the cabin below the quarterdeck. He paused inside the doorway to allow his eyes to adjust.

The remains of a single bunk sat on one side and a broken table and chairs were on the other, suggesting it had once been the captain's cabin. Scattered and broken clay crockery lay on the floor. He picked up a pitcher, but decided it was nothing special. Discarding it, he searched for other, more interesting treasures.

At the far end of the room, a beam of light illuminated a frame on the wall, revealing colors of red and black and blue beneath the green moss. Henrick carefully ran his blade across the panel to clear away the algae. He repeated the process, growing increasingly more excited as he revealed what lay beneath. Finally, he sheathed the knife and gripped the edges of the painting, tearing it from the cabin wall. With his prize in hand, Henrick crossed the room, toward the open doorway. For a moment, he paused and considered exploring further but decided it could wait for another day.

He put the painting beneath his arm with one edge digging into his armpit, his arm barely long enough to wrap his fingers around the other edge. With his other hand, he reached up for the tow rope and gave it two hard jerks. Moments passed, and then, the rope began to pull taught. He walked toward the rope and stepped off the deck when he felt it tug on the harness.

Up and up he went, watching the reef fish eating as he rose toward the surface. Suddenly, his head bobbed above the water, and he held the painting above his head. One of the men took it before both gripped his arms and pulled him into the boat.

Henrick unlocked the helmet, twisting it and pulling it free. The younger man handed him a towel, which he used to dry himself the best he could before wrapping his cloak about himself to shield against the wind.

"Well, did you get what you came for?" the older man asked.

Henrick picked the painting up and used the damp towel to rub away the remaining moss. What it revealed beneath had Henrick's eyes alight with wonder, his mind racing at the possibilities.

"Is that a map?" The old man said, leaning forward as he peered at it. "That don't look like any map I've ever seen."

"Exactly!" Henrick said with a grin. "This is a map of another land."

"Another land?" the younger man sounded confused. "I thought Issalia was all there was."

Henrick ignored the comment, pointing at the starchart at the upper portion of the map. "See these stars? The pattern matches what we see in the distant south just before sunrise."

"What's it mean?"

"It means there is another land, far to the southeast – a new land to explore with new things to discover!"

Henrick fell silent, grinning at the painting in his hands, his fingers nearly purple as he shivered in the wind. His body was cold, but he ignored his discomfort and focused on his discovery.

As he had always dreamed, he had uncovered clues to an unknown history, clues hidden at the bottom of the ocean. The map left him wondering what mysteries might be revealed by following it.

He needed to return to the Ward. It was time to prepare for a new expedition, one that might change the world forever.

BOOKS BY JEFFREY L. KOHANEK

Runes of Issalia

The Buried Symbol: Runes of Issalia 1

The Emblem Throne: Runes of Issalia 2

An Empire in Runes: Runes of Issalia 3

* * *

Runes of Issalia Boxed Set

* * *

Heroes of Issalia: Runes Series+Rogue Legacy

* * *

Rogue Legacy: Runes of Issalia Prequel

Wardens of Issalia

A Warden's Purpose: Wardens of Issalia 1

The Arcane Ward: Wardens of Issalia 2

An Imperial Gambit: Wardens of Issalia 3

A Kingdom Under Siege: Wardens of Issalia 4

* * *

Wardens of Issalia Boxed Set

* * *

ICON: A Wardens of Issalia Companion Tale

23765692R00175

Printed in Great Britain
by Amazon